F MUR MAJDEIN

"I loved this book. It's a really great read;
a proper whodunnit! Who would want to be a police
officer having a whole cast of actors for suspects?
I love mysteries where the characters have
backstories, and these are woven in beautifully.
As a debut novel, this is a cracker!"

JOY ELLIS,
No.1 bestselling author of the *D.I. Nikki Galena* series

"Excellent writing,
with a strong, compelling hook."

LORRAINE MACE,
author of the *D.I. Sterling* crime series

"Relatable characters and a unique storyline.
Realistically written and feels as though you're
watching a blockbuster hit crime movie. Fantastic!"

SHANCURTY IGNACIO,
author of *Maybe This Promise*

"*Murder at Macbeth* is active, suspenseful and utterly thrilling; I couldn't put the book down!"

★★★★★ Write Read Talk Live Book Blog

"One of the best mystery novels I've read this year. I thoroughly enjoyed it. I literally could not put this book down."

★★★★★ Bekah's Bookshelves Blog

"If you are looking for a classic murder mystery with a Shakespearean influence, this is the book for you! It very much read like watching a TV show. Samantha Goodwin is on my 'Watch List'."

★★★★★ Goodreads Reviewer

"Unputdownable! This was a compulsive page-turner that gripped me from the very start. I was so enthralled by all the twists that I stayed up most of the night to finish it!"

★★★★★ Goodreads Reviewer

"I loved reading this book. You are drawn straight into the drama as it unfolds on stage. So many twists and turns made this a thrilling read, I was kept guessing right to the end."

★★★★★ Goodreads Reviewer

MURDER AT MACBETH

Samantha Goodwin

This book is a work of fiction.
Names, places, events and incidents are the product
of the author's imagination. Any resemblance
to actual persons, living or dead, or actual events
is purely coincidental.

A CIP catalogue record for this book is
available from the British Library.

ISBN: 9781798960707

Also available as an eBook.

For Dad, who always wanted to write a book,
Mum, who might read this one,
And Chris, for believing in me to make this happen.

"Let not light see my black and deep desires."

– William Shakespeare, *Macbeth*

CHAPTER ONE

The Way to Dusty Death

Friday 23rd March

Nikki Gowon was dead. Neil Hillton was sure of it. Dumbfounded, he stared blankly down at the young woman's lifeless body. A crimson stain had blossomed on her white dress like a macabre flower and a pool of blood was seeping out from beneath her, discolouring the wooden floorboards. Her dark, tangled hair resembled a spider running across the stage. The sharp knife had clattered to her side, where it lay forgotten, the blade glinting ominously red.

A hushed silence had fallen backstage, punctuated only by Megan's intermittent sobs. A sense of complete and utter panic was setting in fast. Beyond the red velvet curtains currently obscuring the stage, Neil could hear the distant murmuring of the impatient audience waiting for the next act of the play to commence. Of course, they could never have guessed

1

the real reason for the delay.

What exactly was he meant to say? *Oh, so sorry for the temporary setback but our lead actress has just been killed. I do apologise for the inconvenience.*

As a seasoned London theatre director, Neil had experienced his fair share of live disasters over the years, but tonight's current predicament made all those previous quandaries fade into insignificance. He couldn't foresee how the old showbiz adage 'it'll be alright on the night' applied here.

It most certainly will not be, he thought bitterly. *Everything will definitely not be alright in this scenario.*

Neil was painfully aware he should have already sprung into action. But he felt rooted in position, rigid in shock. He was at a loss to explain the circumstances leading to this horrific moment. All he could think about was the motionless body of the beautiful young actress slumped across the stage.

His stage.

He was vaguely aware of the other cast members milling around him in equal states of shock and confusion. A grief-stricken Jimmy knelt on the floor unmoving, staring down at Nikki's still body in disbelief. His trembling hands were pressed against the ugly stab wound in her abdomen in a vain attempt to stem the gushing blood flow.

Neil regarded the desperate lover grimly. It was already too late for such heroics.

Ben stood awkwardly to the side of Jimmy, hand placed stiffly on his shoulder as though it offered some semblance of comfort. Standing behind them was Violet, frozen still as a statue, silent tears rolling down her rosy cheeks. Eyes wide, deep blue pools of despair. The teenage girl frustrated the hell out of Neil. Sure, she served her purpose and had proved eager to offer her help and assistance as a dutiful stagehand. But recently she had taken to following him around like a lost puppy, as though she was afraid to be left alone. It had been driving him crazy.

An inconsolable Megan started wailing hysterically. Clutching her boyfriend, Peter, she sobbed as he gently stroked her hair in a futile attempt to calm her. Neil had half a mind to berate her for crying so loudly the audience might be able to hear, but he restrained himself. While the audience's opinion was usually paramount, this was hardly a run-of-the-mill night.

A good performance was not exactly Neil's top priority today. That train of thought led to a depressing downward spiral as he glumly imagined the critics' reviews and worse still; the headlines. Never before had he known of an actress dying onstage during a theatre performance. He was finished and he knew it. Who in their right mind would want to work with him now?

A true tragedy; his fledgling directing career over before it had even got off the ground. Just last month, *The Stage* magazine had listed him as one of the 'Top Ten Hot New Theatre Directors' currently working in London. Neil was the one to watch, the next big thing. He had felt destined for greatness.

Over the last ten years, he had worked tirelessly to establish Gemini Theatre as one of the capital's preeminent Shakespeare play venues. Of course, unsurprisingly the famous Globe Theatre still boasted the most authentic, historically accurate portrayals. But when it came to modern, gritty takes on the classic plays, Neil Hillton had developed quite a reputation for himself. His captivating productions performed in the heart of Shoreditch were routinely acclaimed by local and out-of-town critics and a growing raft of theatrical awards further testified his growing success.

But tonight, all he could think about was whether his insurance policy covered him against his lead actress dying on the job. The loss of earnings from cancelling the show would be disastrous for his bank balance.

A soft hand touching his arm dragged Neil out of his thoughts and back to the present. Emma looked up at him questioningly. Incredibly, she seemed composed, collected even. An oasis of calm in the centre of the storm raging around them. Not for the first time, he found himself admiring her strength.

"What the hell do we do?" Emma hissed.

Bloody good question, thought Neil grimly as he fought to regain a sense of composure. The mounting hubbub from the annoyed audience could no longer be ignored. They had to be informed there would be no final act. With a jolt, he realised Emma wasn't the only one looking at him for guidance. A sea of worried faces was turned his way, his cast of actors watching him expectantly. After all, Neil was in charge here, now was the time to take control. But he had never imagined he would ever have to manage a situation as dire as this.

Neil still couldn't understand how this could have

happened. He had personally double and triple checked all of the props backstage an hour before the show had begun. There was no way anyone would have been able to sneak a real knife backstage and leave unnoticed. Unless, of course, they had never actually left.

With that unnerving thought, Neil inhaled deeply and braced himself to address the cast. Taking a shaky step forward, he suddenly felt overwhelmingly thankful for Emma's stoic presence beside him. She held his arm reassuringly, silently offering her support. It felt good to not be completely alone.

"We need to take action," he began, voice sounding more confident than he felt. "Obviously we'll need to inform the police right away. I'll take care of the audience; don't you worry about that. They don't need to know the full gory details. I'll simply explain there has been a medical emergency and so unfortunately, we will be unable to continue with tonight's performance. Then, I'll coordinate them leaving the venue in a timely, ordered manner."

It was at that point, just as he was getting into his stride, that Neil was interrupted as Jimmy took a sharp intake of breath. A strangled, gurgling sound. He had been cradling Nikki's limp head in his lap, holding her close. Now Jimmy looked up, his eyes wild with panic.

"She's alive!" he gasped.

Then, all hell broke loose.

CHAPTER TWO

Something Wicked This Way Comes

Friday 23rd March

*   *   *   ONE HOUR EARLIER   *   *   *

The haunting melodies of the three witches drifted through the auditorium as they sang, "When shall we three meet again, in thunder, lightning, or in rain."

Their eerie harmonies had cast a spell over all those watching. Spooky red lighting and wisps of dry ice spiralling upwards from the iron cauldron added to the disturbingly creepy atmosphere.

From behind the thick red curtain, Nikki peered out curiously to observe the scene. From her vantage point at the far-left stage wing, she could enjoy a clear, unobstructed view of the action, with no fear of being spotted. She pushed a loose dark curl back behind her ear and watched on with interest.

The enchanted audience sat in hushed silence, all eyes fixed on the witches. Still singing their sinister chant, the trio weaved skilfully in and out as they circled the bubbling cauldron dominating centre stage. With their carefully choreographed moves they almost looked as though they were dancing. Every few steps they threw in handfuls of grey powder, which produced a bright spark and made the cauldron gurgle and smoke, much to the delight of the audience. The putrid smell of burning chemicals drifted backstage and Nikki was suddenly grateful she wasn't standing any closer.

Each witch was impressively hypnotising. The delicate, bird-like Violet moved as if she was a real-life doll, with uncoordinated long limbs and broken steps. Pretty in a girl-next-door kind of way, she didn't command attention but was rather pleasing on the eye nonetheless. Emma, by contrast, could only be described as stunning. All high cheekbones and sharp features with luscious, golden locks, she looked every inch like a classic Hollywood movie star.

But Nikki had her eyes firmly set on the third witch, Megan. Swirling around on her tip toes, an ethereal beauty with her stylishly cropped auburn hair. Nikki knew she had to talk to her about last weekend. There had been an unfamiliar distance growing between them since then and it was making her uncomfortable. Normally inseparable, they had barely spoken in the past week. If anything, recently Megan had been going out of her way to ignore her and avoid having any awkward conversations. A rift was forming and Nikki didn't like it at all.

Best friends since they started university two and a half years ago, Megan was the one person Nikki could usually count on no matter what. Her confidante, her shoulder to cry on, her dancing buddy and all-round partner in crime. To lose such a close friend would be unbearable. Nothing had to change between them. Nikki resolved to talk to Megan at the first opportunity. Clearing the air seemed like a good place to start, then they could start moving forward and rebuilding their friendship.

A bright red flame suddenly shot up from the witches' cauldron, raining fiery sparks down onto the stage. The spellbound audience took a collective gasp and cheered in delight. Nikki had to admit, for all his faults, their director Neil Hillton was a genius when it came to dramatic staging. His creative flair for pyrotechnics and prop design was evident throughout the entire production, which showcased everything from dry ice to fake blood.

Hearing a rustling behind her, Nikki popped her head back through the curtain and spun around to come face-to-face with a dead pig head. Jumping in fright, she clasped a hand over her mouth to stop herself from screaming. Her skin turned cold and she could feel the blood pulsing through her veins as her heart rate quickened. The pig was bobbing up and down, laughing at her.

Looking beyond the grotesque swine, she could see Jimmy shaking so hard with laughter he was practically crying.

"You should have seen your face! That was hysterical." He doubled over, holding one of his sides to try and control himself.

Nikki pushed him hard in the shoulder, nearly knocking him off his feet. "That was *not* funny."

"Oh, but it was," chortled Jimmy, dissolving into another fit of giggles. "Your expression was hilarious, you looked like you'd seen a ghost."

Nikki rolled her eyes. Even though she loved him, Jimmy was always finding new ways to wind her up. He was such a fool, always happiest when he was clowning around. But still, she was relieved the prior tension that had existed between them this past week had dissipated. For now, at least, Jimmy seemed to have forgiven her and was back to being his normal, cheeky self.

She pushed him away with a light-hearted grin. "Put that disgusting thing away. Seriously, quit messing about."

Reluctantly Jimmy lowered the silver dome lid back down over the pig head platter. That particular prop was another one of Neil's genius ideas, albeit not one Nikki was particularly fond of. One of the director's friends was a butcher and had provided it free of charge for use in the banquet scene in the show. It gave Nikki the creeps, she could have sworn the pig's lifeless eyes followed her around whenever she was backstage.

She shivered just thinking about it. "Eurgh, honestly I think sometimes Neil thinks he's directing an Oscar-worthy horror movie, not an amateur production of *Macbeth.*"

There was an audible intake of breath behind her. Nikki turned to see Peter staring at her with wide eyes.

"You said the M word!" he gasped. "What about

the curse? You know that's bad luck."

Nikki gave a hearty chuckle. "Oh please, don't tell me you actually believe in that superstitious nonsense? It's all complete hokum."

Peter's reaction surprised her. Over the last few months, as Megan's boyfriend, she thought she had grown to know him pretty well. Although if recent revelations were anything to go by, clearly she wasn't as good a judge of character as she had once thought. Tolerating the conversation with a humourless expression, Nikki forced a small smile. She had no particular interest in engaging with Peter at the moment, especially after what she had learnt last night. Still, she never would have taken him for the superstitious type. He had always seemed far too rational to believe in such drivel.

Nikki didn't have much time for the so-called curse associated with the Scottish play. Allegedly a coven of witches had cursed the show for eternity, so speaking the name *Macbeth* aloud inside a theatre during a performance would cause disaster. Supposedly if a person did accidentally say the name, they are required to leave the building and perform a traditional cleansing ritual; turning three times, spitting over their left shoulder and reciting a line from another William Shakespeare play. Nikki found the whole thing frankly ridiculous. Yet the theatre community was rife with tales of *Macbeth* productions plagued with freak accidents, falling scenery and untimely deaths. A theatre in Portugal had even mysteriously burned to the ground after showing the play.

Peter shook his head fervently. He seemed

uncomfortable tonight, distracted even, as though his mind was elsewhere. Nikki suspected she knew what was playing on his thoughts and felt no sympathy for his distress.

"Surely the curse had to originate from true events though?" he insisted. "There has to be a reason it's still such a widely-held superstition after all these years."

Nikki laughed scornfully. "Right. Next, you'll be telling me you wear a rabbit's foot around your neck for luck or throw salt over your shoulder, just in case."

Peter leaned forward, his voice dropping to a whisper. "Legend has it back in the early 1600's the actor playing Lady MacB died during the play's first production run and William Shakespeare himself had to assume the role. I'd have thought you of all people would be inclined to show a little more caution to the folklore." He spoke in a casual yet reprimanding tone, his voice cool, as his eyes bore into her.

Unsettled, Nikki shivered, but she wasn't about to let herself feel intimidated by Peter. She wasn't afraid of him. "Ooh, I don't know. I think tonight will be a great performance of *Macbeth*," she teased, deliberately emphasising the show name with glee. Smiling wryly to herself, she watched in satisfaction as Peter bristled in agitation. "There's no evidence that ever actually happened. Who knows, maybe the Bard made it up himself to sell a few more tickets?"

Peter stiffened, annoyance etched on his handsome face. "In that case how do you explain the string of deaths associated with the play? Like the actor George Ostroska who died of a heart attack while playing the lead role? Or how about Harold Newman? He

11

reportedly didn't believe in the superstition either; he died after his stage battle got too realistic when playing the Scottish King in the forties." Narrowing his eyes, he paused to emphasise what was coming next. "Then, there was the notorious 1942 production, which racked up one of the highest body counts. Three actors died in unexplained circumstances and the costume designer committed suicide on the opening night."

He exhaled dramatically. Clearly he had done his research on the subject, probably just so he could undermine anyone who dared to disagree with him. Peter always hated to be challenged, he tended to react as though it was a personal attack. Usually, Nikki was content to let him get his own way, arguing with him was far too much effort. But tonight, she couldn't care less. Peter studied her closely, his piercing green eyes locked on hers. His brow was knitted and she could sense his concern. Suddenly uneasy, a small knot of doubt formed in the pit of her stomach.

"That's enough," hissed Neil, stepping into view from the stage wing. "You're supposed to be silent when you're backstage, not joking around like children." He glared at the three of them in turn, his scowl softening a little when it fell on Nikki. "Besides, it may be a stupid old tradition but it is our opening night after all. Whether you believe in the curse or not, it can't hurt to be too careful. Best not to tempt fate."

Finally, the countdown was nearly over. All the waiting around backstage had gradually increased Nikki's nerves until she had become a wound-up ball of nervous energy. In rehearsals, it had always felt like forever to get to her pivotal death scene. But now, during the first live performance, time seemed to have come to a complete standstill. Minutes had stretched into hours that appeared to last an eternity, until time had suddenly become elastic and it had all snapped sharply back into place. Her big moment was here at long last and she could feel the nerves coursing through her.

If she had been the praying type, now would have been the time. *Saint Genesius of Rome,* she vaguely recalled as snippets of an old school history lesson came back to her. *The legendary patron saint of actors.* She could sure do with him watching over her. During rehearsals, she had never felt so much as a smidgen of stage fright, she wasn't sure what had come over her tonight. Plus, it wasn't like this was her first live performance; Nikki had been a veteran of the stage for as long as she could remember. Starring in school plays practically as soon as she could talk, the stage felt like her second home. It was where she felt most comfortable, where she truly belonged. Her natural environment.

Except for tonight.

In the midst of her anxieties, Nikki smiled as Jimmy crept up behind her. Slipping his strong arms around her waist, he hugged her close and kissed her neck tenderly. She shuddered involuntarily at his touch.

"You'll be brilliant," Jimmy whispered into her ear. "Believe in yourself."

He squeezed her tightly and Nikki felt her whole

body relax. Exhaling deeply, she released a breath she hadn't realised she was holding in and felt the tension seep out of her body. She had never understood how he managed to have this calming effect on her.

Jimmy nuzzled her neck affectionately. "No amount of bad luck could make any difference. You're going to smash it my love. You'll be amazing out there, I just know it."

Nikki twisted around to kiss him softly on the lips, savouring the brief, intimate moment. Then, she disentangled herself from his embrace and pulled away. Thanking him hastily for his words of encouragement, she prepared herself to go onstage.

From the left wing, a watchful Ben caught her eye and flashed her a wide, stupid grin. His shoulder-length dreadlocks bounced as he nodded enthusiastically and lifted his hand to give her an exaggerated thumbs-up gesture. Nikki felt Ben's gaze linger on her for a moment too long and she looked away self-consciously, hoping Jimmy hadn't noticed.

Rapturous applause thundered through the theatre as the current scene came to an end. The three witches hurried backstage, slipping through the curtains one by one. Violet offered Nikki a small, timid smile before scurrying away quickly. Megan simply averted her eyes and hurried past, deliberately avoiding her. Nikki sighed in exasperation. Her friend could be so stubborn when she wanted to be, one of her less admirable qualities.

Emma was last through the curtain and her face broke into a wicked sneer when her gaze settled on Nikki. "Break a leg," she smirked. Her pretty features had rearranged into a cruel grimace as she glowered at her. Contempt radiated off of the woman.

Nikki returned her glare with a satisfied grin. Technically speaking, Emma had good reason to hate her but two could play at that game.

The stage plunged into darkness as the house lights were extinguished. Nikki took a deep breath, gathered her nerves and stepped out from behind the curtains. Immediately a spotlight found her and the stage was flooded with light. Temporarily blinded by the brightness, she shrugged off the distraction to deliver her opening lines with compelling urgency. Any fear she had possessed beforehand diminished as she got into her stride. Floating through the dappled shadows, Nikki felt like a goddess as she tread the floorboards.

Tumbling down her back in a cascade of dark ringlets, her flowing hair shimmered in the light. Her ivory dress clung to her slim body, accentuating every curve and contrasting sharply with her dark, chestnut-brown skin. She had originally had her doubts when Violet had put together this costume choice. Somehow the dress had appeared dowdy hanging limp on the hanger, but now with it on she felt truly captivating. Five hundred pairs of eyes stared up at her; the independent theatre was at full capacity tonight. It should have been a nerve-wracking experience, but Nikki found it exhilarating. She was buzzing with excitement, blood pulsating through her body.

The Shakespearean dialogue tumbled effortlessly off her tongue as she spoke the rambling verses of Lady Macbeth, who was going mad with guilt. "Out, damned spot! Out, I say!" she cried shrilly, wringing her hands in imagined anguish.

The enthralled audience hung onto her every word as she commanded the stage as though she had been born for this. Somewhere in the sea of faces, her family were watching. Her parents would be proud as always. She knew she was privileged to have their unconditional love and support as she knew only too well not everyone was that lucky. Also present was her younger sister, Aisha. Ten years her junior, little Aisha had always looked up to her as a role model. It thrilled Nikki to show her what could be achieved when you put in the effort. Her heart swelled with love at the thought of her sister. She was fiercely protective of the youngster, after this last summer more than ever.

Upstage Peter paced slowly, the doctor in his current guise. "Foul whisperings are abroad, unnatural deeds do breed unnatural troubles."

Pausing for a beat, Nikki looked into the blinding spotlight. Now was her moment, the time for her big finale. With no further hesitation, she pulled the concealed knife from beneath the back of her dress, holding it up for dramatic effect. She relished the collective gasp from the enraptured audience. They were lapping it up; Neil really was an artistic genius. 'More action, less inference' was his motto and she had to agree this approach to Lady Macbeth's traditionally offstage suicide was far more electrifying. Nikki brandished the knife a moment longer, light glinting off the blade before thrusting it hard into her stomach in one swift, violent movement.

Nikki's eyes widened as a searing pain coursed through her. For a moment she couldn't comprehend what had gone wrong. She glanced down at the knife, still protruding from her body. Gasping, she watched in horror as wet blood dripped off the handle. Her vision clouded and she swayed on her feet unsteadily. Without warning, her legs suddenly crumpled beneath her and she groaned as she collapsed into a heap. She was vaguely aware of the audience cheering as a ripple of applause ran through the auditorium. The sound seemed distant, as though a dark cloak had descended over her.

Struck by a wave of dizziness, she was fast becoming lightheaded. Pulse racing, her heart thudded relentlessly against her chest. Peering up she could see Peter stood over her, an unreadable expression on his face; admiration perhaps. Nikki wanted to scream she wasn't acting but when she tried to call out for help, she found her voice had abandoned her. She couldn't even manage a hoarse whisper.

Turning her head, she spotted Emma watching from behind the stage curtain, arms folded as an unpleasant smile crept across her face. Complete and utter panic gripped Nikki. Struggling to suck enough air into her lungs, her breathing grew wheezy and ragged. Bitter, metallic blood filled her mouth.

Frantically, she scanned the side of the stage searching for Jimmy's face. Or Megan's. They knew her better than anyone. She wasn't *that* good an actress. Surely, they would be able to tell something was wrong and raise the alarm. But alas, neither of them were anywhere to be seen. Nikki felt a wave of desperation crash over her.

Where was everybody? Why weren't they helping?

A pang of fresh anguish hit her as she realised somewhere in the audience little Aisha was witnessing everything unfold. Her younger sister couldn't watch her die onstage right in front of her. Aisha was fragile, an innocent girl with a warm heart. She would never get over that sort of trauma. It would scar her for life.

With renewed determination, Nikki tried desperately to drag herself across the dusty floor. But she had barely moved a few inches when she gave in, her body sagging. The pain in her stomach was unbearable, she had never experienced anything like it. The agony was all-consuming as she felt her vision go dark. Blood throbbed in her head as a flurry of thoughts raced through her mind. She was left with one burning question as her world slowly descended into darkness.

Who would do this to me?

CHAPTER THREE

Out, Out, Brief Candle

The shrill ringtone of his mobile phone ringing repeatedly shattered the blissful peace Detective Inspector Finley Robson had been enjoying. Stretched out on his comfy bed, he had been relishing a rare moment of tranquillity. Susan was nestled next to him, her warm head resting on his bare chest. He took a moment to appreciate the slender curves of her naked body, her long legs still intertwined with his.

But still the piercing ringtone bore into his mind. Robson felt as though he could hardly hear himself think. Rubbing his temples, he was irritated to find his fuzzy head betrayed the onset of a headache that showed no sign of going away anytime soon. He already regretted the three bottles of wine they had finished off earlier. A trace of stale smoke hung in the air; a parting gift from the evening's exploits.

When he could ignore the phone no longer, he took a slow breath and reached across to the bedside table.

Beside him, Susan stirred and peered up at him through bleary, half-closed eyes. "What's going on?" she mumbled into his neck.

"Phone call. Go back to sleep."

"Do you have to get it?"

"It's work. You know how it is."

She traced her fingertips lightly over his chest muscles. Leaning over seductively, she planted a wet kiss on his lips.

For a moment Robson lost himself in the taste of her, allowing lust to wash over his senses. Then, with considerable effort, he pulled away. "Knock it off Susan. I'm on call, I need to take this."

She pouted, annoyed, but released her grip on his arm. With a dramatic moan, she rolled over reluctantly to let him reach again for his phone.

Grudgingly, he answered the call. "Robson here." His voice was like gravel, head pounding with the effort of talking.

"Oh, so nice of you to finally answer." His partner's voice was clipped. Evidently, she had not appreciated being kept waiting.

Robson sighed heavily. "Sorry Zahra. I was kind of in the middle of something." He was half distracted by Susan, who had slid her hand up his back to gently caress his neck.

"Well, in that case I'm so sorry to interrupt." Zahra's voice was dripping with sarcasm.

With another sigh, Robson pulled himself up and swung his legs over the side of the bed. "What have we got?"

"Stabbing at Gemini Theatre down on Commercial

Street in Shoreditch. I'll fill you in en route. I'll be there to pick you up in ten minutes."

"Right. I'm on it. See you soon." Hanging up the phone, he bent down to give Susan a quick peck on the cheek. "Got to go honey. Feel free to stay here. You can let yourself out in the morning."

She dropped back onto the pillow, crossing her arms sulkily. "I wish you didn't have to go."

"Me too, but duty calls."

True to her word, exactly ten minutes later a black BMW pulled up outside his flat. Zahra honked the horn impatiently as Robson peered out of the window noting her arrival below. He grabbed his keys and planted a final hasty kiss on Susan's cheek. Slamming the front door behind him, he raced down four flights of stairs to emerge onto the street.

Pulling open the passenger door, he slid quickly inside the car. Detective Sergeant Nadia Zahra was drumming her fingers distractedly on the steering wheel. She tossed him a curt smile and twisted the key in the ignition to fire up the engine.

Robson leaned his head against the cool glass of the car window, inhaling in ragged, wheezy gasps. Struggling to catch his breath, he resolved for what must have been the twentieth time that he really had to give up the cigarettes. His chest felt like shit. To make matters worse, his brain was foggy and he still felt faintly drunk. Strictly speaking he wasn't allowed to drink when on call, but so far he had managed to get away with it and there had been no major disasters. Zahra was far from condoning his drinking but they had settled into a comfortable mutual understanding whereby it was rarely, if ever, discussed. Plus, they had an unwritten rule that she was always the driver.

Just in case.

It was then Robson noticed, in the rushed scramble to get ready, he not only was wearing a crumpled shirt but had also picked up odd socks and was wearing one black, one brown, poking out from above his shoes.

Great professional image, he thought, pulling down his trouser legs self-consciously.

A cursory glance at his reflection in the car window revealed a somewhat dishevelled appearance. His jet-black hair stuck up haphazardly, he had bleary, blood-shot eyes and coarse stubble was erupting from his chin. Zahra observed him for a brief moment, her astute gaze passing over him, taking it all in. Embarrassed, Robson ran his fingers through his tousled hair.

She must think I look a right state, he mused to himself.

Nadia Zahra in comparison always managed to look immaculate, yet endearingly low maintenance, no matter how quick the turnaround time. Her fresh-faced, youthful appearance warranted only the smallest smattering of make-up. Flawless, dark honey skin framed her deep brown eyes. The shrewd young Muslim detective had an uncanny ability to always know exactly what he was thinking. Zahra could read his thoughts so easily it was as though he had them written all over his face. He had given up trying to hide anything from her a long time ago, it was like being partnered with a mind reader.

Her hair was always secured beneath a bright,

colourful hijab; today's colour was a deep mahogany red, silk with a decorative floral pattern along the hem. Often Robson found himself theorising that beneath her demure hijab she had a flowing mess of aqua-marine blue hair. A rebellious statement against the politics of society dictating how we should look; after all few people would ever know.

"So, I interrupted something?" Zahra enquired cheekily, a sly smile spreading across her face.

"Just watching TV."

Zahra laughed heartily. She clearly wasn't buying that explanation for one second. "Susan?" she guessed. When Robson stared out of the window in lieu of answering she looked at him sharply. "Susan?" she repeated, a trace of urgency in her voice. "Tell me it's still Susan."

Robson relented, giving a heavy sigh. "Yeah, still Susan."

Relaxing, Zahra settled back into the driving seat. She had known about Susan for some time. Zahra knew about all of them, Robson had a habit of over-sharing in that area. Not that he considered himself a lothario, but with his classic good looks he found it all too easy to hook up with the women who tended to gravitate towards him. Plus, he had the whole myst-erious brooding thing nailed. Why that was appealing, he had no idea. But for some reason, women always loved it and consequently he had enjoyed a number of casual flings over the years.

Robson was the first to admit most of his ill-fated relationships had lasted significantly longer than they would have done without Zahra's sage advice. Susan had been around for a few months now and it was a testament to his partner's approval that she had lasted longer than any of his previous lovers. Zahra seemed to be quite taken with her and had even started joking about Susan being 'The One.' She enjoyed watching him squirm at the prospect of settling down into a committed relationship.

Even as he approached his late-thirties he still struggled to make his lovers stick. 'Daddy issues,' Zahra constantly teased. She was right of course, she always was. But he definitely was not prepared to deal with that emotional quagmire just yet. Once that door was opened, there was no going back. The mere thought of his father made a tight knot form in the deepest pit of his stomach. It was much easier to simply make sure people kept their distance so the daunting prospect of commitment never rose its ugly head.

Zahra was driving fast, always a challenge on the congested streets of London. Her beady eyes darted around as she skilfully manoeuvred obstacles as the car blitzed down the road. Robson braced himself as they flew over another pothole and landed with an abrupt jolt. Exhaling deeply, his stomach lurched. He felt far too delicate for this high-speed journey.

Cursing as a taxi cab pulled out in front of them, Zahra swerved recklessly to avoid hitting it. "Bloody London drivers!"

"Good night?" Robson queried conversationally.

"Fine," she replied curtly, shooting him a warning look.

Nadia Zahra was a great partner in many ways;

dedicated, tenacious, brave. She was resourceful and fiercely loyal. But she was a closed book when it came to her personal life. Robson had tried numerous times to crack her impenetrable veneer, but to no avail. He tended to speak a lot about his own personal life to compensate, hoping it might encourage her to share more in return. However, his strategy had failed to date; their deeper conversations remained frustratingly one-sided.

"So, tell me about the crime."

Zahra nodded, back in business-mode. "Right, you're going to love this. Our victim is a twenty-one-year-old black woman called Nikita Gowon. She stabbed herself in the stomach live onstage during an amateur theatre performance of *Macbeth*."

"She stabbed *herself?*" Robson repeated slowly.

"Yep, you heard right. Apparently, she was playing Lady Macbeth in the show and it was meant to be an onstage suicide. Allegedly there was supposed to be some sort of retractable prop knife, all part of a master illusion. However, somehow the fake knife was switched with a real blade backstage. Our leading lady didn't realise until it was too late and well, you can imagine the rest."

Robson slumped back in his seat. Unfortunately, he could picture the gruesome scene all too clearly. He always had been squeamish. Ten years with the Met had never fully prepared him for seeing butchered bodies in the flesh. Suddenly very aware of the copious amount of alcohol swilling around in his stomach, he felt a tad queasy just thinking about it.

"Anyway, she was rushed to hospital with serious

stomach injuries."

"Wait, what? She's still *alive*?"

"For now," said Zahra, grim-faced. "But I'm not going to lie, it doesn't sound good."

After what seemed like no time at all, Zahra turned onto Commercial Street. Mercifully, they had managed to make it across to East London without becoming casualties of a high-speed collision. Just. Parallel parking in the first available space, the pair stepped out of the vehicle and started to make their way up the busy street.

"Neil Hillton is the show's director. Heard of him?"

Robson shook his head, surprised Zahra had.

"He's touted as one of the hottest theatre directors in London to emerge in the last few years. An avant-garde success story. Considers himself to be the twenty-first century answer to radical theatre."

That sounded about right to Robson. Looking around the bustling Shoreditch street, he could see the place was overrun with achingly hip bars and clubs. Naturally, the theatre scene would be trendy and vibrant as well.

"Mr Hillton specialises in modern-day adaptations of old classics, particularly Shakespeare. He has a reputation for being revolutionary."

Robson looked at her, eyebrows raised. "Since when do you keep tabs on London theatre directors?"

Zahra shrugged nonchalantly. "I saw his production of *Romeo and Juliet* last year. He fancies himself as the theatrical version of Stephen Spielberg; a visionary mastermind. All emphasis on the visual effects, whereas the actual acting was pretty mediocre. Too much style over substance if you ask me."

"I didn't know you were into theatre?" In two years, this was the first time she had ever mentioned going to see a show and they lived in London – the hub of the national theatre scene. "Hang on a minute. *Romeo and Juliet?* A romance? Was this a hot date?"

She punched him playfully in the shoulder and smiled noncommittally. "Never you mind that. Right, let's go meet our famous director."

The theatre, as it turned out, was a converted Victorian warehouse that had been refurbished to house a contemporary amphitheatre for Off West End performances. The former industrial building dominated the street and Robson had to admit it was a very cool and edgy venue. As they got closer, he could see to his dismay that there was a small crowd of reporters already camped outside the entrance with several cameramen in tow.

Vultures, he thought contemptuously. He couldn't help himself, he always had hated the media. All the reporters he had ever met would happily sell their soul for a good exclusive; anything for a juicy headline. It had been bad enough in the old days, but now in the era of social media they were insufferable. Constantly scouring the Internet for any breaking news, they had an unnerving tendency to swoop down on crime scenes, sometimes quicker than the police themselves, before the blood was even dry on the pavement.

Robson closed his eyes for a moment and took a deep breath. The noisy crowd was exacerbating his headache, which had now kicked into full swing.

Suddenly, a particularly plucky blonde reporter broke away from the throng and bounded towards them with a spring in her step.

She thrust a microphone towards them aggressively. "Is it true a young woman was stabbed onstage here tonight, in front of a paying audience?"

Of course, that was the angle they would run with, groaned Robson. The press would have a field day with this case. He could already foresee the sensationalist headlines. *Horror at London Theatre. Bloodbath at cursed Macbeth. Tragic stabbing live onstage.*

"We cannot comment on an ongoing investigation," said Zahra firmly, striding past the reporter with Robson hurrying behind her.

A barrage of questions followed as the reporters swarmed around them, but Zahra led the way through the crowd confidently without looking in their direction. Robson felt his heart swell with pride for his young partner. He loved her no-nonsense attitude, even in the most challenging of situations, she never so much as batted an eyelid.

Nadia Zahra had risen quickly through the ranks to become one of the youngest sergeants on the Metropolitan Police Force after being promoted at the tender age of twenty-five. Driven and ambitious, she still maintained a healthy disregard for bureaucracy which he couldn't help but admire. Initially, Robson had been doubtful when he was first partnered with the petite, well-spoken Muslim woman two years ago. But Zahra had wasted no time in proving herself and together the pair had become a formidable team, a force to be reckoned with.

Following speedily in her footsteps, Robson pushed his way through the swarming crowd and up the steep concrete steps. Together they ducked under the yellow crime scene tape and pushed open the heavy metal door to step through into the theatre.

CHAPTER FOUR

Blood Hath Been Shed Ere Now

The bright house lights basked the stage in an eerie, golden glow. The auditorium stood empty, lines of vacant seats strewn with litter. A huge, echoing cavern, alive with expectation. Robson had always found empty theatres hauntingly mysterious; a myriad of possibilities just waiting to be brought to life.

Up on the abandoned stage, a cordoned off area was marked with fluorescent crime scene tape fluttering in a slight breeze. The forensics team were still in transit, on their way to document the evidence. A noticeable chill and the frequent creaking of the old windows indicated the cold evening wind was seeping into the large open space. The interior of the renovated warehouse still showcased a number of original features to preserve the industrial aesthetic. Exposed brickwork and timber beams were complemented with contemporary metal finishes, which resulted in a performance space that was both historically quirky and effortlessly modern.

The only souls in sight stood to the left of the stage; a uniformed police officer alongside a fair-haired man dressed in dark jeans and a bright blue floral shirt.

Walking purposefully over to the pair, Robson flashed his badge with authority. "Detective Inspector Finley Robson and this here is Detective Sergeant Nadia Zahra."

Nodding in response, the police officer motioned to the man beside him. "Good evening, I'm Police Constable Randall and this is Mr Neil Hillton. He's the director of this production and the owner of this theatre. He's the one who called it in earlier."

Extending a trembling hand for a limp handshake, the director smiled weakly at them. "Welcome to the show." A concerned frown appeared on his face as he quickly added, "Have you heard anything about how she's doing?"

Zahra shook her head. "No. She's still at the hospital, best place for her right now. We'll keep you updated as soon as we hear anything." She paused respectfully for a moment before continuing. "We've got a few questions we'd like to ask if you're feeling up to it?"

Neil gave a feeble nod. "Of course. Please ask me anything. I'm more than happy to help in any way I can."

Robson placed a comforting hand on Neil's shoulder and led him to the first row of seats. The deathly pale director shivered as he lowered himself into a seat. Vibrant blue, his gaudy, flowery shirt was indicative of a man who under normal circumstances was flamboyant and charismatic; a larger than life

31

character. But tonight, he seemed completely deflated, a mere shadow of his former self. It was more than the wind being knocked from his sails; closer to his boat being shipwrecked and splintering into a hundred jagged shards.

Zahra leaned against the stage and produced a black notebook from her pocket.

Robson settled into a chair next to Neil. "From what we understand, the victim is a young actress called Nikita Gowon. In your own time can you talk us through exactly what happened here. Tell us everything, no detail is too small."

Neil exhaled a long, shaky breath. His eyes were downcast, fixated on the dusty wooden floor. "Honestly, I'm still trying to get my head around it myself. Nikita... Nikki...was Lady Macbeth in the play. This evening was our opening night. It was going really well; the audience was loving it. Possibly the best reception I've ever had." A glimmer of pride flashed across Neil's face as he puffed out his chest. "Anyway, it was the second scene in Act Five; Lady Macbeth's famous death..." He faltered, voice catching.

Robson placed a hand on his shoulder reassuringly. "Take your time."

"So, by this point of course, Lady Macbeth is overwrought with guilt, haunted by the memory of those she had conspired to kill with her husband in their quest for power."

"I'm familiar with the play Mr Hillton."

"Oh, very well. Anyhow, Nikki had just finished delivering the notable 'out damned spot' speech. She performed it brilliantly too, really moving. Then, she stabbed herself in the stomach and collapsed onto the floor, exactly as we had practised in rehearsals. I was watching from the wings. I didn't realise anything was wrong. She seemed a bit distressed but Nikki was a great actress, I assumed she was embellishing her performance…" Neil trailed off again, dropping his head to his hands.

Robson stole a glance at Zahra who was studiously making notes. For a long moment no one spoke, the silence stretching out between them until Robson pressed on with his next question. "I know Shakespeare's works a little. I thought Lady Macbeth traditionally died off-stage?"

Zahra raised her eyebrows. It was an oft-forgotten fact that in his younger years Robson had studied English Literature at Cambridge University and had graduated with a first class degree nonetheless. He rarely mentioned his university days, not least because of the relentless teasing and 'posh toff' name calling he tended to endure at the hands of his amused colleagues whenever he accidentally brought it up in conversation. However, his elite education had left him with an almost encyclopaedic knowledge of historical literature. Having taken a specific interest in Shakespeare – his specialist subject for his dissertation – he could still recall many of the classic plays, *Macbeth* included.

Raising his head, Neil shot an irritated glance in his direction and threw his hands up in sudden exasperation. "It's called drama! Artistic expression. This is a *modernisation* of *Macbeth*. I've got license to make some bloody changes. Everyone in this city thinks they're a goddamn director."

Robson held his hands up in surrender. "Okay, okay, calm down. I was only asking. So, humour me, can you explain what was meant to happen?"

Neil heaved a huge sigh. "Fake knife. Retractable blade. Pretty nifty idea, right?"

Nodding, Robson attempted to convey the notion he was impressed in his expression. It was fast becoming clear that stroking this man's ego was the key to keeping him talking.

"But that's not all. To add to the illusion, I attached a small pin to the top of the handle. Idea was the pin was sharp enough to pierce through the plastic bag of fake blood sneakily concealed under Nikki's dress strapped to her body. The effect is rather impressive even if I do say so myself." A smug smile had started to blossom on his lips.

"I think I'm following. So, how long was it before you realised your theatrical stunt had gone wrong?"

A dark grimace returned to Neil's face. "After the curtain had dropped. Nikki was meant to immediately move off the stage so we could do a prompt scene change. Only she didn't get up. She just lay there, not moving a muscle. At first, I thought she was being melodramatic, milking it, you know? Megan went across to help her up and suddenly started crying. Then, it was obvious something was wrong. I ran over and she was staring blankly, all glassy-eyed. There was blood everywhere." Neil breathed in shakily and took a moment to compose himself before continuing. "We all jumped into action of course. Her boyfriend, Jimmy, tried to stop the bleeding by applying pressure to the wound. But to be honest I thought it was already too late. At first, I didn't understand how the stunt could possibly have gone wrong. There was an awful moment when I thought the retractable mechanism had jammed, but when I took a closer look I realised it wasn't the fake prop knife at all. It was a real blade; an exact replica."

Zahra's head snapped up. "I'm sorry, did you say the weapon was a *replica* knife?"

Neil nodded. "Precisely. Looked exactly the same, right down to the ornate red jewels embedded on the golden handle. It was very masterfully done, even I couldn't tell the difference at first. You've got to look really closely to see the blade is fixed, there's nowhere for it to retract back into. I'm not surprised Nikki didn't realise when she picked it up."

Robson pondered that with interest. Deception on that scale took time and careful planning, not to mention premeditation. Plus, whoever was behind it would need the means to source an effective replica knife, he wasn't even sure how someone would go about organising such a thing. Evidently on the same wavelength, Zahra paused from taking notes to speak to Neil about how they would start investigating right away, exploring specialist stores to hopefully shed some light on the situation.

"Can we ask, where did the original prop knife come from?"

Neil shrugged, shoulders sagging in despair. "I've got no idea. It's been part of the theatre props collection for generations. It's a favourite of mine in fact, very effective. I use it in a lot of my productions."

"Like *Romeo and Juliet*," said Zahra, smiling.

Neil squinted at her quizzically. "Yes. How did you know that?"

"Lucky guess."

Hands at his temples, Robson mused over the replica knife revelation. "I suppose that leads us onto our next question. How do you think someone managed to swap the knives around backstage? Who had access to the props area?"

"That's what I keep coming back to," admitted Neil. "Thing is, there was limited opportunity. Backstage access is restricted, no member of the public would be able to get through to where the props are stored unnoticed. My front of house staff have all been in their positions since the show started and the technical team who control the sound and lighting operate from the elevated light box in the auditorium. So, that just leaves the cast."

"What about the backstage crew?"

The director shook his head. "There isn't one. I run quite small, streamlined productions here. One of the younger actresses, Violet Underwood, doubles up as a stagehand to make sure all the costumes and props are in order backstage. But beyond that, the actors were each responsible for ensuring they had everything they needed for their upcoming scenes. They coordinated any scenery changes too."

"And how many actors are in the *Macbeth* cast?"

"Seven, including Nikki. But if only the cast had immediate access backstage that means…" He trailed off uncertainly, clearly not wanting to verbalise that particular train of thought.

"That means the culprit has to be one of your

actors," finished Robson.

A haunted look fell upon the director's gaunt face. "I can't believe any of them would be capable of such a thing. But like you say – it's the only possible expl-anation."

"When was the last time you checked the show props and knew for sure the original retractable knife was still there?"

"I checked through all the props myself an hour before the performance started. I can guarantee they were all correct then. Everything was exactly in order, just as it should be."

"Can anyone verify that?"

The director shot Robson an accusing look. "Are you saying you don't believe me?"

Robson stared at him blankly. "Well, sir, you've got to understand you are currently one of our lead suspects. You said it yourself, the culprit has to be someone who had backstage access. Obviously, that includes you as well as the cast."

Neil paled. A flicker of doubt flashed across his face, as though he hadn't considered that possibility.

"So, I'll ask again, can anyone verify that?"

"Yes, yes, young Violet, I think. And Emma might have seen me. Perhaps, I'm not sure. I can check." Flustered, Neil stumbled over his words, like he was struggling to string them together.

"Who would have access to temporarily steal the prop knife so a replica could be made?" Zahra asked.

Neil considered it for a moment. "If truth be told, that could be any member of the cast. We don't do a prop inventory check every night. As long as it was returned in time for when it was next required for a scene rehearsal, I doubt anyone would have even noticed, myself included."

Robson nodded, he had figured as much. "Where is the weapon now? At the hospital with Nikki?"

Flinching, Neil shook his head. "No. It's around here somewhere. Up on the stage I think."

Robson arched an eyebrow, incredulous. "You took it *out*? Isn't that *First Aid 101?* Never remove a protruding object if someone is impaled? Keep it in to help stop the blood flow so they don't bleed to death?"

Neil shrugged helplessly. "I don't know what happened. It was chaos! Someone must have yanked it out in the commotion, I didn't see who. I'm sure they would have been trying to help, an honest mistake."

Robson frowned. "Or someone was making sure the job got finished – that she definitely died."

"Didn't work though, did it?" snapped Neil. "She's still alive."

Sighing wearily, Robson chose not to press the point. Emotions were clearly running high and he couldn't deal with trying to placate the director right now. "Well, we'll get the weapon sent to our forensics team, dust it for fingerprints. See where that gets us."

Neil paled again, edging ever closer to a ghostly white. "Erm, alright. Although my fingerprints will be on it too. I picked it up earlier to inspect it after Nikki was stabbed. Sorry, I wasn't thinking." A slight tremor shook his voice and he stared at them pleadingly.

Zahra raised her eyebrows sceptically. Effortlessly she caught Robson's eye and they didn't need to speak to communicate what they were both thinking. *That was awfully convenient.*

"How about the original retractable prop knife? Do you know where that has ended up?"

Neil gave an apologetic shrug. "I'm afraid I've got no idea. I can't find it anywhere. I guess whoever swapped them around hid it to make sure Nikki definitely picked up the fixed blade."

With a slight, almost imperceptible shake of his head, Robson continued, "So, obviously we'll need to interview everyone in the cast, get their witness statements. Try to work out what happened here."

Neil looked up, worried. "I sent them all home. Was that the wrong thing to do?"

"That's fine, don't worry about it. We can get in touch to organise speaking to them. Have you got their contact details?"

"Yes, yes, I can get them for you."

Robson nodded gratefully. "Great, that would be useful, thanks. We'll instruct them not to speak to each other until they've given their formal statements."

Picking up her notebook again, Zahra chimed in. "It would be helpful if you could give us a quick breakdown of who is in the cast. You mentioned it's quite a small one, is that right?"

"Yes. That's one of my hallmarks as a director. I like to work with small casts with the actors doubling up to play different roles. It adds a new dimension to the show, plus it's more of an interesting challenge for the actors of course."

Zahra nodded. "Quite. So, can you talk us through the main players of *Macbeth*."

A self-satisfied smirk crept across the director's

face. He was back in his element now he was discussing the play again. "Sure. Let's see, Nikki joined the show with her boyfriend, Jimmy, and two of her university friends, Megan and Peter. They were a couple too. Thick as thieves those four, always together. A talented chap named Ben is our leading man, Macbeth. I've worked with him before; he's great. Then there's Emma, another amazing actress, she's quite something. And finally, Violet who…tries her best."

Scribbling furiously in her notebook Zahra barely looked up as she asked, "Was there any conflict in the cast you were aware of? Any disgruntled actors not getting along with our victim?"

Neil threw up his hands theatrically. "Every cast has its politics! There are the good actors, the not-so-good ones, those who dream of being famous and those who don't take it seriously – who are just having a laugh. Then, inevitably some people use acting as pure escapism – a break from their boring, mundane lives."

A scathing tone had permeated the director's voice. Robson stole another quick glance at Zahra. His partner was watching Neil carefully, a small, amused smile on her face.

With an exasperated sigh, Neil continued, "Nikki did get along with most people to be fair, she was a lovely girl. She didn't see eye to eye with Emma, they were self-confessed rivals. Vying for the spotlight, they were at each other's throats for most of rehearsals." Falling silent for a moment, Neil seemed to think better of what he had just shared and started hastily backtracking. "Not that I think Emma tried to kill her of course. She's not capable of that, far too much of a gentle nature. Come to think of it, Nikki's relationship with her boyfriend Jimmy has been pretty strained recently. They keep arguing about something, I have no idea what."

Robson nodded. The director was hardly being enlightening but to some extent he had not been expecting much from him. From experience, he had found the person in charge rarely knew what was really going on. Keeping his expression neutral, he began to wrap up their interview. "Okay, thanks. You own this building too, is that correct?"

"Yes, I live for this place. It's my livelihood, my passion. I guess you could say I'm married to the theatre."

"We'll need to shut it down for a few days. Right now, it's a crime scene first and foremost."

Neil stared at him, affronted. "But what about the show tomorrow night?"

Robson shook his head in disbelief. "In case you had forgotten, one of your actors was nearly killed here tonight. You can't seriously be thinking about the next performance?"

"The show must go on. This was the opening night of a fortnight run!"

Robson failed to hide the sarcasm in his response. "Apologies for the inconvenience, investigating the potentially lethal stabbing of a young woman trumps selling theatre tickets."

After thanking Neil and assuring him they would be in

touch again soon, Robson and Zahra headed to the stage. Their forensics colleagues had appeared on-site and were already busy photographing and cataloguing evidence. Zahra dutifully dug out a bundle of latex gloves from her coat pocket and handed Robson a pair.

Leaving the forensics team to do their work, the two detectives made their way to the left stage wing searching intently for anything untoward that could be a potential clue.

From the corner of his field of vision, Robson noticed two lifeless black eyes staring at him. Walking closer, he saw the unseeing eyes belonged to a macabre dead pig head. *For the banquet scene,* he guessed, with a grim smile. *Disgusting idea, but unnervingly effective.*

Next to him, Zahra sniggered at the strange sight. "Now why doesn't that surprise me? It's drama, darling!" she drawled dramatically, throwing her hands up with an exaggerated flourish.

Robson laughed. It was an uncannily good impression of the flamboyant director. "Now, now, don't go *bacon* my heart."

"Seriously? I'm not even going to dignify that with a response," groaned Zahra, a small half-smile playing on her lips.

"You couldn't if you *fried*."

Zahra rolled her eyes and shot him a disparaging look. It was a poor attempt at humour Robson knew. But still making people laugh, especially Zahra, helped to make the job more bearable. Sometimes he swore it was all that got him through the day.

Looking beyond the decaying swine, an emerald

shimmer caught Robson's eye. Marching over to better inspect the backdrop, he saw something soft had been stuffed behind it. Partially concealed, it seemed like it had been hidden in a rush. Bending to his knee, he reached behind the partition to yank out a crumpled dark green velvet jacket. As the garment was dislodged from its hiding place, a metallic object clattered to the ground in a blur of silver.

"I think I've just found our missing prop knife."

Zahra hurried over for a closer look as Robson picked the knife up delicately and carefully pushed the blunt tip so the blade slowly retracted back into the handle. He lowered his hand so the blade popped out again and repeated the action of pushing it in, this time in super-fast motion. The unsettling result was so effective Zahra actually winced. It looked exactly like Robson had driven the blade right through the palm of his own hand.

"Nice trick," she said, visibly impressed. "I'll go get forensics." With that she ran off, her hijab billowing behind her, a fiery red blur in her wake.

Still crouched down, Robson took a moment to take in the scene around him. It was the first time he had been backstage at a theatre for years. He shivered as all the old memories came flooding back from long before he joined the Met. Much to the despair of his well-meaning parents Robson had enjoyed a brief dalliance of trying to earn a living as a professional writer after graduating from Cambridge University. He was younger then, high-spirited and idealistic, free from the shackles of responsible adulthood. Encouraged by his peers, Robson was naively convinced he would make it as a famous playwright. He had rather fancied himself as a modern-day William Shakespeare, bringing fresh tales of tragedy, comedy and romance to a new generation of theatre-goers.

Frequent excursions to the famous Globe Theatre in London to watch traditional Shakespeare performances had only served to add fuel to his ill-fated ambition. Surrounded by fellow dreamers, he had gone on to have the best summer of his life, full of lazy afternoons seeking inspiration. Always booze-filled, sometimes drug-fuelled, to 'get the creative juices flowing.' Honestly, he couldn't remember doing a whole lot of writing. Not that it mattered in the end. That short-lived dream had come to an abrupt end in the following April when his whole world had come crashing down around him.

CHAPTER FIVE

She Should Have Died Hereafter

After spending another hour scouting out the crime scene, the two detectives left it in the capable hands of the forensics team to finish up and seal the theatre building. Following the discovery of the concealed prop knife, they hadn't found anything else noteworthy, although Robson didn't find that particularly surprising. It was what he called a 'messy crime scene' – chockful of contaminated evidence. Processing hair fibres and fingerprints wasn't going to get them anywhere in this instance. Every person's presence at the crime scene could be explained and even fingerprints on the murder weapon could be dismissed as circumstantial evidence and definitely wouldn't lead to a conviction in court.

Next on their agenda for the night was a short drive to The Royal London Hospital in Whitechapel to speak to the victim's family. Unlike all their previous cases, Nikki Gowon marked their first victim who hadn't actually died at the crime scene. There was still a faint gleam of hope for her, which Robson couldn't help but hold on to. He hoped she was a fighter.

Swerving into a parking space, Zahra only narrowly avoided colliding with an expensive-looking Audi. Without fail, the diminutive detective always drove like she was in some sort of imaginary high-speed car chase. Taking a moment to catch his breath, Robson stepped out of the car into the crisp night air. There was a definite chill in the breeze and dark clouds were rumbling overhead, signalling a storm was brewing.

Walking in companionable silence to the hospital entrance, Robson suddenly felt grateful that it was largely deserted at this twilight hour. It was fast approaching midnight and he lacked the energy to make polite small talk with some chatty receptionist. Thankfully the reception area was eerily quiet, save for a lone whistling porter who pointed them dutifully in the direction of the Trauma Ward on the twelfth floor.

The journey there seemed to take forever as they walked through stretch upon stretch of stark hospital corridors. A random arts charity must have received funding at some point to try and brighten the place up and consequently a smattering of questionable paintings and photographs were strewn haphazardly over the white walls. Rolling green hills, wonky lighthouses and snowy mountain tops. Robson found them more bizarre than comforting, as though he was trapped in the world's most depressing art gallery.

Upon reaching the Trauma Ward, the pair were met by a perky young nurse who proved more than willing to update them on the current situation. Robson had to wonder if the hyperactive nurse was high on caffeine to help her get through the night shift. Intent on speaking a million miles an hour, she nodded her head emphatically to stress certain points and peppered her explanations with a whole load of medical termi-nology he couldn't quite grasp.

"Miss Gowon is still in emergency surgery at the moment. Unfortunately, the stab wound lacerated her liver, which caused serious internal bleeding. The blood loss caused her to go into hypovolemic shock in the ambulance on the way here. She went into cardiac arrest but the paramedics managed to resuscitate her. Dr Glynne's operating on her now, attempting to repair the damaged blood vessels. She's in the best hands, if it was me, I'd definitely want to be operated on by Dr Glynne – her reputation proceeds her. You know she's one of the most renowned trauma surgeons in the country? It's lucky the theatre was so close by for Miss Gowon to be brought here, this hospital has an international reputation as a specialist trauma and emergency centre. If anyone can save her life, it's our medical team."

"Prognosis?" queried Robson, when the nurse fin-ally paused for a breath.

"Hard to say until she's out of surgery, but honestly I wouldn't say her chances of survival are great. But we don't fully know what we are dealing with yet, we've got to take it one hour at a time." Lowering her voice she added, "Her parents are in the waiting room down the corridor with their youngest daughter, all distraught as you can imagine. You know they were in the audience? Saw the whole thing take place."

Robson nodded grimly. In his time, he had met a lot of grief-stricken, heartbroken parents, but had never yet encountered any who had the misfortune of actually watching their own child stab themselves right in front of them. He felt a deep pang of sympathy for her family, he couldn't imagine what they must be going through.

"Are we able to talk to them now?" Zahra asked, business-like as usual.

The nurse hesitated. "You're welcome to try. But, as I say, they're completely devastated. Her mother in particular was verging on hysterical earlier. So, I'm not sure how much sense you'll get out of them. But I'm sure if it would assist the investigation, they'd be happy to help. To be honest it might be a welcome distraction, it's never easy waiting for someone to come out of surgery."

Zahra thanked the nurse who quickly turned on her heel and bounced down the corridor, leading them to the waiting room. Robson knocked respectfully before entering.

No matter how many times they spoke to grieving parents, that part of the job never got any easier. Robson could never shake the feeling he was invading the family's privacy, gate-crashing on an intimate moment of mourning. Unfortunately, in his line of work he spent far too much time meeting family members on the worst day of their lives.

As they stepped through the door, the clinical, blank walls seemed to close in, shrinking around them. Already stuffy, the oppressive atmosphere dominated

Robson's thoughts. He knew from experience hospital waiting rooms were truly terrible places. He felt faintly nauseous at the memory and wondered, not for the first time, how long he could continue dealing with such harrowing cases. Every victim had been taking more of a toll recently until it felt like the weight of despair was starting to crush him.

Zahra's brusque voice jolted Robson back to the present. A well-dressed, tall black man rose from his chair to greet them, shaking Zahra's hand firmly before turning to welcome him in the same fashion. Slender, with sharp cheekbones and warm eyes, the man appeared to be in his early fifties. He looked weary, as if he was carrying the world on his shoulders.

"I take it you're with the police? I'm Mr Isaac Gowon, Nikki's father. This here is my wife, Sade, and this is our youngest daughter, Aisha."

He motioned to his wife, a tired looking woman with soft features and thick black braids who was slumped in one of the wooden chairs. She offered them a weak smile when introduced. Her daughter, who looked about eleven years old, was curled up next to her. Her small head rested on her mother's shoulder, who had an arm wrapped protectively round her. The young girl was half asleep, but still watched them suspiciously through drooping eyes and dark curls that had fallen across most of her face.

"Please allow us to introduce ourselves. My name is Detective Inspector Finley Robson and this is my partner, Detective Sergeant Nadia Zahra. We'll be leading the attempted murder investigation concerning your daughter. We've come straight from the crime scene. I understand this is an awful time, but we were hoping it might be possible to ask you a few quick questions?" Robson spoke gently, his words a soothing balm.

Isaac nodded sombrely and motioned for them to take a seat. "Of course, of course. Anything we can do to help. *Attempted murder,* dear God, help us. We are still in utter disbelief anyone would ever dream of hurting Nikki. She is such a wonderful girl, everybody loves her. This whole thing is a complete nightmare." His voice quivered and he sank back down into his seat next to his wife.

Robson lowered himself into an uncomfortable chair across from the family, with Zahra sitting on his right, notebook already in her hand. Just as he was about to begin, Isaac glanced across at his wife, sharing a knowing look.

Sade stooped down to pick up her leather handbag and started rooting about in it. Nudging her drowsy daughter, she spoke softly, "Aisha, honey, why don't you listen to some music while we talk to these nice detectives?"

Aisha roused herself with a yawn, stretching out in her chair and rolling her eyes. "Mum, I wasn't born yesterday! I know what sort of questions they'll be asking." Fully awake now, her dark eyes darted around, studying Robson and Zahra's faces in turn. She settled on staring at Robson, her expression pleading. "You want to know who would want to try and kill my sister, right? Well you better find them, they need to pay for what they did."

Before he had chance to reply, Sade interrupted

abruptly. "Please Aisha, do as you're told. I'm in no mood to argue."

Reluctantly, Aisha relented and snatched the phone being held out to her. With a resigned sigh, she slipped the earphones into position and snuggled down again, her little head bobbing slightly to the music.

Robson and Zahra exchanged a quick look, silently signalling to each other they would keep it short.

"Let's start with your daughter, Nikita Gowon. What can you tell us about her?"

"Nikki is brilliant. Everything a parent could hope for – friendly, compassionate, kind. She brightens up a room just by walking into it." Isaac beamed, swelling with pride as he spoke. "She's smart too; a straight A student, on course to get a first-class degree. She's studying Theatre and Performance Practice at London Metropolitan University, approaching the end of her final third year now. She always works so hard, a very conscientious student. She took to university straight away, such a social butterfly."

Nodding, Zahra glanced at her notes. "She lived in student accommodation with friends for the first two years, but moved back into the family home for this final year, is that right? What prompted that decision? Seems a bit unusual to leave a shared house with all her friends if she's as social as you say."

Isaac hesitated, looking pointedly at his wife before replying, "It just made sense financially. She was keen to save some money by not paying rent. London prices are ridiculous these days, as I'm sure you can appreciate. Plus, we've had a few family issues Nikki wanted to be around for. We've really valued her support over the last year. She's quite a calming influence, which is exactly what we've needed."

"Care to elaborate on the 'family issues?'" pressed Robson.

"Not particularly," Isaac replied shortly, visibly flinching. Next to him, his wife looked down blinking back fresh tears. "It's personal. Do you mind if we don't talk about it right now? It's not relevant and it's been a tough night."

Robson made a mental note to follow up on that topic at some point in the near future. For now though, he let them off the hook. "No problem. So, are we right in thinking Nikki started working on the *Macbeth* production just under two months ago, at the beginning of February? An extracurricular activity with an amateur cast. But we understand she already knew some of her fellow castmates from university?"

"Indeed. Her boyfriend, Jimmy Walker, is performing alongside her, as is her best friend, Megan Newbold. Meg's boyfriend, Peter Winters, is in the show as well. They're all on the same university course. It was Nikki's idea, she loves being onstage. She's done quite a few amateur plays, dreams of becoming a famous actress."

His voice caught and he turned away sniffing. Beside him, his wife started crying noiselessly, shoulders jerking as tears streamed down her cheeks. Isaac slipped a comforting arm around her and gently kissed her forehead.

"We won't be much longer, we promise," said Zahra. "You're doing great, this is really helpful. What can you tell us about her boyfriend, Jimmy

Walker?"

"Ah Jimmy, a fine young man. They got together halfway through their first year and have been inseparable ever since. She's completely smitten with him. They're great together, Nikki's got a lot more confident since they started dating; he definitely brings out the best in her."

Zahra smiled. "What about Megan Newbold? You said they were best friends?"

Isaac's face visibly brightened. "Yes, that's right. Meg is lovely. As luck would have it, she ended up in the bedroom next to Nikki's in her first-year student flat. They got on straight away and the rest, as they say, is history. They lived together in second year too and even this year when Nikki has been back at home, Meg has always made the effort to come over and visit. She even helps us cook our Sunday roasts. She's a part of the family as much as Jimmy is."

"And Megan's boyfriend, Peter Winters?"

"Quite a new relationship, I think. I believe they started dating just before Christmas, so a few months now. I must admit we've never met him in person, but we hear Meg is quite taken with him."

His wife piped up then, "I think Nikki was more excited about the prospect of double-dating than anything else. She thought it would be fun, all four of them hanging out together. She worries about Meg, you know how it is with girls? She didn't want her to feel like a third wheel all the time."

"Did Nikki ever talk about any of the other actors? The ones she hadn't met before?"

Isaac shared a fleeting look with his wife who

shrugged helplessly. "Not really. She thought the director, Mr Hillton, was a bit of an eccentric. She complained he was always micromanaging, wanting to be in charge of even the slightest detail of her performance. It frustrated her, but in the grand scheme of things she didn't mind too much. She was just so chuffed to be given the role of Lady Macbeth last-minute. All those months as an understudy finally paid off."

Robson frowned. "Sorry, I'm confused. Do you mean originally Nikki wasn't meant to play that role?"

Isaac looked at him, surprised. "No, she was one of the witches. She was swapped in as Lady Macbeth only two weeks ago. Took over from another actress, the blonde one, Emma I think her name is. Mr Hillton didn't tell you? I assumed he would have mentioned something like that."

Shifting in his seat, Robson leaned forward, elbows on his knees, as if he was about to tell a story. "Any idea what prompted that sudden cast change? Seems quite out of character for a control freak director who likes to be in charge at all cost."

Isaac shrugged. "Not a clue I'm afraid. Nikki mentioned something about artistic differences, but she didn't dwell on it. She was thrilled to have the part; the play was quite a big deal. The director's pretty well-known in theatre circles, so she said there was likely to be a few talent scouts attending on some of the nights. Nikki was excited about the prospect of getting spotted, she says the acting industry is all about being in the right place at the right time."

Robson nodded slowly, taking a minute to digest

this new information. "How about the other cast members? Did Nikki ever talk about any of them?"

"She mentioned Ben a few times, he's the fellow with the dreadlocks who plays Macbeth. She thought he was great, really talented. I don't think she was mighty impressed with Emma, I heard Nikki complain about her poor attitude pretty scathingly. Very unlike Nikki to speak unkindly about anyone, so I think she must have properly rubbed her up the wrong way."

"So, do you think any of them would have a reason to hurt her?" asked Zahra.

"Gosh no. Like I say she was popular, she got along with everyone."

"Except for Emma evidently?"

Isaac screwed up his face at that comment. "Well, yes. I don't think they saw eye to eye but there's a bit of a jump from that to attempted murder. From what I've heard Emma seems pretty harmless, I doubt she would be capable of something so atrocious."

Sade spoke up at this point, agreeing with her husband. "Really there is no one who would want to hurt Nikki. She's a great girl. When you speak to her for yourself, you'll see that."

Only if we get to speak to her, thought Robson grimly.

"If it's alright with you, it would be helpful for us to have a quick look around your house at some point when it's convenient? Have a look in Nikki's bedroom, see if we can find anything that might help our investigation."

"Of course. Anything you need. Although, I don't know what you're expecting to find. Can we organise that tomorrow? We'll be staying in the hospital tonight."

"No problem at all. There's no immediate rush. We can get started with our interviews in the meantime."

Robson paused, gearing himself up to ask the question he had been trying to avoid. "Now, I'm sorry but I have to ask, has Nikki ever expressed any suicidal thoughts? Is there any reason why she would want to kill herself?"

Sade took a sharp intake of breath. "No! Absolutely not. She isn't that sort of girl. She has everything to live for. She's so young, she still has her whole life ahead of her."

In her arms, little Aisha had surreptitiously paused the phone's music and was listening carefully to their conversation. Her lips turned downwards as a haunted expression crept across her young face.

Isaac glared at Robson. "I can assure you, no. Her mental health is really good these days. There is certainly no chance she would ever contemplate suicide now."

"*Now?* As in she might have contemplated it before?"

While his wife glared at him, Isaac sucked in a deep lungful of air. He seemed flustered, anxious. "That's not what I meant. Nikki had a few troubled teenage years, she was diagnosed with depression for a while towards the end of high school. But that's ancient history. She's doing well, really well. It's been great to see her finally happy again."

Interjecting, Sade added, "Trust me, we know our daughter well enough to be confident she is definitely not suicidal by any stretch of the imagination. Honestly, I think this whole thing has to be one big misunderstanding. Perhaps it was just a terrible mistake? A mishap backstage?"

Isaac straightened his back in his chair, the warmth gone from his face. "Are you quite done with your questioning? I think it's about time we got back to praying for Nikki to make it through surgery rather than coming up with wild conspiracy theories about why our daughter would want to kill herself."

With an appreciative nod, Robson rose to his feet. "Thank you for your time. We'll keep you updated as our investigation progresses. We are truly sorry for what you're going through. I do hope the surgery goes well." He fished a crumpled business card out of his jacket pocket and handed it over. "Please don't hesitate to get in touch if you have any questions or remember anything else you think we should know."

Walking silently down the corridor, Robson couldn't help but feel relieved they were free from the bleak waiting room. Yet still he was troubled by the kaleidoscope of jumbled thoughts churning around in his mind. *Why would a self-confessed control freak director risk compromising his own show by changing the lead female role a fortnight before opening night? What would motivate someone to source a realistic and deadly stage knife replica? What family issues would prompt a social, friendly student to move back home after experiencing a taste of freedom? And why were Nikki's parents so reluctant to divulge more details about her troubled past?*

Next to him, Zahra gave a little cough to get his

attention. Looking across at his partner, Robson could see she was also deep in thought.

"You think the suicide question was too much?"

"Your timing wasn't great," she admitted. "But I have to say I've been thinking the same thing. It would be wrong to assume it was definitely someone else who swapped around the knives. Nikki had just the same opportunity to do that, more so you could say. I mean it would be a pretty dramatic way to go if she did want to kill herself. But she is an aspiring actress after all, they do tend to love a good audience."

"Exactly. Guess we'll need to first establish if there is actually a crime to solve."

CHAPTER SIX

Fair is Foul, and Foul is Fair

Upon arriving back at the Police Station, Robson was amused to see some enterprising officer had taken it upon themselves to enlarge the monochrome cast pictures from the theatre programme and stuck them on the large noticeboard in the centre of the wall. Each person's name was pinned under their photograph, with Nikki's headshot taking pride of place in the centre of the display. Surveying the assortment of potential suspects, Robson noted they ranged from classically beautiful to plain-looking, and everything in-between.

"A rag tag group of performers if ever I did see one," commented Zahra, clearly on the same wavelength.

Robson smiled in agreement. "Guess that's the draw of amateur theatre, it attracts all manner of people." Hand resting on his hip, he studied the eight faces staring down at him from the wall. "The cast really is small, isn't it? Only seven performers, including our victim, Nikki, and then the director? For a production of *Macbeth,* I'd expect to see a cast of at least sixteen actors, if not more."

Zahra grinned knowingly. "Remember what Neil mentioned earlier about small casts being one of his hallmarks as a director? I remember from when I saw *Romeo and Juliet* last year; he likes to think of himself as pioneering '*Skeleton Casts*'." At Robson's blank expression, Zahra explained, "You know how a shop can be run on a skeleton staff team during quiet shifts, just the bare minimum for what is required? Neil applies the same logic to his theatre productions. He enjoys the challenge of having the smallest cast possible, thinks it adds to the drama."

Robson glanced across at his partner. "So, the cast were all doubling? Or tripling in some instances?"

"Exactly." She motioned to one of the theatre programmes abandoned on the table. "For example, Jimmy, who plays King Duncan, crops up later as Macduff. Peter, who is Banquo, also appears as Menteith and so on. As you well know, it's hardly a new theatrical convention having performers play several parts, effectively doubling, tripling or even quadrupling their stage presence. It can be much more financially viable and it can be more of a challenge for the actors too, giving them the opportunity to show off their versatility in making sure their multiple characters are clearly differentiated."

Robson scratched the dark stubble on his chin thoughtfully. "Now I think about it, I remember reading about how there was some historical justification that William Shakespeare himself would have been familiar with the practice of doubling. He was a practical man of theatre and worked in a commercial culture, that's why some historians think his plays are frequently structured to make that possible."

Zahra nodded sagely. "Precisely. It's nothing unique. Sounds to me suspiciously like our director friend has tried to coin the term '*Skeleton Cast*' as something innovative and new. Dressing up doubling as something groundbreaking and exciting, he seems desperate to hang his hat on something special just to stand out. Ironically, it appears to be working too. His name is a buzzword in the theatre world at the moment. Even though his shows are all low budget, they are commanding an impressive audience presence nonetheless and talent scouts keep popping up too. It's only a matter of time before other more mainstream opportunities are offered to him."

A tentative knock at the door interrupted their conversation. A nervous-looking female police officer poked her head in and sidled apprehensively into the room. Fresh-faced and bright-eyed, she had her strawberry blonde hair scraped back into a high ponytail, which made her look even more youthful than her twenty-something years. One of their youngest new recruits, Robson had been introduced to her last week, but for the life of him couldn't remember what she was called. *A-something. Alicia? Amelia? Anna?* Her name had completely escaped him.

PC A-Something was clutching a pile of papers under her arm, shifting her weight awkwardly from one foot to another as she hovered in the doorway. "Excuse me, Sir, Madam. We've been conducting some preliminary background research on our theatre suspects and thought it would be helpful to share with you both before you set up the interviews to get everyone's formal statements. Is now a good time?"

Robson waved her in with an enthusiastic smile. "Come in, and there's no need for Sir and Madam. Robson and Zahra will do just fine."

The police officer scurried forward and perched on the edge of the nearest desk. Shuffling through her stack of papers, she extracted a handful of summary sheets and started reeling off the information with surprising efficiency. "Right, as you're aware, this particular *Macbeth* play is an amateur production so the cast had to balance evening and weekend rehearsals with their day jobs. Four of the actors, including the victim, Nikita Gowon, are full-time students attending London Metropolitan University. They're all on the same Theatre and Performance Practice course, which is how they knew each other prior to the play."

Taking a deep breath, the police officer continued, "First, there is the victim's boyfriend, Jimmy Walker, twenty-one-years-old. He's a local Londoner, having grown up in Brixton. Seems to be a fairly average student, on target for a mid 2.1. He plays for the university rugby team and is involved in the Film Society. Nothing particularly out of the ordinary. From what we can tell he's been in a relationship with Nikki for about two years, since they got together halfway through their first year. Although they weren't 'Facebook official' until a few weeks ago. Then, there is Megan Newbold, twenty, originally from Leeds.

Close friends with Nikki, they lived together for the first two years until Nikki moved home for her final year. Again, nothing particularly remarkable. She volunteers as a presenter for the Verve student radio station. Evidently, she's struggling a bit with the academic side of Theatre Studies and is averaging a low 2.2 grade for most of her written projects. Which is ironic in fact, as she was originally studying English Literature that she switched from, so you'd think she'd have a better grasp of the written side of the course."

Robson nodded. So far everything was corroborating what they had been told by Nikki's parents, which was a good start.

"The final student is Peter Winters, he's also twenty. He hails from Surrey and comes from a particularly wealthy family. He's been in a relationship with Megan since before Christmas, so about three months. By all accounts Peter is an exceptional student. Not only has he achieved first-class marks in all of his practical and written projects to date but he is predicted to graduate top of his class if he continues on his current trajectory. He's also one of the star strikers on the university football team."

Pausing for a beat, PC A-Something flashed them an anxious smile before continuing. "Regarding the other cast members, they are quite an eclectic bunch. There's Ben Grahame, twenty-three. Originally from Hackney, he went straight into work after high school and has been employed as a car mechanic at a garage over in Hoxton for six years now. He lives in a rented house share with two other guys and plays for a local tennis league in his spare time. Next, there's Emma

Thorpe, twenty-four. She's the high-flyer of the group. Works as a Senior PR Executive for a global consultancy firm based in Canary Wharf. One of their fastest progressing graduates, she joined the organisation three years ago, fresh from achieving a first-class degree in Business Management from Lancaster University. Originally from Bristol, last year she bought her own studio flat in Finsbury. Then, the last cast member is Violet Underwood. At nineteen, she is the baby of the cast and only left high school last summer. Currently she works as a shop assistant at an independent bookshop. An only child, she still lives with her parents in Greenwich."

PC A-Something hesitated and gave them a nervous half-smile. "Finally, there is Neil Hillton, thirty-six, who's the director and owner of Gemini Theatre. As I'm sure you've already gathered, he's something of a big deal in the world of independent theatre. His name keeps cropping up in a whole host of articles on hot young directors emerging from the London theatre scene. One to watch as the next big thing, if you can believe the press. He owns a small flat down the road from the theatre in Shoreditch. We'll keep digging but our initial searches indicate he's in a bit of a financial pickle. While his shows are drawing in large crowds, the theatre itself is getting quite dilapidated these days. Neil's had to remortgage the building twice in the last five years just so he could afford to pay for essential building repairs. It doesn't take a genius to figure out he'll be barely breaking even, never mind making a profit."

Zahra gave an appreciative nod. "That's great.

Thanks for the update. Keep up the good work Amy."

Amy! That was it, thought Robson. *PC Amy Armstrong. Double A.*

PC Amy Armstrong flashed them a final grin and slipped quietly out of the office.

"It'll be interesting to see how our cast of budding actors present themselves online on social media," mused Zahra. "I never cease to be amazed how much a person's digital footprint reveals about them these days. I can imagine that's even more true when it comes to actors who tend to love any kind of audience."

"Ah yes, the good old Instachat," agreed Robson with mock sincerity.

"Instagram," corrected Zahra, throwing him an exasperated glance. "And Snapchat and Facebook."

"True. Will be good to see what the Book of Faces has to say."

Zahra groaned, unamused. "Seriously? Are these your lame attempts at dad jokes?" Then, she caught herself, gave him an apologetic smile and let it go.

Taking a noisy gulp of his steaming coffee, Robson thought aloud, "Strange crime, isn't it? Assuming of course that it's not in fact a suicide, we've got to treat it as attempted murder due to the weapon involved. But technically it was actually the victim who was holding the knife; she's the one who stabbed herself. I bet the perpetrator thought they were being very clever on that front – much easier to elude capture or argue their way out of the situation if they did get caught."

A pensive Zahra considered it for a moment. "I suppose. But technically it's still orchestrating a murder, not all that different from what we've seen before. They were fully aware of the implications of swapping the prop knife. That's no different to tampering with somebody's car brakes or slipping poison into their drink."

She looked pointedly at the coffee Robson was holding.

Suddenly less thirsty, he lowered his half empty mug and set it down on the table. Wearily, he took a deep breath. "Guess we've got our work cut out for us. Everyone had the opportunity and the means to introduce the would-be murder weapon. So, it's up to us to determine who had the best motive to want our young actress dead."

Zahra nodded. "An uncoerced confession is going to be key for a conviction. Obviously, we'll have to stress that all the witness statement interviews are voluntary conversations for now. Let's tread carefully here; with the lack of physical evidence it's more crucial than ever to ensure everything is by the book so nothing can be thrown out in court." Wandering over to the noticeboard, she stared at the smiling faces peering down at them. "So, if it is murder, which of the big four do you reckon it is?"

It was a well-known fact in the Met that the motives underlying nearly all homicide cases usually came down to one of the infamous 'big four'; drugs, money, jealousy or revenge. No matter the subtleties of the individual murder case, the motivation could normally be traced back in some way to one of the four motives.

Robson smiled. "My instinct is jealousy for this one. I reckon a love affair turned sour. It is a theatre show after all. Actors are notorious for that sort of thing. They're always crossing the line and shacking up with their co-stars, just look at Hollywood. I bet there was a lot of hanky panky going on behind the scenes."

Zahra chuckled. "*Hanky panky*? Sorry, I didn't realise we'd gone back to the nineties!"

Robson waved her off dismissively. "You know what I mean. I reckon Nikki was sleeping with one of the other actors on the side. Maybe her boyfriend Jimmy found out and wasn't too happy about it? Or perhaps her lover felt jilted and couldn't face not being with her so thought they would teach her a lesson?"

"Bit of a harsh lesson."

"True. But love drives people to do crazy things. What do you think?"

Zahra considered it for a moment, her face a study in concentration. "Money, or rather success. The director Neil is a pretty big deal, at least in the independent theatre community and Nikki's father mentioned there would be talent scouts coming to see the show. That's a big opportunity for actors who want to get spotted, it could provide somebody's big break. With Nikki out of the way, there would be some big shoes to fill. Could be the perfect opportunity for someone else to shine; the golden ticket to success so to speak."

"You reckon it's one of the girls, her competition?"

"Perhaps. Also, I want to know why Nikki was suddenly swapped into the lead role so late in the day. That sounds plain dodgy to me; what was going on there? And why didn't Neil mention that last-minute cast change when he first spoke to us? What is he trying to hide? Maybe Nikki had something on him? If he was having money troubles, chances are he could be bribed easily."

"You think it's Emma? The girl who got cheated out of the part of Lady Macbeth. Nah, too obvious. And as for Neil being involved, why on earth would he sabotage his own show?"

"No less likely than contrived love triangles."

"We should bet on it."

Zahra laughed. "Or we could just get on with it. How do you want to play this?"

"Start with those closest to the victim and gradually work our way through the list?"

She nodded in agreement. "Sure, why not. Let's organise a preliminary talk with each cast member to get their formal statements. Once we've sussed everyone out and we have a better insight about what's been going on we can organise any follow up inter-views as and when required."

"Sounds like a plan. Let's get started," Robson said with a stifled yawn. He hated the twilight shift. He already felt shattered and in dire need of a drink stronger than coffee.

Four hours later and the detectives had successfully scheduled all seven interviews required. With spare time to kill before the first interviewee arrived at the station, they had also taken the opportunity to get acquainted with the cast's social media accounts. Robson always felt astounded by how much inform-ation was freely available in the public domain. There was a lot to be gleaned about someone's psyche from how they chose to present themselves online. Somewhat depressingly, social media had steadily become their most powerful tool for finding out who someone really was, or rather who they wanted to be.

Carefully orchestrated Instagram posts and gushing Facebook status updates had a way of revealing a lot more about the nuances of peoples' personalities than they seemed to realise. This eclectic group of twenty-something actors was no exception. All the typical clichés were on display. There was the *Self-absorbed Selfie Queen* (Megan) with numerous preening, self-indulgent posts. The *Narcissistic Fitness Freak* (Peter) with countless buff topless gym photos and motivational fitspiration posts about his gruelling diet and exercise routine. The *Attention-seeking Sexy Poser* (Emma) seductively pouting in scantily clad, revealing photos. And the *Mysterious Deep Thinker* (Violet) sharing lofty, intellectual musings and inspirational quotes, usually from famous authors in her case.

Nikki's digital profile was, to her credit, considerably less irritating than some of her peers. Her current Facebook profile picture was a close-up selfie shot of her and Megan smiling at the camera, necklaces glinting in the sunlight. Flicking through her photographs, Robson saw her posing by London landmarks, enjoying herself in trendy bars and restaurants and walking barefoot in grassy parks. She came across as friendly and extroverted, exactly like her parents had described her. Confident, but not vain. Inspiring, but not condescending. Cheerful, but not seeking validation. It had taken a while to find Nikki's social media profiles; all were private and she had dropped her surname and was listed simply as Nikki G. Even then, they had only found her by association with the other student castmates whom she was connected to online.

Engrossed, Robson made his way meticulously through Facebook and Instagram, curious what the young actress felt compelled to share with the world. It was all pretty standard. Smiling, loved-up selfies of her and Jimmy, candid paparazzi-style shots of her and Megan dancing on nights out, the occasional repost of cute animal videos and countless pictures of various meals.

Scrolling through Nikki's earlier posts, Robson continued looking further back on her Facebook timeline. Chewing on his pen, he stumbled across something peculiar he couldn't explain. Flicking to Instagram he confirmed the bizarre case was the same for both. "Hmm, that's strange."

Across from her computer, Zahra looked up in interest. "What?"

"All Nikki's Facebook posts only date back to the September when she first started university. That goes for Instagram too. There's less than three years of activity on her social media accounts."

Zahra frowned. "What kind of teenager doesn't have social media?"

"No one. Plus, Nikki's not exactly a technophobe, she posts quite frequently. At least daily status updates and new photo uploads. I highly doubt she went from nothing to that level of activity overnight. It's much more likely she either didn't have online access for some reason, or more probably she deleted her old social media accounts and started afresh with new ones."

Zahra nodded thoughtfully. "So, she seized the opportunity to reinvent herself when she started university."

"Which means the real question is – what was she trying to hide?"

CHAPTER SEVEN

A Heart to Love

Having left PC Armstrong to conduct a more in-depth online investigation into the seven key suspects, Robson and Zahra now sat on one side of a standard issue desk in the dingy interview room. Cracked paint was flaking off the washed-out cream walls and the scuffed grey carpet was speckled with suspicious stains and trodden-in chewing gum marks. The cramped space was a little too claustrophobic. Harsh, fluorescent lighting a little too bright. Stale air a little too stuffy. All of this under the watchful eye of the large, imposing one-way mirror.

Without fail, the familiar scene made Robson snigger every time. A poor imitation of some random cop show, late night TV at its finest. It never quite seemed real to him. If only they had license to apply the pressure on the suspects like in those fictional shows. Sadly, the reality was far less straightforward. Without compelling, strong evidence and a rock-solid confession, any case could fall apart by the time it finally reached court. Too often he had seen culprits team up with some smart aleck lawyer intent on representing the best interests of their precious client, regardless of whether they were innocent or not. Robson couldn't understand how they slept at night, knowing they were defending a guilty person. It made a mockery of the entire justice system.

Fortunately, or perhaps unfortunately, Robson had an uncanny gift when it came to intuition. Even without a state-of-the-art lie detector at his disposal, he could usually ascertain with spooky accuracy if a person was telling the truth or not. He had lost track of the number of criminals he had seen walk free on a technicality or lack of sufficient evidence, despite the fact he had *known* they were guilty. If only intuition was enough.

The door opened with a creak and their first inter-viewee of the night was ushered in, the victim's boyfriend, Jimmy Walker. Dressed casually in faded jeans and a blue and black tartan shirt, Jimmy was an attractive young man – tall with broad shoulders, well-defined muscles and a messy mop of tousled, reddish-brown curly hair. A light scattering of freckles ran across the bridge of his nose and he had a deep dimple in his right cheek. His warm, bluish-grey eyes were bloodshot and red.

Shuffling reluctantly over to them, he slumped down into his chair looking utterly drained. Silently accepting the tea proffered to him, he wrapped his hands around the hot mug and looked up at them apprehensively.

Robson leaned forward and gave what he hoped was a comforting smile. "I'm Detective Inspector Finley Robson and this is my partner, Detective Sergeant Nadia Zahra. As I explained on the phone, we just want to ask you a few questions and take your witness statement, all very routine. Do you understand everything that has been explained to you by the police officer outside? That you'll have to sign your statement at the end to confirm it's correct."

Jimmy glumly fixed his gaze on the table, "I understand. What do you want to know?"

"Let's start at the beginning. Can you describe your relationship with Nikita Gowon?"

"Nikki," corrected Jimmy automatically. "Sorry, it's just no one ever calls her Nikita, she hates it. Her full name is reserved only for when her parents are really mad at her."

Robson gave an appreciative nod. "Okay, noted. Can you tell us about your relationship with Nikki?"

Jimmy took a deep, shuddering breath. When he spoke, there was a distinct tremor in his voice and his chin quivered slightly. "We've been together for two years, since halfway through first year. She's amazing, she means everything to me. Frankly I still can't believe this is happening, I keep waiting to wake up from this nightmare. I can't get my head around the fact she's fighting for her life in hospital. A few hours ago, she was fine and now she might not survive the day. I don't understand how this could happen." Voice cracking, he hung his head as he fought to hold back tears.

Robson leaned forward, resting his chin on an upturned palm as he watched Jimmy intently. "I understand this might be a hard question, but I have to ask, have you got any idea who might want to hurt Nikki?"

Jimmy shrugged helplessly, an air of desperation settling around him. "I have no idea. I don't understand who could possibly want to do this. Nikki is brilliant, everyone loves her." His words sounded hollow.

"Did she get along with the rest of the cast? Was there any friction we should know about?"

With a sad shake of his head, Jimmy said sombrely, "I'm telling you, Nikki gets along with everyone. She's the friendliest, most loving person I've ever met."

"Surely she couldn't have been best friends with everyone all the time though?"

"Well, no," Jimmy conceded. "I guess she isn't a big fan of Emma, they tend to clash and Nikki ended up getting her role in the play, so you can imagine how that went down. Plus, she could get quite frustrated with our director Neil, he's somewhat of a perfectionist; he often rubbed her up the wrong way. But it wasn't anything serious, neither of them would want to *hurt* her."

Zahra cocked her head to one side as she studied Jimmy closely, her dark eyes narrowed in suspicion. "How about the two of you? How was your relationship?"

"Nikki's the love of my life, I can't imagine ever being without her. I love her more than I ever thought possible."

Robson's lip flickered a half-smile. *Young love. Always so idealistic and romantic.*

Zahra continued relentlessly, "Actually, we've

heard that the pair of you have been arguing recently? What was that about?"

Snapping his head up, Jimmy's face tightened in sudden bewilderment. "Who told you that? We're like any couple, we have the occasional disagreement. Who doesn't? We bicker about silly, petty stuff, nothing important." His tone was defensive now, indignant at the challenge.

"So, you wouldn't say you were having problems?"

"No, quite the opposite. We've been making plans for after graduation. We're committed to each other."

Robson flinched as he saw a glimmer of hurt pass over Jimmy's face. His remorse seemed genuine, but he had nearly been fooled by convincing performances in the past and they were from people who didn't specialise in acting as a pastime.

"How about you talk us through what a typical rehearsal would look like? That might be helpful in prompting you to remember some details you might otherwise overlook?"

Managing a weak nod, Jimmy clasped his hands tighter around the untouched mug of tea sat before him. "Sure, if you think it will help. Any particular rehearsal day?"

"How about when Nikki first stepped into her new role of Lady Macbeth? We understood she took over from Emma two weeks ago?"

Jimmy gave a long, heartfelt sigh. Leaning back in his chair, he began to talk.

* * *

Thursday 8th March

They had exactly one hour until the evening rehearsal began and for Jimmy, it couldn't come late enough. Slipping his fingers underneath Nikki's dark, curly hair, Jimmy pulled her closer. Wrapping her lithe body around his, she pressed further into his embrace, her soft lips brushing his neck. Tracing her fingers across his bicep, Nikki beamed at him, a devilish twinkle in her eye. Jimmy was completely captivated by her.

She was so goddamn beautiful.

Ever since their first conversation about classic Audrey Hepburn movies, he had known there was something different about her. The passion with which she spoke. The sharp wit that permeated her conversations. The endearing way her eyes lit up when she smiled. Jimmy had started falling for her straight away.

They had been randomly paired up for a first-year university assignment, required to act out a scene as a couple from Arthur Miller's *The Crucible*. Out of hundreds of students they had ended up together. Jimmy's mum had called that fate, proclaiming, 'everything happens for a reason.'

Over the next two years Nikki had introduced him to a number of new experiences – eclectic music, arthouse films and delicious food. Plus, Nikki was nothing if not creative. Possessing an undeniable zest for life she had a knack of coming up with quirky, innovative ways to experience their home city of London at its finest, and cheapest. As she had so rightly pointed out numerous times, people had a tendency to forget the wonders on their own doorstep. A myriad of unusual dates had followed. Together they had done everything from making the most of the capital's free summer festivals to taking in the breath-taking views after climbing the dome of St Paul's Cathedral. They had even delved deep below the city to explore a labyrinth of London's secret disused tube tunnels.

The tingling sensation of Nikki's soft lips pressing against his dragged Jimmy back to the present. Forgetting himself, a groan of pleasure escaped from his lips.

Giggling softly, she clasped a warm hand over his mouth. "Shh, we've got to be quiet."

Jimmy chuckled in reply, pulling her towards him to kiss her again. "Sorry, I forgot. I couldn't help it."

A sharp knock shook the bedroom door. The couple froze and Nikki put a finger to her lips. Even in the silence, Jimmy continued to play gently with her hand, interlacing his fingers with hers – white and black, fitting perfectly together like keys on a piano.

Another insistent knock pounded the door. "Guys, come on. I know you're in there. Let me in!" Aisha's plaintive wail drifted through the door.

"Busted," whispered Jimmy, nuzzling against her neck.

"You know when we decided it would be a great idea for me to live at home?" grinned Nikki. "I'm so regretting that right now!"

With a final rushed kiss, the pair swiftly extricated themselves from their embrace and busied themselves retrieving their discarded clothes that had been flung haphazardly around the room.

"Wait a minute," called Nikki, stepping back into

her dress and running her fingers through her tangled wavy tresses. Jimmy hastily pulled on his jeans and slipped his shirt over his head. He straightened the bedding as Nikki hurried over to unlock the door.

Aisha burst into the room, a miniature version of her older sister. She looked around suspiciously before staring at the couple, her eyes resting on Nikki's unkempt hair. "What were you two doing?" she queried, a knowing smile spreading across her face.

"Just watching a movie," Nikki answered quickly, sounding flustered.

Aisha shot a look over at the blank television screen. "Netflix and chilling?" she asked, winking at her older sister with a mischievous glint in her eye.

"Hey missy, none of that cheek!" exclaimed Nikki, ruffling the youngster's curly hair affectionately.

Squealing with glee, Aisha tried to dash out of reach, but Jimmy blocked her way and scooped her up to fling her playfully onto the bed. At that point, Nikki descended on her little sister tickling her mercilessly as she tittered and squirmed. Jimmy joined the girls and all three ended up collapsed in a heap on the bed, laughing breathlessly. For a fleeting moment, Jimmy thought he saw a look of concern flash across Nikki's face as she hugged her sister who was wheezing to catch her breath.

Tilting her small head back, Aisha looked up at them longingly. "So, you said something about watching a movie?"

Nikki laughed and reached over to drop the television remote into her small hands. "All yours.

You can choose anything you want, apart from *Frozen*."

Joyfully grabbing the remote Aisha nestled between them and set about scrolling through the movie choices on Netflix. Over her head, Nikki locked eyes with Jimmy and mouthed *sorry*.

Smiling, he shook his head. During the past few months he had grown used to the untimely intrusions by the pint-sized youngster. As an only child he had never experienced the joy of having siblings. If anything, he was jealous of the sisters' close bond.

Leaning over, Nikki whispered thanks and kissed him lightly on the cheek.

Aisha squirmed between them. "Eurgh, gross! I'm *right here*. That means *no kissing*."

Sniggering at her indignant tone, Nikki held up her hands. "Sorry boss! Won't happen again. Have you chosen a movie yet?"

Nodding, Aisha hit the play button to start a light-hearted comedy film. As the opening credits rolled, she snuggled between them, resting her head on Jimmy's chest. Overwhelmed with love for the pair of them, he was flooded with gratitude for Nikki and her family who had completely accepted him as one of their own. With one protective hand resting on Aisha, he hooked his other arm loosely around Nikki's shoulders. She smiled at him gratefully and dropped her heavy head onto his chest as the three of them settled down to watch the film.

Five o'clock had arrived before they knew it. Leaving a half-asleep Aisha curled up on their bed, the television still playing in the background, they had crept out of the bedroom and tiptoed downstairs. After saying a brief goodbye to Nikki's parents, they had hurried out to Jimmy's car to set off to the evening rehearsal.

Now, they drove in silence, listening only to the spluttering of the engine as it trundled along. The ancient car sounded more than ever like it was in the final death throes of its life as it limped down the busy road.

Jimmy made a mental note to have a proper look under the bonnet later to see if there were any quick fixes that could eke it out a bit longer. He had contemplated asking Ben to take a look at it to see if he could offer any advice, but his pride wouldn't allow him to admit defeat. He knew he should just stop procrastinating and sell it while it was still worth something. A constant drain on his resources, Jimmy could barely afford to keep the car running some months and that was before factoring in countless repair costs. It was increasingly tempting to cash it in so he could actually start saving some money. Yet so far, something had always stopped him.

He liked to kid himself it was because of the status symbol the car brought or because he enjoyed tinkering with the mechanics. But, realistically, he knew that wasn't the case at all. His car provided a comforting safety net – the means for a quick getaway should it ever be required.

Staring quietly out of the passenger window, Nikki watched the blurry streets of London whizz by. She seemed jittery and distracted. His girlfriend always had been a terrible back-seat driver, prone to shouting out loud whenever anyone dared to drive too close to their car. He had lost count of how many arguments there had been over her sudden outbursts. Usually ending with Nikki getting teary, he would always find himself being the one apologising, despite the fact he had done nothing wrong. Today though, she was particularly on edge, as though she was playing something over and over in her mind.

"Nervous?" he guessed, stealing a quick sideways look at her.

She gave a non-committal shrug, being uncharacteristically evasive. "Not really."

Tonight marked her first rehearsal in her new role as Lady Macbeth. Exactly why their pedantic director Neil had experienced such a sudden change of heart four weeks into rehearsals was still shrouded in mystery. But yesterday, he had announced Nikki was to step up into the coveted role, for which she had been a dutiful understudy. Meanwhile, Emma had been unceremoniously recast.

With their opening night fast approaching, it meant there was only a fortnight for Nikki and Emma to master their new roles. The whole situation was plain bizarre and seemed completely out of character for the control freak Neil, as if his hand was being forced. A puppet dancing on strings. Jimmy had an uncomfortable feeling Nikki knew more about the mysterious situation than she was letting on. But every time he had pressed her about it, she had retreated into herself, fallen silent and refused to give anything away.

He wasn't worried about her new leading role.

Nikki had been the understudy for Lady Macbeth since day one, so she had already learnt most of the challenging part back to front, just in case. Undeniably talented, she had the passion and drive that might lead to her actually making a name for herself in the cut-throat industry.

As they approached the end of their degree, she had grown tired of the university-based shows and had cast her eye out further afield for something more raw and challenging. Scouring various options, she had finally stumbled across the amateur *Macbeth* production. Unabatedly enthusiastic, she had spent ages convincing them all to join her in auditioning for the play – him, Megan and Peter.

At the time, Jimmy had thought it was a great idea. Now, he wasn't so sure. Glancing over at Nikki, his heart ached in sympathy. Her deep brown eyes looked so sad. She had endured a rough summer, they both had in fact. And although that horrific situation had not exactly been resolved, Nikki had somehow managed to find some peace.

"Do you want to talk about it?"

Shaking her head, Nikki's expression softened as her lips formed a thin, sad smile. "Honestly I just want to be distracted. Escaping into a world of make-believe is exactly what I need. Mayhem and witchcraft will do me good."

"Exactly. And I already know you're going to be the world's best Lady Macbeth."

Nikki nodded weakly in response and promptly resumed staring out of the window.

Drumming his fingers thoughtfully on the wheel,

Jimmy hesitated a moment before changing tack. "On a different subject, have you got around to telling Megan the news?"

Shoulders sagging, Nikki let out a weary sigh. "No, not yet."

Jimmy bit down on his lip, trying to hide his disappointment. It wasn't the response he had wanted. "Really, because you said you were going to?"

Nikki shot him an exasperated look. "Leave it with me, okay? It's a big deal, I'm trying to find the right moment. I'm capable of talking to my best friend in my own time."

"I know. But I think—"

"Jimmy, can we just drive in peace for a while?"

Taken aback, Jimmy felt a little hurt by her sharp interruption. They continued driving, the heavy silence forming an invisible wedge between them. Nikki gazed solemnly into the distance, purposefully avoiding eye contact. Idly fishing her phone out of her pocket, she tapped it a few times and it buzzed in response.

"Who's that?"

"Meg."

Dark curls fell over her face as she leaned forward to read the message. Eyes glued to the small screen, she was fixated.

Curious, Jimmy peered over her shoulder. "What does it say?"

"Nothing," she replied tersely, tilting the phone so he could no longer see the screen.

Jimmy frowned. They had never been the sort of couple who kept secrets from each other. Early on they had established they were all in, warts and all. He had no idea why she was suddenly acting so secretive. "Come on, tell me."

Nikki gave a long, deep sigh. Reluctantly locking her phone, she returned it to her pocket. "Trust me, it's really nothing. Please just drop it, okay?"

There was an edge to her voice. Something about the way she said it made it sound like a warning.

Pulling up outside the theatre, Nikki wasted no time in jumping out of the car and slamming the door. She seemed relieved to no longer be trapped in a confined space with him. Puzzled, Jimmy stared at her as they walked in. Her eyes remained downcast studying the pavement.

No sooner had they stepped through the door of the auditorium, Megan descended upon them, greeting Nikki with a wide grin and throwing her arms around her in a huge bear hug. She tossed Jimmy a cursory glance and gave a curt nod. Instantly Nikki began talking animatedly with Megan, excitedly catching up about some reality TV show he hadn't even heard of. For some inexplicable reason Nikki loved those shows. By his own admission, Jimmy would rather claw his eyes out than watch such drivel.

Peter sauntered over to them, a slight swagger in his step. Dressed in a tight-fitting white shirt with a low neckline, his outfit simultaneously showed off his tan and his bulging arm muscles. *No surprise there then.* Peter always had a constant air of arrogance about him, as though he was cocky enough to believe he was better than everybody else. Half the time

Jimmy suspected Megan was only with him due to his money and good looks, their relationship didn't seem to have much depth and Peter hardly had a winning personality. Still, Jimmy tolerated him because of his connection to Megan, and thus Nikki by association who shared none of his reservations.

Jovially slapping a hand onto his shoulder, Peter grinned broadly as he greeted him with over-stated enthusiasm. "Jimmy! Mate, did you see the game last weekend?"

Jimmy forced a weak smile. "No, didn't catch that one." Peter knew full well he was a rugby guy and wasn't interested in following football but constantly insisted on talking to him about it regardless. It always came back to Peter in the end.

"Man, you missed out! It was an awesome game. Spurs beat the Terriers two-nil, would you believe? The second goal in particular was a beauty, bloody brilliant. You know this means Spurs are third in the Premier League? I reckon we've got a real chance to win it this year."

Nodding along distractedly, Jimmy feigned interest, continuing their ongoing little charade. Across the auditorium he could see that Ben, their resident Macbeth, had arrived and was joking with the girls about something. Laughing wholeheartedly, his girlfriend was fawning over Ben's every word, touching his arm affectionately.

Breaking away from the conversation, Nikki sidled over to Jimmy. "We're going to go and start rehearsing. We've got a lot to get through." She was smiling now, her face radiant.

Behind her, Ben raised his hand in a cheery wave. With his athletic build and chiselled cheekbones, Jimmy found himself increasingly jealous of the amount of rehearsal time Nikki was going to spend with him.

But unlike Peter, Ben was charmingly oblivious to how attractive he was. There was no arrogance in his behaviour, just genuine warmth and affection. Without fail he always made a conscious effort to chat with everybody, regardless of their so-called status within the show. He had somehow managed to stay out of all the cast's drama. Even the last-minute actress swapping of his onstage wife hadn't phased him.

Nikki kissed Jimmy on the cheek. "I'm sorry if I was a bit standoffish earlier, I didn't mean to snap at you. I've got a lot on my mind, I'm feeling quite overwhelmed." Her deep brown eyes were sad, she almost looked guilty.

"It's alright, I understand. But don't feel you always have to carry everything by yourself. You can confide in me, I'm here to help you."

She smiled gratefully. "I know. I love you. See you later, okay?"

"Sure, love you too. Have fun."

It had only been a few minutes after Nikki had left with Ben when Jimmy spotted her discarded phone which she had left carelessly on one of the chairs. Grinning to himself, he walked over to retrieve it. She always left her phone lying around, barely a day went by when she didn't lose it at least once. He intended to take it straight back to Nikki before she started panicking about losing it, but with the phone in his hand he suddenly hesitated.

They had never been precious about passwords because they trusted the other not to snoop through their messages. True to his word Jimmy never had, but now holding her phone for the first time he felt tempted. There had to be a reason Nikki was acting so cagey. The bombshell of last summer was already behind them, they had been working to move past it. But that didn't explain why she had been acting so differently this last week, downright weird on some occasions.

He knew he was being paranoid, but that only incr-eased his temptation. If he could just check it definitely was Megan she had been texting, then he could breathe a sigh of relief and move on. In the meantime, the growing doubt in his mind was driving him slowly insane.

Caving into curiosity, Jimmy quickly typed in her password before he lost his nerve. He saw instantly there was no recent message from Megan. Or anyone else for that matter. The last text received had been from himself, earlier that afternoon. The messages from whoever Nikki had been speaking to in the car had been deleted. All evidence erased.

Jimmy frowned, confused. *Why would she lie about that? What on earth was going on?*

"What do you think you're doing?"

Spinning around, he saw Nikki had retraced her steps and was stood behind him, arms folded angrily.

"You're going through my messages? How dare you?" Her voice was cold, laced with disbelief.

"I thought you said you were texting Megan?"

"Give me my phone back."

Hesitating, he looked down at her phone uncertainly. Seeing her stony stare, he relented and reluctantly handed it back. "Why did you delete that message?"

"Jimmy, you need to trust me."

"But—"

"This conversation is over."

*   *   *

Taking a deep, shaky breath, Jimmy squeezed his eyes shut and rubbed his forehead. He seemed relieved to have finished sharing his account.

Robson studied him for a long moment. "Did you ever find out who Nikki was talking to?"

Jimmy shook his head apologetically. "No, I tried to bring it up a few times afterwards but she was having none of it. I admit we argued about it. In the end, I didn't think it was worth the hassle so I just dropped it. I could live without knowing. I never imagined it might be important. That her life might be in danger or it could help identify who would do something like this to her." There was a desperate edge to his voice that was painful to hear.

"That's alright, you've still been helpful." Robson shot a quick look across at Zahra, who nodded in response and scribbled in her notepad. They would request Nikki's phone records later.

"Do you think Nikki was getting too close to her co-star Ben?"

Jimmy shifted in his seat, considering the question.

"I'm not sure. I mean, I trust Nikki and naturally they had to spend a lot of time together because of the show. They are onstage husband and wife after all, our leading man and lady."

Elbows resting on the table, Robson gazed at him intently, watching the actor's every move. "You don't think they were seeing each other behind your back?"

Brow furrowed, Jimmy paled slightly. "What makes you say that? What have you heard?"

Zahra chimed in at that point. "For someone who claims to trust his girlfriend, you're pretty quick to believe she might have been cheating on you?"

Jimmy gave a heavy sigh. "Honesty I don't even know anymore. I love Nikki more than anything. But recently, I feel I barely know who she is anymore. It's as if she's a different person some days. These past few weeks especially. There's definitely been something on her mind. She's been distracted, distant."

"Anything she cared to share with you?"

Jimmy blinked. "Afraid not. Truth be told, I was worried about her. She seemed to be retreating into herself, shutting me out. Sometimes it felt as though she was taking the weight of the world on her shoulders on her own, like I wasn't in the picture."

"And you have no idea what was troubling her?"

"No, I already said that. You could try asking Megan?" Jimmy suggested, his voice slightly raised.

"Megan?"

Jimmy laughed, but there was no mirth in it. "You think Nikki tells me everything? Please! I'm just her boyfriend. It's always been Megan she confides her deepest secrets to. They've been best friends since

Freshers week, long before I came on the scene. There's nothing they don't know about each other. I can guarantee if anyone knows what was going on, it would be her." Stifling a yawn, Jimmy stretched out in his chair. "Are we nearly done here? I need to be getting back to the hospital to visit Nikki."

"Almost. But I do have one more question. What happened to your hand?"

"My hand?" Jimmy repeated, staring down at his right hand. All his knuckles had been scraped raw. Angry and red, the wounds looked painfully sore but had already started to scab over, so Robson figured he must have been injured a few days ago at least. Giving a nervous laugh, Jimmy shrugged off the question dismissively. "Oh that? I don't remember. I must have caught it on something. No big deal."

Robson and Zahra shared a look. That explanation rang false, but it seemed doubtful they could prise anything more out of him, at this stage at least.

"Alright, you're free to go. We'll be in touch if we need to talk further."

Visibly relieved, Jimmy wasted no time in pushing his chair back and promptly scampering out of the room.

Zahra rested her head on her palm and looked sideways at Robson. "What do you think?"

Robson shrugged, non-committal. Truth was he wanted to believe Jimmy, he even sort of liked the guy. But he knew from experience people rarely showed their true colours in these initial interviews. Or told the whole story evidently. "Of course, he's going to paint a rosy, idyllic picture of their relationship. I'd be interested to find out what other people thought of the couple. He's clearly not telling us everything."

He raised a quizzical eyebrow when he saw a flicker of disappointment cross Zahra's face. It was always rare for his strictly professional partner to show her emotional side.

She gave a dejected sigh. "You know for once, I'd really love for it *not* to be the boyfriend. That might restore my faith that romance isn't dead."

Robson smiled to himself. *The elusive Nadia Zahra was a romantic, who would have thought?* "Well, there are exactly seven suspects. That's an 86% chance the culprit was someone else. You might just get your wish. Who knows, perhaps this couple might even have a happy future. After all, Nikki's currently still alive."

Zahra laughed. "True. Maybe it will be a fairy tale ending after all."

CHAPTER EIGHT

Double, Double, Toil and Trouble

Zahra pushed a steaming cup of black coffee tow-ards Robson, with a disgusted grimace on her face. "I don't know how you can drink that stuff, it tastes like rocket fuel."

Robson smiled. "Perhaps I enjoy my coffee just like me – dark and strong." That earned him a small grin from Zahra who rolled her eyes as she raised her own mug. Typically, her coffee preference was the complete opposite to him. Essentially hot, sugary milk as far as Robson was concerned. It didn't surprise him; the pair of them were polar opposites in just about everything. They were both Londoners, but that's where the similarities ended.

Robson was embarrassed to admit he had never had to work very hard at anything. Born to wealthy parents in South West London, he had enjoyed a privileged upbringing and an elite education at one of the capital's best private schools before going on to study English Literature at Cambridge University. Naturally intelligent, he had always aced his exams with minimal effort and had never thought twice about frivolously spending a couple of hundred pounds to celebrate in style.

By contrast, Nadia Zahra hadn't had it so easy. Far from Robson's wealthy lifestyle, she had grown up with only the bare essentials. When her refugee parents had arrived in England as teenagers back in the early nineties, they owned nothing but the clothes on their backs. No strangers to hard grafting, the couple had hunkered down, quietly committing themselves to scraping together a living through an assortment of odd jobs before settling as shopkeepers in a small newsagent.

Their committed attitude towards work had clearly rubbed off on their daughter. Zahra had achieved straight A's in her A levels while simultaneously working tirelessly to help out her parents. Contending with ignorant racist remarks from her small-minded classmates and teachers alike, Zahra had been determined to succeed and had won a scholarship to study Criminology at Birmingham University, before joining the Metropolitan Police Force as one of their brightest young recruits.

Their different backgrounds were partly responsible for how Robson and Zahra always came at everything from opposing viewpoints, but somehow the dynamic between them worked.

A brisk knock at the door preceded PC Armstrong ushering in their next interviewee, Nikki's best friend,

Megan Newbold. A slightly plump young woman, Megan had stylishly short, cropped auburn hair which framed her oval face. Clad in a tight-fitting purple top and figure-hugging dark jeans, remnants of black mascara smudges coloured her cheeks and her eyes were red and puffy. Sniffing relentlessly, she continually dabbed at her red nose delicately.

A perfect study in grief.

Sinking heavily into the chair, Megan took a few deep breaths to steady herself. Finally, she rose her head to look at them cautiously, her eyes glistening with unshed tears. When she spoke, Robson could hear a distinct waver in her voice. "Sorry I'm such a state, I guess I'm still in shock. God this is a nightmare, poor Nikki."

"We're here to find out who did this to her. Do you have any idea who might want to cause her harm?"

An uncomfortable silence descended, punctuated only by Megan's sniffles. Her eyes were distant and she had a strange look on her face, an expression Robson couldn't quite decipher. Eventually she tentatively said, "Actually yes. Now that I think about it, there's a few people who could be to blame."

"A few?"

"Yeah I think so. Nikki's beautiful you see, and popular. Certain people were jealous of that. And Neil essentially stole the lead role from Emma to give it to her. That made her a new enemy, one out for blood."

"She told you this?"

Megan smiled coyly. "We're best friends, we share everything. Nikki always confided in me. I know all her secrets."

"Excellent, now you can share them with us."

Megan nodded in agreement, concern suddenly etched in her features once again. "Have you heard from the hospital? How's Nikki doing? Is she going to die?"

"We're not at liberty to say," Zahra said, professional as always.

Megan's lip quivered as she breathed in heavily. "Yeah, that figures. Have you got any leads? Is there any evidence pointing towards anyone?"

"Why don't you tell us what you know and we can take it from there?"

*   *   *

Friday 9th March

A fiery plume of red smoke shot high into the air, raining bright sparks down onto the stage around them. Absentmindedly, Megan wondered if the sparks were hot enough to burn through their clothes should they get too close. It wasn't a theory she planned to test any time soon.

A jubilant Neil was enthusiastically demonstrating the combustible properties of a strange grey powder he was thrusting into the iron cauldron. The director sure did love his pyrotechnics. Flouncing about joyfully, he was like an over-excited child in a toy shop. Struggling to contain his glee, he was reeling off some scientific-sounding mumbo-jumbo that meant nothing to her. Something about an exothermic chemical reaction when mixing with the flammable liquid in the cauldron. An acrid smell of burning chemicals flooded Megan's nostrils and she wrinkled her nose in disgust.

Zoning out, she fixed her attention instead on her two fellow witches. A sceptical looking Violet was stood to one side, well out of reach of the fiery sparks. Wringing her hands together nervously, she appeared worried. But then again, the teenage girl was always fretting about something. She was so uptight Megan couldn't recall the last time she had even seen her smile.

Not for the first time, she was struck by how fragile Violet's waif-like figure looked. Gaunt with long, sinewy limbs and a stomach so flat it was practically concave, she had not an ounce of fat on her. A strong wind could knock her off her feet.

In comparison, beside her Emma stood slender but strong. Megan couldn't help but feel envious of her athletic build and firm muscles. Today Emma was wearing a sheer black top, exposing her taut, toned midriff and her diamond belly button piercing which glinted as it caught the light.

She's probably one of those girls who doesn't even have to try to maintain her slim figure, Megan thought bitterly. She hated girls like that.

Suddenly conscious of her own heavier figure, Megan instantly felt like the fat kid she had once been all over again. At size sixteen she was hardly obese by any means, not anymore. But she was still far removed from the legions of skinny barbies such as Emma. Or Nikki for that matter. Sure, she had come a long way since her teenage days, but the mean high school taunts still haunted her memories. Seared into her mind she always heard the cruel cries of *Mega Meg* whenever she glimpsed her reflection in the mirror.

Losing four stone before starting university, she had relished the chance for a fresh start. Gone were the dowdy clothes, loose dungarees and scuffed converse shoes. In were the towering heels and flattering, figure-hugging dresses to show off her new voluptuous figure. Mercifully during her weight loss her best feature – her large bosom – had remained intact.

The transformation had taken months of dedication, boring healthy diets and far too much exercise for her liking. The struggle had been real. But her motivation had been prompted by her parents' divorce after her dad had abruptly left her mum for a younger, prettier and significantly skinnier woman. Megan had taken a long hard look at herself and vowed never to end up fat and alone.

"What do you think Megan?" Neil's impatient voice snapped her out of her nostalgic daydream. The director stared at her intently, tapping his foot as he waited for her response.

"Erm…yeah. That's cool. I like it, very effective."

Neil gave a small self-satisfied smirk.

Emma rolled her eyes dramatically. "Alright, great. Can we stop playing around with fire now and get on with actually rehearsing?"

Neil narrowed his eyes in irritation but didn't argue with her. He never really did. The director always pandered after Emma's approval in some form or another, as though she was royalty on set. That's why her unexpected demotion from the starring role of Lady Macbeth two days ago had caused such a stir. The cast had been buzzing with gossip ever since. The rumours were endless.

But one thing that could not be disputed was that Emma was absolutely furious. Mad at Nikki for stealing her coveted role and livid at Neil for letting it happen. Emma glowered at Megan as she strutted past. Guilty by association.

Suddenly Megan's phone buzzed, vibrating in her back pocket. Fishing it out she smiled when she saw the new message was from Nikki. Clearly her and Ben weren't doing a whole lot of rehearsing next door.

Hey Meg, Are you free after rehearsal today? Need to chat. xx

A frown creased Megan's forehead. She had no idea what the text was referring to. Why did they need to chat? She didn't like surprises at the best of times. Hastily, she tapped out a brief reply.

Yep, I'm free. Sounds serious. Everything OK? xx

Holding her phone in her palm, she waited anxiously for Nikki's reply with bated breath. After a minute it buzzed again.

LOL! Yeah, don't worry! All fine. Just need to chat. Nothing bad I promise. xx

As much as she racked her brain, Megan couldn't think what the cryptic message might be about. It was enough to cause a little seed of fear to gnaw away inside of her.

Megan beamed at Nikki as she bounded into the auditorium. Dark curls bouncing around her shoulders, Nikki returned her smile enthusiastically. She looked stunning, a vision as always. Megan still had to pinch herself that they were friends. *Beautiful, popular Nikki.* Girls like her weren't normally friends with girls like Megan. A pecking order existed, even beyond high school.

Thrown together by fate, their student bedrooms had been opposite each other in their first year. The pair had instantly bonded over their mutual love of dancing, they were always the last two on the dance floor at every club night. Staggering home tipsy, they were usually still singing and putting the world to rights when they finally got home. Over the years they had become even closer and their friendship had truly blossomed.

Nikki stopped short, a look of horror darkening her face. Smile faltering, Megan squinted at her, confused. *Why did she look so horrified? Had she accidentally done something to piss her off?*

"What the hell has that man done to your eyes?" demanded Nikki, evidently disgusted.

"My eyes?" repeated Megan slowly, then she laughed. "Oh, I'd totally forgotten about them. What do you think of my new look?"

Her formerly hazel eyes had been transformed into a vibrant, yellow reptilian stare. Courtesy of Neil's cobra contact lenses, the snake-like vertical pupils completely changed her appearance. The effect was distinctly unsettling and suitably bewitching.

"They're so creepy. You look possessed!" Grimacing, Nikki pushed Megan away. "Stop it, they're vile. I can't even look at you."

"Ah, but they do make for a good selfie opportunity though." Slipping her phone out of her pocket, Megan flung an arm around her friend's shoulders and pulled her close. Nikki flinched as she flicked the phone into selfie mode, the screen's glare illuminating her reptilian eyes. Snapping a few photographs, Megan busied herself with uploading the best shot simultaneously to Instagram and Facebook, tagging Nikki. Pondering the caption for a moment, she settled with the somewhat unoriginal; *Double, double, toil and trouble! Fab time rehearsing today with @NikkiG #Macbeth.*

Grabbing her arm, Nikki dragged her friend after her. "Come on selfie queen, we should get going and you need to get rid of those hideous lenses. I can't stand them."

Reluctantly Megan expertly popped the lenses out as they walked, discarding them carelessly on the floor. Emma bustled past them as they headed out, giving them a cold stare before storming off in the opposite direction.

"Ooh she's really not happy, is she?" Megan remarked. Turning her attention to Nikki, she cocked her head in interest. "So, how come you suddenly got swapped into the Lady Macbeth role anyhow?"

Nikki tapped her nose conspiratorially. "That's for me to know and you to find out."

Megan laughed. "Oh, come on, do tell. I can keep a secret. There has to be a juicy story to share?"

Chuckling lightly, Nikki shook her head. "No, I'm joking. I have no idea. Neil just made the executive decision it was best for the show. When he told me, it was completely out of the blue. I was as surprised as you."

"Really?"

"Really. Trust me. There's no big secret."

Stepping out of the main theatre door, the pair practically collided with a distracted Ben on the steps. Nikki's gaze loitered on him for a minute longer than was necessary and Megan grinned to herself.

Linking arms with her friend, she looked at her quizzically. "So, what do you think of your new onstage love interest?"

"Who, Ben? He's alright I guess."

Megan raised an eyebrow at her coyness. Back in the day Nikki would have told her exactly what she thought. She hated how distant Nikki had become, lost in daydreams she wasn't willing to share.

Recently it had felt more and more like Nikki was pulling away, gradually shutting her out. Ever since she had started dating Jimmy nearly two years ago, there had been increasingly less time for meaningful conversations. He seemed nice enough, but their dating always got in the way of their friendship and for that she could never quite forgive him.

Nikki giggled as she waltzed into Megan's bedroom, her gaze falling onto a glitzy pair of purple high heels by the wardrobe. "Oh my God, I totally forgot you still had these. Did you ever plan on giving them back?" Kicking off her flat shoes, she stepped into the heels.

"That's rich coming from you still carrying my handbag," Megan pointed out pedantically.

Nikki laughed, a sweet melodic sound. "Good point. That is true my friend."

Not that it really made a difference. Megan had far too many bags as it was. Shoes too, for that matter. A hark back to her larger days – bags and shoes would always fit. It was the perfect way to perk her up and feel good about herself. Although she cringed to think about how much of her sizeable student loan had been spent on impulsive shopping sprees.

For a few minutes Megan stood silently watching Nikki prance around in front of the mirror, admiring her shoes. Ever since they had first met, Nikki had struck Megan as the type of girl who had always felt comfortable in her own skin. Never plagued by insecurities or giving a damn what anyone else thought. It was one of the many things she admired about her.

Nikki did a final spin in the purple heels, taking one last look at her reflection in the mirror before kicking them off and clambering onto the bed, sitting cross legged. Megan sank down onto the opposite end, readjusting the pillows behind her so she could sit comfortably, leaning against the wall with her legs drawn up in front of her.

Staring longingly around the room, Nikki smiled wistfully. "I miss this life. The independence, the freedom."

"But you're still a student."

She nodded sadly. "I know. It's just so different living back at home. It's hardly living the student dream when you need to make sure you're back in time for your mum cooking dinner."

"Well, you're more than welcome to move back in. The new girl is driving me crazy. She never washes her pots, always leaves everything out. The kitchen is a mess all the time. It kinda sucks here without you."

Nikki raised an eyebrow. "What? Because I'm a good pot washer?"

"You know what I mean."

"Believe me, I'd rather be here. It's not like I had a choice Meg."

"Yeah I know. I never said you did. It's just…I miss you."

Nikki sighed. "I miss you too."

"How are you finding it at home now anyway?"

Nikki shrugged her shoulders slightly. "It's fine, think I've finally settled back into the old routine. Although I feel like I'm a teenager again! But at least I'm saving a small fortune. London rent really is ridiculous, even for student houses."

"Tell me about it!"

Smiling, Nikki leaned forward conspiratorially. "So, how is it going with you and Peter? You've both been pretty loved-up at rehearsals this week?"

"Good, I think. It seems to be going well." Megan could feel a slight frustration bubbling inside of her. Nikki was a master at this sort of thing – inviting herself over to chat about one thing and then skilfully steering the conversation in another direction in order to ask Megan questions about her own life instead. She was a master manipulator in that way.

Toying absentmindedly with her silver necklace, Nikki ran the chain through her fingers and twirled the heart pendant. She seemed nervous, as though she was trying to avoid getting around to the topic she had initiated the catch-up for in the first place. Looking up, she caught Megan's eye and winked. "You two make an attractive couple. Both so hot!"

Megan grinned at the compliment. "Thanks! Glad you think so. You're not so bad yourself. But I'm guessing you didn't invite yourself over here just to talk about Peter. What's up?"

Biting down on her lip, Nikki straightened her back and took a deep breath. "Okay, here goes. It's about me and Jimmy. We have some news." Pausing, she left that cryptic statement hanging in the air.

A million possibilities immediately raced through Megan's mind. *Were they breaking up? Did he cheat on her? Did she cheat on him? She had been getting close to Ben recently...*

"Yes?" prompted Megan, staring at her curiously. "Good news or bad news?"

Smiling, Nikki relaxed her posture a little. "Good, definitely good news."

Instinctively Megan's eyes dropped to Nikki's stomach, currently concealed beneath her floaty dress. *That was it – she had to be pregnant. The end of life as they knew it, there would be no going back from that.*

Nikki paused again, each second dragging out for an agonizingly long time. Butterflies were jostling about in Megan's stomach as she waited in frenzied anticipation to hear what her friend was going to reveal.

"We're thinking about getting engaged."

Megan fell silent as she let that bombshell news wash over her. At least her friend wasn't having a baby. It took her a few moments to realise Nikki was looking at her expectantly, anxiety in her wide eyes. "Holy shit Nikki, I thought you were going to say you were pregnant!"

Nikki laughed nervously. "No, not yet. So, what do

you think?"

Megan swallowed, unsure where to start in tactfully verbalising her thoughts. "Wow. Erm, I wasn't expecting that."

Nikki sat quietly, waiting for her to go on.

"What do you mean you're *thinking* about getting engaged? Has Jimmy actually proposed yet?"

"No, we're only talking it through at this stage. He's still saving up to buy a ring."

Megan let out a slow breath. "Okay, good. Don't you think you're rushing into things a bit too quickly? You're both so young. Hell, we haven't even graduated yet."

Disappointment fell across Nikki's face. "You don't think it's a good idea?"

Grappling for the right words to articulate her thoughts, Megan said, "I didn't say that. I think it would be great to get engaged when the time is right. But you haven't even been together two full years yet. You've got your whole life ahead of you. People can change a lot after university. What's with the rush to get hitched?"

"But we love each other." Her voice was small and hopeful, as if that changed everything.

"I know you do. But Jimmy's not going anywhere."

"That's not necessarily true," Nikki said quietly.

Megan shook her head in disbelief. "Christ Nikki, you've only just turned twenty-one! It's hardly the age to be settling down into marriage. You're still a student for God's sake."

"Why does that matter?" she asked indignantly.

"If I'm honest, I don't think now is the time to be

jumping into any hasty decisions. You've not even lived together yet for crying out loud."

"Living together isn't going to change anything. We're hardly going to break up because he forgets to put the toilet seat down or leaves his socks on the floor." Nikki's voice was high and strained, getting defensive as she prepared to fight her corner.

Swiftly Megan changed tack, adopting a gentler approach. "Look, you've had a shit summer. Your emotions will still be all over the place. Maybe now isn't the time to be racing into any life-changing decisions. I'd hate for you to rush into something you end up regretting."

Nikki's eyes welled up with tears. "Who said I'm going to regret it? We're in love."

"Yes, but are you absolutely sure you only want to be with Jimmy for the rest of your life."

Nikki narrowed her eyes. "What exactly are you implying?"

"Nothing. Just something to think about."

"I thought you'd be happy for us. It would have meant a lot to have your blessing." Nikki's voice caught then and she buried her face in her hands.

Quickly, Megan pushed herself up and scooted over to her. Wrapping an arm around her shaking shoulders, she stroked her arm comfortingly. "Of course I'll be happy for you when the time is right. Don't take this the wrong way Nikki, but if you were truly convinced this was definitely what you wanted, would you have really told me beforehand? The fact you're even seeking my opinion suggests you must have some doubts yourself?"

"I wanted to share it with you, you're important to me. It matters what you think," Nikki muttered between sobs.

Megan's heart lifted at her words. Their friendship really was special, one of a kind. "Look, thanks for talking to me, I appreciate it. But I do think it would be sensible to take stock and move slowly on this one. You need to make sure you're ready, especially given your past. Don't forget all the shit you went through with your ex. If anything, Jimmy was the rebound guy."

Nikki stiffened, her whole body becoming rigid with tension. When she spoke, it was through gritted teeth, "This *isn't* about my ex, no need to dredge up old news. Besides, I'm over that."

Megan raised an eyebrow sceptically. "Alright, if you say so. But you'd be a fool to think that sort of thing wouldn't affect you. You can't just walk away from something like that unscathed. We all have baggage, but that's pretty epic. I mean, have you even told Jimmy the full story about it yet?"

Reluctantly, Nikki shook her head, her body still tense.

"Do you not think that would be a good place to start? How can you seriously be entertaining the idea of marriage if he doesn't know about your history? It's made you who you are. A story doesn't make sense if you rip out the earlier chapters, no matter how much you want to pretend they didn't happen."

Fresh tears rolled down Nikki's face. Her voice dropped to barely a whisper. "I can't. It's too painful. Besides, what if I tell Jimmy everything and he doesn't love me anymore?" She crumpled in Megan's arms, convulsing sobs shaking her body.

Sighing, Megan grasped Nikki's shoulders and twisted her to look directly in her eyes. "That's a risk you're going to have to take. If he truly loves you it won't change what he thinks of you, believe me."

Sniffing, Nikki wiped her eyes with the back of her hand. Megan reached over to drop a box of tissues in her lap. Grabbing one, Nikki blew her nose and resumed furiously rubbing her eyes afterwards.

Hesitating for a long moment, Megan tentatively asked, "And what about Ben?"

Nikki looked up. "*What* about Ben?"

"Oh, come on, you can't deny you two have chemistry. Are you really telling me you don't feel something for him?"

Nikki drew away from her, knocking off Megan's arm. "Are you suggesting I'm cheating?" she asked, incredulous. "I would never do that."

Megan shrugged causally. Sometimes she knew her friend better than she knew herself. "Whatever you say. But I've seen the way you flirt with him. I'm not saying you've crossed the line yet, but you've definitely been tempted. Isn't that just as bad? Maybe it's only a matter of time?"

Nikki stared at her, dumbfounded. "What gives you the right to make such outrageous claims?"

Megan grasped her hand tenderly, "Nikki, I'm only trying to be a good friend. I'm just warning you to tread carefully. You don't know what might happen if you go there."

*   *   *

109

"Do you think Nikki was lying about hooking up with Ben?"

Megan paused indecisively. "These interviews are confidential, right? No one else will hear about what we say unless it is used as evidence in court?"

Robson nodded in confirmation and she relaxed.

"Well, I don't want to speak badly about Nikki, but yes I do think she was lying. I've seen the way those two look at each other. There's definitely a spark there, a hunger in their eyes. That much is obvious. And personally, I'm not sure Jimmy is the right one for her. They've always seemed a bit mismatched, an odd couple if you ask me."

"Was Jimmy the jealous type?"

"You mean, would he be pissed off if he found out his girlfriend was cheating on him? Of course! He has a bit of a violent side actually. Normally he keeps his temper under control, but sometimes if he's been drinking he can fly off the handle at the smallest thing. I think it scared Nikki how unpredictable he could be."

"So, you think it was her boyfriend Jimmy who hurt her? Or her supposed lover, Ben?"

Megan blinked. "Perhaps. Nikki's such a lovely person, everyone adored her, I can't imagine anyone hating her so much they wanted to kill her. But perhaps someone didn't hate her at all? Maybe they were in love with her, so infatuated that they couldn't live without her? A crime of passion? It's almost romantic."

Robson and Zahra remained silent, prompting Megan to continue her speculation. "Maybe Ben made a move on her and she rebuffed his advances? The jilted wannabe lover seeking revenge? Or Nikki listened to what I said and called off her soon-to-be engagement. That could have pushed Jimmy over the edge. Like I said, he's got a temper. I dread to think what he'd do if Nikki really pissed him off. Or perhaps it wasn't a love thing at all. Maybe it was revenge, pure and simple. Emma finally had enough of being pushed to one side and decided to make Nikki pay for what she had done?"

"You've certainly given it a lot of thought."

Megan smiled, satisfied. "Hopefully it gives you something to go on."

"It does indeed. In fact, you're practically doing our job for us."

Scowling, Megan crossed her arms defensively. "She's my best friend. Obviously, I want to help find out who did this to her. They deserve to pay."

As Robson watched Megan leave, his mind was reeling with all the alternative scenarios she had laid out before them. None of her theories were particularly insightful or even anything new they hadn't already considered before. But still it had been compelling to hear them told by Megan, an alleged close confidante of Nikki's. However, she had been awfully quick to assign blame to her fellow castmates, even potentially throwing her best friend's boyfriend under the proverbial bus by highlighting his possible guilt.

She could simply have been overzealous in her bid to help seek justice. Yet, something about the way she conducted herself had seemed slightly off. As though she was almost incriminating herself by working so hard to deflect away any attention directed towards her. One of the oldest rules of self-preservation in the book. Although, Robson could think of no possible motive Megan would have. But as he had learned from experience it was usually the ones who were quick to blame other people that had something to hide themselves.

Scratching his chin thoughtfully, Robson said, "I don't think Megan's lying as such, but she's definitely hiding something from us. Did you notice how quick she was to push our attention onto the others? It was as if she were afraid of crumbling under scrutiny herself."

Zahra nodded. "I agree. How much easier would our job be if everyone just told the whole truth from the onset?"

"Truth will ultimately prevail where there is pains to bring it to light," Robson said without thinking. His father's favourite saying; a quote from the late American president George Washington if he recalled correctly.

Zahra looked at him curiously for a moment, before smiling slightly and turning away.

CHAPTER NINE

Is This a Dagger Which I See Before Me?

Shuffling from foot to foot to ward off the icy air, Robson took a long drag of his cigarette, his earlier resolve to give up already forgotten.

Fuck it. Today was a day that called for smoking.

Savouring the feeling of the hot smoke deep inside his lungs, he blew out a stream of smoke thoughtfully. Ominous dark clouds rolled overhead, threatening rain that had not yet fallen. Distant rumbling signalled the thunder that was fast approaching with the coming storm.

It had only been a matter of weeks since Britain had been battered by heavy snowfall and blizzards in some of the worst winter weather experienced in decades. The treacherous conditions had caused widespread disruption across the country and evidently the sub-zero temperatures showed no sign of abating any time soon.

The winter of discontent, Robson thought to himself, amused. How fitting. *Dark. Grey. Dismal.* That figured. It matched his mood perfectly. He chuckled to himself. The thought made him feel like a cliché.

His mind kept flicking back to Nikki's family sat in that godforsaken hospital waiting room. Robson knew only too well the feeling of powerlessness that accompanied that long wait. He wouldn't wish that fate on his worst enemy. Still, perhaps Nikki would be the miracle he hadn't realised he had been waiting for. *Maybe she would live.* Although he felt the cynicism set in before he had even properly entertained that thought. *Doubtful. At best, highly unlikely. What was the expression? That patient's circling the drain.*

Yet, there was still part of him holding onto that small glimmer of hope. He had never been in this situation before, where the fate of the victim might actually turn out alright. As a homicide detective, death was part and parcel of the job. Foolishly, he thought after fourteen years he had become hardened to it. Today, he was re-evaluating that assessment.

Taking a final long pull on his cigarette, he relished the temporary heat it generated, comforting against the cold chill of the bitter morning air. Exhaling a cloud of smoke, he dropped the cigarette butt and extinguished it with the toe of his boot, stubbing it out with more force than was necessary.

Zahra looked up enthusiastically as Robson strolled back into the interview room. He had often found himself wondering how such a mature head could sit upon such youthful shoulders. She truly was an enigma.

Right now, Zahra was grinning broadly. "There's been an interesting development. However, first I should update you that it's been confirmed the only fingerprints on the murder weapon belong to our victim Nikki Gowon and Neil Hillton."

Robson snorted. "Which of course, our director was quick to explain."

"Quite. And the prop knife we discovered has been wiped clean, so no fingerprints there either. But our team did unearth this." She handed him a photograph.

He studied it closely. "Intriguing."

"I thought so too. Something to quiz our leading man about."

He nodded in agreement. Ben Grahame's interview was coming up next. "Let's leave it until the end to mention it. See what he divulges voluntarily before we start pushing."

Zahra granted him a wicked grin. "Crafty. I like your style."

As it turned out Ben was one of those men who was instantly likeable. Disarmingly handsome with chiselled features, flawless dark skin and shoulder-length dreadlocks, he exuded warmth and had a charismatic, easy smile. "Awful situation. It beggars belief."

"Would you say you're close to Nikki?"

Ben hesitated for a moment before answering, as if weighing up how honest to be. "I guess so. I mean as close as I can be. I've only known her for six weeks. Although it feels like longer, working on a theatre play together does tend to throw you in at the deep end. You bond quickly – it's pretty intense, a pressure cooker of emotions."

"What did you think about the last-minute swap of actresses?"

A small smile tugged at the corners of Ben's mouth. "Oh, Neil! That man sure knows how to cause drama. I thought it was completely unnecessary. To be honest, I stayed well away from the politics of everything. I was only there to have fun acting, a bit of light-hearted relief you know? That's all."

"Any idea what prompted Neil to make that unexpected cast change?"

Ben gave a casual shrug. "Like I said, he loved the drama. I wouldn't be surprised if he did it just to ruffle a few feathers, keep people on edge. I tried to stay out of it. Both Nikki and Emma have their merits – they're talented actresses. Nikki's a lot more chilled though, which made my life a lot easier."

"Any idea who might want to hurt her?"

"I really don't know. I'm sorry I can't help you there." Ben fixed his gaze on Robson, a hint of a frown appearing between his eyes.

*   *   *

Saturday 10th March

Ben Grahame had never been a clock-watcher before. He had always lived in a way befitting to his firmly held belief that you only live once. Life was short after all. He had no patience for people who wasted their time moaning about all the things they could easily change – whining about jobs they hated, relationships that had turned sour or exotic countries they had never visited. The solutions were simple to him. Get a new job. Find a new partner. Go on holiday already. Just *stop* frigging moaning.

Ben had a lot to be grateful for and he knew it. He had supportive parents and great siblings, all of whom lived nearby in the capital. Additionally, as a car mechanic he had a job he genuinely loved. Normally the working day flew by. He adored the different challenges each new car threw at him. It was like solving puzzles and he happened to be brilliant at it.

But recently the days had been dragging. Hours stretching out for what seemed like an eternity, elongating the time before the all-important evening rehearsals. *Macbeth* had been dominating his mind for more than one reason.

Ben stole another glance at his watch as the minute hand slowly slid into twenty minutes to five. He sighed wearily. Five o'clock couldn't come quick enough. It was bad enough he had the misfortune to be working on the weekend shift, which meant he had already missed out on the day rehearsal. Returning his attention to the task in hand, he put the finishing touches to installing the new alternator and slid into the driving seat to double-check it was working. He smiled in satisfaction as the engine immediately purred into action. *Another puzzle solved.*

Lingering for a few painfully long minutes, he pretended to fiddle with the spark plugs under the bonnet. It was far too late in the day to be assigned a new job.

He couldn't afford to be any later tonight. Glancing at his watch again he saw it had finally reached five minutes to five. *Perfect.*

Satisfied, he closed the bonnet and nipped into the office to hand in the car key. Hurrying into the staff changing room, he scrubbed the grease off his forearms and hastily dumped his gloves and coverall in his locker.

"You off to the pub with us mate?" Stuart's gruff voice echoed in the small room as he slapped Ben on the shoulder.

"Nah, not tonight. Sorry, busy." Ben replied quickly. The theatre show tended to be a contentious subject among his work colleagues who were fast begrudging of how much of his free time it was consuming.

Stuart sniggered. "Ah yeah, that's right. Ditching us to prance around in your tights again, ain't ya?"

Ben rolled his eyes. He had grown used to the good-natured teasing. Of course his workmates didn't get it. Their idea of unwinding was downing beers, perhaps with some competitive pool or darts thrown in for good measure. Learning Shakespeare for fun was an alien concept to them. But he wasn't interested in their approval, he wasn't doing it for them.

"So, are there any hot chicks involved?" asked Stuart.

Ben couldn't help but grin as an unbidden image of Nikki popped into his thoughts. *Deep brown eyes sparkling and her soft lips curling up as she flashed him an enchanting smile*. "I guess so."

Stuart let out a loud guffaw of laughter and slapped his shoulder again with renewed vigour. "Aha, I knew it! Thought it couldn't just be that oldy worldy talking that keeps you going back for more."

Still grinning, Ben shook his head. Slinging his rucksack over his shoulder, he pushed his locker shut. "Anyway, I really do need to go. I've only got thirty minutes to make it across to Shore-ditch."

"Sure, whatever. Have fun mate."

Nikki flung open the door with enthusiastic zeal and burst into the rehearsal room with a spring in her step. Ben granted her a dazzling smile that had been known to work wonders for him in the past. In return, Nikki wrapped her arms around him for a brief embrace, planting a quick peck on his cheek. Her touch made his skin tingle and he shivered as electricity coursed through his body.

"Sorry I'm late," she said apologetically. "Traffic was a nightmare. Jimmy needs to get rid of that car. I mean, who drives in London anyway? It's ridiculous!" Her voice was a gentle lilt, music to his ears.

From his angle, shimmering light bounced off Nikki's dark skin, illuminating her beautiful face. Her features were drawn together in amusement as she watched him closely, head cocked to one side. "What are you staring at?"

Embarrassed at being caught gawping gormlessly at her, Ben shook himself out of his trance. "Sorry, I was miles away." Offering no further explanation, he quickly turned away and started flicking through the script he had been holding limply in his hand. When he stole a glance back at Nikki, she was smiling at him, amused.

Their rehearsal space for the evening was a small storeroom, tucked away in the depths of the theatre. Fairly cramped and shabby, the room's poor lighting emanated from one flickering exposed bulb. Teetering crates of old props were stacked precariously against the bare walls. It was hardly a creative or inspiring place for acting but it served its purpose well. The large auditorium was far too crowded when the entire cast was simultaneously rehearsing different scenes and Ben always struggled to concentrate with the cacophonous drone of constant background noise.

Plus, an added bonus of rehearsing in the back storeroom was that they could thrash out scenes and explore different approaches free from the judgmental eye of a watching Neil. As a rule, Ben generally got along with everyone. He had a gift for seeing the best in people. But even he found the pedantic director was testing his patience. Especially recently, the man had an opinion on everything, which was gradually driving the cast insane.

Looking up again, Ben was surprised to see Nikki staring at him, an unreadable expression on her face. Lips slightly parted, deep eyes fixed on his. For a moment he thought he detected longing, even desire. But that was probably just wishful thinking.

Ben cocked his head. "Earth to Nikki. Now, *you're* the one staring."

She jumped, as if she hadn't realised he had caught her looking. "Sorry, ignore me."

"What is it?" he asked, tone gentle. She had been acting weird all week.

"It's…you remind me of someone. That's all."

Ben didn't know how to take that. "Is that a good thing?" There was an awkward silence as Nikki turned away. "Will Smith?"

She laughed and the tension was broken. "You wish! Come on, let's get started."

She was wearing a floaty turquoise dress today that accentuated her slim, yet curvaceous, body. Ben noted her jewellery and painted fingernails were colour coordinated to match the turquoise theme. "Nice nails."

Nikki looked down at her hands, clearly surprised he had noticed. "Oh, thanks."

She poured over her script, studying her lines for their next scene. Although she was still learning the part, she had a knack for bringing the character of Lady Macbeth to life in a vibrant, exciting way. By contrast, reading lines with Emma had always been more clinical and business-like. Even their onstage kisses had felt mechanical, one of her eyes always working out the best angle for the audience. Other than her lack of passion, Emma had been a relatively talented acting partner. But her demanding personality offstage had left Ben cold. She was far too high maintenance.

Just as they were about to get into the swing of the scene, a loud knock at the door interrupted them. Jimmy strode purposefully into the room to deliver a *Macbeth* reference guide Nikki had left in his car. Ben raised his hand to wave. Jimmy returned the greeting half-heartedly before turning his attention swiftly back to his girlfriend. The dynamics in the cast had changed since Nikki had been given her new role, as though there had been a subtle shift in power.

121

Now, the couple were stood close, heads bent together, whispering about something he couldn't quite hear. Jimmy's brow was furrowed and he kept glancing across at Ben like he didn't quite trust him. Hesitantly, he finally stooped down to kiss his girl-friend as though he didn't want to leave. Gripping Nikki's arm a little too tightly, his fingers dug deep into her flesh.

Pulling away from the kiss, Nikki flinched as she said goodbye. Jimmy was still holding her arm posses-sively as if she belonged to him. Eventually, he tore his eyes away from her, threw a courteous nod in Ben's direction and disappeared.

Ben watched amused as Nikki ran back over. "What was all that about?"

"Nothing."

"Trouble in paradise?"

"Shut up you." Nikki poked his side playfully and granted him a cheeky grin. "Let's get back to it."

Ben had drawn the short straw this evening and cursed his bad luck at being the nominated cast member to traipse down the street and pick up their takeaway pizza order. Annoyingly, the pizza parlour refused to deliver to the theatre – apparently it didn't count as a 'proper' address. It was a policy Ben had grown to resent as he staggered back with a leaning tower of eight pizza boxes obscuring most of his vision.

Stumbling back into the auditorium, he was thank-ful when Violet ran across to help him. Dressed in a pink floral dress with her light brown hair pulled back into a neat plait, she looked endearingly cute today.

Violet always reminded Ben of a little mouse, scurrying about on tip toes. At some point Neil had convinced her to do his bidding as stagehand, which seemed to be synonymous with being his slave. Consequently, she had spent the last month feverishly running around, doing errands, making programmes, creating costumes. You name it, Violet had done it, even down to fetching the director his daily coffee.

Ben left six of the boxes with Violet to distribute among the other actors and headed back to the rehearsal room with the remaining two pizzas. Upon appearing in the doorway, he was surprised to see Nikki had snapped up another rehearsal partner while he had been away and was halfway through practising one of their earlier scenes. She circled Megan, their bodies close, faces only inches apart as they delivered the dialogue. Nikki's eyes were alive with excitement and a beguiling smile had spread across her face.

Ben found himself wondering if he didn't announce his presence, would they take the scene to its natural conclusion and kiss at the end. The racy thought made his heartbeat quicken but any hope of that outcome was dashed when Nikki caught sight of him and broke character to wave enthusiastically. Megan spun around a second later and offered him a wan smile.

Ben strolled over to them casually. "Geez, things are getting a bit steamy in here. Girl-on-girl action, now that would bring a different element to the show."

Megan rolled her eyes scathingly. "I never get why guys are so turned on by that? It's hardly like they would get a look in."

Nikki laughed and gave him a cheeky wink. "It's

because guys always want what they can't have. Isn't that right Ben?"

Stung by the insult, he shrugged nonchalantly and dumped the remaining pizza boxes on top of the crate pile. "Whatever."

Megan grinned at her friend. "I'll leave you to it. We need to organise another double-date soon, we've not done that in ages."

Nikki nodded. "Sure. I'll speak to Jimmy, try and convince him."

After a quick hug, Megan hurried out. Ben frowned slightly as he watched her go.

"Since when have you been rehearsing with Megan?"

Nikki gave a casual shrug. "A while."

"You know I'm available as a rehearsal partner too. If you need more time together just let me know and I'll make it work. Anything to help you out." As soon as he said the words, Ben could hear the neediness in his voice and started mentally kicking himself. "Anyway, I thought you would have chosen your boyfriend to read lines with."

She let out an exasperated sigh. "Jimmy's not exactly thrilled about the fact I have to act in an onstage romance. The less I say about it the better. Definitely not wise to bring it to his attention unnecessarily."

"But surely that's not an unusual occurrence for a theatre student? Obviously you're going to be kissing other people on stage! He never struck me as the jealous type."

Nikki winced. "Usually he's not. I don't know what's gotten into him recently. It's like he's got paranoid about everything. You know I caught him snooping through my phone a few days ago?"

"What, seriously? That's harsh."

"I know, right? He clearly doesn't trust me anymore." She shrugged again, evidently not wanting to discuss it further. Ben got the impression he had touched a raw nerve. "Anyhow, Megan is a much less judgmental rehearsal partner. We're used to practising together from university anyway."

"Why is Jimmy suddenly so paranoid? Got secrets you're trying to hide?"

Nikki gave him a flirtatious wink. "Everybody's got secrets."

"So, do you think Emma's a better actress than me?" Nikki asked the question quietly, her voice barely a whisper.

Ben looked at her, surprised. "What? Why do you ask?"

"I want to know what you think. Who's the better Lady Macbeth?"

"You are!"

"You really think so? You're not just saying that?"

"Yes. Geez Nikki, I didn't take you for the insecure type. Besides, does it matter? Clearly Neil thinks so, otherwise he wouldn't have swapped you into the role."

Nikki gave a pained smile. "I guess so." Her voice sounded strange, almost remorseful.

They had been rehearsing for four hours straight, well into the evening and both of them were exhausted. Clearly for Nikki her tiredness was manifesting itself in doubts about her acting ability.

Ben gave her a reassuring pat on the shoulder when he saw the genuine concern on her face. "Come on, let's finish the scene, see what Neil makes of it and then we can call it a night."

Nodding, Nikki stepped closer into their embrace. She caressed his arm gently, a tender look in her eyes. Even though she had barely touched him, Ben felt his heart rate quicken as he felt a rush of adrenaline. For a fleeting moment, he allowed himself to daydream what it would be like to be with her in real life. He was no stranger to having girlfriends, but somehow it felt Nikki would be different, more exiting. Perhaps she was right, maybe she was more desirable simply because he couldn't have her. 'The forbidden fruit,' or whatever the expression was.

Nikki slipped a hand softly around his neck and pulled him close to kiss him passionately. It was scripted of course, but still Ben felt a rush of elation course through his veins. To his horror he felt himself go hard. Panicked, he twisted his body away from her, hoping she hadn't noticed the conspicuous bulging in his jeans. Thankfully she seemed oblivious, carrying on with the scene as normal.

Distracted, Ben focused all of his energy on suppressing the sexual urges flooding through his body. Gradually, he became aware of her watching him, a strange look on her face. *Was that desire he could see? Maybe he had been approaching this all wrong? Perhaps the feeling of attraction was mutual after all and Nikki had just been waiting for him to make the first move?*

Suddenly brave, he broke character to move in and kiss her again.

Instantly she pulled away and stepped out of his reach. "Ben! What are you doing?"

"I thought...the way you were looking at me."

"It's called *acting!*"

"Oh...I...erm..."

Ben was at a loss of what to say to explain himself. For a minute, he stood there mute as Nikki folded her arms and glared at him unimpressed. In the end, he was saved by the abrupt arrival of Neil who threw open the door with a loud clang and barged into the rehearsal room. Ben had never thought he would actually be pleased to see the meddlesome director.

Launching into a foul-mouthed tirade about Emma, Neil was evidently pissed off and had no qualms about sharing his outrage. "Seriously, who does she think she is? Swanning around here like she's entitled to the best of everything. No fucking respect for my decisions as a director. It's a bloody joke." Exhaling angrily, Neil turned to Nikki. "Be honest with me, has Emma been harassing you?"

She gave a casual shrug. "Nothing I can't handle."

Neil grimaced darkly. "I'll speak to her. Look, can you do me a favour though? If she threatens you, please let me know."

Nikki laughed dismissively. "I'm not scared of Emma! Her bark is worse than her bite."

Frowning, Neil shook his head. "I mean it. She's on the warpath and I'd hate for you to get caught in the crossfire."

"Fine, whatever." A trace of doubt had seeped into

Nikki's voice. She may have been standing firm and speaking with bravado but she didn't fool Ben, he could see her uncertainty.

Studying Neil closely, Ben could see the director seemed genuinely troubled. He hadn't noticed before today but dark smudges had appeared under his eyes and his usually perfectly coiffed hair was in disarray. His skin had taken on a deathlike pallor and large sweat patches were visible under his armpits. Neil had the air of a man only just holding it together. Maybe the strain of the show had finally got to him, he certainly looked like a man under an enormous amount of pressure. Surely it was only a matter of time before he cracked completely.

* * *

Staring pointedly at the table, Ben appeared reluctant to make eye contact, as though he was concerned he had shared too much.

Robson leaned back in his chair, scrutinising him for a moment. "Would you say you were obsessed with Nikki?"

"*What?* No! I admit I was a little besotted with her. In awe of her talent and everything. But not in a creepy way, nothing inappropriate." His voice was high and strained. He sounded strangled.

"You don't think kissing her was inappropriate?"

Ben flinched as if the words were acid. "That was strictly one-time only. I honestly don't know what I was thinking. It was so humiliating. Come to think of it, I don't know why I even bothered mentioning it.

It's really not relevant to your case."

"So, how was your relationship with Nikki outside of the show?"

He shrugged, nonchalant. "Sadly, non-existent. I didn't ever see her. I'm not sure Jimmy would have liked us meeting up anyway. He can be quite possess-ive, controlling even."

"Can you blame him?" chimed in Zahra.

"Look, I liked her alright. Who wouldn't?" snapped Ben. "But clearly the feeling wasn't mutual. Alth-ough, I could be mistaken but sometimes when she was acting a bit strange this last week I could have sworn she wanted to kiss me too. But something was holding her back."

Zahra raised an eyebrow. "Like her boyfriend?"

The dreadlocked actor gave another casual shrug. "Maybe I'm speaking out of turn, but it seemed to me their relationship was in trouble."

"No thanks to guys like you trying to muscle their way in," Zahra countered coldly.

Narrowing his eyes, Ben leaned back in his chair and crossed his arms defensively.

Swiftly Robson changed tack before he withdrew completely. "Do you think Neil was concerned about having an interracial lead couple with you and Emma?"

Ben let out a derisive snort of laughter. "Hardly! This is twenty-first century London. No one even bats an eyelid at a diverse cast these days, it's not exactly controversial. Neil tends to have a colour-blind appr-oach to casting anyway; the actors who perform best at the auditions get the leading roles, no matter what they look like. Besides I think he appreciated the interracial element, he said it added a new dimension to the star-crossed lovers."

"So, why did he make the change?"

"Beats me. I mean I ain't complaining. Nikki's hot. Nice too, less pretentious than Emma. I wish she'd got the part sooner."

Robson exchanged a fleeting glance with Zahra who gave an almost imperceptible nod. Drawing the brown folder on the table towards him, Robson extracted the top photograph and laid it purposefully on the table.

"Do you recognise this?"

Leaning forward, Ben stared at the photograph for a moment, then gave an awkward attempt at a smile. "Yeah. It's one of my jackets from the show. I wear it in one of the final scenes. Why?"

Observing him closely, Robson deliberately took a long pause before he answered. "We found it stuffed behind the stage backdrop at the theatre. The original prop knife was wrapped up in it, hidden in a sleeve. You know, the knife that wasn't lethal."

The smile vanished from Ben's face and was replaced with a baffled look. His surprise seemed genuine and Robson had to remind himself that he was an experienced actor who could easily be putting on the performance of his life.

"Did you really think we wouldn't find it?"

"You think I put it there? I know nothing about that."

"I thought you said the jacket was yours?"

Panic flashed across Ben's face as he shifted uncomfortably in his chair. "It is, but everyone had access to it backstage. I didn't hide the knife in it. Why would I do that? Man, this is absurd! You've got to believe me, I've got nothing to do with this. I'm being set up, someone must be framing me. It's an underhand tactic that's even stolen from the bloody play when Lady Macbeth plants the blood-stained daggers on King Duncan's servants! I'm telling you, I have no idea how that knife ended up in my jacket."

"Why would someone want to frame you? What reason would you have to try and kill her?"

"Trust me, I have no idea. Of all people I would be the least likely to hurt Nikki."

Robson cocked his head. "Because you have feelings for her?"

Ben fell silent, eyes downcast.

"Let me be clear, concealing the knife is pretty damning evidence. Now, we aren't arresting you just yet, but it really would be in your best interest to tell us everything you know. Why don't you go away and have a long hard think if there's anything else you want to share with us?"

As soon as they were left alone Robson could feel Zahra's eyes boring into him, her eyebrows raised slightly in amusement.

"What?"

"*Damning evidence?* There aren't even any finger-prints on the prop knife to tie Ben to it. We certainly don't have enough for an arrest warrant."

Smiling, Robson winked conspiratorially. "Anything to get him to talk more, right?"

"Be careful. We need to make sure all our evidence

is admissible in court. We don't need any accusations of police coercion against us."

"Don't be such a spoilsport."

Zahra shot him a withering look.

Robson held up his hands, resigned. "Okay, okay, I'll behave. You have my word. So, what do you reckon? Crime of passion by her jilted would-be lover?"

Zahra grunted. "I'm not sure."

"Yeah you're right. He does seem too chilled to be a guy who would fly into a jealous, murderous rage."

"But that's just it, isn't it? This wasn't an impulsive attack. Whoever targeted Nikki took time, deliberation. This took careful planning, it was a considered, calculated murder attempt. Clever enough for the culprit to think they could get away with it."

Robson's expression hardened. "Well, they didn't count on us. Let's make sure they don't walk free."

CHAPTER TEN

Look Like the Innocent Flower

Emma Thorpe sauntered into the interview room with an air of superiority normally reserved for minor celebrities. She carried herself with a sense of entitlement and self-importance that was already irritating Robson.

Although he couldn't deny Emma was a stunningly beautiful young woman. Her deep-set blue eyes and sharp, elegant features were framed by a flowing mane of luscious golden locks. Even her flawless skin seemed to possess an angelic glow.

Gracefully lowering herself into the chair, Emma perched on the edge of the seat as if she wasn't planning to stay for long. Belatedly, Robson threw a hand up in front of his mouth to hide a yawn he hadn't quite managed to stifle.

Cocking her head to one side, she smiled sweetly at him with lightly glossed lips. "Am I keeping you up detective?"

"You didn't have trouble getting to sleep when your co-star stabbed herself onstage right in front of you?"

Emma shrugged, giving a dismissive wave. "We're not very close. Besides, it's important to get my beauty sleep."

Robson shook his head in disbelief.

Glancing at her watch distractedly, Emma tutted. "You know I'm missing an important client meeting to be here? How long is this going to take? It's not exactly convenient."

The detectives exchanged a look.

"I have to say your remorse for your injured co-star is astounding."

The blonde actress let out a frustrated sigh. "Nikki isn't exactly my favourite person."

"From what we've heard, that's somewhat of an understatement."

Emma laughed bitterly. "There's no love lost between us, that's not a secret. It doesn't mean I tried to kill her, if that's what you're implying?" She spoke in a condescending tone that was fast getting on Robson's nerves. Indignant at being challenged, her flirtatious smile had morphed into a pout.

"Why do you hate her so much?"

"Are you kidding? The fucking bitch stole my role! I'd spent weeks mastering Lady Macbeth, working on all the staging, developing the costumes. Then Nikki swooped in right at the end to take all the glory." She spat the last words, pure venom in her voice.

"I thought it was the director who made that decision, not Nikki?"

Emma rolled her eyes disdainfully. "Yeah, well whatever. She clearly had a hand in it. She acts all innocent but she's a manipulative little bitch. Nikki will do anything to get what she wants. There's no way Neil would have willingly changed the parts last-minute of his own accord. That must have been her doing. If you ask me, I reckon she blackmailed him."

"You sound quite worked up about it?"

"Believe me, I am," snapped Emma. "Everyone around here acts like Nikki's some kind of saint, it feels as though I'm the only one who can see her dark side."

"Sounds as if you'd have a lot to gain if she was no longer in the picture?"

Emma grunted scornfully, pursing her lips. "Seriously? You really think I'm that shallow? To try and kill someone to reclaim a part in some stupid play? What kind of idiot do you take me for?"

Robson gave a small shrug. "Just pointing out it sounds like motive to me."

"Perhaps if I were a complete moron," she sneered. "I don't even need this ridiculous play! I don't harbour a lofty ambition to become a famous actress, I'm not delusional. I already have a great career in PR, I was only doing *Macbeth* for a bit of fun. Now I wish I hadn't bothered. But I sure as hell would never jeopardise what I already have."

"You do seem quite possessive of the lead role though?"

Folding her arms tightly across her chest, Emma's lips curved into a sly smile. "Maybe I'm just the best. Did you ever consider that?"

*   *   *

Sunday 11th March 2018

Emma breathed a sigh of relief and took a welcome sip of her slightly tepid tea. Sat at her work laptop, she had eventually finished putting the final touches to a new PR proposal and set about emailing the presentation to the rest of her team for their approval.

She hated working on the weekend. Thankfully, the new client pitch had come together quicker than she had thought it would, no thanks to that idiotic director Neil Hillton. Her manager would be less than understanding if they lost out on a multi-million-pound client because Emma was distracted by an amateur play of all things.

But distracted she was. No wonder she was behind schedule, having spent most of Thursday and Friday sneaking subtle glances at the *Macbeth* script on her phone. *Bloody Neil.* It was taking her ages to learn her new lines. Having literally just memorised Lady Macbeth's complicated speeches, she was now forced to push all those lines from her mind in an attempt to try and remember her new dialogue. She could have killed Neil.

The *Macbeth* show was meant to be a welcome distraction, a fun pastime for the bleak winter evenings. Emma hadn't acted since high school but she had always missed being onstage. It felt invigorating to have all those eyes on her, she always had relished being the centre of attention. She was good at acting too, a natural. Much to her surprise, she had been enjoying the play more than she had expected to.

But now she was starting to wish she had never got involved. Neil had been a distraction from the start. She had never expected to be captivated by the man's directing ability, but he had truly proved himself to be a creative genius. Emma found him remarkably inspiring and had loved spending time with him working on the complex role.

Despite her best intentions, she couldn't get Neil out of her mind. Even the thought of his self-righteous face made her bristle in rage. *How dare he do this to her?*

When he had broken the news to her that he was swapping Nikki into the Lady Macbeth role, Emma had been so stunned she hadn't even argued. Before that day, the director had appeared suitably impressed with her performance and now, four days later, Emma still couldn't understand what she had done wrong. Recently her bewilderment had given way to embarrassment and she had spent yesterday's rehearsal trying to limit her interactions with the other cast members.

But today was different. She had woken up with a new clarity on the situation, as if everything had suddenly clicked into place. *Nikki Gowon was the key to the whole fucking mess.* There was no way Neil would have completely changed his mind so dramatically if his hand wasn't being forced. Emma had seen what the last few days had done to Neil and he seemed like a broken man. Certainly not someone who was comfortable with all the last-minute changes.

Meanwhile, Nikki had gained a shiny new lead role. *The golden girl wins again. How convenient.* Well, today Emma had decided she had finally had enough. Her former humiliation had melted away and was replaced with a burning anger. At the rehearsal tonight, she would confront Neil, and Nikki for that matter, and find out once and for all what the hell was going on.

Crammed uncomfortably into a work toilet cubicle, Emma swiftly changed into a figure-hugging red dress with a plunging neckline and towering stiletto heels to match. Hovering at the mirror to carefully apply a fresh coat of lipstick, it appeared she was heading out for a hot date. Truth be told, Emma would have preferred to be getting glammed up for another reason but sadly it was merely part of her dedication to get answers. She was determined to crack Neil and had found from experience it was much easier to get men to cave when she looked the part.

Ever since she was a young girl Emma had known exactly how to expertly manipulate any situation to get her own way. Naturally pretty, she had found people were always fussing over her and basking in her radiance, which made them very easy to control.

As she got older, she was amused to discover almost every man wanted to be with her and she took advantage of that in every conceivable way. Over the years Emma had craftily learnt how to exploit people's emotions and convince them to do her bidding. It gave her a great sense of power and she was well-versed at getting what she wanted. A mistress of manipulation.

She could lose herself in her own fabrications. Lying had always come easily to her; it was just another form of acting, which at its essence was simply persuasion. And Emma Thorpe could be exceptionally persuasive.

It did however, mean she didn't deal well with things being beyond her remit of control and this latest twist had really thrown her. Emma felt more riled every time she thought about Neil until her blood was practically boiling with rage.

Her phone buzzed to inform her the pre-ordered taxi had arrived. Grabbing her handbag, Emma took one last look at her reflection in the mirror, granted herself a congratulatory smile and set off.

The ear-splitting, heated argument reverberated around the auditorium, creating a cacophonous din of never-ending insults. Or rather, Emma's harsh voice could be heard echoing around the theatre.

Did it still constitute an argument if it was purely one-sided?

Nikki had not so much as raised her voice as Emma stood berating her. She simply stood watching, lip curled slightly in amusement, not taking the bait.

Smart move, thought Emma. *What was it about this girl that always threw her off her game?*

Emma had intended to head straight to Neil's office when she arrived at the theatre, but as fate would have it, she had accidentally run into Nikki beforehand. She had greeted Emma so smugly that something inside her snapped and she lost her temper. She had turned on Nikki so ferociously it was like a wild animal had finally been let loose to ravage its prey. All her inner restraint was laid down and all of her pent-up bitterness came flooding out.

Naturally, Emma had assumed Nikki would retaliate and was all geared up for a battle. However, frustratingly Nikki had refused to be drawn into arguing, which had the annoying effect of making Emma look like a raging idiot. The whole scene appeared completely unbalanced, not unlike an angry rhinoceros kicking a timid balled-up hedgehog. That irked Emma all the more; Nikki was manipulating the situation even now.

Pausing for breath, Emma glared at her. Nikki stood casually, hand on her hip, looking unimpressed. A strange smile crept across her face, as though she was quite enjoying the dramatic scene Emma had inadvertently created.

"Are you quite finished?"

The nonchalance in her tone pissed Emma off more than she had thought possible.

"No! I'm nowhere near finished you fucking bitch."

She raised her hand to slap Nikki across the face. That movement finally made her react. Expertly blocking the strike, Nikki grabbed Emma's wrist and pushed her violently backwards. Emma stumbled as she tripped over her own feet and almost lost her footing. Humiliated she straightened up, wishing looks could kill as she glared daggers at Nikki.

They had attracted quite a crowd; the entire cast had gathered to watch them. Peter stood leaning against the wall with an undeniable smirk on his face, enjoying the spectacle. To his left Megan stood with her arms furiously folded, features drawn together in a dark scowl. She looked like she was contemplating attacking Emma herself if she dared to raise her hand to hit her friend again.

Jimmy had also sprang into action and dashed forward to pull Nikki back protectively and stand between them.

How did Nikki inspire such loyalty in these people? It was as though she was their queen.

"Aww, your own personal bodyguard, how cute!" Emma scoffed. "Can't you fight your own battles?"

Silently, Nikki gave Jimmy a warning look. There was a pleading expression in his eyes but he dutifully stepped back at his girlfriend's request.

Emma sniggered at his obedience. "Down boy! Got him well-trained, haven't you?"

Jimmy shot her an evil look, hands balling into fists at his sides.

Ignoring him, Emma marched up to Nikki, halting only inches from her face as she dropped her voice to a bitter hiss. "That role was *mine*. I auditioned and won it fair and square. You can't just steal it now because you want it. That's not how these things work."

Nikki bit down hard on her lip and dug her fingers deep into her own waist. It was clearly taking every ounce of her self-control not to retaliate and lash back.

"You mess with my life – I'm going to destroy you."

Nikki gave a dismissive flick of her hand. "Ooh I'm quaking in my boots."

Emma scowled as she felt the heat rising to her face. *How dare Nikki undermine and humiliate her like this? Why wouldn't the bitch just fight back?*

"I'm deadly serious. This isn't over. You better watch your back. You'll never even see me coming."

Smirking, Nikki opened her mouth to respond but her witty comeback was lost when Neil suddenly materialised onstage like a phantom.

Stomping down the steps, his face was livid with rage. "Emma! What the hell do you think you're doing?"

"I'm giving her a piece of my mind, what does it look like? Besides, it's not just me."

"Did you hear me raise my voice?" asked Nikki innocently, flashing the director a cherubic smile.

"Fuck you."

"Break it up girls," said Neil authoritatively, adopting a commanding tone in a desperate attempt to re-establish control. Grabbing Emma's arm, he dragged her roughly towards him. "We need to talk. In my office right now."

A furious Neil paced back and forth across the limited width of his small backstage office, veins bulging in his neck. Sat defiantly on his desk, Emma swung her legs distractedly.

The director looked utterly exhausted, but Emma couldn't bring herself to feel sorry for him. Neil had brought this upon himself. His normally immaculate hair was matted against his forehead as though he hadn't showered in a while and there were noticeable food stains on his shirt.

He really had let himself go.

Finally, he lifted his head to glare at her. "What the fuck Emma?"

She shrugged. "It was important to say my piece."

Neil shook his head, exasperated. "We spoke about this. You promised to go along with it."

Emma grimaced. "No, *you* spoke about it. I never got a word in. All of this was very much decided without my involvement."

Neil turned away in frustration, clenching his fists.

Emma glared at the back of his head. The man always knew exactly how to get under her skin. "Are you ever going to tell me what the hell is going on?"

"I don't owe you an explanation."

"Are you joking? You bloody do!"

Neil's voice became a low growl. "It's for the best of the show, you've got to trust me."

She let out malicious laugh. "Of course! Why would I struggle to comprehend that?"

"Nikki is a great Lady Macbeth."

"That's not what you were saying last Tuesday."

The director sighed wearily. "Please Emma, you promised to be reasonable."

Emma's eyes narrowed into dark slits. "Oh, believe me, I *am* being reasonable. Don't forget I could make life very difficult for you."

"Is that a threat?"

"What do you think?"

Neil studied her closely. "Now, let's not get ahead of ourselves."

"I mean it. I've been a good girl, kept my mouth shut. And for what? I could bring a whole world of pain down on you. I deserve answers."

Neil visibly paled as tiny beads of sweat appeared on his forehead. "That's the one thing I can't give you."

Crossing her arms irritated, Emma noticed Neil's eyes linger on her body for a moment. She had almost forgotten about the red dress. She drew her arms up to push her breasts closer together and amplify her cleavage more. "How is the new Lady Macbeth working out for you anyway?"

Much to her annoyance Neil promptly looked away. "That's not going to work Emma."

"Really? After everything you're seriously not going to give me an explanation?"

"Look, I know it's rubbish, but unfortunately my mind is made up. It would be far too disruptive to swap you both back now. We're cutting it damn fine as it is."

Emma stared at him coldly in disbelief. "That's your rationale? It would be too *inconvenient*? Why on earth did you think it was a good idea in the first place?"

"I don't expect you to understand, but sometimes as a director it's my job to make the tough decisions. There's no point making idle threats. There's nothing I can do now. 'What's done, is done'." Smiling sheepishly, he gave her a small, helpless shrug.

She glowered at him. "Oh, believe me there's nothing idle about my threats."

Grimacing, Neil gave her a pleading look. It was only then Emma realised how much power she had over him.

"Emma, what you're talking about would hurt everyone involved, yourself included. Plus, it wouldn't change anything. You've got nothing to gain."

"Maybe. But then again it could be interesting. I suppose I'll just have to decide if you're worth the effort."

*   *   *

"So, you do admit openly threatening Nikki?"

Emma lifted her chin. "Everyone heard me, I can't exactly deny that. I hate her, that's no secret. But like I said before, it doesn't mean I tried to kill her."

"So, your threats were just empty words? No intention to ever follow through?"

She let out a scoffing laugh. "What do you think?"

Robson raised a quizzical eyebrow. "I think you'd have a lot to gain if she were no longer around."

"Weren't you listening to anything I said? Neil wasn't interested in negotiating. His mind was made up."

"Exactly. You weren't tempted to take matters into your own hands?"

Emma stared at him. "Are you insane?"

Zahra shot Robson a warning look and took over the questioning. "What were you talking about when you were threatening Neil? What did you know?"

"That's not really relevant."

"You know we can charge you with obstruction of justice if you try to mislead our investigation?"

"It's only obstruction is it has got something to do with your case and trust me, it has nothing to do with Nikki." With that Emma folded her arms defiantly, making it crystal-clear there was nothing more to be said on the subject.

"Any idea who would want to hurt her?"

Emma gave a nonchalant shrug. "Not a clue. All I know is the bitch has secrets of her own. And I'm convinced Nikki must have something on Neil. Maybe she offered him money to blackmail him into giving her the part? Who knows? She's a conniving little manipulator who's det-ermined to get exactly what she wants." Glancing at her watch, she took a sharp intake of breath. "Look, I've humoured this little charade but I really do need to go now. We've got a pitch for more business this Monday and it's imperative I help sweet-talk the clients today before the presentation. I can't afford to lose my job over this."

Leaning back in his chair, Robson gave her a rueful smile. "You're free to go. Just be sure to let us know if you remember anything else."

After she had left, Robson rubbed his forehead and gave a deep sigh. "Too bad we can't roll the lie detec-tors in."

"You think we're being played?"

"I think we'd be foolish to think a bunch of actors would ever be completely straight with us. They'd be more confident than most at lying to hide anything that might make them look bad."

Zahra groaned, disheartened. "I guess you're right. They could all be feeding us any old story in the hope of duping us. Plus, you can't deny there's definitely professional jealousy involved. What's that old saying? How many actors does it take to change a lightbulb? Ten, one to hold the bulb and nine to say 'it should be me up there'."

Robson grinned half-heartedly. "So, what do you

think of the original Lady Macbeth?"

Zahra let out a short, barked laugh. "Emma? I think she's a snake. I believe the expression is 'look like the innocent flower, but be the serpent under't'."

Impressed, Robson looked at her in surprise. "Wow, good *Macbeth* knowledge."

She smiled proudly for a minute before collapsing into giggles. "Honestly? I googled that before you came in. I couldn't resist it. I was dying to see your face when I started spouting off Shakespeare quotes!"

Robson granted her a quick half-smile, he wasn't in the mood for jokes.

Struggling to contain her laughter, Zahra fought to regain her composure. "Seriously though, I think Emma's a snake in the grass. There's something about her I don't like."

"You think she's lying?"

"I don't think she's telling the whole truth and you're right she does have a clear motive."

Robson scratched at his stubble silently.

"Penny for your thoughts?"

"I was just thinking about the gender differences when it comes to committing murder. Generally speaking, men are more predisposed to violence so it's not surprising they're responsible for the majority of homicides. But when women are the culprits they tend to opt for stealthier, less violent methods. That's why things like poisoning remain a predominantly female crime."

"What you're getting at is that this *wasn't* a violent crime?"

"Precisely. I mean it's not exactly poisoning, but

it's the same principle. The would-be murderer simply stood back and let Nikki inflict the damage on herself. Their own hands are clean of blood, metaphorically speaking. Plus, it's smart, a much lower chance of actually getting caught."

"Basically, you think it's one of the girls? Emma, Megan or Violet?"

Robson shrugged. "It's a theory."

Zahra's phone rang suddenly, interrupting their conversation. She answered it quickly, nodding along in silence. Robson's heart sank as he watched her features darken.

When she hung up, Zahra turned to face him with sadness in her eyes. "Well, unfortunately our attempted murder case has now officially become a homicide investigation. Nikki died from surgery complications half an hour ago."

"That's too bad. I was just starting to like the sound of the girl."

Robson hated to admit he felt a pang of disappointment at the news. Usually he prided himself on maintaining a professional distance and never getting too emotionally involved in his cases. However, this investigation was somehow different. Not only was it all hauntingly familiar being back in a theatre after over a decade, but it was also his first case that could have potentially had a happy ending. He hadn't realised it before, but he had truly allowed himself to believe Nikki could miraculously survive against all the odds. To have that hope wrenched away so abruptly felt like being punched in the gut.

Looking over at his partner, he saw a similar pained

expression etched on her face. Normally Zahra was particularly skilled at hiding any personal emotions, but right now she looked deflated and absolutely shattered.

CHAPTER ELEVEN

The Night is Long

Violet Underwood was one of those people who seemed significantly younger than her age. Robson knew she was a good few months past her nineteenth birthday, but the fresh-faced teenager sat before them barely looked a day over sixteen. A doll-like creature with delicate features and clear porcelain skin, she was dressed casually in a baby-pink jumper. Her mousy brown hair was pulled primly to one side in a simple braid that further enhanced her youthfulness.

She stared at them with wide, blue eyes gleaming with tears, cheeks flushed red, as though she was embarrassed by a question they hadn't asked yet. Twiddling with the frayed hems of her jumper sleeves, she absentmindedly ran the woollen material back and forth through her fingers.

Suddenly aware of Robson's gaze, Violet pulled her sleeves further down self-consciously then clasped her hands tightly together to stop them from shaking.

Was that fear he had observed? Or something else?

"We just want to ask you a few questions," began Zahra softly. "There's nothing to worry about."

Violet nodded feebly, eyes flicking from one detective to the other.

"What can you tell us about Nikki Gowon?"

"Honestly, I don't really know her. I'm not exactly cool enough to hang out with those guys. But from what I do know she's nice. She is…was…kind to me, friendly even."

"Do you have any idea who would want to kill her?"

"No, I'm sorry, I don't know." Her voice cracked and she buried her face in her hands as she burst into tears.

They sat in uncomfortable silence as Zahra produced a small pack of tissues from her pocket and pushed them across the table.

Gratefully grabbing one, Violet dabbed at her eyes and took a shaky breath as she attempted to compose herself. "I'm sorry. I just can't believe she's really dead. I didn't think…"

Looking at her curiously, Robson frowned. "You didn't think what?"

Violet opened her mouth to speak but couldn't find the right words. Instead, she swallowed and lowered her voice to a whisper. "Never mind. It doesn't matter."

"Everything matters, even the smallest details. You have no idea who the murderer could be?"

Violet shook her head but there was no conviction there. She leaned back in her chair, withdrawing into an invisible shell. Robson had always been good at reading people. It was a talent that served him well as a detective and few could decipher a person's emotions as accurately as he could. As he sat studying Violet, in her face Robson saw mainly fear tinged with sadness and guilt. *But what was there for her to feel guilty about? And why was she so afraid?*

The young actress looked up then to meet his stare and Robson realised he was wrong. He could see in Violet's eyes that she was more than afraid.

She was terrified.

*   *   *

Monday 12th March

Late, late, late. No matter how well Violet planned her routine she always managed to find herself running behind schedule. Despite good intentions, she was incapable of ever getting anywhere on time. Usually daydreaming, she had an annoying habit of losing track of time reading a book or scrolling through an interesting article on her phone.

She glanced at her watch. *Crap. Neil was going to kill her.* Setting down her hairdryer, she snapped shut the novel laying in her lap, one of those historical romance tales she adored. A tale of forbidden love set against the backdrop of Elizabethan Britain.

Violet was the very definition of a bookworm. She loved nothing better than losing herself in a good story, escaping into a fictional universe. Her parents always joked if she had spent half as much time on her schoolwork as she had with her nose buried in a book then she would have passed all her A Level exams with flying colours.

As it happened, she had unsurprisingly aced an impressive A grade in her English Literature exam, but had only managed a C in Psychology and had barely scraped a D in French. The mediocre exam results had nudged her slightly below the entry requirement for Warwick University where she had set her heart on studying English Literature, close to William Shakespeare's hometown of Stratford Upon Avon. Instead of opting for an alternative second choice, Violet had decided to temporarily delay university and work in her local independent book-shop for a year while she retook her exams in the hope of achieving better grades. She got the impression her parents were secretly quite pleased their only child was still living at home for a while longer.

Shrugging off her fluffy dressing gown, Violet grabbed a pink floral dress and threw it on over her head before stepping into nude coloured tights. Her novel's main protagonist was still dancing through her mind. A loveable rogue, he had professed his undying love for the young scullery maid; even though he came from a privileged royal background, he wasn't about to let different social classes stand in their way. *True love.* Violet had constructed a mental image of how the character looked in her head so she could swoon over his handsomeness. Embarrassed, she found herself blushing as heat rose to colour her cheeks.

Wow, I really am pathetic, she thought. *If I feel this excited by a fictional character, I can't imagine what I'll be like when a real man finally comes on the scene.*

Slipping on a pair of scuffed ballet pumps, she grabbed her pristine copy of the *Macbeth* script and hurriedly bounded down the stairs. Poking her head into the kitchen, she smiled as she saw her father sat at the table. His shoulders were hunched as he leafed through the daily newspaper with his reading glasses perched on the edge of his nose.

By the oven, Violet's mother was stood stirring a saucepan. *Spaghetti Bolognese*, if Violet remembered correctly from the meal rota. Her parents were nothing if not meticulously organised, which included planning their family meals at least a fortnight in advance. Other teenagers would have found the routine suffocating but Violet loved it.

Auditioning for *Macbeth* had been her mother's idea. After stumbling across a flyer calling for auditions in her bookshop, Violet had mentioned it in passing conversation over dinner, out of interest more than anything else. She loved all the classic plays just as much as she adored novels. In fact, her parents had bought her the complete set of Shakespeare's works for her eighteenth birthday. She treasured that book set; when she read the plays, it felt like she was holding a part of history in her hands.

Upon discussing the imminent *Macbeth* casting, her mother had somehow managed to talk her into getting involved, convincing her it would be a great opportunity to be bold and try something different.

Violet was still smiling at the memory as her mother turned to greet her warmly. "Hi sweetheart. Are you heading out?"

"Yeah, sorry I won't have time for dinner. Save me

some for later? I'll have a snack at the theatre to keep me going."

"Sure thing. Consider it done. Have a good time at rehearsals." She set the spatula down on the counter and drifted over to Violet, placing her hands gently on her narrow shoulders. "We're so proud of you sweetie. It's so great you're doing this. We can't wait to come and see the show."

Violet couldn't help but feel self-conscious as she walked through the grand metal doors of the Gemini Theatre entrance. Naturally shy and retiring, acting had already pushed her far beyond her comfort zone. But now with all the tension in the cast since the dramatic Lady Macbeth reshuffle, she was dreading what drama today's rehearsal might hold. Emma's explosive meltdown yesterday was still fresh in her mind and Violet was fearful of getting caught in the crosshairs of another heated argument.

Back when she had first auditioned, Violet's mother had assured her the play wouldn't be anything like high school; there would be no popular kids to rule the roost. Violet had laughed bitterly at that naïve notion. It was a fact of life that every social circle always had a pecking order. The *Macbeth* cast was no exception. Turns out it wasn't all that different from high school after all. Worse in fact; the cast had come with a readymade clique of the four student friends.

Top of the clan were the popular '*elites*' – Nikki, Peter and Emma, followed by their '*hanger-on's*' – Jimmy and Megan who circled their partners like satellites. Emma by contrast practically lived in Neil's pocket, until recently at least. Then, of course, there was always at least one loser; Violet the quiet do-gooder. She hadn't figured out yet where Ben fit in the whole social strata. He was something of an enigma; a charming, affable guy who happily floated between the various social groups with ease.

By default, Violet had found herself bonding with Ben, not least because he made more effort than everyone else to actually talk to her. Strictly platonic, their friendship was an unlikely one in many ways. Violet was conscientious and uptight, diligent about abiding to the rules. In comparison Ben was more relaxed and laidback, with a somewhat laissez-faire attitude to life.

Ben waved at Violet as she walked into the auditorium. Effortlessly cool, he was wearing a retro band t-shirt. Recently, he had taken to teasing her mercilessly about her lack of music knowledge. Gesturing at his current t-shirt, he winked at her. Black with a yellow smiley face with crosses for eyes. *Nirvana.*

"Wait, I know this one! Isn't that the band with the lead singer who committed suicide? He shot himself, right? Carl Cocaine or something?"

Ben rolled his eyes. "*Kurt Cobain.* Only one of the greatest singer songwriters of all time. Can you even name any of their songs?"

Violet screwed her face up in concentration. "Erm…"

"*Smells Like Teen Spirit. Come As You Are. Lithium.*"

Violet stared at him blankly and Ben burst into laughter. "Wow, you're so sheltered. Remind me to make you a Spotify playlist to introduce you to some real music. You never know, you might surprise yourself and find you like it. It's a lot better than the middle-of-the-road acoustic crap you listen to anyway."

"I happen to enjoy my acoustic music, thank you very much."

Ben grinned. "We'll agree to disagree. Although you're still wrong."

Violet couldn't help but smile as she shook her head. "Anyway, duty calls." She held up the Starbucks coffee cup.

Ben nodded. "Can you send Nikki in my direction when you deliver that to Neil? I've been waiting for her to start rehearsing for ages."

Neil's cramped backstage office was full to the brim of old theatre memorabilia, as if he was fearful of letting go of the past. Row after row of programmes were stashed on his bookshelf alongside an eclectic assortment of books. Faded posters of plays the theatre had hosted looked down upon them from every wall – memories of years gone by.

Rushing into the office, Violet hastily set the coffee down on his desk, nearly knocking it over in the process. Neil's eyes flickered briefly to the steaming cup before he cast a disapproving glance down at his watch.

"Sorry it's late."

"I'm sure he won't mind. Isn't that right?" remarked Nikki, gazing at the director pointedly. Leaning against the desk, there was something almost predatory in her stance.

In contrast, Neil was stood cautiously against the

far wall as if he were under attack. The tension in the room was palpable. Violet got the impression she had inadvertently interrupted an intense conversation.

Ever since Nikki had first stepped into the lead female role, the atmosphere between her and the director had been tense, strained for some reason unbeknown to Violet. She had caught the two of them casting furtive glances at each other across the stage when they thought no one was looking. On more than one occasion, Nikki had returned Neil's stares with a cheeky wink. And recently, Violet had stumbled upon the pair speaking in hushed whispers that faded into uneasy silence when she approached.

Studying the two of them, Neil struck her as a man who was somewhat uncomfortable. *Perhaps he was regretting his last-minute cast change*, mused Violet thoughtfully. Only five days ago the director had announced the Lady Macbeth swap with great enthusiasm. He had pitched the change with such certainty, Violet had genuinely believed he thought it would be the best for the show.

But now she wasn't so sure.

Before when Emma was in the role, Neil had been buzzing with uncontrolled excitement at every rehearsal. Whereas these days he was considerably more restrained. It appeared he had begun to operate more out of a sense of duty and obligation, rather than the passion and drive he had possessed previously. Plus, he seemed distracted, as though his mind was elsewhere.

Tapping her foot impatiently, Nikki looked across at Violet. "Need anything more?"

Shaking herself from her thoughts, Violet gave an apologetic smile. "Sorry, no. I'll leave you to it. But Ben says to head in his direction once you've finished."

"Sure, tell him I'll be right out."

Stood onstage alongside her fellow actors, Violet was relieved for the brief respite from rehearsing provided by Neil gleefully explaining the intricacies of their next scene. Desperately trying to memorise her lines, she snuck subtle glances at her script while the others peppered the director with questions.

The cast were all stood in a tight circle on centre stage. Well, almost all the cast. Jimmy was a no-show, which had not gone down well with Neil who had taken the opportunity to lecture the rest of them about the importance of commitment and being punctual.

"So, are you happy for us to come up with our own personal interpretations for our characters?" asked Peter.

Neil nodded thoughtfully. "Yes, good initiative Peter. I'm sure I'll have some pointers to guide you in the right direction, but that's a great place to start from. It's your own individuality as actors that will bring originality to the play. You should all dig deep and think about what personal touches you can incorporate into your roles to really help them come alive. And remember, 'above all: to thine own self be true'."

"Wise words sir."

"Not mine. William Shakespeare wrote that in *Hamlet*." Neil sighed in exasperation. "Never mind, let's take it from the top."

Hearing loud footsteps echoing behind her, Violet glanced over her shoulder to see Jimmy had finally arrived. Wearing a determined expression, he strode purposefully towards the stage and leapt up the steps two at a time. Conversation came to an abrupt halt as everyone stopped talking mid-sentence, distracted by his untimely intrusion.

"We were actually in the middle of discussing a scene," protested Neil, clearly annoyed at the disrupt-tion. "One you're meant to be in coincidentally."

Ignoring the director, Jimmy made a beeline straight for Nikki. Reaching for her hand he pulled her away from Ben and towards him.

Looking utterly mystified she laughed nervously. "Jimmy, what on earth are you doing?"

"Do you know what today is?" he asked, a boyish grin appearing on his lips.

Confused, Nikki shook her head, squirming under the scrutiny of everyone's stares.

A fleeting look of disappointment flashed across Jimmy's face. "Today's our two-year anniversary. You didn't forget, did you?"

Nikki smiled sheepishly. "No of course not. I just thought we were celebrating tonight, that's all." She seemed tense, acutely aware they were the centre of attention, literally in the spotlight no less.

Evidently unperturbed by their audience, Jimmy reached into the canvas bag slung over his arm. Nikki's whole body stiffened as though she was afraid of what might come next. She appeared to relax slightly when he produced a huge bunch of red roses to present to her.

"Twenty-four roses, one for every month we've been together."

Cautiously taking the flowers, Nikki gave an embarrassed laugh. "Erm…thanks! They're beautiful."

"Not as beautiful as you, my love. My life began the day I met you. I love you so much." Leaning in, Jimmy kissed her deeply on the lips, oblivious to all the people watching them.

Across the room, Emma caught Violet's eye and wrinkled her nose in disdain as she made a pretend gagging gesture. Violet smiled to herself, even though she could understand why Nikki was uncomfortable with the public display of affection, she still thought it was incredibly romantic. She would give anything for a man to stand on a stage and proclaim his love for her like that.

Peter sidled up next to Violet. He was wearing one of his trademark tight-fitting t-shirts that clung to his body over his bulging muscles. "He's so soppy! Nikki's got him totally whipped."

Violet shot an annoyed look in his direction. "Just because you've never made it to two years with anybody doesn't mean you can judge how other people celebrate that milestone."

Peter gave a quiet grunt. "That's a bit rich coming from you. Rumour has it you don't exactly have much experience in that area yourself."

Violet flinched at the insult and turned away before he could see her cheeks turn scarlet. "Shut up Peter."

"Besides, those roses have nothing to do with romance and everything to do with Jimmy staking his claim."

Violet's brow furrowed in confusion. "I don't understand, what do you mean?"

"Seriously? You're so naive. He's practically marking his territory, he might as well have peed on her. What other reason would he have for announcing his love for her in such a public way? I mean take a look at the two lovebirds now."

Looking back to the couple, Violet saw Jimmy had wrapped his arm tightly around Nikki and pulled her close to snap a selfie to capture the moment. He had a wide grin on his face, but Nikki appeared distinctly uncomfortable and was cringing in his embrace.

Behind them, Ben was stood awkwardly staring at the floor in an effort to avert his eyes. Surprisingly, Megan looked annoyed as she watched the happy couple. Features pulled together in a dark scowl she kept staring angrily at Peter who was wearing a bemused expression. It seemed a strange reaction to Violet, although perhaps she was annoyed Peter had never done anything so romantic for her. Even the best of friends still got jealous of each other sometimes.

Violet shook her head. "I reckon they're simply in love. Who says there has to be an ulterior motive?"

Peter shrugged casually. "Whatever you say."

* * *

"Is that all you have to tell us?" asked Zahra gently, as though she was coaxing a timid animal out of a cage.

Violet nodded quickly, eyes darting to the floor. "Yes, that's it."

"Are you sure?"

"Yes, I can't remember anything else out of the ordinary." Her voice was little more than a whisper.

"Alright." Zahra leaned back in her chair, something akin to disappointment on her face.

"You can't honestly think I had something to do with Nikki's murder?" pleaded Violet, a ring of desperation in her voice. "I mean, do I look guilty to you?"

Yes, thought Robson silently. *Or at least you sure as hell look like someone who is hiding a secret.* Her whole body language screamed that she wasn't telling the truth. At their silence, Violet shrank back into her chair, as if she were trying to make herself as small as possible.

"You worked closely with Neil as the stagehand? Any idea what prompted him to swap Nikki into the Lady Macbeth role."

Violet shrugged helplessly. "Not a clue I'm afraid. I had no idea he was going to do that. I found out at the same time as the rest of the cast. He didn't exactly let me in on his thought process." Dropping her voice to a whisper she hesitantly added. "If truth be told, I'd have guessed Neil would have been much more inclined to swap out Ben rather than Emma. It was clear he was besotted with her. Neil rather fancied his chances with Emma if you ask me. I don't think he'd want to jeopardise that."

"Interesting."

"Just an observation."

Rubbing his forehead in thought, Robson looked across at Zahra. "So, what do you reckon it is Violet's not telling us?"

His partner sighed heavily and gave a glum shrug.

"Whatever it is, she's definitely scared of something."

"Or someone."

Pushing his chair back, Robson rose to his feet with a stretch. Strolling out of the interview room, he walked over to the investigation noticeboard his colleagues had set up earlier. In the centre of the display, Nikki Gowon stared down at them from her photograph. She didn't look impressed.

Contemplating the accumulated information pinned to the board, Robson groaned in dismay. Five interviews in and they had barely made any progress since last night.

"Slow going, isn't it?" said Zahra, walking up behind him.

Gesturing at the latest additions to the noticeboard, Robson agreed, "It sure is. But at least the toxicology report has come back clear and the coroner has conducted the physical exam too and there's no sign of sexual assault."

"Great, but that means we're still no closer to solving the case." She sounded thoroughly disheartened.

It had come as no surprise to Robson when he learnt that Zahra's stoic, business-like demeanour and no-nonsense approach had quickly earned her the title of *The Rottweiler* among her colleagues. What she lacked in size, she made up for in tenacity. She was doggedly determined in pursuing any potential lead in a case, leaving no stone unturned in her relentless pursuit of justice. However, even she got frustrated when all their leads led to nowhere.

Forcing himself to sound optimistic, Robson said, "Well, we still have two more interviews lined up for tomorrow – Megan's boyfriend, Peter Winters, and of course the director, Neil Hillton. Maybe they'll prove more enlightening."

"Perhaps." Zahra covered a yawn with her hand. She sounded exhausted.

"How about we call it a day?" Robson suggested gently. "Go home, get some sleep and start fresh first thing in the morning."

Zahra nodded in agreement. "Sounds like a plan."

CHAPTER TWELVE

Sleep No More

How the hell did this happen? Dumbfounded, Robson peered down at Nikki's limp body. Her eyes were wide, glassy stare unseeing. Hesitantly inching forward, his foot slipped on something wet. Glancing down, he saw his shoes were covered in blood. Retching, he hastily drew back.

Suddenly, Nikki blinked. Blood trickled from the corner of her dry, cracked lips as she gave a spluttering cough. "Help me," she croaked, her voice barely a whisper. "Please help me."

Spurred into action, Robson dropped to his knees beside her. Heart thumping against his chest, he leaned forward and pressed his hands firmly against her hideous stomach injury. Deep crimson blood spurted out from between his fingers. Try as he might he could not stop the unending gushing flow.

"Help, please…" Her weak voice faltered.

Holding his trembling hands in front of him,

Robson could see they were stained red. The coppery stench of blood hung in the air.

"I'm right here. I'll save you." Bending over, he whispered in her ear. "Who did this to you?"

Nikki stared up at him through clouded eyes. She attempted to say something but no sound escaped from her lips.

"I can't hear you. Say it again." Robson leaned closer, his cheek brushing against her ear.

As Nikki tried to speak again, she was interrupted by a harsh ringtone slicing through the silence. Frustrated, Robson scrambled to switch off his phone. It slipped through his fingers and clattered to the ground with a resounding clunk. Still it was ringing, loud and persistent.

Nikki whispered desperately, an inaudible, gurgling sound. He could almost make out what name she said.

Almost, but not quite. Half heard, it remained tantalisingly beyond his grasp.

Meanwhile, blood was still gushing freely, pooling on the floor around his feet. She was slipping away. He was losing her...

Robson jolted awake, fragments of the disturbing nightmare still hazy in his mind. Head pounding, he was disoriented until gradually his bedroom came back into focus. The irritating ringtone was still there, part of the dream that hadn't quite left yet.

It took him a few minutes to realise it was his phone, vibrating steadily on the bedside table. Reaching wearily to pick it up, he knocked over a half-full beer can which spilt everywhere, mostly over everything electrical.

Cursing loudly, he made a half-hearted attempt at mopping up the spillage with one hand as he groggily answered the dripping phone. "Hello."

"Hi there. Let me guess, I woke you up?" Zahra sounded amused.

Glancing at his alarm clock, which he noted with annoyance was flickering after getting wet, he saw the gleaming display read 5.50 a.m. "Course you woke me up. It's officially night-time."

"Not for me. I've already been for a short run down by the river. Good to blow away the cobwebs. You should join us sometime."

"Uh huh, maybe," grunted Robson.

That was clearly never going to happen and they both knew it. Through the haze of his hangover, Robson perked up at something Zahra had said. "Hang on a minute. *Us?* Since when do you have a running partner?"

"Never you mind that."

"Hmm, anyway do you actually have a reason for calling?"

"Right. Well PC Armstrong has the digital team working on Nikki's mobile to see if they can work their magic pulling her complete call history and retrieving those deleted texts. Should help to give us a clue as to what has been going on."

"Great, sounds promising."

"As for our next witness, Peter Winters, he's been in touch to ask if we could bring forward his interview two hours so he can still make his university football match later this morning."

Robson laughed bitterly. "Wow, some of this lot really have their priorities straight, don't they? Nikki's death is nothing more than an inconvenience."

"Tell me about it. Anyway, he can get in for seven o'clock. I can pick you up in half an hour so we have time to set everything up beforehand. Could you be ready for then?"

Robson yawned. "Sure, I can make that work. See you soon."

Thoughts of Nikki came flooding back to Robson as he edged himself towards being fully awake. A sense of melancholy overpowered his senses as he laid staring at the ceiling dejectedly. Robson inhaled deeply and let his breath out in a world-weary sigh. His chest felt tight, as though an immovable rock had been placed on top of him during the night and he was slowly being crushed.

Poor Nikki. Her poor family, he thought to himself. *They didn't deserve this.* To be presented with a little piece of hope and have it snatched away was beyond cruel. Worse than if she had simply died onstage in the beginning. At least that would have been merciful. He had thought somehow she might make it, even if the odds had been stacked against her.

So much for miracles.

Robson didn't consider himself a religious man, but when he did occasionally find his thoughts wandering to God, he couldn't help but think of him as a mean, vindictive ruler. *God is the omnipresent king and we are merely his playthings for amusement to do with what he fancies. Akin to a spiteful child stomping on ants purely because he could. Or worse, taking out a magnifying glass in the summer heat and frying them to death just to watch them squirm in torment.* Sometimes it was the only way Robson could make sense of the shit people were subjected to. A loving God wouldn't be so malicious.

With another heavy sigh, he reluctantly swung his legs over the side of the bed. His head was swimming, the bedroom littered with empty beer cans and wine bottles. What was that old adage about the rules of drinking? 'Beer before wine makes you feel fine. Wine before beer makes you feel queer.' He couldn't remember which order he had drunk them, but he certainly felt closer to queer than fine. Groaning, he reached for some paracetamol and got ready to drag himself into the shower.

In hindsight drinking last night had been a bad idea. His mind felt fuzzy and his vision was slightly unfocused. Hopefully nothing a cold shower couldn't fix. Despite the late finish and feeling utterly exhausted yesterday, he had found he couldn't escape the unnerving thoughts circling through his mind, which had made sleep impossible. In the end, he had raided his fridge for alcohol and climbed into bed to watch back-to-back episodes of some nonsensical comedy show, gradually drinking himself into numbness. He couldn't keep dwelling on the past like this, it meant every case tortured him even more than necessary.

Sitting in the interview room, Robson was irritated to discover his headache hadn't budged, despite the cold shower and four paracetamol tablets. The room felt airless and far too hot for comfort. A glowing sheen of sweat had formed on his forehead and he felt faintly nauseous.

Waltzing through the door, Zahra greeted him brightly as she plonked a steaming cup of black coffee down in front of him. "Thought you might need this."

He nodded weakly in gratitude and she gave him a knowing wink. Cheerily reeling through their schedule for the day, his partner was buzzing with energy. She was far too much of a morning person for his liking.

Stifling a yawn, Robson noted Zahra was wearing a bright green hijab today, colour coordinated to match the emerald bracelet dangling from her wrist. A new job present from her father when she had been promoted to Detective Sergeant if he recalled correctly. She had only mentioned it briefly once. Zahra was always careful not to talk about her father too much. She was thoughtful like that.

He had barely had chance to sip his coffee before the next interviewee was ushered in. Peter Winters was a sickeningly attractive young man. With his chiselled looks, fashionable dark-blonde hair and designer stubble, he wouldn't look out of place in a Hollywood movie. Robson couldn't help but feel a sudden pang of jealousy as he glimpsed his ripped six-pack visible beneath his tight t-shirt.

Robson had often been told he was ruggedly handsome in an unconventional sort of way and had never quite figured out whether that was a compliment or not. Peter, on the other hand, was the epitome of conventionally handsome. He could clearly have ladies flocking to him at the drop of a hat. Robson was starting to understand why his girlfriend, Megan, had seemed so self-conscious; it was clear she was punching way above her weight.

The blonde actor stared at Zahra's hijab, his gaze lingering suspiciously.

She narrowed her eyes. "Got a problem?"

Peter jumped, taken aback. "No, it's nothing. You just look too young to be a police officer."

"Detective Sergeant, actually," Zahra corrected tetchily.

Flashing his perfect teeth in a dazzling smile, he winked at her. "Damn, that sounds sexy."

Robson sniggered quietly. Fool be Peter if he wanted to try his luck with his partner. Good old-fashioned charm never swayed Zahra. Her gentle appearance belied a dogged resistance and he often found himself pitying the unsuspecting men who got on her wrong side.

Zahra glowered in reply. "Macduff is your main role in the play, is that correct?" she asked coolly. There was a frostiness to her voice that she reserved for people she really didn't like.

Peter nodded. "Alongside a few other characters too. Neil has us all doubling up to play multiple parts, you know that right? Part of his vision for the production; a small tight-knit cast taking on the mantle of a huge Shakespearean classic." He let out a scoffing laugh.

"You don't sound convinced?"

"Honestly, I think it was less to do with artistic

expression and more to do with saving money. Fewer actors, less pay. We did get paid a little, even though it was an amateur production."

"We've been in touch with your university theatre course leader. Pretty impressive stuff. Not only are you predicted to get a first-class degree, but we've been told that you're one of the most talented actors in your year."

Peter straightened in his chair, puffing out his chest like a peacock ruffling his feathers in pride.

Robson's throbbing head pounded as he struggled to focus on the conversation. Mercifully Zahra seemed happy to take the lead on the questioning for now. Relieved, he leaned back in his chair as small droplets of sweat started to roll down his back.

"Any idea who would have reason to kill Nikki?"

Peter looked at them triumphantly, conviction evident on his face. "I don't have a name for you, but I do have a *date* I think you'll find most interesting."

"Go on then," said Zahra, with newfound interest.

"1672."

Robson and Zahra shared an exasperated look. "Alright, we'll bite. What's so special about 1672?"

"This has happened *before*. Allegedly, in a 1672 Amsterdam production of *Macbeth* the actor playing Macbeth knowingly substituted a real dagger for the fake prop one and killed the performer portraying King Duncan live onstage in full view of the spellbound audience."

"So, what?"

"So, what if the person who did this took inspiration from history. I mean it's a perfect crime if you think about it. Who would ever see it coming?"

"I'm still struggling to see how that's at all relevant for this investigation?"

"Because it's inspiring, isn't it? Just think – it's a foolproof way of getting rid of someone and not getting caught."

"Not getting caught *yet*. And I'd be willing to bet you're the only one aware of that particular piece of historical *Macbeth* trivia. I'm not sure what that says about your innocence?"

Peter's face contorted into a scowl. "Obviously I had nothing to do with it. Why would I mention it if I was? But Nikki showed no respect for the ancient superstitions about *Macbeth*. Maybe she got what was coming to her."

* * *

Tuesday 13th March

"What did you think of yesterday's rugby match?" Jimmy asked conversationally.

Peter stared at him blankly. Jimmy knew he didn't give a shit about rugby, he couldn't even remember the difference between Rugby Union and League despite the fact Jimmy had explained it to him several times. It was typical he selfishly insisted on bringing it up anyway. He shrugged in muted reply, inviting no further comment.

At some point Violet had sidled up to the pair of them quietly. It took Peter a few minutes to notice her as she stood nervously on the fringe of their conversation, not wanting to interrupt.

"Sorry, I was just needing to…when you have chance…to take your measurements. You know, to finish your costumes. No rush though, whenever you two are ready." Violet was stuttering, stumbling over her words as she rushed to get them out. A deep flush rose to her cheeks, painting them a deep pink.

Jimmy smiled at her kindly. "Sure. You can do me now."

"Oh sure, okay. Erm, that's great!" Flustered, her face turned even redder. Dropping her bag to the floor, she fumbled around in it to retrieve her measuring tape and notepad.

Jimmy stood stock-still as Violet measured his body, recording the figures in her book. When finished she stepped back and looked at Peter expect-antly, who had a wicked glint in his eye.

"Alright darling, you can *do me* next." Laughing harshly, he gave Jimmy an over-exaggerated wink.

Jimmy rolled his eyes impatiently.

As Violet shuffled over obediently, Peter flexed his muscles for her benefit and smirked in satisfaction as he saw the colour rise again to her cheeks. Her gentle touch was light on his skin, as though she was stroking him with a feather.

"Ooh steady on love," Peter teased as she ran the tape up his inner leg. "You don't want to get me too excited. Wouldn't that be awkward?"

By the time Violet had finished, she was the colour of a ripe tomato. Grabbing her bag, she hastily thanked them both, flashed Peter a sheepish smile and scurried away.

Jimmy bristled. "There's no need to tease her."

Peter snorted a laugh. "Oh, please! The girl's pathetic. Have you heard the rumour she's still a virgin? Violet clearly likes what she sees in me. She probably loves the attention, let's face it – it's all the action she's getting."

Shaking his head silently, Jimmy led the way to join the girls at the other side of the auditorium. Nikki was huddled over her phone, giggling with Megan as they scrolled through something. Peter could overhear the tail end of their animated conversation.

"Oh my God, we totally have to get rainbow Afro wigs! That would be so frigging awesome!"

Peter sniggered, amused. "*Why* exactly are you buying rainbow Afro wigs?"

Looking up from her phone, Nikki gave him a quick half-smile. "Oh, hi Peter. We're just planning ahead for the Pride in London Festival in July. The Amnesty International Society were chatting about it today. We thought it would be fun to dress up this year. We were thinking multicoloured wigs and we could each fashion a large rainbow flag into some form of dress, or maybe a cape for the guys. What do you think?"

Peter wrinkled his nose. He couldn't think of anything worse. He hated crowds at the best of times and loathed dressing up. At the annual gay rights parade, there was far too much of both. He could do without the garish outfits, exuberant antics and overzealous displays of same-sex affection. "Nah, I think I'll give it a miss. It's not really my thing."

Disappointment fell across Megan's face and she turned away disheartened.

Next to her, Nikki regarded him coldly. "You know it wouldn't kill you to be more supportive."

"Why? I'm not gay. Neither are you in fact."

"So, what? That's not the point. It's about freedom, campaigning for equal human rights for all. Did you know being homosexual is *still* considered a crime in over 70 countries around the world?"

Next to her, Megan nodded along enthusiastically, adding, "There's a whole bunch of us going from our theatre class. Gay and straight, it's great to support each other. Besides, it will be a good laugh, a fun day out."

Peter gave a nonchalant shrug. "It's just not my idea of fun."

Nikki narrowed her eyes and shook her head. "Whatever."

"I think it sounds great. I'll definitely come along," said Jimmy, bending down to plant a light kiss on Nikki's cheek.

Peter glared at him, annoyed. Of course Jimmy would find a way to show him up. How typical.

"Thanks, my love." Nikki beamed at her boyfriend.

Smug little bitch, thought Peter. *Always taking every opportunity to flaunt their perfect relationship.* Stealing a look at Megan, Peter groaned inwardly as he saw her scowling. He was clearly going to pay for that later.

Turning to Megan, Nikki gave her a quick hug before standing to leave. "Got to go. Catch ya later."

As she strutted off, hand in hand with Jimmy, Peter slid into her vacated seat and leaned across to kiss Megan. She returned the kiss half-heartedly and Peter frowned as he pulled away. "Hey, don't be pissed just because I don't want to go to some stupid march."

Megan closed her eyes and sighed heavily. "It's not about the march Peter. It's about supporting me, actually giving a shit about the things I find important. Nikki and Jimmy get that, why can't you?"

Peter was still searching for the right words to respond when Megan grabbed her bag abruptly and said she would see him after rehearsal, before darting off without so much as a backwards glance. Peter seethed as he watched her go. Fucking Nikki always managed to have this sort of negative effect on her. Megan was intense enough as it was without having to contend with her friend who always insisted on stirring up trouble. Nikki was the sort of passionate zealot who was quick to ram her idealistic opinions down people's throats if they dared to disagree with her. Peter had clashed with her over it many times before.

Recently, Nikki had persuaded Megan to join the university Amnesty International Society with her. Not that Megan had taken much convincing, she was like a sheep trailing her shepherd when it came to Nikki. It was as though she became a different, more easily-led person around her. Since then, there had always been some random cause they were busy rallying behind. Last week, it had been campaigning in the run up to International Women's Day, before that fundraising for refugees in Britain.

Now Nikki had gone and caused an argument between them just because he had better things to do than traipse around the city draped in a ridiculous technicolour flag, brandishing some shitty sign. Peter released an aggravated sigh.

He really had to do something about that girl.

It was frustrating the hell out of Peter how mechanically Megan was delivering her lines. Despite the fact they had been rehearsing together for over an hour, she seemed incapable of getting any better. If anything, she was becoming more wooden as time went on. What's more, she was still pissed at him after their earlier argument. He would have thought that should have blown over by now. Peter had a sneaking suspicion she was harbouring the grudge purely to spite him. Or please Nikki.

Megan's moods were as changeable as experiencing all four seasons crammed into one day. The couple had experienced a number of bust-ups over the past few months of dating, normally culminating in Megan screaming at him, even throwing things at his head. But then, just when he figured he had put up with enough and was ready to break up, she would change and be all sweet and endearing again.

And holy shit, the make-up sex was worth it.

It had been a student club night at The Rocket when they had first hooked up. Peter was stood at the bar downing pints with his football team when he had spotted Megan. Dressed in a figure-hugging purple dress with a plummeting neckline that clung to her curvaceous figure, she had been dancing seductively with Nikki on the dancefloor. They had been happily gyrating to the upbeat music when the DJ abruptly changed the pace and switched the music to a slow acoustic song.

Nikki had given Megan an apologetic hug and dashed off the dancefloor to go and hunt down Jimmy. Interrupting the conversation her boyfriend had been enjoying with his rugby teammates, she had cajoled him onto the dancefloor and flung her arms lovingly around his neck. Shuffling awkwardly on each other's toes, they had giggled as they danced, somehow making it look kind of cute.

And just like that, Megan had been unceremoniously dropped, flung aside as if she was a piece of unwanted chewing gum. Dejected, she trudged over to the bar and slumped onto one of the stools. Lips puckered, a dark look crossed her face as she enviously watched the dancing couple.

Peter had made his move straight away and swooped in to buy her a drink. There was nothing more appealing to him than a desperate girl cast aside by her friends. Initially standoffish, Megan granted him a weary smile and said she wasn't in the mood for being chatted up. But she accepted the drink nonetheless. *Playing hard to get.* That was cool, he preferred a challenge anyhow. For the next hour he had been her confidante. Nodding along as she ranted and brushing a tear from her cheek when she got emotional. Together they had put the world to rights.

As he expected, Megan had loosened up after a couple of drinks. Peter was buying, after all it would be rude not to; hopefully she would be paying him back in a different way later. The silver pendant from her necklace was nestled snugly between her breasts, drawing Peter's eyes to her ample cleavage.

Megan giggled flirtatiously as he lined up a row of

shots on the bar. "I don't normally drink like this. Anyone would think you were trying to get me drunk?"

"Now, would I do a thing like that?" He gave her a wink. "Okay, let's down them together. On the count of three. Three!"

Peter grinned as they knocked back the shots. He had to admit he was impressed with Megan's stamina. The girl could hold her drink.

Yet as soon as Megan's last empty shot glass had been lowered, her sad gaze drifted back to Nikki and Jimmy. The couple were still swaying rhythmically on the dancefloor, eyes closed now and lips locked together in a deep kiss. The jealousy on Megan's face was unmistakable. Glancing over, Peter gave Jimmy a dismissive, appraising look. He was alright, but Megan could definitely do better.

Leaning over, Peter whispered softly in her ear, "Hey, do you want to get out of here?"

Megan nodded enthusiastically. "Actually yes, let's go."

Peter was as surprised as anyone that four months after that chance encounter, the pair had become a couple. A somewhat dysfunctional couple prone to heated arguments, but a couple nonetheless.

Frankly, Peter had only intended Megan to be a one-night stand. But it was also his final year at university and he couldn't be arsed with the chase every week. Recently, he had come to the stark realisation he had to actually buckle down and concentrate on his studies if he was going to achieve his lofty predicted grades. He hated to fail. But a guy still had needs. The promise of a regular shag kept him satisfied. Plus, Megan's sexual appetite was almost as insatiable as his, even if most of the time the actual sex never set either of their worlds alight. She always seemed to be holding back, like her heart wasn't completely in it. Or she was wishing he was someone else.

"Hey you, eyes up here." Megan's angry voice startled Peter out of his reminiscing and back to the present rehearsal. Wearing an irritated look, she tilted his chin up away from her breasts and onto her face.

Peter hadn't even realised he had been ogling her cleavage. He laughed dismissively. "Sorry babe. You sure know how to distract me." Stepping forward, he closed the gap between them and kissed her. Sneaking a hand up to grope her left breast, he gave it a little squeeze.

Gasping, Megan batted his hand away. "Peter! We're in public."

"So, what? You're my girlfriend. No one's watching. Don't be such a prude."

Megan frowned. "I'd better be going anyway, it's getting late. You've got a rehearsal in front of Neil next, right? Good luck."

"Break a leg, you mean."

"What?"

Peter sighed. "You shouldn't say good luck in the theatre. It's unlucky."

Megan rolled her eyes, nonplussed. "How do you know that?"

"How do you *not* know that?" admonished Peter. "Call yourself a theatre student? And we're acting in the most famously superstitious play in history."

"What do you mean?"

"Are you for real? Legend has it the play is cursed, so speaking the name *Macbeth* during a performance will cause unmitigated disaster."

His girlfriend looked doubtful.

"There's been so many examples of tragedies in *Macbeth* productions, the curse just has to be true. Serious injuries from falling props, theatres burning down, suicides. One actor playing King Duncan was even killed onstage when his co-star swapped a fake prop dagger with a real blade before their fight scene. Can you imagine doing something so evil?"

Megan merely shrugged.

*   *   *

"That's it?" Zahra sounded distinctly unimpressed.

Peter flashed her a casual smile. "That's it. There's nothing more to say. We came. We read our lines. We went. That's pretty much the extent of it."

As Robson subtly wiped the beads of sweat from his forehead, he was surprised to notice Peter's jagged fingernails were bitten right down to the nail bed. For someone so obviously obsessed with their appearance, it seemed out of place.

Clearly a habit, he thought. *So, what is Peter worrying about so much it's causing him to gnaw his fingernails down to a stump?*

As soon as Peter had left the room, Zahra launched into a vicious tirade. "Who does he think he is? Does he honestly think just because I'm a woman I'm going to be so dazzled by his looks I'd actually let him off?"

"You just don't like pretty boys. You think they can get away with anything."

Zahra shot him a scathing look. "That's because they usually can."

Nodding distractedly, Robson closed his eyes and sank his throbbing head into his hands. He was struggling to hear over the pounding of blood in his ears. It was impossible to concentrate and, far from being refreshing, sipping his strong coffee had made him feel increasingly queasy.

When he opened his eyes, Zahra produced two paracetamol tablets from somewhere and pushed them across the table.

The woman was an actual angel. What would he do without her?

Robson gave her a weak, grateful smile and reached for the tablets.

"It's a tough case," Zahra said, as if that explained everything.

Pushing his chair back, Robson rose unsteadily. "I'm going for a smoke, I need some fresh air."

Zahra nodded as she watched him go and said nothing to point out the irony in that statement.

The stormy weather from yesterday had not abated, but thankfully the rain was holding off for now. Robson shivered violently from the bitter wind whipping around him, but at least it was helping to quell his nausea. He was starting to perk up a bit.

Taking a welcome drag of his cigarette, he pondered about how things had to change. There was only so long he could continue down this road without consequences. He knew he was continually risking putting Zahra in a compromising position too. She was a stickler for the rules in everything, except when it came to him. Then, she was seemingly happy to turn a blind eye but he knew even she would be at her limit if his drinking started to negatively affect his work. Interviews he could just about handle, but anything more strenuous or gruesome would have pushed him over the edge this morning.

Perhaps the time had come to pack the job in after all. He had been on a downward spiral for a while. This coming April would mark fifteen years since that fateful day. Zahra knew he didn't deal well with anniversaries.

Closing his eyes, Robson inhaled deeply on his cigarette.

One inch.

That's all it had come down to in the end.

One inch.

The doctors had said it plainly, matter of fact. As if it offered some semblance of comfort. But that useless nugget of information was no comfort at all. If anything, it was a torment, a cruel jibe that made him live in a land of 'what ifs.'

One inch to the right and the bullet wouldn't have torn through the coronary artery causing massive haemorrhaging. One inch and the right ventricle wouldn't have been shredded, leaving irreparable damage. One inch and the heart wouldn't have failed.

One bloody inch.

That's all it would have taken to make all the difference.

One bloody inch and his father would still be alive.

Try as he might, recently Robson couldn't shake the image of his father from his mind. His face pervaded all his thoughts as though he was scrutinising his son's every move. Almost fifteen years ago he had been shot dead on the streets of London, a random victim caught in the crosshairs of a gang gunfight. It had been April, the year after Robson had graduated from university, back when he had been chasing hopeful dreams of becoming a famous playwright. In many ways, Robson felt like his whole life came to a grinding halt on that fateful day. He could still remember the awful phone call from his mother, hearing her break down hysterically as she told him the news. In that split second, his whole future had been dashed. He had lost not only his father, but his confidante, his advisor, his snooker partner and his best friend.

Robson had been hooked on the resulting investigation for weeks, following the police's every move. Much to his dismay, they never had caught the shooter. Just like that, his father's name had been consigned to history. He had become a statistic, another unfortunate victim of gang violence. *Where was the justice in that?*

For a few years, Robson had drifted around, not knowing what to do other than drink himself slowly into oblivion. His passion for writing was snubbed out, it didn't feel important anymore. Finally, at his mother's insistence, he had straightened himself out – well enough that he could function at least.

Then he bit the bullet, so to speak, and signed up to

start police training. Pursuing justice had finally given him the sense of purpose he so desperately sought and, as his mother continually assured him, at least he knew it would have made his father proud.

Recently though, he had started to have his doubts.

Sighing heavily, Robson stubbed out his cigarette. Fishing around in his pocket, he extracted a battered pack of mints and popped one in his mouth as he headed back inside. With the fresh hit of nicotine still circulating in his bloodstream, he felt marginally more relaxed.

That feeling proved to be short-lived. As he passed a colleague's desk, Robson happened to glance down and spot something. Hands tightening into fists, rage built up inside of him. He felt like a ticking bomb that was about to explode.

How dare they?

Chapter Thirteen

Only Vaulting Ambition

Outraged, Robson barged into the interview room. "Have you seen this trash?" he demanded, slamming the offending tabloid down onto the table.

Startled, Zahra looked up over the rim of her mug of milky coffee and studied the newspaper for a long moment. Immediately, she clocked the sensationalist headline emblazoned across the front page. *Tragic onstage death at cursed Macbeth.* She gave a resigned shrug. "We knew this was coming. The press was always going to have a field day with this case."

Still bristling with barely contained fury, Robson shook his head violently. "But have you seen how they've had the nerve to write it? It's so damn insensitive." Picking up the paper, he scathingly read the opening paragraph aloud, "Life's but a walking shadow, the innocent Miss Nikki Gowon was the poor player, strutting and fretting her final hour upon the stage, and then tragically she was heard no more."

Zahra smiled wryly. "Actually, sounds quite high-brow for that paper. I'm surprised they know enough Shakespeare to bastardise."

Reluctantly, Robson tore his eyes away from the morose headline. Scrunching up the newspaper, he dumped it into the rubbish bin with grim satisfaction. He'd forgotten how much he hated working on high-profile cases. Solving a murder was tough enough without the press getting hold of the story and tearing apart every detail like a pack of rabid dogs. The article had gone into full blown martyr mode: '*In death, the young actress has finally achieved the fame she so desperately craved.*' It was beyond callous, he felt outraged on Nikki's behalf.

It took Robson a while to realise Zahra was staring at him, concerned. When she spoke, it was with a soft, placating tone. "Well, let's crack on and work out who the murderer is. Give them something real to write about."

Neil Hillton practically bounded into the interview room. Bright-eyed and smiling broadly, he was full of energy and seemed a world away from the weary, pale-faced director they had met at the theatre.

Flinging himself into his chair, Neil leaned across the table and spoke enthusiastically. "Have you seen the papers? Have you heard what they're saying? Wow, it's so amazing. Better than I could have ever hoped for."

Robson frowned. "I think you'll have to enlighten us."

"The reviews! They're incredible. The critics are

universal in calling the show groundbreaking, one of a kind. One reviewer even said it could redefine a generation in how Shakespeare is adapted for modern audiences. They're calling me a creative master-mind!"

Underneath the table, Robson balled his hands into fists. "Too bad about the untimely death of your lead actress."

Neil's smile faltered. "Well, yes of course, that is most unfortunate. Tragic what happened. I didn't mean to sound heartless, I'm just excited. The show got coverage not only nationally but also in the intern-ational press. That's a big deal."

"In that case, congratulations."

Without registering Robson's sarcasm, Neil laughed joyfully. "Thanks! You know I got a call from the National Theatre this morning. They're interested in me directing their next production. That's a huge opportunity for me. I can't believe it! It's not how I thought this was going to pan out."

"I imagine Nikki had different plans too," Robson said coldly.

Those words finally extinguished Neil's enthu-siasm. "Yes, yes, I know. Terrible news."

Robson noted there was no longer any sign of the feverish anxiety Neil had been displaying when they first met him at the theatre. Now, he couldn't help but wonder if the director's fear had been more inwardly focused and his true concern had been the impact Nikki's stabbing could have on his own career.

"Directing amateur theatre shows is your full-time job, is that correct?"

Noticeably bristling, Neil quickly corrected him. "I prefer the term *semi-professional.* It better reflects the high calibre of the productions I put on. Plus, they may not be full-time professionals, but I select the very best actors available. Believe me they are better than most *amateurs* you'd normally come across. Plus, I can afford to pay them a nominal fee. Nothing huge, but it helps inspire loyalty and commitment. I have a dedicated group of returning actors who have performed in multiple productions."

"Had you worked with anyone from the *Macbeth* cast before?"

"Only one on this occasion – Ben Grahame. He was in my *Romeo and Juliet* show at the end of last year – fantastic actor, very believable. I invited him back to audition for *Macbeth* and he ended up graduating to the lead role."

"How did you find the rest of the actors?"

"Open auditions. This time of the year is always tricky for a lot of my regulars, so it was a good opportunity to get some fresh blood. It worked well hiring the theatre students – Nikki and her friends. They're used to the quick turnaround time for developing a new play." Neil puffed his chest out a little as though he was rather pleased with himself.

"How long do you work on each show?"

"We rehearse for six weeks and then have a fortnight run of shows every evening with a matinee on Saturday. I'm developing a great reputation for producing exceptional shows given the short timescale, even if I do say so myself."

"You do six plays in a year, one every two months?"

"That's right." The director gave a satisfied nod.

"Sounds intense."

"No rest for the wicked. Besides, the mortgage payments on the theatre are ridiculous. I need four sell-out shows a year just to break even, before taking into account running costs, building repairs and paying myself a salary."

"There can't be much opportunity for any time off?"

"Eight weeks in total for each production. So, I end up with four weeks off a year between shows which I tend to use for any essential maintenance works, things like that."

"You must really love it."

Neil beamed. "Oh, I do. It's a way of life for me, my greatest passion. I don't do it for the money."

Yet, thought Robson sceptically. *You don't do it for the money yet. But you do seem rather taken with the possibility of moving onto bigger and better things.*

"Yesterday was your opening night of *Macbeth*?"

"That's right, the first performance of what was meant to be a fortnight run." The smile fell from Neil's face. "I guess the remaining shows have been jeopardised now."

"Probably. So, would you say there had been any drama between the actors offstage?"

"I suppose a little. But no more than usual. After all the great William Shakespeare himself once said, 'All the world's a stage, and all the men and women merely players.' Although I imagine a detective wouldn't know what on earth I'm talking about."

"'They have their exits and their entrances, and one

man in his time plays many parts.' That's the full quote, is it not? From *As You Like It*."

"Bloody hell. Bravo Inspector, I take it back."

*   *   *

Wednesday 14th March

"It's a difficult scene filled with undercurrents of emotion. Ambition. Betrayal. Loyalty. Remember at this point Macbeth is insistent about asserting his power over his fellow men." Stood centre stage Neil was enthusiastically talking through the scene they were about to rehearse. Surrounded by his young cast of budding actors, he felt his heart swell with pride. He felt every bit as important as a king himself.

God, he loved his job. They were hanging onto his every word, patiently waiting to hear his expert guidance. "The corrupting power of ambition is a key theme here. Remember ultimately that is Macbeth's biggest weakness, his fatal flaw. When Macbeth says 'only vaulting ambition, which o'erleaps itself, and falls,' it foreshadows his own tragic downfall. Even honourable men can be corrupted by ambition. In this case it's what caused the Scottish king to act against his better judgement and aim too high, so he fails and loses everything."

Later, Neil could have sworn Nikki caught his eye at that precise moment and winked.

"Right, okay gang, let's take it from the top."

The cast obediently assumed their positions. Not for the first time, Neil wondered if he would ever fully get the appreciation he deserved for his genius. He was confident there was no other contemporary director in his generation who could present the works of Shakespeare as creatively as he could.

No sooner had the cast begun to get into their stride than a shrill ringtone sliced through the tense atmosphere.

Groaning in exasperation, Neil shook his head in despair. "How many times do I have to tell you people? Turn *off* your phones during rehearsals. This is serious stuff we're trying to achieve here."

Ignoring his passionate plea, Nikki fished out her phone from her back pocket and stared at the screen with a look of dread on her face.

"The rules apply to you too Nikki."

"What? Oh, sorry, I need to take this." With an apologetic shrug and offering no further explanation, she darted offstage to answer the phone call in the privacy of the corridor.

Toying with the idea of continuing the scene in her absence versus granting everyone a five-minute breather to wait for her return, Neil opted for the latter. Everyone really needed to be present to nail this scene. Relieved to receive a brief reprieve, the other cast members milled around chatting among themselves.

Across the stage, Neil fleetingly locked eyes with Emma and gave her a sheepish smile. She bit her lip and averted her eyes in response. Neil grimaced darkly. He had to find some better way of making sure she listened to reason. He dreaded to think of the damage she could cause if she decided to talk. The secrets she could reveal would ruin him.

Neil was ripped from that disturbing thought when a weeping Nikki ran back into the auditorium. Sobbing hysterically, she clambered up the steps and threw herself into Jimmy's arms. Stroking her head tenderly he wrapped her close as she clung to him. Unlike everyone else's stunned expressions, Jimmy looked concerned yet resigned, as though he had known this would happen.

Brushing the tears from her face, Nikki snivelled, "Sorry, I need to go." She said it more to the floor than anyone in particular. Wasting no time at all, she spun around and bolted out of the door.

Jimmy threw Neil an apologetic look. "Sorry, I should go too. We can catch up with things tomorrow."

Before he could even form a sentence to protest, Jimmy had disappeared as well.

Neil felt the heat of frustration burning up inside of him. The sense of control and power he had been so delighted about just minutes earlier was already slipping away. He was the director for God's sake, that should command at least a modicum of respect.

The remaining actors stole nervous looks at each other, clearly trying to suss out what had happened. A frowning Megan squinted quizzically at Ben who shrugged cluelessly. A bored looking Peter tapped his foot impatiently while mouthing something to Violet. Emma had lost all interest whatsoever and was scrolling through Facebook on her phone. And to think Neil had been stupid enough to pay this lot for their time.

"Anyone else have somewhere they would rather

be?" challenged Neil coldly, desperately grappling to reclaim the authority that alluded him. "I'd hate to keep you all here against your will." He took a shaky breath. "I mean it. It's not like we're only one week away from our opening night. We've only got a flipping Shakespeare play to put on! What do I have to do to get you all to start taking this seriously?"

Neil forced himself to take another trembling breath. A cold sweat had formed on his brow and he could feel his stomach starting to churn. He was teetering precariously on the edge of a panic attack. *Slow, deep breaths,* he reminded himself as his heart pounded. Struggling to retain his composure, he fought down an overwhelming sense of anxiety. He couldn't afford to break down and lose the last semblance of respect he had.

Bloody Nikki. How dare she have the audacity to walk out of rehearsal now of all times? After everything he had gone through to get her the leading role, the very least she could do would be to show commitment. Neil had assumed, wrongly as it turned out, that hiring four theatre students would be a sure-fire way of bolstering up the professionalism of the show. He thought they would be driven and ambitious, wanting to elevate the performance to a new level.

Neil supposed he had only been half wrong. While the student foursome were undeniably talented and driven, any sense of teamwork or comradery was woefully lacking. Instead, they all seemed intent on demanding that the spotlight shone brightest on themselves. He should have known they would be more trouble than they were worth.

"How about we start from the top regardless," Ben suggested helpfully. "The main interactions are between myself and Peter anyway. Let's practise rehearsing that. And perhaps Emma could read the part of Lady Macbeth so we can work out the best staging for everyone?"

Looking up from her phone, Emma gave a derisive snort of laughter. "Oh, so *now* you want me as Lady Macbeth?" She seemed set to continue arguing but then she caught Neil's eye and something in his desperate expression made her relent. Sighing, she reluctantly agreed. "Fine, whatever."

"Great, that's brill," said Ben. "So, if you could come over here, stand beside me at the banquet table. Peter let's go back to your line. I'm sure Neil could read Jimmy's part."

Ben was in his element directing his fellow actors. Neil had never seen this self-assured, slightly bossy side of him before. He knew Ben was just trying to help but there was only room for one director on this show.

Don't lose their respect, Neil repeated over and over in his mind. Never before had he had such little faith in a cast. Plastering an enthusiastic smile on his face, Neil stepped forward to claim back the job that was rightfully his. "Okay, that's great. Thanks for your input there, Ben. I'll take it from here."

*   *   *

The director's expression grew solemn. "I take what I do very seriously. This isn't just a job for me, it's a way of life. Creating my shows is my greatest passion. I must admit, I was frustrated at Nikki's lack of commitment, especially after she was recast as Lady Macbeth."

Robson leaned forward curiously. "Coincidentally, why did Nikki end up getting swapped into the lead role? Strange you didn't mention that when we first spoke to you at the theatre?"

"Oh…" Neil faltered, his resolve lost. "Did I not tell you that? It must have slipped my mind."

"Do you think professional rivalry had anything to do with Nikki's death?"

The director choked a half-laugh. "No! Absolutely not. If you're implying that Emma Thorpe is somehow involved, then you're mistaken. That woman's a gentle soul, there's no way she would be capable of such a monstrous act."

"You seem pretty certain about that?"

Neil paled. "Just trust me on this. You're looking for someone else."

"So, have you got anything else to share about your leading lady?" enquired Zahra.

Neil studied her for a long time before speaking. "No. I'm sorry I can't be of more help."

"Well, don't hesitate to get in touch should you remember anything else," said Robson. "And good luck with the National Theatre job. At least that's one good thing to come out of this tragedy."

"Why thanks!" Failing again to register the sarcasm, Neil nodded enthusiastically as a proud smile spread across his face.

After the director left, Zahra laughed humourlessly. "There we have the epitome of a master manipulator."

Robson eyed her with interest. "I agree, but what's your point."

"It's all awfully convenient, isn't it? Neil Hillton is a man far too excited about becoming an overnight sensation. All the sudden press coverage, new directing opportunities. The elevation of Neil's status is far beyond what you'd expect from your average amateur, sorry *semi-professional*, director."

Robson stared at her in disbelief. "You're not seriously suggesting he set the whole thing up for his own personal gain, are you?"

Zahra shrugged. "It was just a thought. I mean Neil is clearly an egotistical publicity whore. What better way of securing the press's attention than if your lead actress dramatically stabs herself live onstage?"

"Wouldn't the death of your main star on opening night be somewhat inconvenient?"

"Perhaps it was only intended to be a flesh wound? The potential for severe harm was a mistake he overlooked? The show must go on. After all he did have another trained Lady Macbeth waiting in the wings. And you can't deny he had more opportunity than most to swap the knives around. He was the one who did the final prop check and his fingerprints are all over the murder weapon."

Robson stared at his partner like she had gone slightly mad. Perhaps she had. Maybe it was the sleep deprivation talking. But still, they had encountered people who had been murdered for much less.

Shaking his head slowly, Robson countered, "But Neil seemed genuinely distraught when we first met him at the theatre? He was devastated by what had happened."

Zahra nodded thoughtfully. "True. But perhaps that was regret about Nikki getting more hurt than he had originally intended. She was never meant to actually die? Or maybe it was all just an act. I guess you don't spend years directing theatre performers without learning a few acting tricks of your own."

Robson raised an eyebrow incredulously. "Well, it's an interesting theory. But what we really need in this case is some hard evidence. We're never going to get anyone to crack and tell us the truth without giving them a compelling reason to do so. Have we heard back about Nikki's phone history yet?"

Zahra consulted her phone. "No, not yet. Should be soon though, give it a few hours. And in the meantime, we've been given the go-ahead from Nikki's parents that we can go and conduct a search of her bedroom."

Allowing himself a grim smile, Robson said, "Well, there's no time like the present. Let's get that done next and hope it sheds some light on what happened to our victim. Even with the first round of interviews done, we're no closer to learning who murdered Nikki Gowon. All we do know is that some, if not all, of the people we've spoken to aren't exactly telling us the whole truth."

Nikki Gowon's bedroom looked like a typical student sanctuary. Scattered books were strewn across her flowery bedspread and an assortment of clothes littered the floor. Piles of paper covered her messy desk, on top of which a purple laptop was perched precariously. A single teddy bear poked out of her bookcase – a memory of childhood Nikki clearly couldn't bring herself to part with yet.

And then there were the photographs. Every inch of available wall space had been plastered with pictures. Her boyfriend, Jimmy, featured a lot, as did Megan, and her family. Scanning the prints, Robson was struck by how similar Nikki looked to her younger sister Aisha.

The two sisters beamed down at him. Canoeing, ice-skating, cycling, hiking, paddleboarding. All of their adventures catalogued and preserved in time on Nikki's bedroom wall.

Clearly the pair have a lot of fun together, thought Robson silently, before mentally correcting himself. *Had fun. Past tense.*

A cough emanating from across the bedroom caught his attention and he spun around to see Zahra looking at him quizzically.

With a perplexed expression on her face, she muttered, "I thought Jimmy said Nikki was his girlfriend?"

Frowning, Robson strode over to her. "He did, why?"

Gesturing to the open bedside drawer, Zahra shook her head. "Nikki didn't seem to think so."

Robson let out a long whistle. "Guess we just figured out who's the first person we need to set up a follow-up interview with."

Nodding in agreement, Zahra meticulously started cataloguing the drawer contents.

Thinking out loud in a halting, considered fashion, Robson recounted what they knew so far. "So, regarding suspects, we've got the victim's boyfriend, Jimmy Walker, who was suspicious enough about Nikki's faithfulness to go snooping through her text messages, only to find out she had deleted all of her phone history."

"And he's nursing an injured hand he refuses to explain," added Zahra.

"Then there's Nikki's best friend, Megan Newbold, who was rather overzealous in providing us with different leads, and her boyfriend, Peter Winters, who was obsessed with that historic production of *Macbeth.*"

Zahra nodded and took over the recount, "Next, there's Ben Grahame, our victim's onstage lover who was besotted with Nikki and may or may not have been texting her behind her boyfriend's back. Not to mention, it was his jacket we found the prop knife wrapped up in."

Rubbing his forehead thoughtfully, Robson continued, "Plus, there's Violet Underwood, who seems like she couldn't hurt a fly, but is very obviously afraid and hiding something from us. And let's not forget Emma Thorpe, Nikki's onstage rival, who was humiliated by losing out on her leading role. Then finally there's the show director, Neil Hillton, who seems to be benefiting greatly from the whole debacle and was quick to explain why his fingerprints were all over the murder weapon."

Letting out a long breath, Zahra groaned. "If there's one thing I've learnt over the years, it's how difficult it can be to understand a person's motive. With this lot, it's like chasing a shadow. Just as we get close at honing in on someone, something else crops up and leads us in another direction."

Scratching at his stubble, Robson sighed in irritation. "And we still don't know the full story of what's been going on behind the scenes at that theatre. Or why Nikki doesn't have any presence on social media prior to starting university or why she felt suicidal during high school."

For a few tense seconds, the detectives stood in stony silence. The investigation wasn't going as planned and neither of them were used to failing.

Eventually, they turned back to searching the bedroom. Beyond the intriguing discovery in the bedside drawer and Nikki's laptop that would be sent to the digital team to explore, they found nothing else of note.

Robson was on the verge of giving up when he spotted something metallic glinting in the light in Nikki's bin. Rooting through the top layers of rubbish, he dug his hand in to pull out a silver heart necklace buried at the bottom.

"Lovers' tiff?" suggested Zahra.

"Maybe," agreed Robson, studying the necklace closely. He was no expert in jewellery, but he thought it looked expensive. The silver heart pendant was adorned with several sparkling diamonds. "Why does this look familiar? I could swear I've seen it before."

Zahra laughed. "You have!" She motioned to the photo montage on the wall. "Nikki wore that necklace all the time. It's in practically every picture."

Robson nodded slowly. "That must be it." But still he couldn't quash the niggling thought at the back of his mind that the explanation wasn't that at all. "Anyhow, if she loved it so much, why did she end up throwing it away?"

CHAPTER FOURTEEN

Life's but a Walking Shadow

Jimmy Walker looked like a man who had lost all hope and Robson didn't blame him. He sat opposite the detectives with his shoulders slumped, a blank expression on his face as if racked by a deep sense of guilt. He was like an ice sculpture that had been gradually chipped away until there was nothing left. Clearly the news of Nikki's death had hit him hard.

Robson gave him a small nod of respect. "I'm sorry for your loss." He said the condolence mechanically, the words sounding hollow. *Your loss. What a stupid expression. Like you had carelessly misplaced your keys. Lost. As though you stood a chance of finding it again.*

An ashen-faced Jimmy shrugged glumly. "I wasn't even there," he said in a quiet voice. "By the time I got to the hospital it was too late, she was already dead." Biting back tears, he hung his head, wretched.

Robson felt a stab of sympathy for the young man, he knew that grief only too well. When his own father had died it felt as though something had been physically ripped out of him, leaving a gaping hole in its wake. Pushing such personal thoughts aside, he forced himself to stay focused on the task at hand.

Feigning a weak smile, Jimmy raised his head. "So, how many times do I have to talk to you guys?"

"Well, that depends. When are you going to start telling us everything?

Jimmy opened his mouth to say something, then seemed to think better of it and closed it again. He lowered his gaze to the table. "What do you know?" he asked cagily, testing the waters.

Robson laughed. "Why, what a tactful question. Let's start with your relationship with Nikki Gowon. She was your girlfriend?"

"Yes, that's right."

"Not your fiancée?" Robson could have sworn he saw Jimmy's shoulders drop slightly in relief.

The actor hesitated for a few minutes before clearing his throat nervously. "Not technically. We had talked about getting engaged but I hadn't actually proposed yet."

Zahra eyed him suspiciously as she opened up an envelope and tipped it up, scattering an assortment of wedding brochures onto the table. "We found these in Nikki's bedside drawer. Seems she was a little further down the route of wedding planning than you think."

Jimmy let out a weary sigh. "Well, she did tend to get ahead of herself, but I suppose in this case she had a good reason."

Robson frowned in confusion. "Why don't you explain?"

*   *   *

Thursday 15th March

"Megan wasn't so thrilled about the prospect of us getting married the last time I brought it up."

Jimmy glanced across at Nikki from the driver's seat. "She's your best friend. I'm sure you'll be able to talk her round to it."

"Perhaps." She didn't sound convinced.

Jimmy's brow knitted together in concern. "You're not getting cold feet on me, are you?"

Nikki shook her head slightly. "No, it's not that…"

"Look, speak to Meg after rehearsal tonight like we agreed. Give her the full story this time, not just the headline. I'm sure she'll understand."

"I guess so."

"Put it this way – if you do still want to get hitched this summer after graduation, then we better get on it with wedding planning. It's only three months away."

"And even then, it might be too late," said Nikki quietly.

"Well, we're going to have to hope that it's not." In a vain attempt to lighten the mood, Jimmy joked, "You'll have to remember to act surprised when I do finally get around to proposing!"

Nikki smiled weakly. "I will, I promise. Just don't ask me in front of loads of people though, I'd hate that."

"Yes, I know. Come on, give me some credit."

An awkward silence descended upon them.

Finally, Nikki hesitantly asked, "So, speaking of

weddings, have you thought about how to broach the subject with your parents?"

Jimmy shuddered involuntarily at the probing question. "Not yet. I'm sure my mum will be cool with it though."

"And your dad? I take it you'll be inviting them both?"

He bristled in agitation. "I wish I didn't have to, but I can't not really. Be prepared for my dad to make a scene though. All that free booze? He'll be in his element."

"I'm sure he'll be fine."

Jimmy laughed scornfully. "It's glaringly obvious you don't know him very well."

Nikki fell silent again. Eventually she cautiously asked, "Is it still the same?"

Jimmy grimaced. "You mean is he still an abusive alcoholic who hits my mum whenever I'm not at home? Yep, same as always."

Nikki flinched at his harsh tone and turned away. "I don't understand why your mum doesn't leave him. Just walk away and be done with it."

"It's a little more complicated than that."

"It doesn't need to be complicated."

Jimmy gritted his teeth and gripped the steering wheel tighter. "You think I haven't tried to convince her to leave? It's like Groundhog Day having the same argument over and over. Why do you think I'm still driving this piece of shit? I keep waiting for the day she finally listens to me so I can drive over, pick her up and we can both escape forever."

Shifting uncomfortably in the passenger seat, Nikki

looked across at him. "Is he the reason you don't like drinking much?"

Jimmy took a deep breath, exhaling slowly. "I suppose I'm scared of what it might do to me. You know my dad's not a bad person when he's sober; he's actually a decent bloke. I guess I've always been worried about losing control if I got hammered and having a temper as bad as his."

Nikki nodded in agreement. "Makes sense."

Jimmy glanced over at his girlfriend thoughtfully. "Why don't *you* like drinking?" He had never thought about it before, but he couldn't remember ever seeing her drink more than one glass.

She shrugged, nonchalant. "I just don't enjoy it. I hate having a hangover, so I only ever have one drink." There was something in her voice that made it sound like she was lying.

A lovely, peaceful quiet had descended upon the auditorium now it was free from the bustle of the earlier rehearsal. As much as it pained him to admit it, Jimmy could understand why Nikki and Ben preferred to rehearse in the private storeroom backstage.

Just one hour ago the auditorium had been a hive of activity – from the cast rehearsing their lines and the lighting and sound technical teams practising their cues, to their obnoxious director barking commands. Now, the former warehouse was eerily silent, with the hushed conversation between Nikki and Megan providing the only sound.

"'Nothing in his life became him like the leaving it'." Megan threw her script on the floor in frustration.

"I'm so utterly lost, what does that even mean?"

Patiently, Nikki bent to pick up the discarded script. "So, this is Malcolm talking about the traitorous Thane of Cawdor who is being executed for campaigning against King Duncan. Basically, he repented at the gallows, which means he died with more dignity than he lived with because he confessed bravely." At Megan's blank expression, she continued to explain, "I guess I'd like to think what Shakespeare is saying here is everyone is capable of change. Just because someone has done bad things in the past doesn't necessarily mean they will always be a bad person. They have the opportunity to repent." Nikki said the words with such fervour it was as if she needed them to be true.

Megan smiled comprehendingly. "Okay thanks, I think I get it. But I guess you didn't stay behind late to tutor me in understanding *Macbeth* dialogue. What is it you wanted to talk about?"

Nikki flashed a nervous glance in Jimmy's direction, as if seeking his approval. He gave a small, gentle nod.

She took a deep breath. "Remember last Friday, the conversation we had in your bedroom when I mentioned we planned to get married soon?"

Megan shot a cold look at Jimmy. "Of course, how could I forget?"

"Well, we've decided to bring forward our wedding plans. Now, we're thinking of getting married this summer after graduation." Megan opened her mouth to speak but Nikki held up a hand to silence her. "Meg, I need to have my little sister as a bridesmaid at my own wedding."

For a moment Megan looked confused, then her jaw dropped in realisation. Her expression softened as the truth dawned on her. "Oh my God, Aisha. What's the latest prognosis? Do you know how long 'she's got?"

Nikki swallowed. "It's hard to say exactly but the doctors reckon its months rather than years."

Silently, Megan wrapped an arm around her friend and pulled her close into a comforting embrace.

Jimmy closed his eyes. The diagnosis had been made last summer – *malignant Grade Four Glioblastoma.* More commonly known as an inoperable, cancerous brain tumour.

The pain resulting from that diagnosis had ricocheted through Nikki's family like a bullet, slowly tearing them apart. Jimmy had found the impending grief of losing Aisha unbearable and she wasn't even his biological sister. Initially hopeful, the doctors had grown grimmer at each hospital visit as countless tests finally confirmed the aggressive tumour had grown back after an initial surgery and the cancer had spread to her spinal cord. The fast-growing tumour appeared to be resistant to treatment and no amount of radiotherapy and chemotherapy would make any difference. The prognosis was terminal. Ferociously private about the situation, Nikki had only ever confided in Jimmy and Megan, and he alone knew about the latest developments.

Fighting back a sob, Nikki said, "Remember that phone call I got yesterday at rehearsal? That was my mum. They had just got back from another hospital appointment. The test results came back conclusive, there's definitely nothing more they can do for her. The consultant also thought the end will come much sooner than they initially predicted. Aisha's expected to deteriorate pretty rapidly over the next few months and is unlikely to make it past Christmas." Nikki's voice caught with emotion and she hung her head in despair.

Megan was silent. Jimmy winced at the pain and betrayal on her face.

"You should have told me sooner."

Tears flowing freely, Nikki bit down on her lip. "I don't like saying it out loud. Somehow it makes it feel more real. It was hard enough telling Jimmy once."

Megan turned her head briefly to throw him a cursory glance, an unreadable expression on her face.

Nikki cast her eyes downward to the floor. "None of this is fair, you know. Aisha's never done anything wrong. If anything, it should be me who has cancer. I would actually deserve it."

Jimmy stared at her in disbelief. "What on earth are you talking about? Of course you don't deserve to die. Why would you say that?"

"You don't know everything about me Jimmy."

Megan failed to suppress a knowing smirk as she grabbed her friend's hand. "You have to stop blaming yourself. It's not your fault."

Jimmy looked between the two girls in confusion. "Blaming yourself for what? You're not a bad person Nikki. There's nothing you could have done that would be as drastic as what you're implying."

Nikki smiled sadly. "Maybe you just don't know me as well as you think."

*   *   *

"Did you ever find out what Nikki was referring to?"

Jimmy slowly shook his head. "No, I guess that secret died with her." Only Robson caught the nuance of hesitation in his reply.

"So, her younger sister, Aisha, was diagnosed with terminal cancer last summer. I take it that's why Nikki moved back in with her parents for her final year?"

"Yeah, she wanted to spend more time with her family. She did consider packing in her university course all together. Nobody would have blamed her. But in a roundabout way, it was Aisha who convinced her to finish her degree. Nikki had always been her role model, she adored seeing her big sister onstage. Their parents figured some normality would be good for Aisha. Besides, I think Nikki found acting a welcome distraction most of the time. A bit of light relief from all the drama going on at home."

Robson scrutinised him for a long moment before asking, "Speaking of which, do you care to elaborate on your own home life?"

Expression darkening, Jimmy gripped the table so tightly his knuckles whitened. "There's nothing more to say. My dad's always been an abusive drunk."

"You know your mum could report him for domestic abuse if things get really bad?"

Jimmy stiffened. "Do you think I've not suggested that? Mum's loyal to a fault, says that would be betraying her own husband." His lip curled in anger, hands balled into tight fists. For the first time, the curly haired actor showed signs of losing his temper. "How is that relevant to Nikki's murder investigation anyway?"

Robson paused. "Well, from our experience the cycle of abuse has an unfortunate habit of repeating itself through generations. It would be prudent to ask—"

He was interrupted by a loud thud as Jimmy slammed his fist against the table.

"I *never* hit my girlfriend."

"I didn't say that you did."

"But that's what you were implying, isn't it? That the apple didn't fall far from the tree? Believe me I'm nothing like my father. I never laid a hand on Nikki and I sure as hell didn't kill her."

Robson held up his hands in surrender and Zahra cast him a reproachful glance. The actor settled back into his chair, squeezing his eyes shut.

After a few tense minutes, Zahra asked their final question, keeping her tone purposefully mild. "Oh, Jimmy, we've been meaning to ask, do you recognise this necklace?" She held the jewellery up casually, as if it was no big deal.

Opening his eyes, Jimmy squinted at it for a moment, then nodded. "Yeah, it's Nikki's. She loved that necklace. She wore it all the time."

"A gift from you?"

"Nah, it's not from me. I think it was a twenty-first birthday present, she's only been wearing it for the last few months."

Zahra frowned. "Any idea who bought her it?"

Jimmy's face sagged in defeat. "Sorry, I've got no idea. I'm not very observant when it comes to jewellery, I never thought to ask."

After Jimmy had left, Zahra leaned back in her chair, tapping her foot against the table leg. "Plays the part of the grieving boyfriend well, doesn't he?" she said, a note of disdain creeping into her voice.

Robson looked quizzically at his partner. "You're not convinced?"

Shaking her head, Zahra took a sip of coffee. "I think Mr Walker is keen to present himself in a certain way and let's not forget this lot know better than most how to play a part convincingly."

"I guess you're right. I do get the impression nearly everyone is holding something back and not telling us the whole truth."

Slamming her empty mug down on the table, Zahra groaned in frustration. "Our job would be so much easier if only people would stop lying to protect themselves."

Robson's eyebrows rose. Normally calm and collected, it still shocked him to see Zahra so irritated. Only one previous case had ever caused her to get this riled. That had been one of the earliest cases they had worked on together, in which a man was convicted of sexually abusing his fourteen-year-old niece. Zahra had been incredible with the young victim, demonstrating an extraordinary gentleness he hadn't seen before. It had been purely down to her interviewing skills that they had managed to elicit a witness statement, securing a conviction that gave the victim's uncle a one-way ticket to jail.

At the time, Zahra had told Robson she couldn't stand predatory men who preyed on vulnerable young women. He got the distinct impression there was a whole lot more to that story, but that was all she had ever been willing to share on the subject.

CHAPTER FIFTEEN

My Dearest Partner of Greatness

Emma Thorpe sat with her arms folded, silently scrutinising Robson as he fired up Nikki's laptop that had been provided by the digital team. There was a hint of a smirk on her lips. "Couldn't you wait to see me again detective?" Chuckling, she flicked her golden hair over her shoulder.

Robson's eyebrows rose. "You don't seem awfully concerned about being called in again?"

Emma shrugged. "My conscience is clear. I didn't do anything wrong. I am intrigued though."

Robson squinted up at her from behind the laptop sitting on the table. Her bored, disinterested tone was already irritating him. It was clear she couldn't care less about her co-star's death. "It appears you haven't been entirely honest with us," he said, impatience seeping into his voice.

Emma merely stared back at him curiously and chose not to reply. Beside him, Zahra bristled in agitation, Emma was evidently getting under her skin too. With no further preamble, Robson spun the laptop around so it faced the blonde actress. Her eyes widened when she saw the still image captured on the screen. Robson paused for a second before hitting the play button to start the two-minute long video.

As it played, he watched Emma keenly to see her reaction. Skilled actress as she was, even she couldn't hide her initial shock. A stunned expression remained etched on her face long after the short video had ended. After a few minutes of silent contemplation, Emma composed herself with a little shake. Settling back into her chair, she pursed her lips as she adopted her signature unimpressed look.

She truly is a talented actress, thought Robson to himself. *How easy it would be for her to conceal what she was really thinking.*

"Nikki recorded that video one day before she mysteriously landed the Lady Macbeth role two weeks ago. Do you reckon that's significant?"

Understanding dawned on Emma's face. "That's *Nikki's* video?"

"It sure is. Care to tell us how she ended up with it?"

"Nikki's video," said Emma again, repeating the phrase as if it were something incomprehensible. Then, she laughed. "Voyeuristic bitch. See, I told you it was blackmail. I knew she had something on Neil."

"You probably should have mentioned this before."

"Mentioned it? I've only just found out it exists."

"You know what I'm talking about."

A sly smile crept onto Emma's lips. "It didn't come up in conversation."

*   *   *

Tuesday 6th March

Emma hadn't meant for it to happen. She hadn't planned it. But ever since her initial audition when the director had first laid eyes on her, she had clocked the way he stared longingly, eyes lingering a shade longer than necessary.

Emma was no fool. She knew she was beautiful and, what's more, she enjoyed the thrill of the chase. It was intoxicating to feel so desirable. Young, free and single, she had nothing to lose. The director was attractive too. Not movie-star handsome, but good looking in a more attainable sort of way. She always had found herself drawn to older, most sophisticated men and at almost ten years her senior, Neil Hillton fit the bill exactly.

It had started out as a game. Furtive glances, a sly wink here and there, meeting his eyes fleetingly from across the stage. Before long she was consciously considering her outfits, applying an additional dash of perfume before rehearsals, ensuring her lips were glossed. She knew how these things worked. Men were so predictable.

Sure enough, Neil gradually began to find more reasons to spend time alone with her. He insisted Lady Macbeth was a challenging, deeply involving role and, as a director, he would benefit greatly from discussing how she planned to play it. There was always some excuse. To give him credit, Neil did seem genuinely invested in the play, annoyingly so in Emma's opinion. But it was more than that. She could see it in his eyes; he was falling for her. And honestly, that was the thing she enjoyed the most. Having power over someone like that, it was exhilarating.

Then, one day Neil had casually thrown into conversation that he had made some in-depth notes on her role and inquired if she was free to pop around to his house after rehearsal to go through them.

Notes, Emma had smirked to herself.

Unsurprisingly, a few hours later they were curled up on his sofa, locked in a passionate embrace. It wasn't hard to identify when they had stepped over the line into something infinitely more complicated. Things had escalated from there. What started as a casual fling quickly grew into something more serious.

Emma had never believed in fairy tales, in knights in shining armour, and she had definitely never anticipated falling head over heels for an amateur theatre director. She always figured she would end up with some suave, powerful businessman. But much to her surprise, Neil had completely swept her off her feet. Against her will, she had been enchanted. The director had a charismatic personality and a deep voice that made her tingle when he spoke. His throaty laugh was so infectious she couldn't help but giggle along at his jokes. Plus, he had a way of making her feel safe when she was with him, like he would always protect her no matter what. In many ways, Neil was the ideal man – charming, sexy and kind.

And married.

Emma still couldn't believe she had managed to get

herself into this situation. It was only ever meant to be a bit of fun, there was no harm in fooling around. She had no idea their relationship would grow into something so much more than that. If she had even the slightest inkling about what would happen between them, she would never have got involved in the first place. But it was already too late for regrets. The past couldn't be rewritten.

Watching Neil from across his miniscule backstage office, Emma felt her heart swell with love. How someone she had known for only four weeks could stir up such strong feelings in her, she had no idea. Neil was currently twisting his wedding ring round and round his left index finger. He had an endearing habit of fiddling with it when he was nervous. There was something vaguely ironic about that.

She leaned back against his bookcase and inhaled the comforting scent of old books. She loved the smell of his cosy office – warm and earthy with distinctive notes of vanilla and an underlying mustiness. It was their private sanctuary, safely hidden away from prying eyes.

From behind his desk, Neil suddenly raised his head and locked eyes with her. With a warm smile, he held up an unopened bottle of Merlot and cocked his head questioningly. Emma grinned in response and nodded approvingly. Padding barefoot over to him, she relished the warmth of the wooden floorboards underfoot. She had kicked off her heels as soon as they had stepped into his office. It had become an unspoken signal between them; the roles of director and actress could be left outside for now.

Expertly uncorking the bottle, Neil poured her the first glass and handed it over. Emma took no time in lifting it to her lips and savouring a long sip. *Delicious.* She sighed in pleasure. He smiled at her reaction and poured a second glass for himself. Merlot – that was the director's influence. Before him she had only ever drunk cheap white wine, usually whatever the local supermarket had on offer, but Neil had taught her how to appreciate the finer things in life.

Brushing a golden wisp of hair out of her face, Neil kissed her lightly on the forehead. "'My dearest partner of greatness'."

Emma pulled back from him with an amused giggle. "Are you quoting *Macbeth* on me? Hardly the model couple, were they? Conspiring together to murder people and then both winding up dead?"

He swept her up in his arms. His face always came alive when he quoted Shakespeare, eyes sparkling with enthusiasm. "Okay, okay, I can do better. How about 'I would not wish any companion in the world but you'."

She grinned at him. "Better. *The Tempest?*"

Neil smiled proudly. "Wow, well done!"

Accepting the praise, Emma winked at him. It wasn't really all that impressive. She'd figured out early on that Neil wasn't as well-read as he liked to think, so all of his romantic quotes always came from the same five most well-known Shakespeare plays. The way she figured – she had at least a twenty per cent chance of guessing it right.

It was a game Neil adored playing with her, quoting

classic Shakespearean lines about love and encouraging her to guess which play they were from. Emma found it endearing, in a cute, goofy sort of way. She liked that it was something just the two of them shared.

"'Love looks not with the eyes, but with the mind'."

"Ooh hang on, I think I know this one too." She screwed her face up in concentration. *"A Midsummer Night's Dream?"*

Neil nodded in agreement, visibly impressed.

Edging slowly away from him, Emma reached over to the precarious piles of books and notes strewn across his oak desk. Somewhat dramatically, she gave them a sharp push to fling everything onto the floor.

She had always wanted to do that.

The heavy books thudded onto the hard floor with a louder bang than she had intended. Handwritten notes she hadn't realised were loose drifted haphazardly across the room. Ignoring the mess, Emma jumped onto the desk, pulling herself up in one swift movement. Turning to face Neil, she swung her legs in a seductive manner as she beckoned to him.

The director glared at the scattered paper on the floor. "You're lucky I numbered those pages."

"*That's* what you're thinking about?"

Neil allowed himself a small smile as he approached her. "No."

"Good. Now, get yourself over here."

She reached to clutch his shoulder tightly and gasped as his lips brushed against hers. Sliding a hand under his shirt, Emma lifted it up over his head. His skin was smooth, taut over the toned muscles of his arms and chest. A besotted expression had appeared on Neil's face as he stared down at her, as though he was stupefied in her presence.

"Irresistible," he mumbled into her neck.

Neil took her shoulders and pulled her gently towards him. Emma closed her eyes as his fingers slid into her hair. Their lips met and Neil kissed her deeper this time, the warmth of his breath mixing with the acidic taste of wine and the smell of his aftershave. Emma slid nearer, hands pushing inside his clothes.

In one deft move, he unzipped her dress and she wriggled out of it obligingly. Reaching to grab his neck, Emma kissed him again and Neil moaned in pleasure. She could feel her heart pounding in her chest as she fumbled with his jeans.

In the height of their passion, neither lover noticed an unsuspecting Nikki walk through the unlocked door into the office. Shocked, she hastily pulled back and retreated through the doorway. Hesitating in the corridor Nikki leaned her head against the wall, silently weighing up her options. A cunning expression crept across her face as an idea suddenly occurred to her. Quietly, she slipped her phone out of her jacket pocket and stealthily resumed her position peeking through the open door. She hesitated for only a second before drawing a deep breath and hitting record.

* * *

Emma stared down at the incriminating video, arms still folded defiantly across her chest. Eyes narrowed, she gave Robson a cold stare. "So, we were sleeping together. What's the big deal?"

"Nikki clearly thought it was a big deal. Scandalous enough to capture on film at least."

"Yeah well, she always was a manipulative little bitch. I've met girls like her before. All starry-eyed with dreams of becoming famous. The real world just isn't like that. Reality tends to bring them crashing down quickly. Nikki had it in for me from the beginning. The jealous type, you know?"

Robson nodded. "It's interesting footage though, don't you think? Any idea what Nikki planned to do with this video?"

Emma's thin lips formed a tight smile. "I think we all know exactly what she did with this video. She's had Neil wrapped around her little finger for the past fortnight. Now I guess we know why."

There was mockery in her tone but Robson noticed the blonde actress was taking great care not to sound too condescending. Not to let her innocent mask slip.

Emma spread her open palms on the table, looking at them imploringly. "Look, I've told you about the affair. I've been completely honest with you. What more do you want from me?"

"Well, it's not like you had much choice but to come clean given the video. Funny how you didn't mention your relationship with the director when we spoke to you before."

She snorted scornfully. "Oh, please! There is *no* relationship any more. That was as good as dead when Neil double-crossed me to promote Nikki into that bloody role. The coward never did bother to explain himself."

"You really did lose a lot because of her."

Emma threw Robson a look of pure loathing. "I guess I did. I suppose that's one mystery solved. Thanks a lot Nikki."

Robson's expression grew thoughtful as he considered the possible motives of the attractive young actress sat before him.

No wonder she hated Nikki Gowon. To lose both her coveted role and her budding relationship because of her was a high price to pay. What was that famous saying? Hell hath no fury like a woman scorned. And Emma Thorpe was clearly a woman adept at manipulating other people to do her bidding. Even if she hadn't swapped the knives herself that didn't mean she wasn't somehow involved. Especially if she knew more than she was letting on.

Robson's face tightened. "Are you sure you didn't know about this little spy video? Neil never mentioned it? I'm sure it would make anyone mad that someone had been spying on them. Invading your privacy, it's just not right. It wasn't tempting to shut her up before she exposed the two of you? Who knows what Nikki was planning? Maybe it went beyond sending it directly to his wife. Why not upload it onto the Internet, let it go viral and be done with it? That negative publicity would be pretty damning. Sure, you're both consenting adults. But an actress who's willing to sleep with a married director to worm her way into a starring role? That never comes across well in the press. I highly doubt your reputation would emerge from the scandal unscathed."

Out of the corner of his eye, Robson spotted Zahra

shoot him a warning look.

Gritting her teeth together, Emma sneered. "That's an interesting story you're concocting there, detective. Pure fiction of course. You couldn't be further off the mark. Besides, as for my reputation as an *actress?* I'm a Senior PR Executive for a global multi-million consultancy firm. Theatre is just a hobby, I'm hardly concerned about my acting career! To think I would be is frankly preposterous. Perhaps Neil would stand to lose his reputation, but it wouldn't affect me at all." Emma leaned back in her chair, suppressing a smirk. "So, to answer your earlier question, no I didn't know about the video. I think I'd remember seeing something like that."

Of course you're in PR, thought Robson bitterly. *A master spin doctor adept at weaving a web of intricate lies in an attempt to make us believe whatever you want.*

Emma threw him a critical look. "I think you should probably talk to Neil."

CHAPTER SIXTEEN

The Love That Follows Us Sometime is Our Trouble

Shifting uncomfortably in his seat, Robson pulled at his collar in annoyance. His starchy shirt felt stiff and restrictive on his arms, his tight tie a noose around his neck. He would give anything right now to slip into a comfortable hoodie, the clothing equivalent of a hug.

Opposite him, Neil Hillton appeared equally uncomfortable. Gone was his earlier boyish excitement, now he looked only worried and tense. He let out a slow breath as he fidgeted in his chair like he couldn't keep still. "So, why do you need to see me again? Surely I've told you everything you need to know?"

Robson's face broke into a smile. "We've been speaking to Emma Thorpe."

"Oh?" Neil's tone feigned disinterest, the look on his face, uncomprehending. But his hands gripped the edge of the table, his entire body rigid with tension.

"She had some interesting things to say."

The director gave an anxious laugh. "Well, that girl always did have a rather fanciful imagination. Honestly, I wouldn't pay too much attention to whatever she is claiming."

"I couldn't agree more," admitted Robson. But no sooner had Neil exhaled a deep sigh of relief, he added, "That's why I prefer to watch the evidence instead."

Immediately Neil paled. "Watch?"

Robson tapped the laptop on the table. "That's right. They say a camera never lies."

A sheen of sweat appeared on Neil's forehead and he shook his head violently. "I don't know what you're talking about—"

"Oh, cut the bullshit," interrupted Robson as he waved the feeble protestation aside. "This particular home movie is rather enlightening. Stars a certain married theatre director and a young actress hooking up in his office. Care to watch it?"

Wincing, Neil lowered his gaze. His face was a picture of contrition, of deep shame.

"I believe there were certain aspects of your story you opted to leave out when you spoke to us before?" challenged Robson.

Still staring at the floor, Neil swallowed and gave the tiniest nod of his head.

"How about we try this again? This time we want your full, unedited account. No deleted scenes to spare yourself any embarrassment."

Still hunkered over the table, the director coughed to clear his throat, his wheezy breathing quick and shallow. Finally, after a long moment of silence, Neil gave a shaky sigh and began to talk.

*   *   *

Wednesday 7th March

Neil stretched out across the full length of the bed, curling his toes into the cool sheets. His heart was racing, blood pounding in his head. Cheeks still flushed from the recent exertion, his bare chest heaved as he caught his breath. The room was dark, air sweet with the smell of them. There was nowhere in the world he would rather be.

Satisfied, he turned to steal a glance at Emma who was sprawled spread-eagled next to him. Her eyes were closed, lips curled up in a hint of a smile. She squinted open one eye to peer at his face before rolling over and draping her arm lazily across him. Snuggled close, she ran her fingers lightly across his chest, tracing his muscles absentmindedly.

Neil shuddered at the sensation. A few weeks in and Emma's touch still made him tingle. It was hard to believe they had only been together for less than a month, it already felt like a lifetime. Never before had being with someone felt so natural to him. In many ways, he had found his kindred spirit in Emma. He finally understood what people were talking about when they spoke about finding their soulmate.

Next to him, Emma stirred and blinked open her bleary eyes. *God, she was beautiful.* Even with tousled bed hair and drooping eyelids, she was still the most exquisite woman he had ever laid eyes on. He felt like the luckiest man alive. Neil leaned over to kiss her forehead softly, his fingers brushing her cheek.

Emma grinned sleepily, nuzzling her head into the nook of his neck. "So, how did it go?" she murmured, still half asleep.

Distracted by the curve of her lithe young body, Neil outstretched his hand to caress her breasts softly. Why she thought now was a good time to strike up a conversation was beyond him. "How did what go?"

"Last night. Telling Lily," she continued, kissing his cheek lightly.

If truth be told, Neil hadn't given his wife, Lily, a second thought. She had got back from her business trip the night before and was already in bed when he had arrived home from the theatre, laptop balanced on her knees furiously typing away responding to emails. Lily had nodded at him distractedly and said her trip was fine, before turning her attention back to her work. Disinterested, she neglected to ask him anything about his own week so Neil had stormed off to watch television in peace. It was hardly the right time to bring up the topic he had been avoiding for weeks.

Too late, Neil realised he had been silent for too long.

Emma stopped kissing him and pulled away, looking at him accusingly. "You didn't tell her, did you?"

He sighed wearily. "Em, it was late. I didn't get chance."

Cheat. Such a dirty word. Reputations had been destroyed over the revelation of being a cheat. And straying with a hot young actress no less. *What a cliché.* Far from ideal for an aspiring theatre director poised to make it big time. The public could be far from forgiving when it came to such scandals. Neil was determined not to allow his career to be tarnished by such a dirty association.

No. This situation was delicate and he had to handle it carefully, not unlike a ticking bomb that could explode at any minute if a wrong move was made. The right timing was paramount. Asking for a divorce was hardly something he could just drop into casual conversation over dinner. Although he couldn't see Lily being anything but relieved. Their marriage had been as good as over for years. He couldn't even remember the last time they had slept together. Honestly, he would be surprised if his wife hadn't cheated on him first during one of the numerous business trips she was always away on. National work conferences had to be a breeding ground for affairs surely?

Neil still clung desperately to that idea. It helped him to deal with the overwhelming guilt that had been gnawing away at his insides. *His marriage had already crumbled. His wife was probably already hooking up with one of her alpha-male colleagues. No one would ever blame him for seeking solace elsewhere. And the lovely Emma had been all too willing to provide it and then, wonderfully, they had fallen in love.* It was a compelling story. A better narrative at any rate than *horny director shags sexy young actress while his faithful wife works away.*

Neil stooped down to touch Emma's cheek but she turned her head away indignantly.

"'The course of true love never did run smooth'," Neil tried hopefully. The classic quote from *A Midsummer Night's Dream* was one of his favourites.

Emma threw him a humourless smirk, clearly she was in no mood for playing games. Instead, she pushed herself up into a sitting position and glared at him. "You promised."

"I know. And I will tell Lily, I swear. I just need to find the right moment."

Emma scowled, distorting her pretty features. "You've been finding the right moment for weeks now. We can't keep doing this. I'm not some slutty mistress you can use and fling aside."

"You're not. Em, you're so much more than that I promise. You know how much I love you."

Drawing her legs up protectively towards her, Emma shook her head. "Do you have any idea what it's like for me to make love in another woman's bed? It feels cheap, dirty even. I don't appreciate feeling like a whore."

"Em! Don't say that." There was a new sheepishness in Neil's voice. He tried to stroke her hand but she snatched her arm away.

"You need to show me you're actually committed. To prove to me that you're in this for the long haul. That you're not just going to bugger off and leave me when things get messy." She paused, looking down at him. "I mean I could be *pregnant*!"

He stared at her, stunned. "Are you?"

She hesitated for a long moment. "Well…no. But I could be. Point is, I still need you to commit."

Neil breathed a sigh of relief. "That's not funny Em."

There was a mounting frustration in his voice as his tone became more irritated. He hated this brattish, selfish side of Emma. The side that made him feel pressured, as though he was always going to be a disappointing let-down, no matter how hard he tried. Surely she should appreciate the precarious position he was in. He had to ask for a divorce *before* there was any chance of Lily finding out about their affair. It was crucial all their assets were divided equally. His wife had always been the breadwinner in their marriage. Driven and ambitious, she had worked her way up into a national sales representative role meaning the vast majority of their joint income came from her job, freeing Neil up to explore his more creative pursuits. Hell, Lily's name was even on the mortgage agreement for the theatre. He dread to think what would happen if he couldn't keep that. He stood to lose everything. Tact was definitely the way forward. But every time he came close to being honest with his wife, he lost his nerve and bottled it.

Emma gave an angry shrug and malice crept into her eyes as she offered slyly, "If you prefer, I could tell Lily myself. In fact, I could just stay here in bed and wait for her, naked. I think she'd get the picture pretty quickly."

"Em!" Neil choked, eyes bulging at the thought.

"I mean it, you can't keep fobbing me off. It's only a matter of time before I take things into my own hands."

"Don't you dare make threats like that! I thought our relationship was built on mutual love and understanding, not ultimatums."

"It's not an ultimatum, it's a deadline. As in you're dead to me if you don't sort this out really soon."

Neil shivered as he felt a familiar sense of dread start to take over. *He couldn't lose her. It would destroy him.* Even in her anger he still felt ridiculously attracted to her. Neil breathed out shakily as he felt his chest tighten, a tell-tale sign of a looming panic attack. *Not now.* He hated showing weakness in front of her. "When are you going to start believing me Em? You're the love of my life. I only want to be with you."

Emma smiled coyly. "Prove it."

"I will. I promise. Look, I'll talk to Lily this evening. I'll tell her everything." Stroking her cheek gently, he tilted her chin up to look directly in her eyes. "Please trust me."

For a long moment she hesitated, then finally she gave a satisfied nod.

Neil sighed, relieved. He never ceased to be amazed at the effect she had on him. Emma had awoken hidden desires he hadn't realised he had and made him feel more alive than he once thought possible. He found himself yearning for not only her touch, but her companionship. She understood him in a way no one else ever had. As his naked body intertwined with Emma's once more, he felt a fresh rush of desire course through him. *He really did love her.* Feeling a new resolve to do right by her, he vowed to leave his wife as soon as possible. He owed Emma that much.

Tonight, he would tell Lily everything.

Neil hummed to himself cheerily as he tidied his backstage office. His mood was still lifted after spending the morning with Emma. She never failed to put a smile on his face.

And tonight was the night!

Finally, after weeks of anxious deliberation, tonight he would be asking Lily for a divorce and he would eventually be free. Neil was so preoccupied in his own thoughts, it took him several minutes to realise Nikki had snuck into his office behind him and was stood quietly to one side. Leaning casually against his bookcase, she was watching him carefully, her eyes full of intensity.

Startled, Neil felt his heart skip a beat. "Nikki! You made me jump. What do you want?"

"What do I *want*? I want lots of things," Nikki mused thoughtfully. She was toying with her phone, turning it over distractedly in her hands as she spoke. "Tell me, is it true there are talent scouts who routinely come to watch your shows?"

Puzzled by the question, Neil nodded slowly. "Usually yes. Obviously, I can't guarantee they'll definitely turn up but there are normally a few that make an appearance these days."

"So, theoretically this play could provide a spring-board to kickstarting someone's career? That's all it takes, isn't it? To be spotted in the right place at the right time."

Neil frowned, confused. He had no idea where she was going with this. "I guess so. Why do you ask?"

"I was thinking about how those talent scouts would probably be more interested in watching the lead performers. I mean, they're generally the most talented, aren't they? The ones to watch?"

Neil's frown deepened but he remained silent.

"Thing is, my family could really do with the money if I was to land a big role. It would make a huge difference to my little sister and time is of the essence. I know it's a long shot but it's worth being in the spotlight, just in case. It's best to aim high, right?"

Neil's brow furrowed. "Sorry, I'm confused. I don't understand what you're asking?"

She looked right at him, dead straight in the eyes. "I'm asking to play the role of Lady Macbeth."

Neil let out a derisive snort of laughter. "What? That's ridiculous! Auditions were over weeks ago. Why would you even entertain the idea I would swap the cast around so late in the day? It would cause complete chaos."

Smiling slyly, Nikki teased, "Oh, I think I can make it worthwhile for you."

Neil shook his head abruptly. "Sorry, my decision is final. There's no bribe you can offer me that's going to change my mind."

Nikki gave a hearty chuckle. "Oh, don't you worry. I'm not planning to give you anything. I could however choose to take something away."

A shiver ran through Neil's body. "Is that right?"

Nikki shrugged nonchalantly. Glancing down, she tapped her phone a few times and handed it over to him.

Neil's blood ran cold as he stared down at the incriminating video. His sexual tryst with Emma in this very office, forever immortalised on film. *How the hell had Nikki managed to record it? He could have sworn the theatre was empty and they had been there alone that night.*

As if reading his mind, Nikki explained, "I was in

237

the area so I popped in to ask about the weekend rehearsal plans. Needless to say, I found you were a little preoccupied."

Groaning internally, Neil cursed himself. *He knew it had been a foolish idea to give all the cast members a spare key so they could come and go at the theatre as they pleased. How could he have been so stupid?*

"It's not what you think. I swear my marriage is as good as over. In fact, I'm planning to ask my wife for a divorce this evening."

"Whatever helps you sleep at night."

"And Emma is—"

"Your mistress?"

"She's so much more than that. We're in love."

"Of course you are."

"Please I'm begging you, that video needs to be deleted."

A razor smile spread across Nikki's face. "I could, I guess. But that's no fun at all is it? Besides, I already have a backup copy saved on the cloud, as well as my laptop."

Neil's heart pounded as a tight knot formed in the pit of his stomach. "What do you want?"

"I've already told you."

"Lady Macbeth?"

"That's right."

"Nothing else?"

She shook her head. "I'm a reasonable person Neil. I'm not here to screw you over for fun. I owe my family a lot of money. Money that would make a real difference to my sister right now. If I have even the slightest chance of earning some big bucks, I need to give myself the best possible chance to be spotted in order to make that happen."

Neil sighed in exasperation. "How very noble of you. Truth is, it's rarely that simple. But the fact remains – it's too late. There's only two weeks left until our opening night. You'll never learn the part in time."

Nikki shook her head, looking rather pleased with herself. "That's where you're wrong. I'm the under-study remember? I already know pretty much the whole part. It won't take me long to refine it."

"And what about Emma?"

"If Emma's half as good as you seem to think she is, she won't have a problem learning a few consid-erably smaller parts in a fortnight."

Neil felt his chest tighten as anxiety threatened to overcome him. "It's still too late, it would be far too disruptive. You'll risk ruining the whole show."

Nikki gave an exaggerated sigh. "That's too bad. I guess I'll just have to send my little candid video to your wife in that case. Lily Hillton, isn't it? I found her on Facebook right away."

Neil froze. His entire body stiffened as beads of sweat formed on his forehead. *Surely she was bluffing. Wasn't she?*

"You can't."

Smiling in agreement, Nikki continued, "Actually, you're right. Talking directly to the wife is so passé these days. Maybe I should simply upload it to You-Tube and go from there? Hope it goes viral. I could forward it onto a few news outlets and theatre critics for good measure. You're beginning to make a bit of a name for yourself in the theatre industry aren't you Neil? I'm sure there would be some websites that would love to do a feature about how you have a tendency to sleep with your lead actresses? So cliché, don't you think?" She let the thinly veiled threat hang in the air, a hint of amusement creeping onto her face.

Neil's mouth was completely dry, even his shallow breathing felt scratchy and forced. "You overestimate me. I'm no big deal. No news website would be interested in running that story."

He was clutching at straws and Nikki seemed to know it. Giving him an appraising stare, she asked innocently, "Are you willing to gamble that? This is your reputation we're talking about here. Not to mention your marriage. I'm guessing you wouldn't be entitled to much if you were exposed as a cheating liar?"

The director had no answer for that. *How had he got himself into this predicament?* Just minutes earlier, life had been so much simpler. It had been the first time he had felt properly happy in years.

Suddenly lightheaded, Neil grasped the back of his desk chair to steady himself. Fainting in front of Nikki was hardly going to help matters. She was watching him closely, a small triumphant smile on her lips. Waiting for his next move, although she already knew she had won. This was checkmate.

"Let's talk about Lady Macbeth," she said cheerfully.

Sweating profusely, Neil swallowed nervously. "How exactly do you expect me to explain this to the rest of the cast?"

Nikki shrugged. "Not my problem. I'm sure you'll

come up with something."

"What could I possibly say? They'll know something's up."

"Look you've made your bed, now you've got to lie in it." She let out a bitter laugh. "Although, I guess if you'd done that in the first place you wouldn't be in this mess. I mean seriously Neil, on your *desk*? Have some class."

Still feeling dizzy, Neil sank into his chair before his legs gave way. It meant Nikki towered over him but he was through playing power games. It was clear who was in control here. Struggling to catch his breath he shook his head in growing despair. "How can I ever explain this to Emma? It would devastate her. She'll be furious, she'll never forgive me."

"You should have thought about that before hooking up in your office."

"I can't lie to her," he pleaded. "I would never want to compromise our relationship. We're in love."

Nikki snickered mockingly. "How sweet. You've barely known her one month. Although I've heard people fall head over heels quickly when it's out of wedlock. See the thing is, I have people I love too who would be thrilled if I got this role."

"Jimmy?"

Frowning, Nikki shook her head. "Keep Jimmy out of this."

"But you just said—"

"I know what I said. I'm talking about my sister. And I'm not saying a word of this to Jimmy. Or Emma. Or anyone else for that matter. I don't care what elaborate cover story you come up with. I don't care if it costs you your secret little love affair. All I care about is that by the end of the day, I'm announced as the lead role."

Neil was silent, lost for words. For one of the first times in his life he could think of nothing to say.

"I trust I don't need to remind you what will happen if you don't stick to the rules of our little agreement?"

Neil nodded mutely.

Nikki beamed a satisfied smile. "Great! That's sorted then. I better get going, I guess I've got some new lines I should start practising."

As Neil watched her waltz out of the office, he felt a burning hatred grow inside of him, like nothing he had ever felt before.

* * *

Neil stared glumly at the table. He looked almost catatonic, absorbed in his own thoughts.

Robson traded a sideways glance with Zahra who merely shrugged and gave a small nod. Turning his attention back to the director, Robson peered at him intently over tented fingertips. "Sounds like a strong motive to me."

Finally, Neil tore his gaze away from the table and stared straight at him. "I didn't kill Nikki, I swear."

"She blackmailed you. She cost you your relationship. She compromised your show. And she threatened to destroy your reputation, wreck your marriage and cripple you financially. None of which you thought to mention to us beforehand, even though we've spoken to you twice."

"I know that doesn't sound good. But I swear I didn't do it." The director's voice was ragged with worry, unsettled by the accusation.

"Not to mention your fingerprints are all over the murder weapon," added Zahra. "And you were the last person to do a final prop check on the opening night. If anyone had the best opportunity to swap the knives around, it would have been you."

Robson stole another glance at his partner. While her voice was business-like, he knew her well enough to know her tone lacked conviction. She didn't believe Neil was the culprit.

The flustered director exhaled sharply, his face contorted in desperation. "I've told you. I can explain all that."

"You have to admit though, it is awfully convenient for you now Nikki has been silenced permanently. Makes me wonder what lengths you might have gone to in order to keep her from talking."

Neil's lip quivered as he answered, "Look I admit, Nikki made my life hell for the last fortnight, but truthfully I have only myself to blame. It doesn't mean I wanted to hurt her. I'm no killer…" His voice caught in his throat.

Robson scrutinised him for a moment longer and then relented. "Okay, well I suppose you're free to go."

A perplexed expression passed over Neil's face. "Really? I am?"

"For now. But don't leave the country just yet."

Giving a hurried nod of thanks, the director bolted for the door. But when he reached it, he lingered in the doorframe and turned around hesitantly. "And you won't be telling my wife about any of this?"

"Rest assured we have bigger things to worry about than your wife finding out about your little love affair. That is, if she doesn't already know. In my experience, I've found women usually know more than they let on."

Neil nodded thankfully and scampered out of the door as if he couldn't exit the room quick enough.

Turning to Zahra, Robson remarked, "You're not convinced?"

His partner grimaced and shook her head slowly. She was toying with the edge of her hijab, twirling the hem around her fingers absentmindedly. "I know it's a compelling motive and most of the evidence seems to point towards Neil, but there's just something about the man that makes it hard to believe he's capable of murder."

"I know what you mean. A bit of a wet lettuce."

"Exactly. I'm more compelled to believe he'd be content to wallow in his own misery, feeling sorry for himself, than ever take definitive action."

Nodding pensively, Robson added, "True. And the fact of the matter is we still don't have enough to arrest him even if we were convinced he was the murderer."

"Which leaves us right back where we started. With nothing."

Robson exhaled in frustration. Normally, he prided himself on being able to identify the perpetrator early on. But in this case, he felt none the wiser having interviewed all of the cast. The murder of Nikki Gowon was starting to edge uncomfortably towards remaining an unsolved crime. That would be rather embarrassing for the Metropolitan Police Force, especially given the media frenzy around the case. And Robson as lead Detective Inspector stood to be ridiculed.

Pondering the lack of evidence they had unearthed so far, Robson found his mind drifting back to the mysterious heart necklace found discarded in Nikki's bin. He couldn't shake the nagging feeling he had somehow seen the familiar jewellery before and that memory could be the key to unlocking the whole case.

A strange moment of clarity pierced his weariness, he was convinced he had hit upon something important. But the critical details of his half-formed memory eluded him, remaining tantalising just beyond his grasp. If he could only focus all of his attention, he might be able to remember where he had come across it before.

It was at that precise moment they were interrupted by a brisk knock at the door. PC Armstrong poked her head into the room, a grim expression on her face. "Sorry to interrupt, but you really need to see this."

After being ushered in, the young police officer hastily set the laptop she had been carrying under her arm onto the table. The two detectives huddled close behind her, curious as to what she was about to reveal.

Looking up, PC Armstrong explained, "So, remember how we requested the CCTV footage from outside Gemini Theatre? Well, I've had the team working on it and they've come across something interesting. Maybe it's nothing, but we thought all things considered it could be important."

Robson nodded eagerly in anticipation. Any lead would be appreciated at this point. The investigation had all but dried up regarding meaningful evidence. PC Armstrong efficiently opened up the two brief CCTV videos in question and played them in respectful silence.

Afterwards the three of them stood speechless around the table, all staring down at the grainy CCTV footage – still images frozen in time.

PC Armstrong was the first to break the silence. "I'm sorry it's taken so long to find this. For obvious reasons we've been focusing on the day of the murder, trying to spot anything amiss. There's nothing we could find relating to that, all the knife swapping must have happened backstage. So, we started to systematically go back further, through the footage from the previous days. That's when we came across this."

A sly smile spread across Zahra's face. "I knew it!" Her tone was triumphant, almost celebratory. "I *knew* they were lying to us." She turned and gave Robson an earnest look, eyes bright with conviction. "I think I know what happened to Nikki."

"What? How can you possibly know that? She's not even on that footage."

"Don't you get it? Of course she's not. She doesn't have to be." Zahra shot him a wicked grin, something knowing on her face.

Robson frowned in confusion.

"Please, just trust me on this." Zahra's expression hardened into a determined grimace. "I know exactly the person we need to speak to."

CHAPTER SEVENTEEN

Yet Do I Fear Thy Nature

Robson was the first to admit that the unexpected CCTV footage had piqued his curiosity. As PC Armstrong had so sagely pointed out, it could amount to nothing. But maybe it would prove to be more than merely a coincidence.

This case deserved a break.

Setting a fresh cup of coffee down in front of him, Zahra hesitated at his side as if she were about to say something before thinking better of it and looking away.

Robson was attuned enough to her to detect the internal struggle she seemed to be waging with herself. He looked up curiously. "What is it?"

Zahra chewed on her lip. "Look, no offence or anything, but do you mind sitting this one out? Watch the interview from behind the mirror?"

Mystified, Robson studied his partner closely. Clearly Zahra had raced ahead to a conclusion he couldn't fathom himself. "Why go it alone?"

"I just have a theory I might have more luck one-to-one on this occasion."

Robson gave a nonchalant shrug. "Fine then, you go ahead." He couldn't tell where his partner was going with this, but he was more than happy to follow her lead. Her instincts had proved good before.

Ensconced behind the one-way mirror, Robson mulled over what Zahra had said, turning it over in his mind like a puzzle to be solved.

How could she possibly know who murdered Nikki Gowon?

There were a number of possibilities that could have led up to that CCTV footage, but frustratingly it still proved nothing concrete. To unearth the truth would come down to asking the right, insightful questions and that responsibility was with Zahra alone.

Unscrewing the lid of the opaque water bottle he had smuggled in, Robson raised it to his lips to take a satisfied gulp. To the casual onlooker it appeared innocuous enough. Only he knew the bottle's contents were laced with gin. Just enough to take the edge off. It had been a long time since he had stooped so low to drink while he was working, but desperate times called for desperate measures. Besides, it helped him think and he needed clarity now more than ever.

Beyond the mirror, the door opened with a loud clang and Robson watched silently as the interviewee was ushered in. Violet Underwood sank down into the chair, eyes darting fearfully around her as she took in the surroundings once again. Gripping the chair to steady herself, her whole body tensed. Robson was struck again by how fragile the teenage girl looked, like a wounded bird.

Zahra leaned across the table, with kindness in her eyes. "Remember me? I'm Detective Sergeant Zahra, but you can call me Nadia."

Violet nodded feebly. Ashen-faced, she was evaluating Zahra warily, clearly afraid of what she might be asked. With one hand, she tugged at the hem of her cardigan, absentmindedly pulling at the frayed sleeves. *It had to be a nervous habit or a sign of compulsive behaviour.*

For a few minutes Zahra sat opposite her in companionable silence. Then, she smiled and asked the young actress what her favourite Shakespeare play was. Her brusque, professional voice had morphed into something warmer and more personal.

Taken aback by the random question, Violet seemed thoroughly puzzled. "I don't know, maybe *A Midsummer Night's Dream*?"

Zahra chuckled. "Ah great choice, a classic! For me, I guess it would have to be *Romeo and Juliet*. I love the romance in that story, the star-crossed lovers. It's all so beautiful and tragic."

Violet blinked, then nodded in agreement. Already her body was less rigid as she started to relax.

"The thing is Violet," continued Zahra. "What happened to your friend Nikki is a real-life tragedy. It wouldn't be honouring her memory if we didn't find out what happened to her. So, here's my problem – I know you're keeping things from us, not telling the whole truth. What I don't understand is *why*. Although, I think I could make a good guess."

Biting down hard on her lip, Violet's eyes shone with unshed tears. Her gaze slipped over Zahra's shoulder to the mirror. Watching her carefully, Zahra spun around the laptop on the table to reveal the still CCTV footage on the screen.

Violet froze, eyes wide with fear. "Where did you get that?"

"There's a camera outside the main theatre entrance, captures everyone going in and out."

"Oh my God." Violet's voice was so faint it was barely a whisper.

"Why don't you tell me what happened?"

All the colour drained from Violet's face. She cast another nervous glance towards the mirror, behind which Robson held his breath in trepidation.

"It's okay, you're safe here," said Zahra softly. "You just need to talk to me."

Shaking her head, Violet gulped back a sob and shrank back into her chair. "You don't understand. I can't…"

"You *can*. All you need to do is tell me exactly what happened."

"The last person I confided in ended up dead."

Zahra's eyes grew sharp for a moment. "In that case, don't you think it's even more crucial you tell us everything? Prevent another death?"

"It's my own life I'm worried about," said Violet, barely audible.

"We can protect you. I promise."

Zahra had adopted a gentle, soothing tone Robson

had only ever heard her use once before. His grip tightened around the bottle as that distant memory came flooding back. His pulse quickened as his entire body went cold. Zahra's theory about what had happened finally dawned on him and he shuddered at the creeping realisation.

He knew exactly where this conversation was going.

*   *   *

Tuesday 20th March

Surrounded by mounds of *Macbeth* programmes in varying stages of completeness, Violet looked around in a state of ever-growing despair. The show opened in just three days. Earlier in the evening, she had commandeered Neil's cramped backstage office to put the programmes together in what she had assumed would be a relatively quick task. Glancing down at her watch, she was distressed to see it was already twenty minutes past midnight.

Crap! She had totally underestimated how long this would take. Her parents were going to kill her.

Grabbing the long-armed stapler, Violet efficiently set about constructing the remaining programmes with new, speedy determination. *Print, fold, staple, repeat.* Foolishly, she had been overly confident to get the job done quickly and was already regretting turning down Neil's earlier offer to help. She had just wanted to be helpful, everyone could see how stressed he had been over the past fortnight. Anything to take some weight off his shoulders would be a kind gesture.

Violet suspected the control freak director was fast reaching breaking point. His behaviour had become more erratic by the day and he had been verging on frantic ever since the Big Bust Up last Friday. The explosive showdown had resulted in both Nikki and Jimmy storming out of the theatre and left a distraught Ben close to tears. Not much had been said about it since, but it didn't take a genius to work out what had happened. And now everyone was on edge. Even Megan seemed irritated, although Violet failed to see how she factored into the situation.

A loud bang jerked her out of her focused, orga- nised zone.

Was that the main entrance door? But it couldn't be. Who on earth would come to the theatre at this twilight hour? Perhaps it was Neil returning to check up on her? Or maybe it was an intruder…

She froze as the vibrations of thudding footsteps echoed from the auditorium. Grabbing her phone in one hand she prematurely dialled 999 and hovered her thumb over the call button, poised to phone the police. Light-footed, she crept out of the office, padding quie- tly down the corridor.

Carefully, she made her way to backstage. While the stage itself was shrouded in darkness, the house lights provided a muted illumination of the audi- torium. Peering cautiously out from behind the curtain, her shoulders dropped as she breathed a sigh of relief.

It wasn't an intruder after all.

A familiar figure staggered into view. Clearly

drunk, he was fumbling with the entrance door, swaying unsteadily on his feet. It took him ages to lock the door successfully and turn the key. As he stumbled around, Violet finally got a good look at his face to confirm it was indeed who she suspected.

Peter Winters.

Albeit a distinctly more dishevelled Peter than she was used to. His normally immaculate dark blonde hair was greasy and matted and a visible sweat patch had spread across the back of his shirt. Violet stepped out from her hiding place into full view on the stage.

Clocking the movement, Peter visibly jumped when he saw her. "Fucking hell Violet, you scared the shit out of me!"

"I could say the same about you. I thought you were a burglar coming to rob the place. I almost phoned the police!"

"It's past midnight. What the hell are you doing here?"

"I'm finishing off creating the show programmes. I thought I'd be done hours ago, I didn't realise how long it would take me. The real question is – why are *you* here?"

Peter gave a dismissive laugh. "Thought I might sleep here. Didn't think I'd have to fight for privacy in the middle of the night."

Rocking unsteadily on his feet, he brandished a bottle of alcohol of some description in his left hand. Violet crept tentatively closer. With a second glance, she realised she was wrong. Peter wasn't just drunk at all; he was absolutely wasted. His piercing green eyes were bloodshot and bleary. A sheen of sweat covered his face, as though he was running a fever. She squinted at the bottle he had clutched to his chest. Whisky. It was over three quarters empty.

Peter took an unsteady step forward and swayed dramatically. For a fleeting moment, Violet thought he was going to collapse. Hurrying over, she ducked under his arm to steady him. With Peter leaning heavily on her for support, she helped him over to the stage. His weight was almost too much for her delicate shoulders. On more than one occasion he veered suddenly to one side nearly forcing them both to topple over. After what felt like an eternity to get him to the stage, it then took even longer to coax him into a seated position until he was, somewhat precariously, sat on the edge of it.

Peter took a swig from the whisky bottle, sighing in satisfaction.

Violet stood back, arms crossed as she looked him up and down, unable to keep the disdain from her face. "So, care to explain why you plan to sleep at the theatre tonight?"

Smirking, he waved her off with a casual flick of his hand. "None of your business missy. Now, scoot along. You're currently standing in my bedroom." He gave a loud hiccup that seemed to take him by surprise. He was still swaying even though he was sat down. Violet wondered briefly if he might fall off the stage.

She groaned wearily. Clearly, he was going to be impossible. "Alright fine. I'm going to go and get you some water, okay?" With that, she hurried away to fill a glass from the kitchenette.

She had never understood the desire to get ridicu-lously drunk. Violet enjoyed a glass of wine as much as everyone else, but she knew her limit and always stopped at one or two glasses. Happily tipsy, she just preferred it that way. Looking at Peter reminded her why. No doubt he would have a stinking hangover tomorrow.

When she returned, he was sat limply on the stage, his head hung. All the bravado he possessed before had leaked out of him and he sat deflated. He raised his head as Violet approached and she was shocked to see his eyes were watery, full of unshed tears.

"Peter! What's wrong?"

"We broke up. Me and Megan. That's why I didn't want to go back to my flat. Too many reminders of her. I couldn't face it." His voice was cracking, over-wrought with emotion.

"Oh my God, I'm so sorry." Violet pulled herself up to a seated position next to him on the stage. "Do you want to talk about it?"

Sniffing, Peter shook his head. "Not really. I don't understand what went wrong. I thought things were going fine. I feel like such an idiot." Words slurring, his voice came out a hoarse croak. He hiccupped a second time.

Violet placed a comforting hand on his shoulder. "These things happen. It'll work out for the best in time I'm sure." She passed him the glass of water which he glanced at briefly, unimpressed, before setting it down and having another swig of the whisky instead.

"Christ, break-ups are shit, aren't they?"

"I wouldn't know," admitted Violet, surprised by

her own candour.

Peter raised his eyebrows. "Seriously? You've never been with *anyone*? I thought that was a rumour."

Violet averted her eyes, her face growing hot. "I'm just waiting for the right person."

Peter snorted derisively and took another gulp of whisky.

Violet frowned. "I may be no expert in break-ups, but I know drinking yourself into oblivion isn't going to help matters. Don't worry about Megan. You're a catch Peter. A good-looking guy like you will find someone else in no time."

He stared at her, suddenly meek. "Why are you being so nice to me? I've always been so awful to you."

"That's not true."

"It is though. I tease you all the time. I'm mean, I say cruel things."

"You're not that bad." She could feel her cheeks burning.

Peter gave a small, sad smile. "You're a good person Violet." He let out a third drunken hiccup, followed by a loud belch. Smile fading, he turned away in embarrassment. "Shit, sorry. I'm such a fucking mess, no one was ever meant to see me in this state."

"Don't worry about it," said Violet kindly.

He hiccupped loudly again, the sudden spasm shaking his shoulders. "For Christ's sake, why can't I stop fucking hiccupping. It's so bloody annoying."

"Take deep breaths. And drinking the water will help," she said pointedly, gesturing to the untouched glass.

Peter stared at it and considered it for a brief second before looking at the whisky bottle in his hand and choosing that necked back another large mouthful.

Violet rolled her eyes in exasperation.

Holding up the near empty bottle, he shook it meaningfully, the last dregs sloshing about inside. "Shame to waste it. I'll drink the water after."

Taking a final gulp, Peter set the finished bottle down on the stage. He at least had the decency to turn away from her as he belched again, noisily into his hand. Sniffing, he hung his head in shame. This miserable wretch of a creature was a far cry from the confident, attractive man Violet admired. He looked broken, as though something had snapped inside of him.

Closing his eyes, he put a hand to his forehead. "Shit, I don't feel so good."

"I'm not surprised," Violet said coolly, sympathy fast fading from her voice. "Maybe the water would be a good idea?"

Peter lowered his hand shakily and hesitantly picked up the glass. He glowered at it as though it might hurt him and took a tentative sip.

"Go on, drink some more," encouraged Violet. *It was like mothering a small child.*

He took another tiny sip and grimaced.

"If you're going to puke, try and make it to the toilets okay? I don't fancy mopping the floor."

Peter shook his head slowly. "Nah, I'm alright." He didn't sound convinced.

Shoulders convulsing, he let out another tired-sounding hiccup, followed by an exasperated groan.

Brightly, Violet said, "My mum's method for

stopping hiccups never fails. Basically, you drink water but with your head tilted to one side. It's simple, but effective."

He looked at her sceptically.

"I swear! I know it sounds like an old wives' tale, but it really does work."

Shrugging, Peter tilted his head and drank to give it a go. He did look utterly ridiculous. Violet couldn't help but grin at the funny sight.

Noticing her glee, Peter poked her playfully in the ribs. "Hey, quit laughing. Or is this just a cunning ploy to make me look stupid?"

Giggling, Violet shook her head. "No! And look, it's worked, hasn't it? They've stopped."

Peter was silent for a moment, before nodding in surprised agreement. "You're right. How about that? Maybe you're a witch after all." Raising his head, he looked at her quizzically. "So, when's the last time *you* got drunk?"

Violet shrugged. "I wouldn't say I'm much of a drinker."

He arched an eyebrow. "You don't say? Alright, better question – when's the last time you did something you regretted?"

Violet's forehead creased into a slight frown. "Erm, dunno. I always try to focus on positives rather than regrets."

Peter cocked his head, incredulous. "Oh, come on, that's so lame! You've got to do better than that."

"Alright…how about I regret totally not realising how long it would take me to put the *Macbeth* programmes together and having to stay here past midnight."

"Ah, but then we wouldn't have met here tonight to have this conversation." His green eyes sparkled as he flashed her a dazzling smile, full of charm.

Violet could feel the colour climbing back to her cheeks and she dropped her head, embarrassed.

Oblivious to her blushing, Peter reached over to push a loose strand of hair back behind her ear. His hand lingered gently on her cheek, his breath warm on her neck. "Anyone ever tell you you're really pretty?"

Violet laughed. "Wow, you really are drunk!"

"I mean it. You're beautiful, an English rose."

She could feel her face turning scarlet. *Why did she always have to blush so easily?*

Peter grinned at her rosy cheeks. "Something I said?"

She returned his smile sheepishly. Before she knew what was happening, Peter reached over and kissed her hard on the lips. With his classic good looks, Violet had harboured a secret crush on him ever since they first met on the show. She was embarrassed to admit she even fantasised about being intimate with him.

The reality wasn't at all like how she had imagined. The kiss was slobbery, rushed. He fumbled clumsily with his hand, stroking her leg. She could smell the stench of stale whisky on his hot breath and could feel the sweat dripping from his upper lip.

But despite all that, Violet still found herself kissing him back. Peter slipped his hand onto her lower back and pulled her closer. She could feel herself getting flustered. Suddenly too hot, there was a relentless flutter in her stomach.

Was this what it felt like to be turned on?

But as Peter pressed himself against her and kissed her with such force she could barely breathe, Violet was gripped with a sudden sense of unease. Extricating herself from his embrace, she pulled away. "We shouldn't be doing this. You've got a girlfriend."

"*Ex*-girlfriend. We broke up, I told you."

"But you're drunk. It's not right. I'd be taking advantage."

He let out a low, mocking laugh. "Now's not the time to be a goody two-shoes. You're not taking anything. I'm right here – giving you the advantage."

Violet hesitated, chewing her lip nervously. Peter edged closer and caressed her nearest shoulder. She recoiled slightly as if she'd been stung. Up close he was physically intimidating – broad-shouldered and tall, towering over her even as they sat. The feeling of unease didn't abate, instead a sense of panic slowly consumed her. In one swift move Peter pushed her back onto the stage and clambered on top of her, his mouth locked on hers.

Struggling to catch her breath between kisses, Violet felt a spasm of fear shoot through her.

Things were moving far too fast.

Writhing under his body, she squirmed to move away. "Peter, wait. Let's take it slow."

Peter didn't respond. He had a glazed expression on his face and an insatiable hunger in his eyes. He fumbled with his jeans, pulling down the zipper.

Breathless, Violet struggled as she wailed, "Peter, I said *stop*. Please stop it. Get off me."

Her hands were on his chest, trying to push him

away. He was so much stronger than she was. A mouse attempting to fight a lion. She yelped in pain as he grabbed her wrists forcefully and slammed them onto the wooden floorboards.

"Quit whimpering. I thought you wanted this." His charming smile had vanished and his lips were twisted into a sneer.

"*No*. Peter stop! Not like this."

Panic rising in her throat, Violet's heart hammered in her chest. She kept straining against him, but he had her pinned down. She screamed, fully aware the theatre was so isolated no one would hear. A quick, sharp movement of Peter's hand brought a searing pain to her right cheek as he slapped her hard.

The pain stunned her for a moment, which was all the time Peter needed to get into position straddling her. Struggling desperately, she tried to claw her way out of his grasp. He tightened his hold, digging his fingernails deep into her wrists.

His expression had changed completely now to something she didn't recognise. He looked purely predatory. He was the hunter and she was the prey. A mere rabbit caught in his trap.

Still writhing beneath him, Violet's strength deserted her completely. Defeated, she squeezed her eyes shut and waited for it to be over.

After Peter was done, Violet wriggled free of his grip and clambered to her feet. Bolting for the entrance door she was relieved to see the key still in the lock. She had already started hastily opening the door, when Peter's hand appeared, pushing it firmly shut again.

Grabbing her shoulders tightly, Peter spun her around aggressively, slamming her body against the door effortlessly as if she weighed nothing. A rag doll in a child's hand.

Blood pounded in her ears as she stared up at him fearfully. The expression on his face was pure rage. Peter's eyes were wide, nostrils blaring. There was an explosion of excruciating pain as he smashed her head backwards against the wooden doorframe. Violet felt a wave of nausea come over her, but swallowed it down. His strong hands were at her throat, applying just the slightest pressure as his fingers caressed her windpipe.

"Didn't anyone ever tell you it's bad manners to go running off like that?"

Violet could muster nothing more than a whimper in response. His grip tightened and she found herself fighting to breathe.

"I think this should be our little secret don't you agree? I wouldn't want Megan to get jealous."

She tried to nod, but couldn't move under his vice-like grip.

"Tell anybody about this and I will kill you. That's a promise." His voice was low and menacing, almost a growl.

He crushed her windpipe a minute longer to emphasise his point. Violet felt her vision cloud and for a brief moment thought he would follow through with that promise there and then. But suddenly his fingers relinquished their grip.

Violet grappled with the door handle and, blinded by tears, darted out into the night.

Thursday 22nd March

The cast party would always have been a toe-curlingly awkward affair, even at the best of times. In his infinite wisdom, Neil had decided on the cost-effective option of bringing the party to the theatre instead of booking a restaurant or hitting a bar. The decidedly pathetic outcome was Neil's questionable iPhone music playlist on speaker and an embarrassingly low-budget selection of cheap beer and wine with a sorry-looking pile of supermarket buffet snacks.

In fairness, it could have worked out alright if it wasn't for the undeniable tension in the room. It seemed everyone in the cast was at loggerheads with someone. Neil and Emma were evidently still furious with each other and were going out of their way to avoid speaking. Whatever Nikki and Jimmy had been arguing about last Friday clearly wasn't fully resolved. Even though they were obviously still together, snuggled close, the mood between them had shifted somehow. Jimmy was acting distant and Nikki was being cloyingly clingy and overly enthusiastic about everything he said, as if she were trying to make something up to him.

Ben, to his credit, was the only one being close to sociable and had dutifully been working the room, chatting with everyone in turn. But even he seemed distracted, as though his thoughts were elsewhere.

And then there was Peter.

Apparently, his break-up with Megan had proved

short-lived as the pair had been giggling and holding hands for most of the night. Violet studied Megan closely, searching for any sign they had gone through a dramatic break-up, only to reunite two days later. Nothing in her behaviour seemed to indicate as such. If anything, Megan appeared to be more taken with Peter than ever, ignoring even Nikki to focus all of her attention solely on him. Violet wondered if he had simply lied and made the whole thing up in order to get close to her. It was an unnerving thought, stuck playing on a perpetual loop in her head.

Violet had spent the best part of the night skulking silently around the edge of conversations, quietly weaving around her fellow castmates and the technical team, trying to avoid being fully drawn into their banter. Naturally introverted, she always hated large social occasions such as this with so much awkward small talk and forced laughter. She would much rather be curled up at home with her nose in a good book.

She had been dreading tonight. For a while she had debated whether to go at all. But eventually she had come to the conclusion not showing her face would end up attracting unnecessary attention and raising too many difficult questions she couldn't face answering.

Violet was wearing a long-sleeved baby pink dress and kept tugging at the sleeves self-consciously. Her wrists were still tender to touch and there was a dull ache between her legs that hurt when she walked. Peter had caught her eye a few times from across the room, but so far she had managed to avoid him. It was as though they were playing a macabre version of cat and mouse and she was tired of feeling hunted.

Across the room Nikki suddenly threw her head back in an exaggerated reaction to laugh hysterically at one of Jimmy's jokes. One of her hands rested firmly on his leg and he had a protective arm hung loosely around her shoulders. But they both still seemed tense, on edge.

They're trying too hard, realised Violet. After the dramatic showdown during their blazing row, they both were clearly over eager to patch things up and to repair what had been broken. Consequently, they were both being far too keen to put on a show to convince everyone, or perhaps mainly themselves, that everything was fine.

It was only then Violet realised she had let her guard down, allowed herself to become distracted. Peter had sidled up next to her with Megan in tow.

"Violet, so great to see you." Feigning a smile, Peter stooped down to give her a quick embrace. He allowed his hand to rest for a moment too long on her arm.

A warning.

Stepping back, he slipped a casual arm around Megan's waist. It was as if he were silently challenging Violet, daring her to enquire about their relationship.

Peter's lips curled upwards into his signature sneer she remembered all too well. A world of meaning conveyed in one look. Megan begun talking about something but Violet couldn't focus on her words. A flood of panic overwhelmed her and nausea began to rise in her throat. Quickly excusing herself she darted away, hurrying past the couple.

Breathing a sigh of relief, Violet relaxed a little when she reached the safe refuge of the ladies toilets.

Peter couldn't follow her in, could he? Glancing uncertainly at the door, she took a moment to convince herself she was safe. Standing in front of the mirror, she steadied herself by gripping onto the sink basin. Lightheaded, she felt sick to her stomach. For a moment she worried she might actually throw up.

Catching sight of her reflection in the mirror, she grimaced. She looked a right state. There were dark bags under her sleep-deprived eyes, her skin was pale and her whole face had taken on a haunted demeanour. Peeling back her dress sleeves, Violet winced as she gingerly prodded at the tender inky black and blue bruises that had spread across both wrists. Somehow it comforted her to be reminded the bruises were still there. To know she was justified in her feeling of betrayal. It assured her she had every right to feel as wronged as she did. That no one deserved to be treated like that. Anger, sadness and fear all welled up inside her, a swirling whirlwind of emotions.

Too late, Violet heard the metallic clang of the door as someone stepped into the room behind her. Hastily she pulled down her sleeves, took a breath to compose herself and turned around in what she hoped was a casual manner. Nikki was stood in the doorway a shocked expression etched on her face. There was no doubt she had seen the bruises.

"Violet! What the hell happened to you?"

With a small groan, Violet attempted to push past her. "Nothing. I don't want to talk about it."

Instantly, Nikki blocked her way and placed a reassuring hand on her shoulder. "It's alright, you can tell me."

Flinching at her touch, Violet shrank back. Nikki's expression softened as she shuffled forward and pulled the door gently shut behind her.

"Did one of the guys do this to you?" There was a note of disbelief in her voice.

Shaking her head, Violet pleaded, "I really can't talk about it."

A look of understanding dawned on Nikki's face, a penny dropping into place. "Someone threatened you. Said you couldn't talk, is that right?"

Lowering her head, Violet gave a tiny nod.

Nikki edged closer to her. "You can trust me. I'll help you, I swear. You just need to tell me what happened."

Violet looked doubtful.

"I will do everything in my power to protect you. But I can't do that unless you talk to me."

Hesitating, Violet drew in a deep, shaky breath. *For some inexplicable reason there was something about Nikki that made her feel safe. She felt like she could be trusted.*

Closing her eyes, Violet made a snap decision and told Nikki everything.

The taxi Nikki had called for her had arrived at the theatre in no less than five minutes. That had to be some sort of record, even for London. Nikki had already disappeared to pick up Violet's coat and bag from the auditorium and had promptly returned to their safe haven of the ladies toilets as promised.

Violet had been taken aback by her kindness and compassion. They had never been particularly close, but Nikki had listened to her with the sympathy of a best friend. Despite Peter's death threat still looming over her, it had felt good to confide in someone. It was though a burden had been lifted and she could breathe a bit easier again.

Without judgement, Nikki had taken everything on board and had sensitively talked through their options. Then she had sprung into action, booking a taxi so Violet could leave the dreaded cast party.

That was Step One.

Violet wasn't sure she would have the guts to follow through with the next steps, but that wasn't tonight's problem.

Wrapping a protective arm around Violet's shoulders, Nikki guided her briskly to the theatre entrance. They both avoided meeting the confused stares of their fellow castmates. Nikki would deal with them afterwards, she had a cover story all sorted.

Just as they were about to step though the door, Nikki cast a hard glance over her shoulder. Cautiously, Violet peered back too. Across the auditorium, Peter stood silently in the midst of the small crowd milling around him. His cold eyes were locked onto Nikki's. His expression hardened as a dark shadow fell across his features. The calculating look on his face was unmistakable.

He knew Nikki knew.

*　　*　　*

Wringing her hands anxiously, Violet lowered her eyes to the floor. She was shaking slightly, shivering as though she was cold.

Zahra glanced triumphantly at the mirror. Out of sight, Robson took a deep breath, interlacing his fingers behind his head as he considered this new information.

So, Nikki was the only person to know about how Peter had attacked Violet. That gave him a strong motive to keep her quiet. After all, he was the one who had been so knowledgeable about previous incidences of onstage deaths at the cursed Scottish play.

Wearing a neutral expression, Zahra asked calmly, "Can I see your arms Violet?"

The young actress paled and instinctively grabbed the hems of her cardigan.

Patiently, Zahra continued, "Please, it's important. We need to corroborate your story."

Sighing wearily, Violet relented. Tentatively, she peeled back her sleeves to reveal a messy web of dark, ugly bruises spread across both wrists.

Behind the mirror, Robson grimaced as he chewed on a fresh mint. Disjointed details that had been swimming in his mind finally came into focus. He understood now why the teenager had been so cautious about never showing her arms. Zahra must have figured out what the young actress was trying to hide.

"So, what happens next?" asked Violet quietly.

Zahra gave her a reassuring smile. "We have a sexual assault nurse who specialises in this sort of thing. She can do an exam, take photographs of the bruising on your wrists. Then, we'll have to collect any forensic evidence, such as the clothes you were wearing that night."

Looking up in alarm, Violet shook her head firmly. "What? No way. You heard what Peter said. He'll kill me if he ever found out I had told you."

"Like I said before, we can protect you."

Violet shrank back into her chair, tears pooling in her eyes. "But you know what he's capable of. You saw what he did to Nikki?"

"You think Peter killed her?"

Violet stared at her with watery eyes. "It's the only explanation. It's my fault she's dead, I never should have told her."

Observing through the mirror glass, a disturbing thought suddenly occurred to Robson. *From what they had heard, Nikki Gowon was headstrong and determined. There was no way she would have let Peter get away with rape. She would have certainly confronted him about it. So, was she killed because Peter was trying to save himself? Or perhaps, it was in fact Violet who had decided to take it upon herself to make sure Nikki never spoke?*

After all, from experience, Robson had learnt to always watch the quiet ones.

CHAPTER EIGHTEEN

There's Daggers in Men's Smiles

Peter Winters sat opposite the two detectives, failing to suppress an amused smirk. Leaning back casually in his chair, his posture was relaxed as if he did this all the time. Much to Robson's irritation, the actor looked arrestingly handsome today, dressed in an expensive looking jacket, crisp white shirt and snug, tailored trousers. His dark blonde hair was coiffed, immaculately in place.

Beside him, his oily-haired lawyer shuffled through the towering stack of papers in front of him. The stout man's appearance was distinctly toad-like, with a round, chubby face, pockmarked skin and a snub nose.

Of course Peter lawyered up, thought Robson bitterly. *The guilty ones always did.*

Clearing his throat noisily, the lawyer sniffed and stared at them with beady eyes. "Let me get this straight – you're currently conducting a *murder* investigation, are you not? Yet you've dragged my client in here to address a supposed rape allegation. Is that right?"

"Who's to say the two crimes aren't connected?" said Zahra stonily. "It wouldn't be a huge jump from rape to murder."

Peter snorted. "I'm guilty of neither. This is a complete farce!"

The lawyer glared at him and Peter shrank back into silence. Turning back to the detectives, he continued, "So, this allegation came from Miss Violet Underwood?"

"*False* allegation," interjected Peter.

The lawyer's brow knitted together disapprovingly. "Do you have any idea how damaging that sort of accusation can be to an aspiring young actor? That sort of negative press has a habit of sticking around and clouding people's judgment. It could tarnish my client's reputation before he's even had the chance to properly establish himself in the industry."

Underneath the table, Robson balled his hands tightly into fists. *Fuck your precious client. Rapists don't deserve lawyers.*

"Mr Winters is a first-class student, predicted to graduate top of his class later this year. A star striker, head boy at his grammar school. There's nothing in his past to suggest he is capable of such a violent act."

"There's a first time for everything," Zahra muttered, unable to hide the contempt in her voice.

Across the table, Peter looked at her shrewdly. He showed no reaction, his face completely blank.

Unperturbed by the interruption, the lawyer continued, "Surely it's more likely this defamatory claim is merely a fabrication from a disgruntled co-star?"

Zahra bristled in agitation. "We can assure you our source is credible."

The lawyer shook his head dismissively. "I very much doubt that. What evidence do you even have against my client?"

Robson gave him an especially sour glance. "I can guarantee we will soon be able to have DNA evidence confirming Peter was intimate with Violet. And as you already know the CCTV footage places them both at the scene of the crime, they were definitely at Gemini Theatre last Tuesday night."

Robson caught the barest flicker in Peter's eyes that registered doubt. For a fleeting moment, he seemed beaten. But the blonde actor quickly composed himself and forced a humourless smile "I'm not denying sleeping with her. But it was all consensual, I swear. In fact, she initiated it. She was practically gagging for it."

"That's not what Violet told us."

Peter shrugged nonchalantly. "She's probably ashamed. I mean it's not exactly the most romantic way to lose your virginity, is it? No one's writing love songs about shagging onstage at a grimy theatre."

Zahra frowned, clearly unconvinced. "So, what's your version of events?"

The lawyer tried to protest, but Peter silenced him with a dismissive flip of his hand. The lawyer may have been the professional, but there was no doubt who was running this show.

"I'll tell you what happened. But it's no *version*, it's the truth."

*   *   *

Thursday 22nd March

Ever since Violet had left the cast party, Peter had been studiously avoiding Nikki, who was glaring daggers at him from across the auditorium. He couldn't be bothered with any more drama tonight. He already had his hands full with Megan; to say she had been hot and cold with him for the last few days was the understatement of the year. It was like comparing a scorching summer day with the depths of winter. He never knew what he was going to get.

Today at least Megan was being warm and affectionate – the model girlfriend. A far cry from when she had coldly broken up with him just two days ago.

"Peter, got a minute?"

Damn. How had Nikki managed to creep up next to him unnoticed?

Her voice was light, conversational. But she had an insincere smile plastered on her face that didn't quite reach her eyes.

Peter hung back for a moment, then relented. He could play along in this little charade.

Nikki edged tentatively closer. "Got anything to tell me?" Her voice had changed, now it was low and angry.

He gave a little shrug, keeping it casual.

"I was talking to Violet earlier. She sure had some interesting things to say about you."

Peter blinked and chose to stay silent.

Her voice dropped to a whisper, so quiet it was almost inaudible. "Tell me it's not true. Tell me you didn't *rape* her?"

He let out a strangled half-laugh that echoed against the high walls. It sounded more jovial than he had intended. "Is that what she told you? Damn, that girl has an active imagination."

Nikki frowned a little, confused. "So, you *didn't* have sex with her?"

Wagging his finger condescendingly, Peter shook his head. "Now, I didn't say that. We may have slept together, but she was into it. It sure as hell wasn't rape."

Nikki's face tightened. "That's not what she says."

He smiled innocently. "I imagine she's embarrassed. Afraid to tell Mummy and Daddy. You know she was a virgin? It wasn't exactly the most romantic first time. I have to admit I was pretty drunk. I wasn't exactly showing her my best moves."

"So, what happened?"

"Well, I did come to the theatre late on Tuesday night. That much is true. I was still reeling after the unexpected breakup with Megan; I'm sure you've heard all about that. Anyway, I'd been out drinking alone, you know drowning my sorrows and all that shit. I was an idiot, wasn't paying attention to the time. I left it too late, didn't realise the tube had stopped when I tried to get home. A taxi would have cost a fortune to get back to Islington and I would have had to wait for ages. Then, I remembered I had a key for the theatre, which was close enough to walk to. Figured I would crash there, leave early before Neil got there in the morning and he would be none the wiser."

Nikki nodded doubtfully. She didn't look convinced. "Right, so that's why you turned up at the theatre, I wasn't disputing that. What happened afterwards? How does Violet come into it?"

Peter took a slow, steady breath, choosing his words carefully. "I ran into her completely by chance. She was at the theatre late too, burning the midnight oil putting those show programmes together. Neil really has got her wrapped around his little finger, hasn't he? Anyway, we got chatting and one thing led to another and we ended up kissing."

"And then?"

A smirk crossed Peter's lips. "Well, can't you imagine what came next? Things got more heated from there and before I knew it, we were making love."

Regarding him coldly, Nikki sniped, "How romantic of you. It was barely a few hours since you broke up with my best friend and already you were jumping onto another new girl?"

Peter narrowed his eyes. "I think you're forgetting Megan's the one who dumped me. If anyone deserves any pity here, it's me. If I'm totally honest with you I felt humiliated by the whole thing. Everyone knows Megan was punching way above her weight, I was well out of her league. As if *she* had the audacity to dump *me*."

Haughtily folding her arms, Nikki scowled at him fiercely.

Right, they were friends. Probably not the best way to endear her to him. Swiftly changing tack, he continued, "Look I'm sorry. I know you're friends. It's just been like walking on eggshells with Megan recently. You know how she can be. I can do nothing right, everything I say pisses her off in some way and she flies off the handle over the smallest thing."

Nikki's expression softened slightly and she pursed her lips thoughtfully. "Did Meg talk to you at all? Before you broke up?"

"Not really. The whole thing took me by surprise. I didn't see it coming. One minute she was in my arms kissing me, the next she was screaming we weren't compatible and that we were over. Then she stormed out before I could even get a word in."

Nikki nodded comprehendingly. Something in her eyes made Peter think she knew more than he did. "Let me guess, then the next day she took it all back. Apologised for making a scene and begged you to get back together?"

Frowning, he said, "Something like that. Although I wouldn't say I welcomed her back with open arms. I'm still trying to figure out if she's worth the effort."

"I'll speak to her. Meg's not being entirely honest with you."

Peter's frown deepened. "And what exactly is that supposed to mean?"

"You'll know soon enough. Anyway, let's get back to Violet. You hooked up with her at the theatre?"

"To be truthful, I was absolutely shit-faced. I wasn't thinking straight. Violet just happened to be there at the right time."

"And she was a willing participant in all of this?"

He suppressed another smirk. "She was into it, yeah. Come to think of it, it was her who made the first move."

Nikki grimaced slightly. "I saw the bruises Peter. Her arms are black and blue. It doesn't exactly scream consensual sex to me."

For a brief moment Peter faltered, then he quickly regained his composure with a smug grin. "What can I say, she likes it rough."

"Who, *Violet?* That seems pretty unlikely, especially for a virgin."

Shrugging dismissively, Peter agreed, "I know, right? Who would have guessed?"

Nikki fell silent, lost in her own thoughts. For the first time in the conversation Peter felt as though he had the upper hand.

"I'm not sure…"

"I'm telling you," he insisted. "She loved it. I was shocked too, but decided to go along with it. Suppose she had no scope of comparison if you catch my drift."

Brow creased in confusion, Nikki stared at him. "Then why would she cry rape?"

He gave an angry snort. "How the hell am I supposed to know? Maybe she's just trying to get attention? Or perhaps she simply regrets it? Violet's a romantic. Probably wanted a better first-time story to reminisce about."

"Well, whatever you did, Violet's pretty upset about it. I think Neil should be made aware of the situation."

She was testing him, he could tell. Peter held up a hand in a cautionary gesture. "Now, we don't need to make any rash decisions. Do we really need to involve more people?"

"I thought you said you didn't do anything wrong? That you have nothing to hide?"

"I don't! But it's embarrassing enough as it is without dragging my name through the mud anymore. I mean *Violet the Virgin*? Seriously? I could do so much better than her. I'm kinda pissed at myself. I'm going to end up with a reputation for hooking up with sub-par chicks."

"Wow, you really are a creep, aren't you? I can't believe I've let you date Meg for so long. How did I not see it?"

Peter glowered at her. "Coincidentally you might want to spare a thought for Megan in this sorry saga. Especially now we're back together. It's not exactly going to fill her with joy to hear about all of this, is it? Particularly when, if you think about it, the whole thing is really her fault."

Nikki raised her eyebrows. "You have a funny idea about where to place blame." Then, she sighed and relented. "Okay, let's keep Meg out of it. She's dealing with enough already. She doesn't deserve to be caused any more pain by you. I've got an idea about what we could do about this."

Peter gave her a cold, reproving stare. He could feel the anger vibrating off himself. With a final, severe look thrown in his direction, Nikki turned on her heel and started to walk briskly away.

His expression darkened. *That girl was going to be a problem, he could tell.*

Impulsively, he stepped forward and grabbed her arm roughly. He spun her around so his face was only inches from hers. "Now, don't do anything stupid. Believe me, you don't want to piss me off."

His tone was flat, cold. Intended to instil fear. But if Nikki was afraid, she didn't show it.

Ripping her arm out of his grasp, she glared up at

him defiantly. "I wouldn't want to do that, *would I?"*

Feigning a smile, she left the threat hanging there as she edged away out of his sight.

* * *

"So, you *did* sleep with Violet Underwood?"

Peter grinned. "Last I checked, there's no law against that." There was a note of satisfaction lingering in his voice. He had told his story so convincingly that Robson had almost believed him.

Almost.

He was struck once again by how calm and relaxed the actor was. Like he had been preparing for this moment. As though his previous interview had simply been a rehearsal for this master performance. "And you'd been drinking?"

Peter let out a low chuckle. "So, what if I had? That's not a crime. If you're going to start arresting people for having drunken sex, you'll have to lock up half of London! Granted, I didn't show her my best moves, but she was into it regardless. Not that she had anything to compare it to, mind you. Besides, Violet's had a major crush on me since day one, anyone can tell you that."

"She tells a different story."

Peter gave a non-committal shrug. "Guess it's my word against hers." The actor's voice was maddeningly calm. Next to him, Zahra stiffened in frustration.

"But why on earth would she put herself through such hell if she wasn't telling the truth? What would she stand to gain?"

Peter gave a disinterested grunt. "Beats me. All I can say is she was willing on the night."

His lawyer nodded in approval. "Women who have sex with someone and regret it later do not have the right to call their partner a rapist."

Skin prickled with heat, Robson's breath shortened as his anger was roused.

At his side, Zahra straightened herself with a grimace. "And how about the fact Violet's wounds are consistent with forcible sexual assault? The bruises on her arms, the internal damage?"

"Don't answer that Peter," interjected the lawyer, murmuring something inaudible in his ear. "As my client has tried to explain, it appears the young lady in question had a certain sexual preference."

"Yes, I can imagine that," said Zahra sarcastically. The look of incredulity on her face was unmistakable.

Robson groaned in exasperation. He could feel this interview starting to slip away from them. There was no denying Peter was crafty. He knew exactly what to say and how to say it.

An excellent performance.

Narrowing her eyes, Zahra continued, "Let's talk about Peter's friend, Nikki Gowon. Our murder victim and coincidentally the only other person who knew about this. What do you have to say about her untimely death? Awfully convenient, wouldn't you say?"

Peter said nothing. There was something unkind about the set of his face.

Shifting uncomfortably in his chair, the lawyer cleared his throat. "I'm not sure I appreciate this line of questioning. I think you'll find that is pure conjecture. A completely unsubstantiated and unjust accusation against my client."

Biting his thumbnail absentmindedly, Peter seemed distracted. Robson remembered how he had noticed earlier that all his nails had been chewed down to stumps.

A nervous habit indeed.

Zahra frowned. "Here's what I think Peter. I believe you were terrified of the ugly truth being exposed. Kind of threatens your golden boy status, doesn't it? Being branded a rapist would be somewhat damaging to your career prospects after graduating, not to mention a possible jail sentence."

Gritting his teeth, Peter muttered, "You can't prove anything. You've got nothing on me."

"Give us time." Try as he might, Robson couldn't stop his voice from rising. Underneath the table he clenched his fists tight.

The lawyer coughed harshly. "Are you done intimidating my client? I suppose by now you've realised the obvious flaw in the logic of your ridiculous theory of him being the murderer?"

The detectives traded concerned glances. Neither could work out why the lawyer suddenly looked so pleased with himself.

"What do you mean?"

Shuffling the papers in front of him into a neat pile, the lawyer gazed at them with a smug expression. "We all agree the cast party took place on Thursday 22nd March, is that correct?"

With a sinking feeling, Robson nodded grimly and

dug his fingernails deep into his palms, relishing the brief distraction the pain brought.

Drawing himself up to full height in his chair, the lawyer concluded scathingly, "So, your somewhat ludicrous claim is that Mr Winters somehow managed to source an exact replica of the ornate prop knife to murder Nikki Gowon in less than twenty-four hours? Ask any knife shop, master craftsmanship like that certainly takes longer than a day."

The words hit Robson like a punch in the stomach. He swore quietly under his breath. *Damn, the lawyer was right.* There was no chance Peter would have been able to commission the bespoke knife in such a short space of time. Nikki's murder was pre-meditated and if Peter had only argued with her the day before, he couldn't be the killer.

After everything, they were right back at square one.

Peter gave a triumphant snort of laughter. "*See?* Told you it wasn't me."

Robson took a deep breath. It took every ounce of his strength not to leap across the table and slap him. "So, Peter, got any ideas of your own about the case?"

The blunt question caught the blonde actor by surprise. "Erm…I dunno. Anyone tell you about the 'Big Bust Up,' as we coined it? Quite the spectacle. I think maybe Ben would be the best person to fill you in on that one. I'd hate to steal his thunder."

Peter smirked, a wicked glint in his eye. His smugness made Robson lose the small semblance of self-control he had left. Without warning, he slammed a fist on the table and leaned in to address Peter in a snarl, "Don't think for one second you've got away with everything. You're still a goddamn rapist, we're going to bury you so fucking deep you're going to wish you'd never set foot in that theatre."

"Robson!" Zahra glared at him stonily.

With another harsh cough, the lawyer rose to his feet, motioning to Peter to follow suit. "I think we're finished here. Do get in touch if you come across any actual evidence."

Peter loitered in the doorway after the lawyer had stomped out. "I guess you better destroy your records of that interview. Unless you want me to file an official complaint against police harassment. I'm sure your superiors would love to hear how you threatened me and tried to coerce me into giving a confession." With an ugly smile smeared across his face, he slipped quietly out of the room.

For a moment, neither of the detectives said anything. Then, Robson sighed heavily. "I bloody hate lawyers."

Shaking her head, Zahra scowled darkly. "Why couldn't you just stick to the script for once?"

Robson dropped his eyes to the floor, he couldn't bring himself to see the disappointment he knew would be etched in her face. "Look, I'm sorry. It's just we're investigating a murder and we've already stumbled across a rapist. It's like they're bloody cockroaches, always more coming out of the woodwork. I can't stand it."

Zahra shot him a reprimanding stare. "No, you know what, I'm past hearing excuses. Don't you realise you might have cost us that case? Where's the justice for Violet then?"

"I said I was sorry."

"I don't want to hear it. Just take a break Robson, we'll push back the next interview a few hours. And pull yourself together, I need you on the ball. I'm fed up of being your minder, rather than your partner." Pushing back her chair, Zahra stood. "Oh, and another thing – if you think for one second you have me fooled with that so-called water bottle, you're an idiot."

Robson's mouth dropped open, a little O of surprise.

Zahra paused in the doorway, hand on the handle. Without looking back, she added under her breath, "I thought you wanted to make your father proud."

CHAPTER NINETEEN

Come What Come May

Two hours, four coffees and twelve mints later, Robson and Zahra were reunited back in the interview room, the uncomfortable tension an unspoken wedge between them. They had both been relieved when half an hour earlier PC Armstrong had delivered another update confirming that all of the deleted text messages and call history from Nikki's phone had been retrieved. Unsurprisingly, the director Neil Hillton featured strongly on the long call list, but interestingly he hadn't been the only one she had spoken to at length. That honour belonged to the actor currently sat in front of them.

"Can I remind you once again of your right to a solicitor? You're being questioned under caution now, as we've explained it's a little different than when we spoke before."

Ben Grahame gave a hollow laugh. "Different in the sense that you think I did it?" He shook his head resolutely. "No way! I'm innocent. I've got nothing to hide. I don't need a lawyer."

"Fine, suit yourself. We've called you back in to ask you a few more questions about your relationship with Nikki Gowon. I thought you said you didn't talk outside of rehearsals?"

"We don't…we didn't." Correcting himself, Ben's shoulders sagged. "I still can't believe she's really gone. I always assumed she'd make it and we'd all just continue on with our lives as normal."

Robson regarded him with a grim smile. "That's understandable. But unfortunately, we're now dealing with a murder investigation."

"I would never want to hurt Nikki. I adored her. Someone must have planted that prop knife in my jacket. I swear I know nothing about that."

Robson held up a hand to silence him. "We're not here to talk to you about the prop knife again."

"Oh," Ben slumped back in his chair. "What's this about then?"

"You maintain that you didn't have a relationship with Nikki outside of the show?"

"That's right."

"So, can you explain why she called you three times last Friday evening?"

Ben froze. "You know about that?"

"We sure do. Just because a call history log can be deleted doesn't mean we can't trace the calls."

Ben's mouth dropped open, his next words silenced on his lips.

"Now, one of those phone calls between you lasted over an hour. What on earth were you talking about?"

Ben shook his head in alarm. A new darkness seemed to be emanating from him as though Nikki's death haunted their conversation. "It's not important, at least I don't think it is. Nikki was just calling to apologise. She'd been arguing with Jimmy earlier that day at the theatre. I kind of ended up getting caught in the middle."

"Pretty long apology, don't you think?" Zahra cut in. "Her boyfriend had good reason to be paranoid, didn't he?"

Visibly flustered by the question, Ben squirmed uncomfortably in his seat. "There were a few things we had to talk through, some things that happened. But I didn't hurt her, I would never do that."

Robson watched the dreadlocked actor closely as he spoke. He could hear the hurt in his voice. There wasn't the slightest doubt in his mind that he had adored Nikki. But that didn't mean he hadn't killed her. He wouldn't be the first person to kill for love.

Elbows rested on the table, Robson leaned forward. "Why don't you tell us the full story about what happened on Friday? No omissions this time."

*   *   *

Friday 16th March

"'Mock the time with fairest show: false face must hide what the false heart doth know'." Ben delivered his lines flawlessly without even glancing down at his tattered script.

Faint sounds of distant talking floated through the

thin walls. At Nikki's request, they were back in their familiar backstage rehearsal room, both safe for now from the prying eyes of Neil. The director had been insufferable for the last week, snapping constantly and criticising everything. Ben couldn't remember him being this pedantic about *Romeo and Juliet*. It was slowly driving the whole cast insane, Nikki especially. Today she seemed particularly distracted, drifting through their scenes on autopilot with a deep sense of melancholy hanging over her.

Ben kept catching her staring at him with a wistful, faraway look in her eyes. There was an unreadable dreamlike expression on her face.

It looked like longing.

But no, he had to be mistaken. He had attempted to go down that road before and still felt embarrassed about his earlier rejection. There was no way she would have flipped one hundred and eighty degrees to be suddenly enamoured with him just six days later.

Yet, still she was looking at him in a way he had never seen before.

"What are you staring at?"

Giving her head a little shake, Nikki forced herself out of her daze. "Nothing. Sorry. You remind me of... never mind, it's not important," she said apologetically, then cast her eyes back down to her script.

Following suit, Ben began reading from where they had left off.

Interrupting, Nikki asked sheepishly, "Do you mind if we revisit Act One, Scene Five?"

"Sure." He shrugged casually, a satisfied smile tugging at his lips.

They could practice that scene as often as she wanted.

Nikki read her lines in a soft voice, almost hypnotic. Ben couldn't help but stare in admiration. It was hard to believe she had stepped into the role only eight days ago. Lady Macbeth was clearly a part she had been destined to play. She had already memorised the vast majority of the role to flawless perfection.

Nikki's voice trailed off as her gaze came to rest on his face.

Damn, he'd completely missed his cue.

"Sorry! I totally messed it up."

Her lips twitched a bittersweet half-smile. "No worries."

Ben returned the smile with a wide grin. "I was just thinking about how awesome you are. I can't believe how quickly you've nailed this part. You should be really proud, it's so impressive."

She gave an embarrassed shrug. "Not really. I was the understudy after all. I knew most of it already."

"Yeah, but you play it perfectly. You're amazing. It's an honour to play Macbeth opposite you." He was acutely aware he was gushing and mentally reined himself in.

Luckily, Nikki didn't seem interested. Her eyes were fixed on his, but she was looking right through him, not listening to what he was saying. A strange look was on her face again. An expression he couldn't decipher.

Smiling kindly, Nikki touched his arm encouragingly. "Come on, let's get back into character. The best bit is still to come."

What exactly was she implying by that? Could she

really mean what he thought?

Thoughts whirring around in his head, Ben fumbled his way through the dialogue. Suddenly nervous, he fluffed his lines a few times, but Nikki nodded reassuringly. Her lips kept flickering, as though she was about to smile.

When the time came for their onstage kiss, he could have sworn Nikki was uncharacteristically nervous too. She shifted her weight from one foot to another, squinting at his face intently as though she was seeing him for the first time.

Stepping forward to embrace her lovingly, he felt her body stiffen in his arms. But when his soft lips touched hers, he felt her press back with commitment. When Ben moved to pull away and continue the scene, Nikki hooked a hand gently around his neck and guided his face back towards hers, kissing him with renewed passion. For the briefest moment Ben was taken aback, then he swallowed down his confusion.

This is *what she had meant. The best bit indeed.*

Still gripping his neck, Nikki pressed her curvaceous body against his chest and wrapped her arms around him, squeezing tight. Ben let her lips brush against his and reached up to feel the smooth, flawless skin of her cheek. He heard her breath catch at his touch.

He had no idea what had prompted Nikki's sudden change of heart. Last time when he had kissed her hopefully, she had been quick to assure him it was never going to happen. The woman before him now seemed like a different person. Ben's mind was racing as he tried to stop himself obsessing over it.

This is what he had wanted all along. So, what if he didn't know what had finally convinced her. Just go with it.

Heart pounding, the pulsing deafened him as it filled his ears. Slipping a hand beneath Nikki's top, Ben caressed the supple curve of her back. Not to be outdone, her hand dropped to his crotch as she unzipped his jeans and reached inside. Gasping, Ben looked down at her. She wore a slightly glazed expression and there was a desperate sadness in her eyes. He felt a sudden pang of guilt.

Was it irresponsible for him to go along with it, with no questions asked?

Reluctantly, he pulled himself away. "Nikki…"

Shaking her head, she put a finger to his mouth. "Don't ruin the moment Ben. You're the one who wanted to get me alone."

"You're putting words into my mouth."

"And ideas into your head? Oh, please, I don't think so. Those ideas were already there, isn't that right?"

Ben faltered, unsure of how to respond.

Eyes glistening, Nikki smiled and seized his face in her hands. "Don't talk. Just…be with me."

Without a second thought, Ben relented. He wasn't going to argue with that. She was clearly giving him the go-ahead. Heart still thudding, goosebumps erupted on his arms as her tender touch made him shudder. A sense of elation flooded his body, he felt intoxicated by her. It was everything he had dreamed of and more. Forgetting his doubts, he threw caution to the wind and began to lose himself in her.

In the heat of the moment, neither of them noticed the shadowy figure stood at the door, silently watching them.

*   *   *

Ben stared at the large one-way mirror, quietly contemplating something.

"Why didn't you tell us this before?"

"Oh yeah, that would have sounded brilliant, wouldn't it? You know that girl whose stabbing you're investigating? Well, I slept with her even though I knew she was in a relationship and we got caught by her boyfriend who stormed off in a jealous rage? That doesn't sound so great for me, does it? Or Jimmy for that matter. Makes us both look guilty as fuck."

"Better than trying to hide it from us," Zahra said reasonably.

Ben let out an exasperated groan. It was a while before he spoke again. He was still staring absently at the mirror, thinking about something else. "God, maybe I did kill her after all."

Robson frowned in confusion. "Care to explain what you mean by that?"

"I know it sounds like I'm incriminating myself, but what if we pushed Jimmy over the edge? What if he killed her out of jealousy because she cheated on him? Maybe I am to blame after all." Ben's head sagged and he dropped his eyes to the table.

"There were two people there; Nikki was just as much at fault as you. Cheating is in a different league than murder though. Jimmy walked in on you both shortly after that point? And then there was the infamous showdown which happened between the couple at the theatre that everybody has been referencing?"

Reluctantly, Ben nodded. He had a searing, tortured look in his eyes. "I think you're best speaking to Jimmy directly. He'll be able to give you a more detailed account than I can."

Zahra gave a world-weary sigh. "Do any couples actually stay together without cheating? Is no relationship sacred these days?"

Robson chuckled dryly. "Spoken like a true cynic!"

"Seriously though, I've never known a case so steeped in depravity. Are all theatre shows this scandalous?"

"No idea. Maybe I should have stayed in the theatre business after all! Also, didn't I tell you from the beginning there would be secret love affairs?"

Zahra smiled a little. "Slow down Sherlock. The case isn't solved yet. I never disputed there might be some, what did you call it? *Hanky panky.* But a good old-fashioned love triangle doesn't necessarily provide the motive for murder."

"But you heard what Ben said. Jimmy caught them in the act, literally. That's enough to drive anyone crazy."

"And set Nikki's jealous boyfriend on a murderous rampage? Fits a bit too perfectly, don't you think?"

"So, what's your alternative theory?"

"I'm not sure exactly," she admitted. "I just believe it's rarely that simple."

CHAPTER TWENTY

The Grief That Does Not Speak

R obson sucked in a deep breath and focused his attention on Nikki's boyfriend, sat before them for the third time. "So, just to confirm, you've chosen to waive your right to free and independent legal advice and you understand your rights as they've been explained to you?"

"Yes, I bloody understand," snapped Jimmy, failing to disguise his anger. "How many times do I have to tell you? I didn't kill my girlfriend." His hands were on the table, tightened into fists as he gave the detectives a hostile stare.

Robson shrugged. "Alright, so you agree to proceed with the interview without a lawyer. I guess that's your choice. We need to ask you a few questions, pick your brains on some areas we're still trying to get clear on. Partners often know more than they realise."

The curly-haired actor nodded silently, his clenched fists shaking slightly.

"Okay then, let's start with your argument with Nikki a week ago last Friday."

A chagrined smile flickered on Jimmy's face. "That bloody argument. I was wondering when you'd find out about that."

"Probably would have been a good idea to tell us yourself."

Jimmy shrugged idly, not really paying attention. He looked annoyed or maybe just resigned. Robson couldn't fully read his expression.

"Ben already told us about hooking up with Nikki," continued Robson. "We already know about your fiancée's infidelity."

Jimmy tensed, lowering his voice to a murmur. "So, you think I killed her out of jealousy, is that it?" His tone was even, but his composure was starting to slip, his breath shortening. Not for the first time, Robson got the distinct impression the actor was wrestling with some kind of self-censorship, as though he was weighing up how honest he should be.

"We just want to understand what happened after that confrontation."

After a brief silence, Jimmy suddenly slammed his fist down onto the table. Leaping to his feet, his chair clattered loudly to the floor. "What exactly are you accusing me of?"

"Like I said, all we want to know is what happened next," said Robson evenly.

Jimmy's expression was grim, all the colour drained from his face. "I'll say it again. *I. Did. Not. Kill. My. Girlfriend.*"

*   *   *

Friday 16th March

"William Shakespeare was a master at creating exqui-sitely tragic figures. Just look at Macbeth and his wife. Driven by greed and ambition they become comp-letely consumed by their bloodthirsty quest for power, which ultimately led to their downfall," explained Neil in a surprisingly authoritative tone.

Jimmy's phone buzzed in his back pocket. Ignoring it, he tried to focus his attention back on Neil who was explaining the intricacies of the current scene. His phone vibrated again insistently. Waiting until the director turned away, he surreptitiously pulled the phone out and glanced down at the locked screen.

Megan Newbold.

Jimmy frowned in confusion. Megan and him never texted each other. Other than Nikki, they had no shared interests whatsoever. Curious, he tapped in his pin number to read the full message.

Come quickly to the backstage storeroom. Hurry, it's important. You need to see this.

Pinpricks of sweat erupted all over his body as Jimmy felt a billowing sense of dread.

Nikki was rehearsing with Ben. What if…

He didn't allow himself to finish that thought. Mumbling a hasty apology, he promptly rushed offstage. As he raced down the backstage corridor, he tried to ignore his stomach doing somersaults as he fought off a rising feeling of nausea. Without hesit-ation, Jimmy flung open the heavy storeroom door.

And his heart sank.

Nikki and Ben jumped, pure terror on their faces.

He had certainly caught them in a compromising position.

Nikki squealed and hastily squirmed to extricate herself from their semi-naked embrace. Pushed up against the far wall, she peered at him from over Ben's bare shoulder.

"Jimmy! What are you doing here?"

He stared blankly at the pair, his face a study in contempt. Ben scrambled to pull up his jeans from around his ankles. From his vantage point Jimmy could only see his naked butt cheeks rather than the full-frontal view. That explicit view was reserved for his girlfriend, who was speedily attempting to dress herself.

Jimmy's face darkened as he felt a flash of intense rage flood through him.

Ben stepped forward, hands still fumbling with his jean zipper. "Jimmy, mate, it's not what it looks like."

"Is that right? Because it looks like you're fucking my girlfriend."

Ben flinched as though the words had stung him. "But this is the first time, I swear. Just this once. We haven't been fooling around this whole time."

Jimmy laughed scornfully. "Well, great! That's the best fucking news I've heard all day."

Nikki shot Ben a sharp look and he shrank back into silence. "Jimmy, my love, we need to talk." She spoke in a measured, placating tone, hands raised like she was calming a wild animal.

"No shit." Jimmy spat the words. "Really Nikki?

Screwing around with your onstage lover? What a bloody cliché! I thought better of you." He spoke through gritted teeth, hands clenched into fists.

Ben hung his head, staring at the ground as though he hoped it would swallow him whole.

Nikki bit her lip and looked at him tentatively. "It's not what you think. Just let me explain." There was a desperate edge to her voice as she pleaded that Jimmy had no time for.

"Oh, believe me. I understand perfectly."

Cocking her head, Nikki studied him curiously. "How come you turned up here anyway?"

Jimmy snorted, incredulous. "That's the issue here? That you got *caught*?" He was yelling with a fury that made Nikki wince. As she recoiled, he could tell he was scaring her. She had never seen him this angry before.

"Sorry, no that's not what I meant," said Nikki desperately. Drawing a deep, shaky breath, her dark eyes pooled with unshed tears. "You deserve to know everything. It's time I told you about Max."

Jimmy stared at her in disbelief. "*Max*? Who the fuck is *Max*? Don't tell me you've got a third guy on the go as well?"

"Max is my ex-boyfriend." Her voice caught and a single tear rolled slowly down her cheek. "I need to tell you about him. It's the only way you can possibly understand."

Jimmy shook his head violently. Face hardened, his eyes remained cold. "Believe me, I have zero interest in understanding. We're over." Turning abruptly, he stormed out of the room, blinking back tears that threatened to blind him.

Stomping across the auditorium, Jimmy could feel the weight of his castmates' stares as they all paused what they were doing to gawp at him. A patter of hurried footsteps echoed behind him as Nikki ran to catch up.

"Jimmy! Wait, please. I can explain." She was sobbing freely now.

He shot her a scathing look. "I've told you, I'm not interested."

She grabbed his arm tightly. "You can't just walk away from me like this."

"Watch me." Jimmy's voice was loud and harsh, reverberating around the cavernous hall. He was vaguely aware of the other actors shuffling awkwardly about on the stage, unsure of what to do.

"You're making a scene." Nikki's voice had dropped to a hushed whisper.

He laughed bitterly. "And whose fault is that? I don't care. I'm leaving." Yanking his arm away aggressively, he turned his back on her and walked out.

Jimmy and Nikki drove in stony silence, unspoken words a gaping chasm between them. Tightly gripping the steering wheel, Jimmy glared straight ahead, paying little attention to the oncoming traffic. He still couldn't believe he had allowed himself to get talked into this situation.

After storming out of the theatre, Nikki had raced after him in floods of tears and pleaded with him desperately to go with her and meet Max. "It'll only take ten minutes to get there, then you'll understand.

Please Jimmy, you owe it to me to give me ten minutes to explain myself."

He had stared at her as if she had gone insane. "I owe you nothing."

With that, he had abandoned her to get into his car. But before he had chance to lock it, Nikki had scooted nimbly to the other side and slid defiantly into the passenger seat. Swearing at her, he had shouted at her to get out and leave him alone. But Nikki had simply shaken her head and obstinately refused to be moved.

Crying hysterically, huge tears streamed down her cheeks, as she continued to argue. "You have every reason to be mad at me. But please just give me a chance to explain why I acted like I did. You might understand my motivation if you meet Max."

Jimmy shook his head in stunned disbelief. "So, your solution to me walking in on you fucking your co-star is to drag me off to meet your ex-boyfriend, who for all I know you're still shagging as well? Are you crazy?"

"Please. It's only ten minutes. You owe it to us to learn the truth."

"There is no *us*." He said it with a flat finality.

But he also knew how stubborn Nikki could be, she would argue for hours until she got her own way. Sighing heavily, he finally relented. "Fine, fuck it. I'll meet him. Although I can't promise I won't kick the shit out of him when I do."

She smiled, evidently relieved. "I won't hold you back. Come on, I'll show you the way."

That had been ten minutes ago, they must be fast approaching their destination. Unless Nikki had lied about that too.

He wouldn't put it past her. If someone had asked him this morning if Nikki was capable of cheating, he would have defended her without hesitation. She had been nothing but loyal to him for two years, or so he thought. But now? He was starting to doubt if he knew the real Nikki at all.

"Turn left here."

"Left? *Here?*" Jimmy repeated uncertainly.

Nikki nodded. "Trust me, I'll tell you everything soon."

Pulling into a parking space, Jimmy turned off the engine and stared dumbfounded at her. "I think you've got a lot of explaining to do."

She swallowed. "I know. But first, I'll take you to meet Max."

Quietly, Nikki led the way down the winding path. The temperature had plummeted earlier in the after-noon and now glittering snowflakes drifted down soundlessly, enveloping everything in a ghostly cold-ness. Shafts of sunlight illuminated the whitened scene ahead as the snow began to settle, dusting the ground like icing powder. Only the gentle breeze broke the peaceful sound of silence as they made their way forward, leaving shallow footprints in the freshly lain snow behind them.

After what felt like forever, Nikki came to an abrupt halt under a bare birch tree. She turned to look nervously at him. A million questions were buzzing around in Jimmy's head. He didn't know what he had been expecting, but it definitely hadn't been this.

"Jimmy, meet Max. My ex-boyfriend. The first man I ever loved."

Silently he stared down at the dark grey, granite gravestone.

In loving memory of Max Goldspink. Beloved son, boyfriend and friend. Rest in peace.

He noted the fresh flowers, someone had visited recently. Perched at the foot of the gravestone was a single weathered photograph. The handsome young black man smiling up at them bore a striking resemblance to Ben. They shared the same cheeky grin and similar sharp facial features, jutting cheekbones and a strong jaw. Even their hairstyle was similar, except Max's dreadlocks were a lot shorter, cropped just below the ear.

"Today would have been his twenty-first birthday. His parents always bring flowers on this date. It's their way of keeping his memory alive."

Jimmy looked across at Nikki who stood solemnly beside him, head bowed in respect. "What happened?"

"I killed him."

"What?"

She let out a cruel laugh. "Not like that. Although is there ever a good way to kill someone?"

Jimmy didn't answer, awaiting further explanation.

Nikki gave a long, heartfelt sigh. When she spoke, her voice was so soft he could barely hear her. "He died in a car accident when we were just teenagers. He bled to death right in front of me. I still have nightmares about it. I tried my best but I couldn't save him." She hung her head, wretched. "I was driving. It was me who caused the crash. I've never forgiven myself."

There was a different quality to her voice now, haunted, overwhelmed with guilt. She sounded so upset that, despite himself, Jimmy felt some of his anger dissipate.

Damn Nikki. Even in her discretions, she made it hard for him to hate her.

"But it's like you said. It was an accident. It wasn't your fault."

Nikki sniffed and shook her head. Eyes still down-cast, her voice faltered as she continued. "I'd been drinking. I was well over the limit. We figured we could get away with it. It wasn't a long journey, we thought we'd be alright. It all seems so stupid now. I only got distracted for a minute but that was all it took. Before I knew it, our car collided head on with a lamppost. Max was dead before the ambulance even arrived."

Jimmy was silent. *What could he say to that?*

"Obviously Max's family were completely distr-aught, inconsolable about their loss. They blamed me for everything. His parents tried to charge me with manslaughter. It cost my family a fortune in legal fees, but my lawyer somehow managed to get me off the hook and kept my name out of the press thankfully. I was only seventeen at the time, so in the end the judge let me off with no prison sentence, just a ten-year driving ban and a fifty-thousand pound fine."

Nodding slowly, Jimmy was starting to understand why Nikki felt so guilty about Aisha's expensive priv-ate medical bills. Her parents would still be paying off that hefty fine and legal fees, it must have decimated their savings and drowned them in debt.

Nikki cleared her throat. "However, Max's family

were mad as hell I wasn't given a jail sentence. But it didn't matter, I was already living in my own personal torture. I was beyond devastated, consumed with grief. Max was the love of my life, my childhood sweetheart, and I was responsible for killing him. How do you start to deal with that?" She shivered as she continued, "We'd been together for four years, since we were fourteen. Max was everywhere I looked, everything reminded me of him. Places we had gone on dates, friends we used to hang out with together. Even Facebook taunted me, with that bloody 'look back on your memories' feature. Not to mention Max's friends were trolling me every chance they got. Every post I uploaded was flooded with abusive comments. I even got death threats."

Comprehension spread across Jimmy's face. It was fast becoming clear why he had never been able to find a digital footprint for his girlfriend's high school years.

Nikki clasped her hands together and squeezed her eyes shut. "I was diagnosed with depression for a while, the grief made me almost suicidal. In the end I couldn't cope anymore. I deactivated everything, permanently deleted all my social media accounts and cut ties with everyone who knew me from high school. It was all too painful, I had to get away from it all. It was driving me insane." She shuddered as a rush of old memories swept through her. "When I started university, I seized the opportunity to reinvent myself, start from scratch. Created new Facebook and Instagram profiles, being careful not to reference my surname so none of my schoolmates could ever find me online. I relished the new start, no one knew what I had done. I could finally start over and just be Nikki again. Not the 'Poor Drunk Girl Who Accidentally Killed Her Boyfriend'."

Turning to face him, she took a deep breath. "I hadn't intended to ever tell anyone about my past, but eventually I did confide in Meg. She had the bedroom next to mine in first year and could hear me crying in my room at night. Everything was still so raw, I was dealing with it the best I could. I could just about hold it together during the day, but I often fell apart at night. I couldn't hide it from Meg. Honestly, I don't know what I would have done without her. She got me through that horrific time."

Shaking his head, Jimmy felt a chill wash over him. "You should have told me. I could have helped too."

Nikki flinched. "I know that now. I'm sorry."

Eyes lingering on the gravestone, a sickening thought struck Jimmy. *Max had died just four months before she started at university and less than a year before they had first got together.* Looking warily at Nikki, he reluctantly asked the question he was dreading. "Was I just the rebound guy?"

Nikki hesitated, chewing on her lip nervously. "When we first got together, I wasn't looking for anything serious. Just a bit of fun. I must admit I liked how you were the polar opposite to Max. Not only in looks, but personality too. He was always more of the strong, silent type, whereas you're more chatty and goofy. He was into cricket and thriller novels, you prefer rugby and comedy films. You get the picture. It was nice to be with someone so different. It was a good distraction."

Jimmy's heart sank. His chest became so tight he could barely breathe. He lowered his head, disheartened. "So, that's all I was to you? *A distraction?*"

Nikki's eyes widened. "No, no, I swear. That's how it *started*. But that was before I really knew you. Before I fell in love with you."

Jimmy sucked in a ragged lungful of air. "You have a funny way of showing how much you love me."

Nikki hung her head in shame. "I'm so sorry. I never meant for anything to happen with Ben. You have to believe me. Max would have been twenty-one today. His birthday is always difficult. My emotions were all over the place."

"And you think that gives you a free pass? That it makes all of this okay?"

"No, of course not. Ben was just…there. You see how similar they look? I know it doesn't make it right. I know it's not an excuse, but he reminded me of Max so much. I know it sounds weird, but it felt like I could be with him again one last time."

Swallowing, Jimmy forced in another deep breath. He hated the sound of Nikki's voice, the wheedling note of desperation. As if that made everything fine again.

She turned to face him, her face full of hope. "Please forgive me. I love you. I always will."

Shaking his head in disgust, contempt seeped into his voice. "Are you kidding me? You think this changes things? Not only have you been screwing around with another guy, but you've also been lying to me about who you really are for the past two years. I feel like I barely know you. A sob story about your dead ex isn't going to magically get you out of trouble."

He could see the pain in her face as her eyes grew moist again. "Jimmy, *please.* I love you."

"You should have thought about that before you shagged someone else. How could you do that to me?"

Nikki turned to face him, fresh tears rolling down her cheeks. "I'll make it up to you, I promise."

"You can't. You cheated on me. How am I ever supposed to trust you again?" Jimmy rubbed his own watery eyes furiously. *He wouldn't cry in front of her, he wouldn't give her the satisfaction.*

She reached to clutch his hand, but he stepped out of reach. "You've had your chance. We're finished. You can make your own way home."

Distraught, Nikki sank to her knees before the gravestone of her ex-lover and dropped her head into her hands in despair. Turning his back on the pitiful sight, Jimmy strode away without so much as a cursory glance backwards as Nikki wailed in anguish, surrounded by snowflakes swirling around her like confetti.

*   *   *

The atmosphere in the interview room had changed. A heavy silence descended upon them in the wake of this latest revelation. Robson and Zahra exchanged stunned glances.

Robson gave what he hoped was a calm, composed smile, but inside his mind was reeling. "As I understand it though, you did end up getting back together?"

Jimmy brushed a tear from his cheek with the back of his hand. "Yeah, one day later. I'll spare you the embarrassing details of that reconciliation. There was grovelling on both sides, it wasn't pretty."

"So, you'd forgiven Nikki?"

The actor's forehead creased into a frown. "Well, I wouldn't say I'd forgiven her exactly. It wasn't something you could just sweep under the rug and pretend didn't happen. The lies bothered me more than the cheating if I'm honest. I couldn't believe she hadn't told me about the accident. I felt as though our entire relationship had been built on a lie."

Robson raised an eyebrow.

"Not that I wanted her dead," Jimmy added quickly. "We were working to move past it." His voice came out croaking.

Robson examined the grieving young man critically. His eyes were distant and his hands were still balled into fists on the table. "Why didn't you tell us any of this before?"

Jimmy sighed and ran a hand absentmindedly through his curly hair. "Honestly, I was trying to forget all about it. To find out my girlfriend had been lying to me about her past for over two years was a slap in the face. Hell, we were talking about getting married! Then, it suddenly felt like I barely knew who she was anymore." He held out his hands apologetically. "But also, I didn't want you to think badly of Nikki. She's made mistakes, we all have. And tragically someone died. But she's a good person. I didn't want you to not take your investigation seriously." He shifted uneasily in his chair. "Tell me, was

Nikki involved in that impromptu Lady Macbeth swap?"

"We're not at liberty to say."

Slumping in his chair, Jimmy's shoulders sagged. "I guess that's a yes. I was afraid of that. She'd become obsessed with being spotted, making it big time. I kept trying to tell her it doesn't normally work like that. You have to pay your dues as an actor for a while, but she wouldn't listen. She would have done anything to make quick money." He swallowed nervously, his mouth fixed in grim resignation. "You don't think that swap had something to do with her death, do you?"

"There's a number of leads we're pursuing."

Robson let out a slow, weary sigh. "So, let me get this straight. Our victim, Nikki Gowon, inadvertently killed her then-boyfriend Max Goldspink in a car crash three years ago. Due to her age and a bloody good lawyer, she managed to escape without a jail sentence, but ended up with a hefty fine and loads of expensive legal fees, effectively bankrupting her family. Which coincidentally explains why we couldn't find any social media presence prior to her university years. But also, it reveals why she was so driven to blackmail Neil and manipulate her way into stealing Emma's lead role of Lady Macbeth. The chance of being spotted by a talent scout and landing a lucrative role would have been tempting so she could finally start paying back her parents what she owed them and contribute towards Aisha's medical bills."

Zahra nodded. "Despite moving on with a new

boyfriend, Jimmy Walker, Nikki was clearly still hung up on her ex-boyfriend, Max, and the role she played in his death. So, she was thrown when Ben Grahame came onto the scene as her onstage lover, who bears an uncanny resemblance to her ex. Nikki gave into her desires and crossed the line to be with him, only to be caught in the act by her boyfriend."

In a low, thoughtful tone, Robson added, "Then, as an aside, Nikki also served as confidante for her younger castmate, Violet Underwood, who was raped by one of Nikki's friends, Peter Winters. Am I missing anything?"

Zahra shook her head slowly. "Think that just about covers everything. This case gets more ridiculous by the hour. But what's frustrating is we still can't pin the murder on anyone."

Closing his eyes, Robson willed himself to think clearly. "Everyone had the means and opportunity to swap the knife and a whole host of people had a compelling motive to do so."

Zahra grimaced. "All the evidence we have is all circumstantial and can be easily explained. There's only Neil's fingerprints on the murder weapon and the hidden prop knife which was found wrapped in Ben's jacket. The call history and the sex tape video point towards motive, especially for Neil and Emma, but they are even less conclusive in proving anything concrete."

"And then there's the discarded heart necklace," added Robson thoughtfully. For some reason his mind kept returning to that. Thinking about it almost brought something to the forefront of his memory, but he couldn't quite grasp what it was. All he knew was it was significant.

"And a heart necklace," repeated Zahra, evidently unimpressed.

Robson looked across at his partner. "You know, I'm still not convinced Nikki didn't kill herself. She was clearly racked with guilt about Max's death and was distraught by cheating with Ben, not to mention the prospect of losing her younger sister. Seems she was tormented by demons she couldn't shake."

Zahra raised a sceptical eyebrow. "So, why was there no suicide note? Plus, her parents were convinced her mental health was better now. I don't buy it. And it sure would be convenient for a lot of people if Nikki suddenly decided to take her own life. Perhaps that's exactly what someone wants us to think?"

Robson shrugged. "Maybe. I guess it all comes down to the murder weapon. Let's chase up if there's been any progress identifying where the replica knife was sourced from. If we could determine who commissioned it that would provide the conclusive evidence we need. Whoever bought that knife had grand plans for her onstage death, whether that was Nikki or one of her co-stars remains to be seen."

Zahra let out a slow breath. "The web of lies and scandal continues to get deeper and more convoluted."

"Technically, Nikki's heart was usually in the right place. Often, she was only trying to do the right thing. To help a vulnerable co-star, to do right by her family, to come to terms with her grief."

Zahra's eyebrows rose again. "By blackmailing the director and cheating on her boyfriend? Sad as her story may be, I think we can both agree Nikki's moral compass has definitely strayed."

Robson sighed. "I suppose. But I don't believe she was necessarily a bad person, just desperate."

"'Tempt not a desperate man,' or woman in this case."

A half-smile twitched on Robson's lips. "*Romeo and Juliet.* So, you *are* a theatre buff after all. You're full of surprises Nadia Zahra."

A light knock at the door preceded PC Armstrong popping her head into the room. "We've been doing some more digging on our suspects and thought you might be interested in this. Last Saturday, Jimmy Walker was caught on a traffic camera speeding in a 30 mile an hour zone in Finsbury. The fine is still being processed, which is why it didn't get flagged before."

She handed over the incriminating speed camera photograph to Robson. Peering down, he arched an eyebrow in surprise and handed it across to Zahra.

"Want me to call Jimmy back in?"

Robson shook his head. "Not just yet. Check out who's sat in the passenger seat."

Zahra smiled. "Interesting. Guess we better set up another interview."

CHAPTER TWENTY-ONE

Blood Will Have Blood

Emma Thorpe glanced at the photograph for a few seconds before settling back into her chair, folding her arms defensively as she adopted her signature unimpressed look. "Yeah, it's me in that photo. But then, you already knew that. I'm not sure what you expect me to say?"

"How about what you were doing with Jimmy Walker outside of rehearsals? I didn't think you two were close?" Robson asked, more sarcastically than he had intended.

"You make that sound suspicious! I was only in his car," scoffed Emma, her pretty face a mask of confusion.

"Did you not think fraternising with the victim's boyfriend might be a good thing to mention to us?"

Emma let out a long hiss. "Believe me, I'm *not* involved with Jimmy!"

"Care to explain then how you came to be a passenger

in his car last Saturday evening?"

Emma opened her mouth to speak, but Robson held up a hand to silence her. He was in no mood for playing games. "And don't pretend he was giving you a lift home from the theatre. My team's already done some digging into your whereabouts that evening. They know where you were before."

*   *   *

Saturday 17th March

Emma hadn't intended to even go into the quirky Station Bar, tucked away on Rivington Street. It was one of those trendy refurbished railway arch bars, a hidden gem nestled in the heart of London's East End.

Eyes bleary with unshed tears, she had been rushing with purpose, set on getting back home as soon as possible. The snowfall had picked up pace throughout the day and Emma braced herself for another bitter onslaught as she hurried down the crowded path.

She had anticipated the frosty temperature and the cold sting on her exposed face, but not the unforgiving wind that forced her eyes to water as she squinted ahead. Wet snowflakes had found their way into her jacket and her feet were freezing as she traipsed through ankle-deep snow, the ground mushy underfoot. Bowing her head until her chin touched her chest, she struggled onwards, all the while thinking about her cosy flat and hot chocolate.

Neil had already spent far too long dominating her

mind. Even the frigging hot chocolate reminded her of him; one of their early morning traditions to accompany breakfast in bed.

That man was such a bloody idiot.

Much to Emma's frustration, the director had stayed true to his word and refused to reveal anything more to her about the cryptic actress swap. The mystery surrounding the bizarre decision was driving her crazy. Plus, if Neil thought the way he was treating her was acceptable, he had another thing coming. She deserved better than to be used, then flung aside like a piece of trash when it no longer suited him.

As fate would have it, a clumsy passer-by collided into her as she turned the street corner. Nearly knocked off her feet, she looked around angrily ready to shout at the rude man who had jostled her. But he was already nowhere to be seen, having disappeared into the heaving crowd of people, completely oblivious to her. Glowering, Emma took a moment to steady herself and readjusted her handbag onto her shoulder, ready to set off again.

That's when she saw it.

Station Bar was directly in her eyeline and parked right outside it was a familiar faded blue Honda. She recognised it straight away as Jimmy's car.

The unexpected opportunity was more than tempting. While she was livid with his manipulative girlfriend and the part she played in her current misery, Jimmy himself had always been pleasant. A genuine charmer, he always made a conscious effort to strike up conversations with everyone, including her. Miraculously, he had somehow managed to stay clear of most of the cast drama. Well until yesterday at least, when the golden couple had blown up in a furious row and Jimmy had stormed out of the theatre after their public showdown. If anyone needed a good drinking partner right now, it would be him.

With the seed of an idea already forming in her mind, she hurried towards the bar entrance before she lost her nerve.

Stepping through the door was like walking into the past. Neglected for decades, there had been a recent resurgence in converting London's old disused railway arches into achingly fashionable venues. Exposed brickwork and distressed features contributed to the chic, industrial style, effortlessly capturing the historic heritage of the bar while remaining hip and modern.

Scanning the bar, Emma spotted Jimmy straight away, huddled into a corner booth. Hunched over his drink, he was scrolling absentmindedly through his phone, only half paying attention.

Sidling up to the bar, Emma wasted no time in learning what Jimmy was drinking; Gin and Tonic, no ice. The bearded barman was quick to oblige. He leered at her gormlessly as he prepared two drinks for her, set up a bar tab and watched her strut over to Jimmy's booth.

"Room for one more?"

Jimmy looked up, surprised. "Emma! What are you doing here?"

"Same as you, I guess. Fancy another drink?"

He shrugged and she slid into the booth opposite him, pushing his drink across the table. Tentatively, she took a sip of her own. She had gone for Gin and Tonic too. In all honesty she would have preferred wine, but she remembered reading an article once claiming people were more likely to open up and share if they were drinking the same tipple. Something about the subconscious mirroring effect and feeling more comfortable.

It was worth a shot anyhow.

"Thanks for the drink." He raised it to his lips and took a large gulp.

Emma smiled sweetly. "No problem. Anything for a fellow castmate."

Jimmy grunted. "I wish we'd never got involved in that stupid show. Then, none of this would have happened."

Taking another sip of her drink, Emma watched him carefully, trying to work out how far she could push it. "Still broken up?"

He gave a small, sad smile and ran a hand through his ruffled reddish-brown curls. "I just can't bring myself to forgive her."

Jimmy had a cute dimple that carved a deep groove in his right cheek when he smiled. She hadn't noticed that before. His curly locks always reminded her of a hobbit. An image she found particularly amusing as it was so at odds with Jimmy's typical rugby player physique. Tall and broad-shouldered with strong, bulging arms, distinctly un-hobbit like. Emma had to admit, while she was normally attracted to older, more distinguished men, Jimmy had mastered his boyish charm down to an art.

Maybe this would be easier than she had thought.

"Nikki had it coming. There's only so long you can play with fire and not get burnt." She expected Jimmy to challenge her and defend his former girlfriend but to her surprise he nodded in agreement.

"Who does she think she is? I can't believe she thought she could get away with screwing her co-star behind my back by telling me some convoluted sob story. I mean, who does that?"

Emma leaned forward, intrigued. "Why, what did she say?"

He shook his head, distracted. "Not important. I can't get over her nerve."

Adopting her best listening face, Emma reached across to touch his hand. She was good at playing the role of sympathetic confidante.

"Did she really expect me to forgive her, no questions asked? To come crawling back like a lovesick puppy. I deserve better."

Emma squeezed his hand softly. "You *do* deserve better. You're one of the good guys. No one deserves to be cheated on."

Jimmy nodded sombrely. "It's over. I don't understand how we could ever come back from this. Clearly Nikki doesn't respect me and I don't know how I can ever trust her again. I feel like I don't even know who she is anymore."

Not for the first time, Emma got the distinct impression Jimmy was talking as though she wasn't there, using her as a soundboard to vent his frustrations. That suited her just fine.

"Exactly. You think you know someone and then they go and stab you in the back. Like they can screw you over to get their own way. We're good people, we don't deserve to be treated like shit." Letting out an aggravated sigh, Emma grabbed her glass and downed the remainder of her drink. Slamming the empty glass back on the table with a clang, she found Jimmy watching her, bemused.

"Forget about Nikki. Who are *you* talking about?"

Emma turned away sheepishly. "No one."

"Hey, no fair! All my cards are on the table. Now, spill."

He prodded her arm teasingly and Emma grinned at his touch. Jimmy was the reserved type. Any form of physical contact was a sign he was letting his guard down, allowing the alcohol to loosen him up.

Catching the eye of the barman, Emma gestured for more drinks to be brought over. "He's no one special. Just my ex. No one you know," she lied.

The obedient barman appeared to set the new drinks down on the table. Emma gave him a curt nod of thanks.

Jimmy leaned back in his seat. "I probably should stop drinking. I only came in to catch the end of the rugby game. I couldn't face going home straight away."

Wrinkling her nose, Emma threw her hands up in mock despair. "But they're already made now. It would be a tragedy to waste perfectly good gin."

Jimmy laughed. "Well, that is true."

Emma pushed a glass towards him with an innocent smile on her face.

Reluctantly, Jimmy picked it up. "Anyone would think you were trying to get me drunk."

"I'm doing nothing of the sort." She picked up her glass. "Hey, we should make a toast."

"To what?"

"How about to new beginnings?"

Smiling wryly, Jimmy raised his glass. "To new beginnings."

Their glasses clinked.

Staggering out of the bar two hours later, Emma giggled as she gripped tightly onto Jimmy's arm for support. Tottering forward, she felt like a baby deer learning to walk for the first time.

"How are you getting home?" Jimmy asked, a touching note of concern in his voice.

"Tube, I guess. Or taxi."

"I'll give you a lift," Jimmy offered, fishing his car keys out of his pocket.

Emma's forehead creased into a frown. She had lost count of how many drinks they had consumed, but she was fairly certain it would be enough to put him over the legal limit. "Are you sure you should be driving?"

Jimmy laughed and waved her off dismissively. "Don't be silly. It's only a fifteen-minute drive and your flat is en route. It would be stupid to pay out money for a taxi when we have a car right here. Besides it'll take forever to be picked up in this weather."

Emma shook her head anxiously. "I don't know. I'm not sure that's a good idea."

Jimmy smiled reassuringly. "Honestly, I'm fine. I can handle my drink. I wouldn't be suggesting it if I didn't feel up to it, I wouldn't risk it. Anyway, it's like the Artic out here!"

Emma opened her mouth to protest but was silenced when a large snowflake fell on her forehead.

Jimmy did seem more sobered up now they were outside. And a lift would be helpful. Not to mention, it provided a good opportunity to finish what she had started. But still, her better judgement was screaming at her not to be reckless.

As if sensing her inner turmoil, Jimmy wrapped a protective arm around her shoulders. Tone serious, he assured her, "It'll be fine, I promise. It's just because you're a miniature person, alcohol affects you more. Us strapping lads can handle it." He tapped her head playfully, joking about her diminutive size.

The light sleet was giving way to heavier snowfall; they'd be drenched and frozen by the time they reached the tube station. Part of Emma still wanted to argue with him, but he was convincingly reassuring. Reluctantly, she swallowed her fears and climbed into the passenger seat.

The car journey proved to be surprisingly uneventful, despite the fierce snow battering against the car window as if it meant to wash them away. White flakes swirled around in an angry vortex, so thick it obscured their view almost completely. No sooner had their car tracks been imprinted on the road, they vanished, covered instantly by a fresh flurry of snow. Outside the familiar sights of Emma's street had been swallowed in white, the world slowly being erased around them.

True to his word, Jimmy was alert and focused,

paying careful attention as he drove. Chatting non-stop, they both relished the easy, no-strings-attached conversation in each other's company. They were fast approaching her flat, Emma's little slice of urban suburbia in an up-and-coming area of Finsbury.

Emma stole a look at him. "So, do you want to be an actor when you graduate?"

Jimmy sighed. "Honestly, I haven't given it much thought."

"You're talented you know. Modest too."

He grunted a short laugh. "Why, thanks."

"I mean it. If you wanted to, I reckon you could make it."

He grinned sheepishly. "Cheers. What about you? How come you never went into acting full time?"

Emma gave a casual shrug. "I wanted a more stable career, get myself on the housing ladder. Who knows, I've still got time to try it out in the future."

"Leaving it a bit late, aren't you?"

Her lips flickered into a smile. "You saying I'm past it? I'm only three years older than you!"

"Nah, you're not past it. You still look youthful. Well, you know, for a golden oldie."

Smile broadening, Emma thumped his arm play-fully. Jimmy turned his head to flash her a wide grin, digging a deep groove in his cheek. The moonlight cast a warm glow across his face, illuminating his freckles. His eyes had a twinkle in them as he met her gaze.

Distracted, Jimmy turned his attention back to the road a minute too late. By the time he glimpsed the glaring headlights of the oncoming van, there was no time to react. The van hurtled towards them at break-neck speed. Their spinning wheels lost traction on the icy road, wipers moving frantically across the wind-screen as they were blinded in a sea of white.

Emma screamed and squeezed her eyes shut.

Bracing herself for the collision, she waited for the crash. Jimmy slammed on the brakes and the car came to a screeching halt. Emma's seatbelt sliced into her neck as she was thrust forward. A harsh horn blared. The smell of burning rubber flooded the air.

Then, nothing.

Cautiously, Emma opened her eyes. Having swer-ved to avoid them, the van was already speeding away from them, the driver madly gesticulating at them in his side mirror.

She glanced across at Jimmy. He was gripping the steering wheel, knuckles white. Sat rigid in shock, Emma could see he was trembling.

"Fuck, that was close." He looked over at her, concerned. "You alright?"

She nodded silently, breathing hard.

Jimmy exhaled a sigh of relief. "Sorry, that van came out of nowhere."

Emma grimaced. "Let's just get out of here."

They drove in stilted silence. Pale and edgy, Jimmy still looked shell-shocked. His clammy hands stuck to the wheel and his breathing was ragged and uneven.

Shaken herself, Emma sensed there was a new opp-ortunity their near miss had presented that she could use to her advantage. Prevent their moment from being ruined. As he pulled up to park outside her flat, she burst into tears right on cue. Turning on the water-works had never been an issue for her.

Jimmy stared in shocked bewilderment as Emma collapsed into heaving sobs.

"Shit, Jimmy we could have *died*. Do you realise how lucky we are?" Unclipping her seatbelt, she leaned across to snuggle against him.

He wrapped his arms around her comfortingly. "I'm sorry, I'm so sorry."

Emma felt hot, wet tears running down her neck as he started to cry too. *Gross, she hadn't taken him for a complete cry-baby. Still, now was the time to capitalise on his vulnerability.*

Sniffing, she drew herself up to look in his eyes. "Makes you think, doesn't it? Life's too short to waste it on people who don't appreciate how good they've got it. We could teach them a lesson?"

"What?" He sounded confused.

Geez, for someone so clever he sure was slow. Without hesitating Emma made her move, pushing her body against his chest and pressing her lips against his.

She expected him to follow suit, but Jimmy drew away almost immediately. Brow furrowed in surprise, he stared at her blankly. "What the hell are you doing?"

Emma smiled coquettishly. "What do you think I'm doing?" She leaned forward to kiss him again, but Jimmy moved away.

"No way. Emma, that's not going to happen."

Biting her tongue, she looked at him beseechingly. Dropping a hand to his knee, she ran her fingers seductively up the inside of his leg.

Firmly Jimmy grabbed her wrist and pushed her

away. "I said *no*. I think you should leave now."

"But—"

"Goodnight Emma." There was a resolute firmness in his voice. He had fixed his eyes back on the road, avoiding any further eye contact.

Dejected, she pouted her lips and cast him one final forlorn look before clambering out of the car. Her feet had barely touched the pavement when Jimmy started the engine up again. He wasted no time in speeding away, leaving Emma stood, sulky and alone, on the snowy kerb in the moonlight.

*   *   *

"So, essentially you tried to seduce Nikki's boyfriend? What for? Revenge?"

Emma's mouth tightened. "I know it sounds petty but I was so mad at her and Neil. I felt like the pair of them had double-crossed me. I just wanted them to feel some of the pain they had inflicted on me."

Robson shook his head in disgust. Zahra was right, Emma really was a sly, little snake.

"Not that it mattered in the end. That guy has the resolve of steel. No one has ever turned me down before."

"That must have pissed you off?"

Scowling darkly, Emma nodded. "Yeah, it did. I guess they must have kissed and made up at some point. They were very much back together at the cast party five days later."

"So, what next? You decided to stab Nikki in the front rather than back?"

Emma let out a short, humourless laugh. "Seriously? No, like I said before, I had nothing to do with her death."

Robson examined the blonde actress critically. *If only they had actual evidence.*

"Alright, you're free to go. For now."

Alone in the interview room, the detectives exchanged exasperated looks. Pressing her lips tightly together, Zahra asked, "Want me to set up another interview with Jimmy Walker?"

Closing his eyes, Robson sighed. "I guess so. I'm intrigued how him and Nikki ended up getting back together. Remember how he conveniently glossed over that part?"

They were interrupted by a frantic pounding at the door as an overexcited PC Armstrong barged into the room. "Sorry for the intrusion," she said breathlessly. "But you need to see this."

Hurriedly, she handed over a file. Peering inside, Robson found himself speechless. The contents triggered a recollection. Suddenly he remembered why that heart necklace had looked so familiar. The hazy memory of where he had seen it before that had been floating tantalisingly out of reach finally became crystal-clear as everything clicked perfectly into place.

Next to him, Zahra whistled as she looked down at the file's contents. "Well, this changes everything."

CHAPTER TWENTY-TWO

Let Not Light See My Black and Deep Desires

R obson was so engrossed in his own thoughts that he could barely concentrate on the interviewee sat before them. Finally, just when the investigation was looking bleak, they had got the break they so desperately needed.

"We do have to remind you that you're under caution. You do not have to say anything. But it may harm your defence if you do not mention when questioned something which you later rely on in court. Anything you do say may be given in evidence. Do you understand?"

"Yes, but I didn't *do* anything! I'm *not guilty*. You've got this all wrong," came the terse reply.

Leaning forward and placing his hands on the table, Robson said calmly, "In that case, this is an opportunity to tell your side of the story. Can I remind you of your right to a solicitor?"

Megan Newbold hesitated for a moment before shaking her head. "I'll do without. I have nothing to hide."

Robson allowed himself a satisfied smile. "Alright. Well remember you have the right to free and independent legal advice which you have chosen to waive and that is an ongoing right should you change your mind during the interview. Now, let's get started. You were with Nikki last Saturday night, weren't you?"

The brunette actress folded her arms defensively against her chest. "So, what if I was?"

"Well, we were hoping you could help out with a few questions we still have about that night. Fill in some blanks, so to speak."

Megan relaxed slightly, shoulders dropping. Her gaze darted over to Zahra, before settling back on Robson. "What sort of blanks?" she asked uncertainly.

"Well, we know Jimmy broke up with Nikki after catching her hooking up with Ben. It was you who discovered that, wasn't it? You're the one who texted Jimmy to come and see for himself?"

Robson detected a note of apprehension in Megan's response before she agreed. "Yes, that was me. I couldn't believe what I was seeing. Jimmy deserved to witness that with his own eyes."

"That discovery led to the couple's public showdown at the theatre last Friday when they broke up. We also know in an attempt to win him back, Nikki eventually told Jimmy about the tragedy concerning her ex-boyfriend Max. But you were already in the know about her ex, weren't you?"

Megan nodded silently. It seemed to Robson like

she was playing a part in her own imagined play.

"Anyway, we also know later that day Jimmy hit the bottle to drown his sorrows with Emma before being caught speeding in Finsbury."

"He was with *Emma*?" repeated Megan slowly. Then, she laughed. "Well, I suppose that does make sense in hindsight. I did wonder how Jimmy had got so drunk. He's normally really careful about that sort of thing, always worried about losing control."

"However, what we don't know yet is what happened next. How did the couple get back together? And coincidentally why did you break up with Peter around the same time?"

A flicker of doubt flashed across Megan's face. "Peter told you about that?"

"It came up."

"But that breakup only lasted two days."

"It was long enough."

Megan frowned a little. "Long enough for what?"

"Let's focus on Nikki and Jimmy for now."

"I really don't understand why you're asking me? Why don't you just talk to Jimmy about what happened?"

"Oh, we will, don't you worry. But you mentioned earlier you had concerns about the couple. It would be helpful to get some more details about that. What exactly were you worried about?" Robson mustered a weak smile. "It's important for us to understand everything about that night. Do you think you can do that for us? For Nikki?"

Megan raised her head, looking at Robson dead in the eye. There was a new steely determination on her face. "For Nikki, I'll do anything."

*   *   *

Saturday 17th March

Nikki Gowon was utterly inconsolable.

Megan had never seen her like this before and, if truth be told, it scared her. The pair had returned to Megan's house after the evening rehearsal, at which Jimmy had been conspicuously absent, much to the director's annoyance.

Now they were curled up on Megan's bed, Nikki wrapped in her arms as she wept. A damp patch had spread across Megan's cardigan as her friend's warm tears soaked into the fabric. Outside the torrential snowfall pelted against the window like a hail of bullets drowning out every other sound.

"I feel like...I can't...breathe," gasped Nikki between heaving sobs.

"Oh, come on, stop being so melodramatic."

"I mean it! How did I mess everything up so badly? Jimmy's not speaking to me. Ben's doubtlessly mad at me too. And I feel worse about Max than I have done in years. I'm such an idiot."

"You're not an idiot," Megan said softly.

Nikki sniffed. "Well, I feel like one. I don't think Jimmy will ever get back together with me. I've ruined our relationship for good."

Megan let out an exasperated sigh. "Maybe that's not necessarily such a bad thing."

Nikki stared at her curiously. "What do you mean?"

Turning away from her, Megan took a deep breath.

331

"I've thought for some time now, perhaps you guys aren't right for each other. He was only ever supposed to be the rebound guy after all, you've said that yourself. And especially recently with all this talk of weddings, he's putting far too much pressure on you to get married."

"But Aisha—"

"Yes, I know Aisha would like to be a bridesmaid. But you can't marry someone just to please your little sister."

Nikki dropped her eyes to her lap. "That's not what I'm doing."

"You need to be with someone who accepts you fully for who you are and can look beyond what's happened in your past."

Swallowing hard, Nikki blinked back fresh tears. "I thought that's who Jimmy was. I thought he'd be more forgiving."

Megan regarded her coldly. "He's not here though, is he?"

Nikki lowered her head into her hands. "I guess I was wrong."

Megan patted her knee comfortingly. It pained her to see her friend this upset. She wished she had the power to do something about it.

Nikki touched Megan's hand unintentionally and gave her a bashful look. "I don't know what I would do without you. Thanks for being there for me, no matter what."

Megan smiled. "Always."

Slowly, Nikki's crying subsided. Her hand brushed Megan's again. This time she wasn't so sure the contact had been accidental. The thought of mentioning it brought a lump to Megan's throat. But before she could verbalise her thoughts, there was a sudden hammering on the front door.

"Who the hell—" began Megan, then Jimmy's thundering voice answered her half-spoken question.

"Nikki! Nikki, are you in there? I need to speak to you."

Nikki's eyes widened. Quickly clambering off the bed, she darted downstairs to let him in, Megan trailing behind her.

Fumbling with the lock, Nikki flung open the door so forcefully it smashed into the wall. Jimmy stood on the step, drenched to the skin. The savage blizzard thrashed around him as the snowstorm continued to rage outside. The deluge of whirling snow whipped around relentlessly, sending gusts of biting wind into the house. Jimmy's straggly reddish-brown curls were plastered to his forehead, partially straightened by the clumps of snow clinging to his hair. Bedraggled and pale, his eyes were red-rimmed and bloodshot, his breath pale against the numbing air.

"You haven't been answering my calls?" he said accusingly, his tone a perfect reflection of the grey sky above.

Nikki shook her head. "My phone battery's dead. Come in, you look freezing."

Gratefully Jimmy shuffled across the threshold and Nikki pulled the door firmly closed, shutting out the apocalyptic deluge.

Thanks for asking my permission before inviting people into my home, thought Megan bitterly but she didn't protest.

For a few long minutes no one said anything, the uncomfortable tension descending upon the three of them like a snake slithering around their necks. Jimmy shivered as his soaked clothes dripped steadily onto the floor. Quietly, Megan sank into a seated position on the stairs. Drawing her legs in close she watched the couple with trepidation.

Finally, Jimmy broke the silence, his words cutting into the strained atmosphere. "We need to talk."

Nikki nodded silently, as if not trusting herself to speak.

Sighing heavily, Jimmy whispered. "How could you do this to us?"

Nikki bit down hard on her lip. "How many times do I need to say I'm sorry?"

"I'm not a jealous guy. I trusted you and this is how you repay me?"

"I tried to explain…"

Jimmy chuckled darkly. His laughter had a hysterical edge. "Yeah, yeah, I know. Dead ex-boyfriend, dead ringer for Ben, bla, bla, bla. It still doesn't excuse what you did, never mind lying to me for so long." A pulsating vein in Jimmy's neck throbbed as he spoke through gritted teeth.

Reaching for his hand, Nikki pleaded, "Please try to understand."

"I understand perfectly," snapped Jimmy, his voice low and strained. "You'd rather shag someone else who kind of reminds you of your ex than come to me and explain you were struggling."

Megan saw the muscle tense in Jimmy's jaw. He

was clenching and unclenching his right hand. When he raised his eyes to meet Nikki's they were cold. "How are we ever meant to rebuild what we had? How am I supposed to trust you now?"

Nikki flinched as if his words had been hurled with violence. "I swear I'll be faithful, I'll never stray again, I promise."

Face twisted with rage, Jimmy turned away from her and spat something under his breath. Balling his hand into a tight fist, he suddenly raised his arm. For an awful moment Megan thought he would hit Nikki, but instead he slammed his fist down hard in an aggressive strike against the wooden front door.

Megan yelped in surprise as the wood splintered in a loud snap and the door cracked open.

Her landlord was going to kill her.

Shaking his fist, Jimmy rammed the door again in another violent blow. The jagged hole deepened, the wood now smeared with blood. His face darkened, eyes livid with anger. For the first time, Megan felt afraid of him.

"*Stop it!* Jimmy, please stop!" cried Nikki as she grabbed his arm.

"Would you prefer I hit you?" he snarled, nostrils flaring as he jabbed a finger in her direction.

Fearfully, Nikki shrank away from him without saying another word.

Grunting in pain, Jimmy inspected his hand tenderly. His knuckles were scraped raw and blood trickled from the gaping wounds. Cradling his injured hand against his chest, Jimmy was speechless for a long moment. When he spoke, his voice was so low

Megan struggled to make out the words. "Being faithful isn't even the only issue. You *lied* to me for *two years* Nikki. How could you not tell me about Max? How could you think I wouldn't understand?"

Slowly, Nikki crept back closer to him so her face was only inches away from his. "I wanted to tell you so many times, but I just didn't know how. I was worried about what you might think of me."

Jimmy shook his head, lips pressed tightly together. "But how could you think I wouldn't understand?" he repeated, louder this time and more insistent.

Nikki sighed and said nothing.

Not for the first time, Megan felt invisible. Sat quietly on the stairs, she doubted the couple even remembered she was there. Part of her knew she should leave to give them some privacy to try and salvage what was left of their relationship, but she couldn't bear to turn away from the drama unfolding right in front of her.

Sniffing, Nikki wrinkled her nose and looked at Jimmy accusingly. "Have you been drinking?"

He groaned. "Why does that matter?"

"It matters. *You* matter to me," Nikki began and then her words trailed off as another thought occurred to her. "How did you get here Jimmy?"

He didn't answer.

"How did you get here?" repeated Nikki, a harder edge to her voice now. "Is your car outside? Did you *drive* here?"

Jimmy swallowed. "Maybe."

Nikki's eyes widened in disbelief and her voice dropped to a bitter hiss. "Are you seriously telling me after everything I told you about what happened to Max, that you drove here *drunk*? Are you fucking kidding me?"

Jimmy dropped his head. "Sorry, I wasn't thinking."

"No, you bloody weren't! Trust me, bad things can happen when people don't think. People can end up dead."

Nikki fixed a cold stare on him. Megan had never seen her this enraged.

Tentatively, Jimmy looked up. There was fear in his eyes, desperation. Megan could tell his anger was still there, yet already his face was tinged with something else. Guilt perhaps?

"Maybe we need to start over?" he suggested hopefully.

Something inside Megan ached at those words. She would give anything to hear them said to her. Looking across at Nikki, she saw her expression soften.

Now he had stopped arguing Jimmy was shivering violently, teeth chattering and his whole body shaking uncontrollably from the cold.

"Come on," Nikki relented. "You need to get out of those wet clothes. I think there are some blankets on the sofa." She glanced quickly at Megan who nodded in confirmation. Placing her hand gently on Jimmy's shoulder, Nikki guided him carefully towards the lounge. At the door, she hesitated and cast a casual glance back over her shoulder. "Just give us some space, okay?"

It was the first time she had even acknowledged Megan's presence since Jimmy had arrived. Without waiting for a response, she disappeared into the lounge, pulling the door firmly shut behind them.

And just like that, Megan was cast out in the cold yet again.

Alone.

The injustice of it stung her. A small ball of resentment slowly expanded in her stomach.

Loitering awkwardly on the staircase, Megan leaned her head against the cool, wooden bannister. If she stayed quiet and controlled her breathing, she could hear faint snippets of the couple's hushed conversation.

"…I still love you."

"But how can we…"

"…we can make this work."

"I forgive you…"

"…a fresh start."

"I can't imagine not being with you…"

"I care more about you than I do about myself."

Megan's breath caught as she listened to those words. A little wrench of jealousy started to gnaw away at her insides.

Time seemed to have ground to a halt in the draughty corridor. Megan swore even her watch had come to a standstill as she sat frozen in position. She had started to lose hope of Nikki ever emerging when suddenly the lounge door cracked open. Tiptoeing out, Nikki shut it softly behind her.

Turning around, she noticeably jumped when she saw Megan sitting on the staircase. "Jesus Meg, you scared me. How long have you been sat there?"

Megan shrugged. "A while."

Her friend stared down at her with a mixture of pity and dismay on her face. "Alright…let's head back upstairs, shall we? Jimmy's asleep, I've left him wrapped up on the sofa." As an afterthought she added, "I hope that's okay?"

"Why wouldn't it be?" Megan's voice came out harsher than she intended and Nikki stared at her confused.

Traipsing in silence back to her bedroom, Megan was suddenly thankful that all her housemates were out tonight. She could do without their annoying interruptions. Already the house felt too crowded with the three of them.

Resuming their earlier position on the bed, the pair sat in uncomfortable silence. Nikki was sat more stiffly now, tense.

Megan bit down hard on her lip. "So, are you two back together?"

"We're going to see how it goes. Start dating again. Try and work things out."

A wave of sadness hit Megan. She felt numb, completely removed from the room in which they sat.

Nikki swallowed and turned to face her with suspicion in her eyes. "You like him, don't you?"

Megan let out a short, sharp laugh. "What? You honestly think I have a thing for Jimmy?"

Nikki's resolve faltered. "Maybe. Peter seems to think so anyway. He's mentioned it to me before."

"Yeah, well Peter can be a fool sometimes."

Nikki frowned. "Perhaps. But I thought he might be onto something. I've seen you staring at us before and you've looked…jealous."

Megan smiled grimly. "Oh, Nikki, maybe you are an idiot after all."

Nikki's frown deepened. "What do you mean?"

"Maybe you have caught me looking at you guys, but it's not your boyfriend I've been pining after."

"I don't understand…" Nikki's expression was blank, uncomprehending. Then, her mouth dropped open in realisation. "Oh."

Instantly Megan reached across to grab her hand. "Please don't freak out or anything. I just couldn't work out how to tell you."

Shaking her head in confusion, Nikki said, "But Peter…"

A smirk crossed Megan's lips. "I guess I'm a better actress than people think."

For a long moment neither of them said anything. Then, Nikki asked in a quiet voice, "How long?"

Sighing, Megan admitted, "I guess it's always been you Nikki. Right back from when we first met. Why do you think I swapped onto your Theatre Studies course?"

Nikki's eyes widened. "You did that for *me*?"

"Yeah, I wanted to spend more time with you, see where it led. And it was going somewhere too, wasn't it? At least before Jimmy came onto the scene."

Nikki grimaced. "You can't blame him Meg."

"We did have a connection though, didn't we? I know it wasn't just me who felt it." Megan squeezed her hand affectionately. Nikki flinched as if it stung and instinctively drew her hand away.

A strange atmosphere hung in the room, as they

both sat in a foreboding silence, lost for words.

Eventually, Nikki drew a deep breath and hesitantly spoke, "Meg, you're my best friend. I'd be lost without you. But that's all it is to me – friendship. I'm afraid I don't feel the same way as you do."

She's trying to be conciliatory, thought Megan. *Attempting to be a grown up about this.*

"I'm really sorry."

Shuddering, Megan tried to ignore the heaviness in her chest and the burning behind her eyes. It was as if the emptiness that sat at the centre of her soul had finally expanded and swallowed her whole. "Perhaps if Jimmy wasn't…"

Shaking her head, Nikki said gently, "This isn't about Jimmy. I promise you, even if he wasn't around, my answer would still be the same. I just don't feel that way about you." A sob fractured her voice as she fought back tears. She looked so sad, so vulnerable.

An abrupt wave of annoyance struck Megan. *That was so typically Nikki. Always finding a way to play the victim.* Heat rose to colour her cheeks, little red circles of embarrassment and rage.

Suddenly Nikki's hand flew to her heart necklace as understanding dawned in her eyes. "Is that what this represents?"

Megan dropped her eyes. "Not exactly."

"Oh, Meg." She started to unclasp it from her neck.

"No please, it was a gift. Keep it, it's yours."

Nikki didn't look convinced but her hands fell back into her lap. She shifted awkwardly on the bed. "Maybe we should take a step back. Spend a little less time together for a while?"

The weight of despair ballooning inside of Megan pressed down harder. "That's really not necessary." Her voice was low and strained.

"No, I think it would be wise," insisted Nikki. "It wouldn't be forever. Just while you figured things out. It must be confusing trying to deal with everything you're feeling with me there all the time."

Megan was silent.

"I mean, have you even come out to your parents?"

Closing her eyes, Megan sighed. "Not yet. I can't imagine it will go down very well. My mum's been crazy about having grandchildren for as long as I can remember."

Nikki nodded. "I can help support you in that if you like. When you're ready to tell them, I mean."

Megan frowned. "Just stay out of it."

"I was only trying to help—"

"Well don't." She cringed at the hurt on Nikki's face. This conversation wasn't going how she had planned it. For years she had rehearsed this speech a hundred times over and it had never turned out like this. A disturbing thought suddenly occurred to her. "We'll still be friends though, right?"

"Yeah, of course we will!" Nikki's tone was bright but Megan swore she could hear a note of hesitation in her reply.

"Good, because I need you." Megan regretted her choice of words as soon as she had said them.

Nikki gave her a look full of pity as she stood and edged to the door. "Okay. I'm going to go now, alright? I think it's probably best I sleep in the lounge downstairs with Jimmy tonight."

Without so much as a backward glance she slipped out of the bedroom, closing the door firmly behind her. For the second time that evening Megan was left alone, sat rejected on her bed with hot tears streaming down her cheeks.

*   *   *

Light shimmered as it bounced off the silver heart pendant dangling from Robson's hand. "It was *you* who bought Nikki this necklace, wasn't it?" he asked calmly.

Megan smiled wistfully. "Yeah, for her twenty-first birthday. She loved it. She wore it all the time, it was one of her favourite pieces of jewellery."

"You own the same necklace too, don't you? It's been bothering me, trying to figure out where I've seen it before. Then I realised it was in Nikki's Facebook profile picture. The one of you two together; you're both wearing the same necklace."

Megan nodded. "That's right. I thought it would be kind of cool to have matching ones. Like a grown-up version of those childhood friendship necklaces. You know, when you each have half a heart and they fit together to make one."

Robson's hand tightened around the necklace. "We found Nikki's buried in her bedroom bin. Clearly she didn't want to muddy the waters further by continuing to wear it."

The smile slipped from Megan's face. "Really? She actually threw it away?"

Robson leaned back in his chair. "Tell us, why did

you kill her?"

Megan gave a nervous laugh. Her expression was inscrutable but when she spoke her voice was high and strained. "What on earth are you talking about? All you've got is a discarded necklace, that's hardly conclusive evidence for murder!"

"No, it's not. But this is." Silently, Robson opened up the brown folder on the desk and laid out the photographs side by side.

Megan froze. The battle of keeping her emotions concealed was lost. Robson could see in her face she knew she had been caught.

"As you can see, this is CCTV footage of you buying a certain replica dagger last Sunday. Paid for in cash of course, very clever: no paper trail. But you forgot about the security cameras, didn't you? And the shop owner has positively identified you too and was more than obliging in handing over the knife specifications as well, just in case there was any doubt in confirming exactly what you bought."

Momentarily lost for words, Megan's face contorted in anguish.

"You think you're pretty smart, don't you?" continued Robson. "I particularly liked the questions you were asking us when we spoke to you before. Enquiring if we had any leads, testing how much we knew. Telling us about Jimmy's temper and how angry Emma was about losing her role. And planting the prop knife on Ben, that was another genius move. You did an awfully good job at casting suspicion on other people. I have to say, I'm impressed. To give you credit – you almost got away with it."

Remaining silent, Megan blinked back tears.

"The thing I don't understand is *why* you wanted Nikki dead? Was it simply a tragic case of unrequited love? If you couldn't have her, no one could – is that it? Getting the ultimate revenge by manipulating her to kill herself onstage so the two men who loved her were forced to helplessly watch her die? There's somewhat of a poetic brilliance in that, William Shakespeare himself would be proud."

Stirred into action, Megan shook her head desperately. "It wasn't like that. I swear I didn't mean for Nikki to die."

"You swapped a prop knife with a real blade and you didn't mean her to die?"

"Really, I mean it. I didn't realise the stab wound would be so deep. I thought the injury would be more superficial, perhaps enough to hospitalise her but she'd survive, no long-term damage. Just enough to make her re-evaluate her life choices. I figured if I put that prop knife in Ben's jacket it would look like he tried to kill her out of jealousy so Jimmy would confront him about it. The two of them would end up tearing each other apart. Then Nikki would come crying to me for comfort. So, maybe finally…"

"You'd be together?" Robson raised a quizzical eyebrow.

Biting down hard on her lip, Megan's eyes glistened with unshed tears. "I just hated the thought of her abandoning me. I couldn't cope if she wasn't in my life."

"But Nikki never said anything about abandoning you?"

"She didn't have to, I knew what she was thinking."

There was a ring of desperation in Megan's voice, like she was trying to convince herself. She sounded more delusional by the minute. "Haven't you ever loved someone so much you feel like you couldn't live without them?" She was talking more to herself than to the detectives, as if she had forgotten they were there at all. "Now, what if not only could you never be with the person you loved but you had to stand by and watch as they married someone else? And to add insult to injury they even use your feelings for them as a reason to cut you out of their life."

"I don't think that's what Nikki was planning to do to you," said Zahra evenly.

An embittered Megan shook her head furiously. "You weren't there. You don't know that. I worshipped that woman and she treated me like a piece of trash, ditching me whenever it suited her. It drove me to the brink of insanity."

Now she had started talking, she couldn't stop. It was as if someone had uncorked a bottle and all her pent-up emotions were coming tumbling out. Maybe Robson couldn't fully understand the subtleties of her motives, but he wasn't entirely baffled by them either.

"I think I'm following your rationale. But I'm curious – why go for the onstage stabbing? It's a rather dramatic way of making a statement?"

Megan smiled proudly. "Actually, in a strange way that was Peter's idea. He had been talking about some historic *Macbeth* performance in which one of the actors died after getting attacked with a real blade instead of the prop one."

"The seventeenth century Amsterdam production.

He mentioned it to us too."

"Exactly! Anyway, it all just sounded so bizarre, so *theatrical*, it had been playing on my mind. It's kind of fitting, don't you think? I thought I would follow my instincts and go ahead with a similar plan."

Robson nodded comprehendingly. It struck him once again that Megan wasn't just talking to them anymore, she was confessing. In his mind, he ran through the sequence of extraordinary events that had led to the convoluted murder at Gemini Theatre. All the pieces of the jigsaw were finally slotting into place. "So, let me get this straight. You first met Nikki Gowon when you started university and you've been best friends ever since. She trusted you enough to confide in you about her past and the role she played in her ex-boyfriend Max's death and you returned the favour by swapping onto her Theatre Studies course to spend more time with her. At some point you realised you had feelings for her, but you were always too fearful to voice them in case they weren't reciprocated. Before long, Jimmy Walker came onto the scene and you were forced to watch Nikki fall in love with someone else. Then, that's when you started dating Peter Winters?"

"That seemed like the right thing to do at the time," explained Megan. "I've always felt as though I've had to play a part in some way. Plus, it meant we could all go double-dating, so at least I got the opportunity to see Nikki more."

"Right, so the four of you sign up to act in an independent *Macbeth* production and that's when things got infinitely more complicated. Not only did you find out Nikki was planning to get married to Jimmy in a few months time, but she also hadn't kept you fully in the loop about her sister's illness. Both of which must have felt like quite a betrayal. Then, you accidentally stumble upon Nikki hooking up with her co-star Ben Grahame, so you tip Jimmy off in the hope it would lead to the couple breaking up. Which it did, much to your delight, but unfortunately Nikki's newfound singleness was only short-lived and you witnessed their teary reconciliation. After which, you confessed to Nikki about your true feelings for her which she rejected and confirmed there could never be a future for the two of you. So, at that point you decided to take matters into your own hands and orchestrate a real-life onstage stabbing drawing upon inspiration from a seventeenth century *Macbeth* performance? Am I missing anything?"

Slowly Megan shook her head.

Robson could tell from her expression she believed it all made perfect sense. He scratched at his stubble in concentration. "So, let me see, last Sunday was the eighteenth of March, the day after the couple's emotional reunion at your house. That's when you commissioned the bespoke dagger. Was your mind really made up that quickly?"

Silence fell for a few seconds as Megan slumped in her chair.

"You weren't sure you could follow through with it though, were you?" chimed in Zahra. "That's why you were so standoffish with Nikki this past week, keeping your distance. You couldn't bring yourself to face her in case she made you doubt your conviction."

"I guess I was testing her," Megan admitted with a long sigh. "I was giving her the chance to make amends, to prove I was wrong about her. But Nikki didn't bother trying to bridge the gap between us. I doubt she even noticed it, she was so blindsided by rekindling her romance with Jimmy I didn't exactly feature on her radar."

Robson's brow furrowed. "So, she deserved to be stabbed? Onstage, in front of hundreds of people?"

Megan flinched slightly. "I only wanted to teach her a lesson."

Another thought suddenly occurred to Robson. "Was it you who removed the knife from Nikki's stomach wound as well? Why'd you do that? To increase the blood loss to make sure she definitely ended up in hospital?"

Eyes widening, Megan gasped. "Oh, I thought I was helping. I figured the shorter time the knife stayed in her body, the less damage it would do. I didn't realise yanking it out might make things worse."

Robson sighed heavily. He couldn't tell if she was speaking truthfully about that, but either way her actions had ensured Nikki wound up dead. "So, do you want to further clarify anything we've discussed?"

"No, I have nothing further to say," Megan replied, her voice suddenly meek.

To Robson's side, Zahra darted a quick look at him. *A silent gaze of perfect communication.*

Turning his attention back to the brunette actress sat forlornly in front of them, Robson rose to his feet. "Megan Newbold, you are being charged with the murder of Nikita Gowon by your intent to cause grievous bodily harm. This interview has now been concluded."

Once Megan had been escorted out, Zahra turned to face Robson with a look of utter shock on her face. "Well, normally I'm pretty good at sussing out who the culprit is early on, but even I didn't see that one coming. What was it you said earlier? That someone completely infatuated by love might be obsessed enough to commit murder?"

Robson nodded grimly. "I guess I was right. Nikki Gowon's death was a crime of passion after all, just not the one we thought. I suppose you could say it turned out to be more of a love square than a love triangle in the end – Nikki, Jimmy, Ben and Megan."

He slouched back into his chair. Now the thrill of the investigation was over, he felt utterly exhausted. He could practically hear his bed calling to him.

Zahra let out a weary sounding sigh. She looked equally spent. "So, what next?"

A small smile crept onto Robson's face. "Well, I don't know about you, but I could sure use a drink."

CHAPTER TWENTY-THREE

What's Done, is Done

A huge box of Thorntons chocolates materialised on Robson's desk as if by magic when Zahra sauntered into the room.

He looked up, surprised. "What's this?"

"It's from Nikki's parents. I did try and explain we're not really supposed to accept gifts but they insisted. In the end I gave up arguing."

Robson managed a weak smile. "That's nice of them."

"They're just so thankful we finally managed to discover what happened to their daughter," explained Zahra. "It doesn't bring her back but at least it gives them some sort of closure. There's peace to be found in knowing who is to blame."

"How are they taking it?"

"Much like you'd imagine. They're still reeling from the shock of finding out it was Megan who was behind everything. She's been a good friend of the family for years, they let her into their home and even cooked for her when she visited. They can't believe what she ended up doing."

A dark grimace fell across Robson's face. "Love can make people do crazy things."

"Speaking of which, I understand Jimmy has been seeing Nikki's family a lot too, trying to work through and process what's happened and come to terms with everything. I think they'll help each other cope with their grief."

"That's good."

Zahra took a deep breath. "Coincidentally, we've heard back from Megan's lawyers. Turns out she's now been diagnosed with Bipolar Personality Disorder, which was previously undetected."

Robson nodded sagely. "To be honest I did wonder if something like that might be the case. In hindsight all the warning signs were there – intense, highly changeable moods, problems in controlling her anger, an unstable sense of self identity and she mentioned impulsive behaviours as well, didn't she? Like her obsessive shopping sprees and sleeping with Peter the first night she met him?"

Frowning in thought, Zahra said, "Exactly. People's personalities aren't fully formed until their early to mid-twenties so that disorder rarely manifests itself fully before then, hence why no one recognised the early symptoms Megan was exhibiting. Even something as innocuous as her parents' divorce could have led to it surfacing in her late teens."

Robson sighed. "And Nikki's perceived rejection of Megan when she revealed her true feelings was the stressor that pushed her over the edge. I know people with that condition can have extremely intense relationships with their friends and loved ones. Not to mention, they can feel worried about people abandoning them and would do anything to stop that happening. So, to Megan her frantic actions to prevent Nikki from leaving her probably made perfect sense. In some twisted logic, she might have even thought she was helping her by protecting their friendship. It doesn't exonerate her behaviour but it does go a little way to explain why she reacted like she did."

Zahra gave a gentle nod. "Her lawyers are going to plead not guilty due to diminished responsibility."

A sombre smile edged onto Robson's face. "You know this might be one of those rare occasions when the lawyers are actually right. I think everyone would agree Megan is already suffering enough. Inadvertently killing her best friend and possibly the only person she's ever truly loved; that will haunt her for the rest of her days."

Zahra's brow knitted together. "How easy it would have been to save a life."

"True. This whole tragedy could have so easily been avoided. If only someone had picked up on the warning signs, there's plenty of effective treatment out there for that condition. What's more, Nikki's family are convinced she definitely would never have abandoned Megan. Nothing had to change. If only Megan had taken the time to properly talk to her friend and discuss everything rather than avoid her and rush to the worst possible conclusion, then Nikki would still be alive today."

Zahra's expression grew more serious. "There is

one positive thing to come out of this mess though – Jimmy's mum has finally left her abusive husband. I understand she figured life was too short to be unhappy given everything that has happened. She's been referred to a counselling service and I think she's planning to rent a small flat with her son while she works out what the future holds."

Robson nodded approvingly. "That's great news."

"And one more thing: Violet's rape kit came back showing signs of forcible rape and they also found Peter's semen on her clothes from that night. That combined with the bruising on her wrists and the CCTV footage of him staggering about drunk and Violet fleeing the scene in distress adds up to a compelling body of evidence against him. The prosecution team believe they have a strong case to make a conviction. Apparently even his smarmy lawyer is starting to panic."

"Brilliant." Robson couldn't help but grin at Zahra's righteousness.

"That is, of course, if the case doesn't get thrown out due to claims of police harassment." She gave him a pointed look.

Averting his eyes, Robson hung his head in shame and quickly changed the subject. "What about Neil and Emma?"

Zahra gave a dismissive shrug. "Who knows? Guess it's up to those two to work out where to go from here. That's if they're still speaking of course, but I have a sneaking suspicion that sort of infatuation doesn't easily get snubbed out."

Robson grimaced. "That reminds me, speaking of Neil, I saw he's managed to bag himself a front-page interview with *Shortlist* magazine. Clearly he's still clinging desperately to his fifteen minutes of fame."

Zahra shook her head in disdain and Robson stifled a snigger at her obvious disgust.

Rising to his feet, Robson stretched out his body in satisfaction. Now the harrowing case was finally over, he felt like he could breathe more freely again. To his surprise, he had discovered that he could still feel a glimmer of hope shining through. He had assumed that had been contingent on Nikki surviving, but he realised now it was more to do with working out what had happened to her. Finally bringing her murderer to justice in what had been for him one of his most personally challenging cases to date. Something inside of him felt rejuvenated.

Turning his head, Robson locked eyes with Zahra. "So, what do we do now?"

"Well, actually after our shift, I've got tickets for *Hamlet* at the Globe Theatre tonight if you and Susan fancied it?"

Robson raised a quizzical eyebrow. "Seriously? After this case you really want to see another Shakespearean tale of bloodlust and murder?"

Zahra shrugged defensively. "What can I say? I guess it's put me in the mood for theatre."

"Were you not paying attention to what happened onstage?"

She punched his shoulder playfully. "Stop teasing! I've already bought four tickets, are you coming or not?"

"*Four* tickets?" Robson repeated slowly. "Me, Susan, you and…"

Laughing, Zahra rolled her eyes. "Oh, do keep up. Call yourself a detective?"

"So, who is this mystery person?"

"Come tonight and you might just find out," Zahra said with a cheeky wink. "What do you say?"

Robson hesitated for only a moment before a smile crept onto his lips. "Alright then. After all, as they say, the show must go on."

ABOUT THE AUTHOR

Samantha Goodwin has written professionally for her business career as a Chartered Marketing Manager for over a decade before turning her hand to fiction. As an avid crime fiction fan, she regularly participates in the renowned *Theakston Old Peculier Crime Writing Festival* in Harrogate and completed their prestigious *Crime Writing Creative Workshop.* She also relishes attending literature festivals across the country as well as engaging in numerous online writing communities.

Keen to support upcoming authors, Samantha recently launched the *#IndieWritingWisdom* initiative on Instagram to collate and share inspiring, original quotes from a wide range of different writers to encourage others.

When she is not writing, Samantha enjoys reading, countryside walks, movies, musicals and almost all chocolate (but controversially not Oreos). She lives in Leeds with her husband, Chris, and son, Jack.

Murder at Macbeth is her first novel and was longlisted for the international *Flash 500 Novel Award* in 2017.

Enjoyed This? Leave a Review!

If you enjoyed reading *Murder at Macbeth,* please consider leaving a short book review online.

It would be greatly appreciated and really does make a difference to new authors.

- www.amazon.co.uk

- www.amazon.com

- www.goodreads.com

Connect With The Author Online

- Web: samanthagoodwinnet.wordpress.com

- Instagram: @samanthagoodwinauthor

I love connecting with my readers from across the world. Please feel free to share a photo on Instagram of you reading this book from wherever you live or travel and I will repost! Remember to tag me and/or use the hashtag *#MurderAtMacbethWorldBookTour*

ACKNOWLEDGEMENTS

I will always be eternally grateful for my wonderful parents, Graham and Glynis Finnerty, for instilling in me a great love of reading, a passion for writing and providing unwavering love and support.

To to my amazing husband, Chris Goodwin, thank you for your constant encouragement and for always believing in me; you knew I could write this novel before I did. Thanks for being my very first reader and for creating such a striking and beautiful book cover design; it has been a joy to create this with you.

To my son, Jack, thank you for being my daily inspiration and for learning how to sleep in the cot so I could finish writing this!

For their editorial support, constructive criticism, and many brilliant ideas, huge thanks to my eagle-eyed editor, Akindele Michael Abisoye, my fantastic proof-reader, Rebecka Yaeger, and my exceptional team of first-time readers; Kelly Finnerty, Gillian Finnerty, Laura Hodgson, Andrew Randall and Robyn Taylor McEwan. You've all helped immensely to shape this story and really bring it to life.

For their valuable professional insights into police procedures, thank you to Emma Armstrong and Craig Newbould. Needless to say, any legal or procedural errors are entirely of my own making.

Thank you also to Jack Sage for your wonderful knowledge of London which helped to inspire the setting for this story, and to fellow author, Stewart McDowall, for your wise advice on how to make it through the long journey of writing a novel.

And finally, to you, my readers. Thank you for choosing to spend your time with this book. I couldn't be happier to share it with you.

BOOK CLUB QUESTIONS

Topics for discussion

1. Did you suspect who the murderer was? What clues did the author leave?

2. Did it take you time to get into reading this book or were you immediately drawn into the story?

3. Did the characters seem authentic and believable? Whose revelations surprised you the most?

4. How did your opinion of Nikki change throughout the course of the novel? What did you think about her character?

5. How do you think the dynamic between D.I. Robson and D.S. Zahra contributed to the story?

6. What do you think were the main themes of the novel and how were these conveyed?

7. Why do you think the author chose *Macbeth* as the setting for this novel? Why not a different Shakespeare play?

8. How effective do you think the story structure was (using the flashbacks and the different points of view)?

9. How did this murder mystery compare to other crime novels you have read?

10. Is there a message in this novel that you think the author would want readers to grasp?

11. What changes would you make if the book was to be adapted into a movie? Who would you want to play the different parts?

12. If you could have coffee with one of the characters, who would it be and why?

Author Interviews

To read interviews with the author
please visit Samantha Goodwin's website:

samanthagoodwinnet.wordpress.com

Printed in Great Britain
by Amazon